I0645762

Home of the Braves

Pamela Ackerson

HOME OF THE BRAVES
by *Pamela Ackerson*

© Pamela Ackerson

All rights reserved.
No part of this book may be reproduced or
utilized in any form by any means, electronic or mechanical,
including photocopying or recording, or by any information
storage and retrieval system, without permission
in writing from the publisher.

Cover Art: Roland Dempsey
Layout: Sharon A. Dunn

LCCN: 2002095420
ISBN: 1-887472-72-X
Printed in the U.S.A.

Disclaimer:

This is a work of fiction.
Any relation to real people, living or dead,
are creations of the author's imagination.

This Book is Dedicated to:

My husband, who gave me the freedom to fly with my eagles.

My mother and my sister, who watch over me from the heavens.

Acknowledgments:

Special thanks to **my family and friends**
for giving me their love and support
throughout my life.

Also, to **Ruth and Dave**
for giving me the opportunity to
be able to follow my dream.

I send heartfelt thanks to those
from the **Native American community**
as well as my friends online.

Last but certainly not least, to **Rodney**
for giving me the chance. And for
becoming not just my publisher
but a friend as well.

PART ONE

Pamela Ackerson

Chapter ONE

A slight breeze moved the French lace curtains as Karen leaned against the verandah doorframe. She watched the men struggle with the awkward and heavy feather mattress she had re-upholstered. The ornate bed was large and high off the carpeted floor. She had fallen in love with it the moment she and Bonnie had seen it at the estate sale.

The antique maple bed and steps matched her furnishings in the room to perfection. This room for some particular reason was the only one in her home furnished with antiques, right down to her eagle photographs in ornately carved frames. Normally, Karen was comfortable with anything and everything modern. It wasn't until the past year that she'd started replacing her bedroom furniture with antiques.

After the men left, she spent the afternoon organizing and moving the rest of her bedroom. Nodding her head in agreement with herself, she looked about the room with a critical eye. It was almost as if the bed was the last piece of the puzzle. Its headboard was strategically placed against the wall with the two windows from floor to ceiling on each side. The bed faced the verandah, the armoire to the right of the bed, the bureau and matching vanity to its left. Karen smiled. The room looked comfortable and inviting.

Hot and exhausted, she lay back on the bed for an afternoon nap. It was soft and enveloping, like a huge hug. The linen sheets were cool and she felt herself relaxing immediately. As she dozed into a restful sleep, Karen felt as if she was floating on water and then upward as if she was flying. It was an exquisite dream. In the dream she closed her eyes and felt as if she was flying. Opening her eyes, she surveyed her surroundings. Karen could feel the dirt and grass beneath her bare feet.

She was spiraled into the mid-1800s by the mystical antique four-poster bed. At first, Karen thought she was dreaming but the threats of the menacing look on the man's face seemed just too real to ignore.

One minute she was reeling in the luxury of the soft bed and the next, she was staring at an extremely handsome and virile looking Indian. As she watched his face, she could see a look of complete astonishment that had quickly turned to anger.

Standing Deer was quite perturbed. He was just getting ready to eat his morning meal when out of the blue heavens this white woman appeared. All of a sudden, there she was. This white woman had long wavy hair with curls cascading down from her shoulders to her waist, like a waterfall. The sun made it sparkle like the rays of sunshine through the clouds and sky. There were so many streaks of colors in it that he wasn't sure what color to call it. It appeared to have all the colors of autumn leaves one saw in the mountains just before the winter snows.

How ironic that she would appear just when he thought the whole trip was a waste of his valuable time. He had been scouting for days and had not seen any Pawnee war parties or scouts. This woman was dressed in clothing he had never seen before. Quite different from the clothing of other white women he had seen. What has the Great Spirit planned for him by bringing this woman to him? Where did she come from? How did she get here without him seeing her? There was no horse that he could see and no possible way she could have entered the campsite without him seeing her. He didn't move, nor did Standing Deer want to move. If he scared her, she might leave in the same way she arrived. From his own experiences and those of others, he knew white women were cowards. They tended to get very skittish when they were around Indians. He did not want to scare her away. He wanted answers to his questions.

The training of a Hunkpapa warrior prepared Standing Deer to be ready for anything. But, this was different. It was magical how she appeared before his eyes. She was a very beautiful woman. Standing Deer could feel his palms sweating, and his heart beating faster. He felt an attraction he hadn't allowed himself to feel in years. What kind of spell had she cast over him?

Standing Deer was thorough as he stood silently admiring and observing her. She was a little woman just barely able to reach his shoulders. She was indeed in strange attire, with practically nothing covering her body. This woman with the colorful hair and strange clothes did not appear to be shaken by his presence. Grinning, her attire did not leave much to the imagination. She was quite striking; her body was well formed and well endowed. She appeared to be strong and healthy for a white woman. It pleased him to see the muscles throughout her arms and legs. Yes, she was quite a specimen. This woman was a strong one.

She would be able to work hard, stand her own ground among the other captives and possibly even among the Indian women of the tribe. She would surely bring him good fortune and many horses when he traded her to the Cheyenne. Maybe he is to take this white woman back to camp with him. He could keep her for himself. He decided that he would definitely like to keep her for himself.

Standing Deer hadn't felt this kind of desire for a woman for too long a time. His body was starting to react to the beauty before him. He closed his eyes for a brief second as he fought to gain control of his thoughts of taking her. Was that lust he saw in her eyes too? The Great Spirit has brought him a jewel from the skies of the Pawnee country.

Karen was scrutinizing him just as he was her. Her eyes left a languorous trail of desire. He was indeed a very good-looking man, built like a god. It had been quite a long time since she looked at a man that actually interested her at all. To look at a man and feel her pulse quicken and her heart pound in her chest was an unusual reaction for her. She could sense his animal magnetism. The sexual attraction was strong. She had to use all her control not to walk over and touch him.

He was tall, at least six feet in height, with a massive, muscular body, tanned to a golden brown. His facial features were rugged and well defined with dark, charcoal eyes that didn't waver, like the look of an eagle when it's hunting prey.

He was not moving. Every muscle she could see was flexed, waiting for action as she imagined a warrior would. Karen could see the ripples of the muscles throughout his entire body. She just wanted to walk over to him and touch him, caress him and feel the hardness of his legs, arms and chest underneath her fingertips and lips.

This was her dream. He was her rendition of Apollo. There was no harm in following through with this uncharacteristic fantasy of hers. Licking her lips, she envisioned herself stroking him gently but firmly. She could feel his strength in her hands, going through her own body, down into her unreachable soul. Oh, how good it would feel. How good it would feel to be his woman and have him desire her as much as she did him. Karen envisioned herself caressing that strong, massive body, while he was gently touching and stroking her most intimate places, making her tremble and quiver like no other man could. She was stroking his long black hair, smooth and shiny, as it was falling onto her chest when he laid her onto the ground. His hair was so beautiful and thick, enough to make a woman jealous. She could feel his hair tickling her chest as she entwined her fingers through it in ecstasy.

Shaking her head, she blinked away the lascivious thoughts. Oh, they were such wonderful feelings. It obviously has been too long since she had been with a man. What a dream, too bad this wasn't real life!

Karen could feel a breeze gently blowing and pushed her bangs out of her eyes. How odd, does that happen in dreams? She could feel the sun beating relentlessly off her back and realized she was sweating. Maybe, she had the temperature of the air-conditioner on the wrong setting.

She was the first to look away. Uncomfortable with the journey her mind was taking, she looked around and saw a landscape that was unfamiliar. From where she was standing, Karen could hear a river somewhere nearby but couldn't see it. She watched the slight wind touch and tickle the leaves. The trees must be cottonwood or aspen. Horticulture was not one of the subjects she had bothered to learn. She didn't have much knowledge about different trees and plants but couldn't recall ever seeing this kind in Florida before.

Clearing her throat, Karen surveyed the campsite, avoiding the Indian's eyes. It had been a while since she had gone camping. She noted the absence of camping gear, tent, propane lamps or equipment. In comparison to the way it appeared that this Indian lived, she was a bit spoiled.

Neither one of them had moved. Karen was beginning to feel uncomfortable under his penetrating gaze. She realized he was staring at her legs. The man appeared to be perplexed. His head was slightly tilted, eyes squinting as if he was trying to understand a complicated problem. Her brown silk shorts were a bit shorter that she usually wore but they were comfortable to sleep in when she wanted to take a midday nap. Why was his face looking so puzzled as if he hadn't ever seen shorts before? What planet was he from? This was her dream, her imagination running wild, why should he react so strangely. This Indian acts as if he has never seen a woman before.

Standing Deer had finally gotten control of his senses and began to speak to her in a deep, rhythmic voice. It seemed almost hushed, as if he did not want to break the spell. Karen could feel the strength of his personality in the sound of his voice. It was almost a whisper. She couldn't understand the foreign words he spoke. Well, it isn't French, and it certainly isn't Spanish. He must be speaking a form of Indian dialect. How could she be dreaming and hearing a language she had never heard before? Why wasn't he speaking English?

He motioned for Karen to sit. Shaky and unsteady, she gratefully sat beside him. Her legs were getting a little shaky anyway.

He offered her a piece of homemade jerky. Surprisingly, it didn't taste that bad. Not quite like the ones you can buy at the grocery store. Karen wasn't hungry, just curious.

Assuming he didn't speak English, she believed they needed to find a way to communicate somehow. Maybe if she tried sign language, the language is considered universal and she would be able to continue conversation, if he understood her. Karen had been learning to sign for about a year. She hoped that although she did not have much knowledge of sign language, it would be enough. Well, she might know enough to keep some conversation going, even if he signed differently than she had learned.

"Where am I?" She signed and spoke at the same time.

"Here." The Indian pointed to the ground.

"Oh, well thanks a lot." It's nice to know he has a bit of a sense of humor. "I couldn't have figured that one out without your help. Where is here?" She spoke and signed back to him with obvious irritation in her actions.

"This is the land of the Scili." He spoke in his language and signed back to her.

Confused by the strange sign she inquired, "What is Scili?"

"Pawnee." Standing Deer said in English with exasperation.

"Are you Pawnee?" She shivered out of fear and hoped he wasn't. Though she felt compassion for the demise of the Native American cultures and people, she didn't have much knowledge of their tribes except from novels or television. She had read stories about the Pawnee and was worried, even if it was a dream. Karen certainly didn't want it to turn out to be a nightmare.

Standing Deer laughed and smiled at her. Karen liked his laugh. It was a refreshing and pleasant laugh, a deep and honest one. Still, the laugh did not relinquish her fear that he may be Pawnee. She waited for his response in complete silence.

"No. I am not Pawnee. I am Hunkpapa. I am from the Lakota, Sioux." Standing Deer said with unmistakable pride.

It dawned on Karen that he had spoken English and spoke excellent English. Why was she trying to communicate in sign language when he could speak English? She wondered why he had not responded to her in English before. Why did he hide his knowledge of the language?

Why was she taking this dream so virtually? This dream seems so real. Was her imagination playing tricks on her? Did she have to keep reminding herself that it was just a dream?

"You speak English. Why didn't you speak English earlier? How did you learn?"

She scolded herself. Of course he speaks English. How can a person have a dream and talk to someone without speaking the same language? He knows English because this is America. In America, you speak English. Well sometimes, she chuckled to herself. This is a dream, Karen reprimanded herself. Why did she have to keep reminding herself?

It was normal for dreams to have twists and quirks that sometimes never make sense. She needed to understand that she couldn't take this as normal everyday life. Dreams weaved intricate symbolism from the sub-conscience mind.

"There have been white men here for a long time. I learned." He shrugged. He was blunt, short and direct in his answers. Karen admired people who were direct and to the point. No games were involved.

"What is your name? I am Karen." This dream could last a while or it could pass by in seconds. Maybe it'll turn out to be a really delightful dream. We might as well call each other by name.

"I am called Standing Deer."

"Well, hello Standing Deer. It is nice to meet you." Karen said formally with a huge grin on her face and puts her hand out to shake his. Standing Deer just touched her hand. It puzzled her that he did not shake it. She couldn't be insulted by the refusal to shake. He had touched her hand and she could still feel the lingering spark. Maybe it was a custom to greet people that way in his tribe. She reprimanded herself again. "In his tribe," listen to yourself rationalize.

Karen spotted a bow and arrow that was leaning beside Standing Deer. She reached over to point to it and before she could react he grabbed her wrist, twisted her around and had her face down on the ground.

Karen rarely swore. This particular time, she screamed a few colorful metaphors as she scrambled up and away from him. She knew Standing Deer had let her go. Otherwise, she would still be on the ground with a mouthful of dirt. She wasn't sure if she should feel angry or relieved.

Shaking with anger, frustration and humiliation that he could have gotten her on the ground so fast, she thought that she should be taking self-defense courses.

She responded to his menacing glare cautiously. Explaining her intrigue with the bow and arrow would take some time. Archery had been a sport she had been interested in learning but never pursued. Karen thrived by learning and knew she would have to learn to survive in the wilderness. Now why would she think that? It didn't make sense. Obviously, she needed to slow down and take the time to watch what was going on around her. She explained her actions to Standing Deer.

"I only wanted to ask you if you would show me how to make one of those and teach me how to shoot. I've always wanted to learn how to survive in the wilderness, like they did before the country became civilized. I'll need to learn how to use one if I'm going to continue to be here. Please, show me, I learn fast."

Why would she need to learn? Karen wondered. Want, yes; need, no. It was only a dream.

"Yes, I am sure there is a lot I could teach you and I would make you a very willing student," Standing Deer chuckled, a deep-throated chuckle. The sexual undertone was rather blatant and lustful. The desire she heard in his voice was unmistakable.

Well, that was a typical male response. She squirmed. Karen was not comfortable with that type of banter. She was used to being treated by men on a professional level. As far as she knew, none of her colleagues looked at her as anything but another professional.

"I am serious," she said, angered by her discomfort.

Standing Deer grinned, enjoying her discomfort. "You do not need to learn. You are coming with me. It is too dangerous here in the land of the Pawnee. And it is even more dangerous for a white woman who does not know how to survive in this land." He stared at her legs. "Or wear the appropriate clothing."

Karen's mouth dropped in astonishment and then quickly closed it in anger. How dare that arrogant man reprimand her for the clothes she was wearing. It's not as if she planned to come here. Besides, she should be able to wear anything she wanted!

Standing Deer meant every word he said. It was a statement. It was a command, and it was a fact. As far as he was concerned, nothing was going to change the fact that she was going with him. Standing Deer got up and Karen silently and cautiously watched him as he prepared to leave. When Standing Deer finished packing his belongings, he walked over to her, picked her up and proceeded to carry her to his horse.

Karen could smell his manliness. The scent of horses and leather tickled her nose. His breath smelled as if he had chewed on mint. Enveloped by how intoxicating he was, she could feel the steel strength of Standing Deer's strong and massive body as he was carrying her in his arms. Her body stirred with desire. The touch was electrifying. Karen wondered if Standing Deer could feel it, too.

It was so very pleasurable to be in his arms .... .

Reality hit Karen on the backside when Standing Deer plopped her on his horse. Fear gripped her while self-preservation took control. What if he was a savage? He didn't look very civilized. It was obvious his bow and arrows were not used for entertainment. What normal man would be dressed in the costume of an Indian, living off the land and riding around on his horse like it was the 1800s? This is not going to happen, she thought. He is not taking me anywhere. This will not turn into a nightmare.

Karen started to get off the horse when he grabbed her waist. Struggling with her as he pulled himself up onto his horse, she closed her eyes when he managed to subdue her without much of a struggle. She wished she were somewhere else. She did not intend to be taken anywhere by some savage and uncivilized man who dressed up as an Indian and was stuck in his warped world of living alone without civilization. I want to be anywhere else, she thought, please anywhere but here.

Stunned and confused, Karen found herself standing in front of the most glorious, beautiful waterfall she had ever seen. She could see a rainbow reflecting off the mist. Oh, how breath taking, she whispered. Karen never realized she had such an explicit and vivid imagination. She looked around for Standing Deer. Her dream had taken her to a paradise away from the threat of the menacing Indian called Standing Deer. She was alone.

Where was Standing Deer? How did she get here? She decided that this was an unusual dream. In every direction, Karen could see hills and trees surrounded her. The hills in the background were dark, almost black. The trees were lush and full, majestic, she concluded. About twenty-five feet from the waterfall, she saw a cave opening. She would have to explore that. In the meantime ... .

Karen wandered over to a pond of sparkling clear water. Oh, it looked so wonderful! She was hot and the water beckoned to her. It was a dream and no one would know, she rationalized, as she quickly stripped off all her clothes and jumped into the refreshing cool water. She could never have skinny-dipped when she was awake, but in this dream, it felt natural. Karen knew she was much too inhibited to do anything like this in real life. It seemed so, so wanton to her. An exhibitionist she will never be, and even though she many not remember her dreams when she awakens, it felt delightful to be able to experience this.

There wasn't a moment's hesitation. She quickly stripped off her clothes, dropping them in a pile on the ground. At home, she'd be afraid to swim in any of the ponds. She was terrified of alligators and water moccasins. This couldn't be Florida, not with those hills and that waterfall.

Nobody but you knows what happens in dreams unless you chose to tell someone. No one to judge you or chastise you. Oh, if only she could relax like this at home. Karen felt all the stress of the past few years float out of her. Now that she had her surgical license, she can finally find a position in a hospital, and have her own office in the future. Karen would be able to help those who could not afford an expensive doctor. She was going to make a difference.

She looked at her body and scrutinized it as she was floating around the cool water. Knowing she looked good now satisfied her. A year ago, she had taken a long look at herself and decided that things were going to change. Things were going to be different. She was not going to be a frumpy person ever again, and wasn't going to allow men to control her anymore either. She had quit smoking, lost thirty pounds, started working out on a daily basis and liked looking at the muscular cuts in her arms and legs. Proof of the hard work she had put into her body, improved considerably by the bike riding she had started on a regular basis.

Karen hated running, bouncing around all over the place, and listening to the cat calls and obnoxious remarks from men driving by in their cars. Besides, running was boring and tedious. A person could cover more territory on a bike and that gave you a larger area to discover. For someone who, a year ago, had little self-esteem as a woman, she had come a long way. Always the brain, she contemplated, never the desirable woman.

"Well, I changed that. Didn't I?" Karen said aloud. Well, almost, she pondered and smiled, knowing she still had a long way to go to build up her confidence and self-esteem. She was confident in herself when it came to her career and everyday life but when it came to relationships, forget it. Total disasters. Karen just let them walk all over her.

She changed that when she broke off with David. That was her first step, getting rid of David, the one destroying her self-esteem. She could look back objectively now and see a trend. She would become involved with men she thought were strong like her father, but found they had felt intimidated by her intelligence and would hurt her emotionally just to prove their manhood.

Karen caught some movement out of the corner of her eye. She groaned and knew the peace she had been feeling was over. Well, at least it lasted a little while. Starting back to where she had dropped her clothes, she cautiously watched the figure come out of the trees. Karen could see blood all over the man's chest. She swam quickly to the shore. As Karen was running to her clothes, she watched the man collapse onto the ground. His horse stood close by, as if guarding him, not moving away from the man. She noted there was a considerable amount of blood on the horse, as well.

Karen pulled on her shorts, grabbed her T-shirt over her head, and sprinted to the injured man. When she reached him, she skidded to a halt. He pulled a knife on her with a viciousness and speed that she could not perceive from someone who was as injured as he appeared. Stunned she realized the man behind the knife was another Indian.

"Put that away, I'm here to help you," Karen gasped. She was out of breath. What is this with Indians all of a sudden? She had never had dreams about them before. Maybe, this dream was trying to tell her something. Maybe there was a message here.

Karen scanned the area quickly and saw they weren't far from the opening of the cave she had spotted earlier. Hoping he would understand her, she explained the necessity of needing to move him to a better place. Karen helped him onto his feet and together they made it to the interior of the cave. Once there, he collapsed again. Before he passed out, he grabbed her arm and mumbled in a foreign tongue.

"Tashunca." My horse.

She had no idea what the Indian had said. The only thing on her mind was to attend to the injured man. She hurried outside to the sparking cool pond of water that she had just so thoroughly enjoyed, and again, took off her shirt. This time, she planned to use it to clean the Indian's wounds. She plunged it in the water. As she was running back to the cave, Karen wished she had him in a proper facility with electricity and medical supplies. She closed her eyes and wished for anything modern and everything she could possibly need to attend to his injuries and care for him.

As she entered the cave, Karen saw and realized that what she had wished for was right before her eyes. Stunned, she dropped the shirt on the floor of the cave, now a huge room, completely modern, with the Indian lying on a bed beneath crisp white sheets. Karen was delighted. Dreams were definitely wonderful, even if they were unpredictable. Too bad real life couldn't be this way. Thank God she wasn't in Salem during the witch hunting years. She would be burned at the stakes.

She picked up the shirt and draped it on the back of a chair to dry.

Karen was meticulous and skilled as she cleaned and bandaged the Indian's wounds. Two of the wounds were very deep, long lacerations. She had sewn them quickly and skillfully.

After she completed her task and made him comfortable, Karen wrapped a towel around herself and went outside to check on the man's horse. Karen tied the horse to a nearby tree so it would be in the coolness of the shade. The horse's wounds were minor and she nursed them easily. Most of the blood appeared to be the Indian's. She believed the horse would be safe and comfortable in the shade of the trees.

As Karen went back into the cave, she saw that her Indian had awakened. He was pale from the loss of blood and she knew he was in much pain, although he did not show it.

"I am Karen, do not worry I am a doctor," she explained, not sure if he understood her. Smiling, with her best bedside manner, she assured him to ease his fears, although he didn't show any.

"I can help you. You are seriously injured and you must rest." She was gentle as she moved him to lift his head so she could help him drink some water

He whispered in his language. When he realized she didn't understand him, he spoke in broken English. Moving his hands to point to himself he said, "Jumping Bull."

His voice cracked so badly that she could barely understand him. He was weak from the loss of blood and would be sleeping soon. The medication she gave him would help him relax and get the needed rest.

Karen sat down in the chair next to the bed. Jumping Bull wouldn't be moving for a while. It will be a long wait unless, of course, her dream decided to take her somewhere else. She loosened the towel so it rested across her chest; a rest is what she needed. Dreams can be exhausting. At least, this one was. There were too many questions. Why was she dreaming of Indians? There had to be a meaning to what was happening.

Maybe she had been idle too long. She disregarded that thought. She needed the break after all the schooling she had been through. Her mind was trying to tell her something.

Karen woke up with a chill. As she rolled over, with her eyes still closed, she thought about the odd dream she had just had. As she lay there waiting for the grogginess to go way, she realized her hair was wet.

Wet? She bolted up and looked down at herself. She did not have her shirt on! Dazed from her sleep, she felt the towel slip off onto the bed next to her. She stared at it, shaken and speechless. Karen leaned over the sides of the bed in search of her shirt. Not there! Reaching down, she pulled up the dust ruffle and looked under the bed. It was nowhere in sight. She jumped out of bed and threw on another top, grabbed a dry towel, wrapped it around her hair. What if maybe, just maybe, she had taken a shower in her sleep? She had never walked in her sleep before, but one never knows.

Her heart thumping, Karen looked in the bathroom for her shirt and then continued to search the rest of the house. She couldn't find the T-shirt anywhere.

It was as if it never existed.

Chapter Two

Karen felt confused about the whole situation. It was all so extremely peculiar. The breeze in her hair, the sun pounding on her back and the tingling sensation she had felt in Standing Deer's arms. The electricity she had felt reeling through her being engulfed her. Everything seemed so real. Then, of all the strangest things in the world, to wake up without her shirt on and not find it anywhere in the house. How did her hair get wet? Why was she dreaming about Indians? How can anyone dream something that turned out to be so realistic? She had never experienced anything quite like it.

The T-shirt had just disappeared as if it was really left behind with the injured Indian. Karen shook her head thinking everything was so odd. There had to be a reasonable explanation. Someone somewhere had to know something. But whom could she tell? Who could she trust? Who would believe her? It is such a strange situation.

Karen couldn't shake the dream from her mind. She kept picturing Standing Deer. How stoic and proud he looked to her. She recalled scars on his chest, wondering where he had gotten them. What kind of battles had he been in to obtain such odd wounds?

His features were strong with prominent cheekbones, his body lean and muscular. There was absolutely not one ounce of fat on the man. She was lusting after him even now. Get a grip, she scolded herself. This was a dream. Let's try to stick to reality. This man was built so well because he was a dream, a warrior to have fantasies over.

Karen wondered why she was having a battle of wits with herself. This was so unusual and out of character. It's not as if she doesn't know the difference between reality and dreams. Where did that shirt go?

Puzzled and curious about her experience, Karen decided to do some research into these extraordinary dreams about Indians. The Internet would be an excellent source to start.

Knowledge had always been a major thirst for her. Karen decided to start her research with the Sioux Indian tribe. As she was walking into the den, she noticed that the answering machine had messages on it. That was odd, she thought. She usually woke up when the telephone rang. She must have really been in a deep sleep. But then, if she was in such a deep sleep, how could she remember the dream so vividly, as if it happened yesterday?

As Karen was listening to the messages and jotting down whom she needed to call, she heard an unfamiliar voice. It was the woman she had bought the bed from at the estate sale. She had said she had forgotten the canopy that came with the bed and if Karen was interested in having it, to please call her so they could make arrangements. Karen returned her call immediately and made plans to pick up the canopy the next morning.

She settled herself in front of the computer for a complete search through the Internet. There was information on every tribe one could wish for. She found a multitude of sites just on the Lakotas. They were quite an interesting tribe and there was more than enough information available to absorb. She saved site after site in her favorite places.

Karen was so intent on her reading that again, she did not hear the phone ringing but heard her girlfriend Bonnie's voice talking on the machine. She quickly grabbed the telephone before Bonnie could hang up. They confirmed their plans for dinner and Karen decided to wait to tell Bonnie about her unusual dream. Bonnie was into anything that was not the norm; maybe she had some ideas why Karen had this weird and unusual dream. Bonnie could interpret what the dream meant, but how would she react to it?

As Karen was preparing herself for dinner, she felt as she was just going through the motions, as if she was not supposed to be there. She felt removed from the real world as her mind kept returning to the memory of Standing Deer and Jumping Bull. For some reason, Karen felt there was a connection between them and could not understand why or how. Bonnie always said she had psychic abilities but Karen never took it seriously. She just believed she had good instincts, good intuition. Why couldn't she shake the idea that there was more to this than meets the eye? There had to be answers somewhere. Karen decided to swing by the library before she met Bonnie at the restaurant.

At the library, Karen found a wealth of information about the Sioux Indians. She decided to concentrate on the Lakota Tribe. She could come back and read up on the Pawnee and the other tribes later. As she was leaving the library, Karen made a quick about-face and picked up a couple of books on self-defense. Now, she believed she would be prepared. Karen was ready to learn what was going through her mind about Indians.

Looking at her watch, she realized she was running late. Bonnie was never on time for anything but work, but Karen knew Bonnie would be irritated because of her tardiness. She would definitely understand when she heard about Karen's unusual dream.

Interested wasn't the word. Every few minutes, Bonnie would get so excited about the dream that she would interrupt Karen with questions. The whole night revolved around discussing Karen's dream. Even at the bar when they were shooting pool, Bonnie kept questioning Karen about the dream.

Bonnie believed there was a very definite message to Karen. She believed there was Indian spirits coming to Karen in her dream to let her know that she was to go and live near an Indian reservation and be a doctor for them. She felt that it was Karen's calling in life to medically serve the Indians. The Indian dream was God's way of telling her what road she needed to travel. Bonnie was so genuinely excited about the revelation that Karen just didn't have the heart to disagree. Besides, what else could it be?

She wasn't sure about Indian spirits coming to her in her dreams. This wasn't a script from a movie, the extraordinary imaginations of writers. Spirits didn't visit you in dreams, did they? Bonnie knew she wanted to help people who couldn't afford proper medical treatment. Could this dream really be a guide to where her future lies? Dreams can tell you many things if you know how to interpret them.

Thoroughly exhausted, she arrived home just as determined as ever to learn about the Lakota Indians. What if Bonnie was right and Indians had the special powers, powers given by God to reach her in her dreams. She wanted to find out as much as she could about the rituals and customs of the Indians. What if Bonnie was right?

Karen was amazed to find out how religious Indians were and how much they depended on their religious ceremonies. She had always considered them pagans.

Pagans! They were called savages. Yet, many of their religious beliefs were comparable to the Christian religions of today. It was almost as if the Great Spirit might well have been called God. Lord help me. Is that blasphemous? Should I even compare the religions? I wonder what the Sun Dance ceremony would be like to watch. That didn't sound very Christian to her.

Karen found the Lakotas had been naturalists, still are, for that matter. They loved the earth and all its beings. They treated all life with a respect that is rare in modern civilization. They took only what they needed and left the rest to thrive and grow. The Lakota studied the trees, the plants and animals. Those were their lessons as they grew. They were taught to be reserved and it was a necessity to possess self-control to be a good Indian. Maybe that is why Standing Deer hadn't said anything to her right away. Maybe he had been waiting to see what she was going to do or say.

Continuing her reading, she discovered that Sitting Bull was a Lakota. He was a chief and a very prominent one from what the information gave her. Tatanka Yotanka was his Indian name. Tatanka, it must mean bull, Karen decided. Tatanka was one of the words Jumping Bull had spoken. She tried to recall other parts of his name but couldn't remember. She could just barely understand him to start with.

Karen was becoming tired and her eyes were starting to blur from so much reading. Besides, she did have a few drinks with Bonnie. Deciding to call it a night, she slipped on her white lace nightgown, closed the books and left them next to her on the bed. The last thing she thought of as she lay back on her pillow was Jumping Bull. Was he the same man she had read about in the research books?

Karen had just dozed off when she heard a noise. She bolted upright, and looked around at the unfamiliar surroundings. It was dark and cool. She was back in the cave.

Jumping Bull was moaning and moving about the bed restlessly. As she walked over to him, Karen felt confused and concerned. She thought that now that she knew what the dream meant, she wouldn't have another one. Maybe there was something else to this dream besides letting her know she was to serve as a doctor on a reservation.

She walked over to Jumping Bull and found that he had a high fever. She put a thermometer in his mouth while she checked his pulse and blood pressure.

Puzzled, Karen checked his wounds and did not see any signs of infections anywhere. She went to the corner and grabbed a bucket to get some water. She would bathe him and hopefully break his fever. His temperature was 104 degrees. She had to break it fast. She knew she shouldn't give him aspirin because his body might have a reaction to it. As far as Karen knew, he had never taken any kind of modern medication before. Karen did not question how the bucket got there. She just knew it would be there because she needed it. She was becoming used to having whatever she needed, at least in her dreams.

As she was bathing Jumping Bull, she put an antibiotic mediation on his wounds. Karen decided to wet his hair down so she leaned him against her shoulder. She could feel his clammy skin through the thin material of her nightgown. She was soaking down his hair on his neck when Jumping Bull yelled in pain. She took a closer look. At the back of his head, near his hairline was a puncture wound, a hole festering away, just having a blast because of her neglect. It was having its own private party, she thought. She admonished herself, feeling frustrated and disgusted because she missed it. If she had found it earlier, it probably wouldn't have become infected. She cleansed the wound, put a topical antibiotic on it and prayed that whatever injured him was not poisonous.

Karen had read that sometimes Indians poisoned some of their arrows and such. She prayed that this was not the case.

Jumping Bull was resting easier and Karen decided to go outside the cave for some fresh air. She was hungry. She would search for some berries or something to eat.

As she was walking around, she could feel a soft breeze billowing through her nightgown. The day was hot but it was pleasant, similar to a Florida spring day. Karen felt so much peace in these hills. It was her own private little world.

Karen could understand why the Indians felt the way they did about their land. She decided she was going to leave Florida, find this place, and live here. It had to exist. It just had to. Now the question was, how was she to find out where she was? If she kept forcing herself to keep thinking of Jumping Bull, she would keep dreaming about him and ultimately he could tell her where she was. There was something to what Bonnie was talking about after all. She groaned. But what?

Jumping Bull's horse neighed as she approached the entrance to the cave. She had forgotten the poor animal. It was probably hungry and thirsty. She had left the animal tied up just a few feet from the water. How cruel and unthinking can a person get?

Karen hurried over to the horse and found that it was fine. Not great, but it was doing fine. Relieved she untied the horse and watched it walk straight to the water. Good, now the horse could at least get what it needed. She wondered what the horse was called. Indians had such colorful names for everything. She let the horse wander around. Unlike herself, the horse would know what to eat. She doubted very much that the horse would go far. Karen believed that this horse knew exactly where her master was.

Karen climbed along the cliff, next to the waterfall, and sat down on a rock. She laid back, soaking up the sun. She could feel the spray of the water from the falls. Her nightgown was getting wet but it didn't concern her. The droplets from the spray of the waterfalls ticking her skin made her more relaxed than she was when she was walking through the woods. Karen felt she could stay forever. Just don't ever wake up, she thought, and live in this fantasyland. No one but Bonnie would miss her. Other people would wonder what had become of her, but she doubted they would miss her.

She giggled. Now if Standing Deer would appear, she could have a bit of sexual excitement and really enjoy herself. Karen closed her eyes and pictured the two of them entwined in a deep embrace under the waterfall. Oh, one does get an over-active imagination here. she thought. Silly girl.

With a wide grin she stood up and gave herself a big stretch. Sparked by her never-ending curiosity to discover and learn, she looked behind the waterfall. Time to explore. There wasn't much space to get inside but it appeared to go further than she could see.

She knew she couldn't go too far into the cave without a flashlight. She had done enough cave exploring to know she'd only be able to go a few feet into the cavern. As she walked cautiously into the cavern, Karen waited for her eyes to become accustomed to the darkness. She could feel the cool damp air grip her moistened skin. Her nightgown clung to her smooth, soft body. The cool, damp interior of the cavern caused goose bumps all over her. She chose to ignore them. Satisfying unquenchable curiosity was much more appealing to her than having the chills. As her eyes became adjusted to the dark, she could see two different pathways.

Karen felt the smooth, wet walls with her fingertips. Underneath her bare feet, she could feel the slippery and wet ground. Only a few feet from the cavern opening, she could hear the muffled sounds of the falls.

A mysterious darkness seemed to encircle her. She felt as if she was intruding on sacred ground. Karen stayed to her right as she walked slowly and cautiously through the cavern. She was extremely careful, not wanting to slip and fall.

When it was too dark to see anything, she turned around and entered the main cavern. Carefully Karen explored the second pathway. She did not see the Indians tracking and scanning the area. She was so engrossed in the mysterious unknown of the cavern that the world outside seemed nonexistent. She didn't know that members of the Lakota tribe were looking for their chief, Jumping Bull.

Unknown to Karen, the Indians found Jumping Bull's horse and continued to search the area for their chief. They believed the chief must be nearby, otherwise the horse would have tried to make it back to the village.

The Indian warriors saw the footprints on the ground but they were scattered and kicked around. Standing Deer thought he recognized the prints, but was unsure because the ground was so difficult to read. He suspected they were the prints of the white woman he had encountered. It didn't make sense. She was days away. The Indian warriors were discouraged. The sizes of the prints were that of a woman or child but the ground did not offer the means to interpret direction.

They did not see an opening to a cave. Though they knew the area well, they didn't have knowledge of a cave in the area. The cave was sealed from their sight, concealed by the powers unknown to man. Karen didn't know that she was the only one who could see the cave entrance and release

Jumping Bull from the confines of the cave. There wasn't access for anyone to enter or exit the cave unless Karen was there with them. Karen was the key.

The Indians had been gone for a while when Karen came out from behind the waterfalls. She had found a few bones but it appeared no one had been in the cavern for a long time.

She hadn't any concept of the time she had been inside the cavern. As she climbed down from the rocks, she realized the sun was close to setting. When she walked toward the entrance to the cave, she noticed the horse was not in sight. She figured the horse could probably take better care of itself in this rugged, savage land than she could. She did not worry. For some reason, she knew the horse was safe. Somehow, she knew the horse would return to her master.

Hungrier now after her lengthy exploration, Karen went searching through Jumping Bull's bags hoping to find something to eat. Her stomach was growling louder than Jumping Bull's snoring. She dug a little deeper and found some dried fruit and jerky.

As she munched on those, she went over to Jumping Bull to check on his bandages and fever. His fever was down but not gone. Karen was very worried that the knife or arrow had been poisoned. Jumping Bull should have been recovering a little faster. Karen cleansed his wound and applied antibiotic cream on him. She did not want his death on her hands and was determined to heal this man.

If he was hit with a poisoned arrow or knife, she should have enough medical knowledge to get him through this. Just what kind of poison did Indians use? How could she heal him if she did not know how to treat him? How would she know if she had to use penicillin or administer some other form of anti-toxin?

Karen was tired and ready for sleep. She knew she would be going back home, ending this dream and returning to her own bed. She would be able to research what the Indians used for poison. If her strange dream continued as it was, she would be able to return and help Jumping Bull.

She closed her eyes and thought of the beauty and magnificence of everything she had seen. As she dozed, the inner peace that she felt surrounded her, warming her like a favorite blanket. Karen could not recall the last time she had felt so serene.

Chapter THREE

Karen awoke more refreshed than she had in years. Unlike most mornings she didn't walk blindly to the coffee pot for her morning caffeine boost. She didn't need a cup of coffee but out of habit, had a couple of cups anyway. The first thing she did after she poured her second cup was to eat a feast. She was starving. She had cooked herself up a couple of eggs and sausage and was now popping a couple of biscuits and sweet rolls in the microwave. She needs to watch out. She did not want to gain any of her weight back.

The telephone rang and of course it was Bonnie. Bonnie started babbling and running on about the dream Karen had the day before. When she finally had a chance to stop her motor-mouth friend, she let Bonnie know she had another amazing dream.

Bonnie insisted on hearing about the new dream. Karen repeated everything she could recall and realized that she wasn't feeling as if it was a dream anymore. It felt more and more to her that it was really happening.

Throughout the whole conversation, Bonnie was silent. That made Karen even more wary. Bonnie silent? Something isn't right. After Karen finished telling about her dream, she had to prod Bonnie into saying something, all the more scary in Karen's opinion. All Bonnie said was that she had to look into it. Look into what? Karen wondered. What was happening? Bonnie hung up the phone mumbling that she had to get to work early and left Karen feeling like she was loosing her grip on reality.

What was going on? Karen wondered why she felt as if the dream was another life, as if she was leading a dual life. She felt so confused by everything right now. Maybe she was starting to lose her hold on reality. Oh Lord please not now, not after all those years of studying. I have spent too much time, money and energy to lose everything now. Please, I want to be a doctor. She prayed to God. I refuse to be confined in some institution somewhere. Why was she feeling so anxious?

Frazzled, Karen started getting ready for her appointment to pick up the canopy from the woman she bought the bed from. As she was preparing herself to take a shower, she sat down to clean and polish her fingernails. While she was doing her right hand she stopped short. There was dried blood! There was dried blood and antibiotic cream underneath her nails!

"Oh my God, help me," she spoke aloud. Shocked by seeing the blood and cream, Karen panicked.

Oh, please hold on to your sanity. There is too much to lose. Why is this happening? Why is it happening to me? What is going on? What is happening? These dreams were real. They really happened. How?

These Indians existed somewhere, but where and when? They can't be real. How? It's impossible. This isn't normal. Things like this don't happen in real life. Something was definitely going on and Karen needed to resolve it fast. She knew Bonnie was knowledgeable about paranormal experiences. Perhaps she could explain what was going on.

As she was driving to pick up the canopy, Karen's mind was reviewing the last two dreams. Bonnie would cover the paranormal aspect, so she needed to research anything and everything she could about the Sioux Indians. She needed to find out what type of poison their enemies used. It wasn't just to satisfy her curiosity anymore.

It wasn't just a curious dream anymore. Now the knowledge was needed to save a man's life. If Jumping Bull was poisoned, she had to help him. There was a reason why she was caught in this other world or dimension. Jumping Bull was it. She had to save his life. Why else would she be chosen to go to this unknown land and have this paranormal experience? She had to save Jumping Bull for some reason and when she did, the dreams would be gone.

Jumping Bull must be a descendant of the Jumping Bull in history, Sitting Bull's father. Why would she be needed? She was sure there were plenty of Native Americans who were qualified to help Jumping Bull. Why would these spirits, as Bonnie referred to them, come to her? She didn't know anything about the Native American people. Of course she knew about what happened in history but not of the people, nations, or traditions.

If she was going back, she needed to study on some self-defense courses, also. There wasn't any way of knowing how long this paranormal experience was going to continue. How would she know what kind of dangerous predicament she could get into by being in such a wild and uncivilized land? What if she was interrupting some kind of ritual or ceremony? She doubted they would accept her explanations. Oh, sorry. I was just sent here by my dream spirits. They'd have her confined in a mental institution.

She was so absorbed in her thoughts that Karen had arrived at the woman's home before she realized she was there. She knocked on the door and a tall dark-haired woman answered and let her in. Karen was brought to a side porch area. The tall woman left them alone.

The woman she bought the bed from was seated on a patio chaise lounge. She was a petite, elderly woman with a happy and peaceful look on her face. She looked comfortably dressed in a long black cotton skirt and blouse. Her snow-white hair was pinned up, fashioned in a bun, with decorative pins circled around it. They re-introduced themselves and Bea offered her some coffee. Although Karen felt she had enough coffee for the day, she welcomed the offer. She had many questions to ask this woman.

Karen and Bea traded the usual polite chatter and then Karen finally had the chance to question Bea about her mother's bed.

"Bea, I'd like to ask you a few questions about the bed." Karen paused and watched for Bea's reaction. A startled look crossed Bea's face but she seemed to recover quickly. In Karen's mind, Bea's change of expression could not be misinterpreted. She knew something.

"What would you like to know, dear?" Bea asked calmly.

"Well, you see, I've had some strange and peculiar dreams since I've bought the bed. I was wondering if possibly you or your mother may have experienced anything similar."

Karen spoke slowly and hesitantly. She did not want to frighten the woman.

Bea looked at her with an expression of concern. Looking toward the gardens with a distant look, she started to recall memories from the past.

"Well, dear, I never slept in the bed. I wasn't allowed. My parents were very strict with us about going into their bedroom. We couldn't enter their room without permission. The door was always locked at night. When I was very young, my mother was classified as a schizophrenic. Her best friend turned her in to the authorities to have her confined. They said that my mother had a dual personality."

Bea paused a moment and continued slowly.

"My father refused to give her the medication that was prescribed to her. He insisted that she did not need it. He was such a good man. He used to humor her when she spoke of her other personality. My mother would talk about George Washington and the American Revolution as if they were actually living in that time. She would talk about all sorts of people from that time period, as if they both knew them and had just spoken to them the day before. My brother, sister, and I would eavesdrop at their bedroom door sometimes and hear the strangest conversations between the two of them."

Taking a deep breath, she reached up and pushed an imaginary hair away from her face. She seemed to need the moment.

"I remember one time when my father had to rush my mother to the hospital because of a stab wound. She must have inflicted injury to herself with a knife while he was asleep. How my mother got a knife like that into the bedroom without anyone knowing, I couldn't tell you. Where she got the knife, we'll never know. None of us had ever seen it before. As I recall, we never saw it after that night either.

They kept questioning my father about the stabbing. I don't think the authorities believed my parents. It was something about the way the knife wound was inflicted. She kept telling the authorities that my father didn't do it. They were trying to deliver an important message to Washington's troops when she was stabbed. The authorities wanted to institutionalize her immediately but my father wouldn't let them take her away. My father was known and respected in the community. He must have had a lot of influence because they didn't take her away from us."

Bea inhaled a deep breath and sighed. As she continued with her memories, Karen started holding her breath. She looked down at her hands and saw how sweaty they were. A lump settled in her throat making her feel as if she was being asphyxiated.

"I remember one time, as a surprise, my father had painted the bedroom for her. He had taken the canopy out of the closet and put it up. It was the only time the canopy was ever up on the bed. That's probably why I forgot about it. Well, anyway, I remember my mother was hysterical after a few days. She kept telling him that it was the canopy. They had to take down the canopy because they had to get back. That was the only time I ever heard her raise her voice. She was yelling, screaming, and crying. I remember how scared I was. I had thought my father was going to have to commit her to an institution and I would never see her again. But, she didn't go, thank God. I was so scared. I guess I learned the hard way not to eavesdrop on other people's conversations.

"She was just like all the rest of the mothers of my friends. She kept the house immaculate and enjoyed watching television and reading. Mama was always involved with our school and activities when we were younger. And always there, with her support, when we became adults.

"I never quite understood her dual personality. It didn't really affect our lives. She only spoke of it with my father in their room. My father seemed to understand her. He must have known that the bed had given her inner strength. Just before he died, he had told me to never put up the canopy and to sell the bed after my mother died. I don't understand why, but as you know, I followed his wish. She was such a wonderful and spirited woman. I miss her very much."

Bea wiped her eyes and excused herself.

"I'm sorry," she sniffled. "I miss her."

"How old was she when she passed away?" Karen asked.

"Oh, she lived a good long life. She was ninety-eight years old," Bea said with a broad smile.

"And your father? How old was he?"

Bea frowned and shook her head.

"Well, dear, I have no idea. I never knew how old my father was. Couldn't tell you what year he was born. We celebrated his birthday on March 16th, but he would never tell us how old he was. I always thought that to be a little odd, but I guess some people are like that."

Bea smiled. One could tell she had very happy memories of her parents.

Karen felt like a sponge. She absorbed the incredible story that seemed so similar to her own experiences. Everything Bea had told her was swarming in her head. Karen found out quite a bit of information. More than what she needed or wanted to know, as far as she was concerned. She felt as if she had to get out of there, now.

As if reading Karen's mind, Bea had finished her cup of coffee and walked over to a box. She motioned Karen to come over to the table. As she pulled out a section of the canopy, Karen took a quick short breath of excitement.

It was exquisite. There was hand-embroidered appliqués of flowers covering and smothering every available piece of fabric. A kaleidoscope of colorful flowers seemed to be overwhelming and overflowing on top of each other. It was like a thick blanket of flowers. The cotton-like fabric was yellowing from age but that just seemed to increase the beauty of it. Karen stroked the soft material.

Bea carefully folded the section she pulled out to fit it back into the box and handed it over Karen. The box was awkward to hold but wasn't as heavy as Karen had expected.

"Thank you for telling me about your parents. I'm sorry you had to recall such painful memories from the past. You have relieved many of my worries. I appreciate you calling me about the canopy. Most people would have just forgotten it and not bothered to call."

Karen started walking toward the front door.

"I've bothered you long enough. I must be going. I'm glad we had this chat, and I will take excellent care of your mother's bed. By the way, would you happen to know how old it is?"

Bea shook her head no in response to Karen's question.

"I imagined that it is at least a couple of hundred years old but really couldn't tell you, dear. I don't know much about things like that. I couldn't even give you an educated guess."

They spoke a little longer at the door about the weather and other minor things and Karen left after thanking Bea again.

Bea turned to her sister and said, "I hope she understood our message."

"I hope you didn't tell her too much," the tall woman replied as they watched Karen walk to her car.

Karen got into her car as quickly as possible. Her head was spinning. So much information and Bea had no idea how much she actually knew. Karen believed that bed had some form of mystical power to allow time-travel and transmit a type of kinetic power. Karen wondered if Bea's mother had these powers, as well.

She may never have the answer to that question.

She was appalled at the thought that this woman was classified as a schizophrenic, but the father knew she wasn't. Could that happen to her? He knew what was going on. Could Bea's father have been from the past? Why were they so protective of the bed? Were they afraid that the children would be classified as schizophrenic as well? Her father had to have been from the past. Otherwise, why keep his age hidden? Why did Bea's parents lock the bedroom door? And what about the canopy? Why did the mother panic like that when the canopy was up? Did it stop the transport into the past? Was the bed a key to the door of the past and the canopy a lock? Were her Jumping Bull and Standing Deer from the past as well?

It isn't necessary to study quantum physics or time-travel, she decided. It's all theories, anyway. She couldn't believe she was taking this seriously. What does anyone know about time-travel anyway, she thought. No one would believe it. They would classify anyone who claimed that they experienced time-travel as a lunatic. They would put them away, lock the door and throw away the key.

What is she up against? They could put her away if she told anyone. Fear overtook her; she could lose everything! Everything she worked so hard for. Karen wondered what Bonnie would think about all of this. She couldn't wait to tell her what Bea had spoken of. Bonnie would probably be the only person in the world who would believe Karen and not think she was losing her mind. She had already told Bonnie almost everything. She was the only one Karen could trust to sort through this extraordinary mess.

Karen received many answers from Bea and ended up with even more questions. She was exasperated.

She glanced at the canopy wondering if what Bea said was true. Did the canopy stop the time-travel, as Bea believed? She wasn't feeling tired. Obviously, time-travel didn't make you lose sleep. She could test the canopy and if it stopped her from going to the past, then, she would know that the canopy was some form of lock to prevent time-travel. Karen would definitely have to wait on testing the canopy until she knew that Jumping Bull was healthy again.

If the time-travel was getting to be too exhausting then, she could put up the canopy until she was ready to go back.

Return to the past, she thought if that was truly where she was going. She wanted to return. Conservative, down to earth Karen was looking forward to returning to the irresolute past. Oh dear, you are nuts.

Karen arrived home, checked her answering machine and returned the necessary calls. One was to set up an appointment for a conference with an administrator at the Regional Medical Center. Good. That was the hospital she was hoping would respond to her inquiries.

Dual lives, it might get to be a bit too much. Bea's mother and father did it, she rationalized. Nevertheless, look what happened to Bea's mother. She was classified as a schizophrenic. In those days, they didn't know as much about psychology, especially paranormal occurrences. Karen realized she had to be extremely careful and couldn't get too involved. What if she was caught in the past and couldn't return?

She brought the canopy into the den and placed it on the coffee table so she could show Bonnie. She grabbed some lunch and then gave Bonnie a call at work. Of course, she was out with a client. She thought acrimoniously, why in the world would she be there when she had so much to tell her?

Karen gathered the books on the Sioux Indians and went outside to relax and read on the patio. She sat herself next to the pool, while she waited impatiently for Bonnie to return her call.

Karen could not concentrate. Restlessly, she kept jumping up and checking the telephone to see if the ringer was on. When the telephone finally rang, it was a solicitor. Irritated by the unwanted call, she returned to reading the book.

Time seemed to be moving at a slow crawl. Finally, the telephone rang again. This time, it was Bonnie. Karen felt foolish. She could not stop talking and she felt as if she and Bonnie had switched personalities. After Karen was finished rambling, Bonnie said she would be over as soon as she could. Her husband was working late and she didn't need to go straight home. Karen was relieved knowing that Bonnie was coming over. It took a big weight off her shoulders. Bonnie would not think she was crazy. Karen knew she would not tell a soul.

Although she hired someone to do the landscaping and yard work, Karen puttered around the back yard pulling weeds out of the garden and debris off the ground. She kept herself busy trying to get her mind settled while waiting for Bonnie's arrival. Karen needed reassurance that she was the rational person she believed she was.

Bonnie beeped the horn as she pulled into the driveway. Karen walked around the front and saw Bonnie bending over into her trunk trying to retrieve an armful of books. With a determined expression, Bonnie told Karen she wanted to go with her.

"What?"

"I want to go with you. The next time my husband goes hunting over the weekend, I want to go into the past with you. I want to experience this paranormal encounter. What an adventure we could have!"

"Are you nuts? An adventure?"

"No, I am not nuts," snapped Bonnie. "Just help me get these books into the house. I have a lot to show you, starting with the bed you bought at the estate sale."

Bonnie placed the books on the kitchen table and pulled out one on Christian symbols.

"What did you do? Dig all your old college books out of the closets?"

"Yes, as a matter of fact, I did. Now, come here. Let me show you something." Bonnie walked into the bedroom and went to the headboard.

"Look at the carvings on here. Remember when we were checking them out when you first bought the bed? Well, I thought I recognized some of the carving but I wasn't sure. It had been so long since I had studied the arts.

Karen, when you started telling me about those dreams, I thought there might be a connection somewhere but I wasn't sure what it was. Your dreams didn't start until after you purchased the bed, therefore, I knew the powers from the bed were from a higher power, but I wasn't sure if it was from witchcraft or from God."

Karen's heart skipped a beat before it clenched into a hard knot. "Witchcraft? What are you talking about?"

"Just hush and listen." Bonnie opened the book containing the Christian symbols. Throughout the book, she had pieces of paper marking certain pages.

"Look, right here at the top of the headboard. See this symbol? That is the symbol of the seven gifts of the Holy Spirit. If you read right here, you'll see that each dove represent the seven gifts ... wisdom, understanding, counsel, fortitude, knowledge, piety, and fear of the Lord."

"It says it's from the book of Isaiah." Karen pointed to the passage.

"Yes. 'And the Spirit of the Lord shall rest upon him, the spirit of wisdom and understanding, the spirit of counsel and might, the spirit of knowledge and the fear of the Lord.' 11:2."

"11:2?" Karen asked.

"You should read the Bible more often Karen. Chapter eleven, verse two."

"Oh."

"Look over here, it's amazing, Next to the angels on the right side of the headboard, see? This carving of a ship in a circle refers to Noah. The mast symbolizes the cross of Jesus. The World Council of Churches uses this as an emblem representing the mission of the church. See the letters? 'OIKOUMENE,' it means the entire inhabited world."

Karen nodded her head and let Bonnie continue. She didn't have the knowledge Bonnie had. Karen believed in God, Jesus, and the Holy Spirit but she didn't attend church every week like Bonnie. She just tried to be the best person she could.

"Now over here, the Chi Rho is the symbol of Christ, the wreath circling it is a symbol of victory. And if you look at the angels surrounding the symbols you'll see that some are holding universally recognized symbols of Christ. Now let's go look at the foot board."

Both Karen and Bonnie sat down on the floor to see the foot board detail. Karen pushed the bottom of the comforter off the footboard onto the bed.

"Look …"

"A pentagram! I never noticed it before. Isn't it a symbol of Satanism?" Karen asked in dismay.

"Yes and no." Bonnie turned to another page and handed the book over to Karen. "Here. It would be easier if you read it yourself."

As Karen read the section Bonnie got up and retrieved another book.

"The pentagram on the bed has the star upright. This," Bonnie pointed to the other book. "The star is tilted or upside-down."

"Okay, and ..." Karen inquired.

"The pentagram on your bed is used as a sign to ward off witchcraft and the Evil Eye. Some people call it Solomon's Seal or The Endless Knot. As the book says, these letters S-A-L-V-S in the points are a symbol of health."

Karen rubbed her hands over her face and sighed. What happened to her simple life?

"Also," Bonnie said, "the star can be considered as three overlapping triangles. A symbol of the Trinity."

Both stared at the bed. The silence was thick, but it was a peaceful silence. Karen's fears seemed to slowly dissipate.

Karen was intent on studying the intricate detail of the angels, doves and fish. How talented this person was, she surmised, to be able to carve everything so intricately and intertwine all the symbols. It amazed her that someone could create such a breathtaking masterpiece.

"Karen, you know the angels all represent guidance and protection. It reminds me of the Angel of God prayer. You know it: 'Angel of God, My guardian dear ... .'"

"Yes, I guess it does. But it really isn't telling me what I'm supposed to be doing. Is it?"

"Karen, you're going to be fine. Just fine! Just remember that prayer and use it." With a big smile on her face, she leaned over and gave Karen a huge hug.

"Yeah, I guess I will be. Just stick by me, Bonnie. Be there for me. You're the only one who can know," Karen whispered unnecessarily.

Karen and Bonnie walked back into the kitchen to make some coffee for the two of them. She told Bonnie everything that had occurred during the day. After a while, she asked what was in Bonnie's bag. Strangely enough, she said, "Clothes."

"Clothes? I don't need any clothes. I don't have room in the closet now."

Bonnie laughed. "You can't keep wearing those clothes you're in now. And you certainly can't wear your nightgowns."

"What in the world are you talking about?"

"Clothes, dear. You need clothes for when you go see your gorgeous Standing Deer and all the rest of the people you will meet in the past. You need clothes to wear so you can fit in. I don't think our way of dressing is appropriate for that period. Do you?"

Bonnie laughed as she pulled the clothes out of the bag.

"Maybe," Bonnie said, "that's why Standing Deer was looking at you so strangely. The other Indian you're helping ... ."

"Jumping Bull."

"Jumping Bull never saw you. Not really. He just thinks you're some angel that has come to save his life." Bonnie laughed and hugged her good friend, "You're a good and honest person, but an angel? Just remember, I know all your secrets."

"Ha, ha, ha. Let me see those clothes." Karen walked over, handed Bonnie a cup of coffee, and started to look over the bag of clothes.

"Oh goodness. I'm going to have to wear these things? I'm a tomboy. Tomboys don't wear dresses. Not dresses down to the floor. Can't I wear jeans?" Karen complained.

"Oh, quit your whining. Think of the adventure! Think about how exciting this is going to be. I've got moccasins here, too. Two pairs. Try them on. The dresses, too. I'll need to adjust them so they'll fit you right."

"Oh, for Pete's sake," Karen snapped.

"Just humor me, will you?" It was obvious that Bonnie was quite amused by the whole situation. As she watched Karen struggle into the dress, her smile couldn't get any wider. She was much more accustomed to seeing Karen in gym shorts and pumping bar bells.

"What period are these clothes from?"

"I picked them up at a second hand store. The sales lady said they are copies from the late 1800s. But I think you're in a time period earlier than that."

"Why do you say that?"

"Well, you mentioned that Standing Deer was Sioux. Hoping to find other names, I looked up information on Sitting Bull because he was a famous Sioux Indian chief. When I found the information at the library, I found that his father's name was Jumping Bull. Just maybe, your Jumping Bull is one in the same."

"I found a Jumping Bull in my research as well. Oh Lord. Are you trying to tell me I'm in the middle of the Indian wars?" Karen yelled.

"Karen, quit stressing. No, you are not. What have you been researching? The wars didn't start until around the time Sitting Bull was chief. We don't even know if Sitting Bull is even born yet or if this Jumping Bull is his father."

Bonnie had all the calmness that was characteristic to Karen and completely out of character for Bonnie. Wasn't I the one who was supposed to be staying calm, wondered Karen?

"Oh, he's born. Unless he had Sitting Bull late in life, Sitting Bull is alive and well."

Karen shared all the information that she had researched about the Lakota Indians. Between the two of them, they felt as if they were almost experts. They knew all too well that living with the Indians would be a whole different world. Books never really prepared you for reality. She had to learn about the People and their ways.

Karen continued trying on the dresses, all the while mumbling to herself about how uncomfortable the clothes were to wear. The time went by so fast that when they looked at the clock, it was after ten. Bonnie made a quick apologetic call to her husband and ran out of the house. Karen watched as she drove off. She smiled to herself, knowing that Bonnie's husband was used to her running late all the time.

Karen put all the clothes and moccasins that Bonnie had given her and placed them on the bed. She decided to take a couple of pairs of jeans with her and her hiking boots as well. Her bed was piled with clothes. Hopefully they would go with her when she falls asleep. Maybe if she held them in her hands they would surely go with her.

Bonnie was right. She could not continue to go into the past dressed in modern clothing. Oh goodness, thinking about her last trip, she remembered that she had on a thin nightgown when she was there. She had believed she had been dreaming. Karen was thoroughly embarrassed. She walked around like that. Jumping Bull saw her in her nightgown.

As Karen laid her head down onto the pillow, she decided to get back up and put one of the dresses on, just in case. Restless, she picked a solid sky blue chintz. It was very quaint. The dress had a very low, plunging and ruffled neckline with small shoulders attached to sleeves that went to her elbow.

The dress had a gathered waist that buttoned up the front. Ruffles started from the middle of the waist, circled down to the bottom of the dress, and then went all around the hem in triple layers. The dress seemed inappropriate for the savage west, but it was the plainest dress that Bonnie had brought her. Jeans would be better but I'll try this for now, Karen decided.

She walked over to the closet and retrieved her 357 from the shelf. She wondered if she should bring her rifle as well but decided to wait. Karen went over to the bureau, grabbed the bullets out of her drawer, loaded the gun and slipped it into one of the deep pockets of the dress. Then, she thanked her father silently for teaching her how to hunt at a young age. She slipped the boot moccasins on and lay down to fall asleep for her trip. She was tired.

Tired, restless and anxious, Karen got up again to pick out clothes she was going to wear for her second conference with the hospital administrator. Then, she went into the kitchen and made herself some hot chocolate, grabbed the book on self-defense and went back to the bedroom.

Karen was only a few pages into the book, when she realized she would need to go to a class. She wrote a note to herself to register for classes tomorrow and lay down. She sighed. This bed is so comfortable. The last thing she recalled was that she had forgotten to thank Bonnie for all she had done.

Chapter FOUR

Karen was slowly waking to the coolness of the cave and the stale smells that surrounded her. She could hear slight movement but was not shaken or surprised by it. She knew where she was and was glad to be there. Standing up and stretching she looked over at her patient.

Jumping Bull was wide-awake and sitting up in the bed. She smiled at him as she walked over to see how his wounds were healing.

Unfortunately for the very modern Karen, walking in floor length gowns and petticoats was not a normal everyday occurrence. Karen stepped on the bottom of the dress and tripped. She went skidding across the room, landing face first, smack dab at the foot of the bed. She started laughing at herself as she pulled herself up off the floor of the cave. Karen wiped off the dirt from the long, flowing dress and mumbled that she had to learn to walk in the blasted things.

She looked up at Jumping Bull and saw absolutely no expression from him whatsoever. If she had looked a little closer, she would have seen the amusement in Jumping Bull's eyes. It was obvious to him she wasn't accustomed to the attire she was wearing. He recalled what she had been wearing before. He wondered why she changed her style of clothing.

Jumping Bull knew there was something different about her but could not quite put his finger on it yet. How she managed to bring these white man's belongings into Sioux territory without being seen by anyone were beyond his comprehension, but he would wait and see.

For some reason, Jumping Bull felt that he was going to get to know this woman and they were going to be lifelong friends. She had come from somewhere and the Great Spirit had brought her to him.

Karen walked the few steps around the side of the bed slowly and cautiously. She definitely did not want to trip again and make a complete fool of herself. It was going to take practice maneuvering herself around in the dress.

As she checked her patient over, she could see there obviously had not been poison involved or he would still be very sick. Jumping Bull sat there, still as can be, and let her check his wounds without saying a word. Karen found the silence to be refreshing, especially after being with Bonnie most of the night.

She recalled a few occasions when her patients would babble from nervousness no matter how much she tried to keep them relaxed. She applied more ointment on Jumping Bull's wounds and pulled out the thermometer from the drawer to check his temperature. Jumping Bull leaned back and gave Karen a wary look. She laughed as she nudged it under his tongue and proceeded to check the wound at the nape of his neck. He was healing well.

"Let's go outside and get you some fresh air."

Jumping Bull got up slowly from the bed. "I not find how to leave."

"Well, I'm glad you didn't leave until I knew you were better. The door is right there." She pointed to the right of the bed.

With eyes wide with astonishment, he looked to where she pointed. Jumping Bull had not seen the door earlier. He gave Karen a puzzled look and followed her as she exited the cave. He had gone over the whole cave and had not found one exit. The Great Spirit had brought him something indeed. How had she gotten in the cave without him seeing her enter? How did she get in? One second, his eyes were closed and no one was around and the next second he opened his eyes and there she was. She must be very powerful. Maybe she was a daughter of the Great Spirit come to earth to help the Indian Nation. He nodded his head. She has come at a good time. The ceremonies would be starting soon.

The sun was bright as they went through the cave passage to the outside. Karen reached into her pocket and put on a pair of sunglasses. She was glad she had thought of getting her gun. When she retrieved the bullets out of her bureau drawer, she grabbed her sunglasses as well.

"What those?" Jumping Bull asked as he pointed to the glasses.

"These are for your eyes. They are called sunglasses. They protect them. Do you want to try them on?" Taking them off she handed them to him.

Jumping Bull took them out of her hand. He twirled them around and looked at them from every angle possible. He put them on and looked around.

"It makes sunshine dark. I use them, a while." He nodded his head in acknowledgment.

Karen smiled at the man. His natural coloring had returned. His graying hair, adorned with feathers, was down to the middle of his back. He looked funny in modern sunglasses with his deerskin pants and feathers in his braided hair.

Not any funnier than she looked, she mused, as she looked down at the dress she was wearing. None of the other clothes came with her. She concluded that in order for her to bring anything back with her, she must be wearing or holding whatever she wanted to take.

Jumping Bull was looking around and surveying the area. "My horse be back. Warriors come to find me, did not. Warriors took her with them. I go get something to eat."

Jumping Bull turned around to enter the cave to get his bow and arrow. He was startled when he did not see the opening to the cave. "Where cave opening?" he asked Karen with amazement.

Karen turned around and pointed to the opening. She watched Jumping Bull's eyes widen with disbelief and excitement. He took off the sunglasses and looked closer, inspecting the exterior of the cave and entrance.

"Door not there until you turn around, point to it," said the astonished Jumping Bull. Jumping Bull was convinced she had much power to make things appear and disappear.

Puzzled, Karen stood at the entrance to the door as she watched him grab his bow and arrows and walk back out of the cave. She was puzzled by his comment about the door. It didn't make sense. What did he mean, it wasn't there?

Jumping Bull turned around and told her he would return. Karen walked over to the pond and reflected on everything that was happening to her. The cave opened and closed to her only. How can that happen?

She could transport herself from area to area by willpower. The limitations and the possibilities could be endless! Just imagine what she could accomplish!

Try something small, one step at a time, she thought. She noted to herself that there wasn't any wind. She decided to try to make the leaves stir on the tree nearest to her. She stared at a small section and concentrated on moving the leaves. After a few moments the branch and leaves moved. I did it! She was ecstatic. She did it.

Next, she looked at a branch that was on the ground. She was concentrating so hard to lift the branch off the ground that she did not hear the three Indians approach on their horses.

The Indians paused to watch this strange white woman staring at the ground as if she was possessed. They conversed among themselves quietly wondering what she was doing. They looked around to see if anyone else was around or hiding. They spotted no one and cautiously approached her. This woman could not possibly be alone. There had to be a white man around somewhere, but where? As they gradually came closer, one of the horses neighed.

Startled, Karen turned around. She did not want Jumping Bull to see what she was doing. To her astonishment, she was looking straight at three of the fiercest looking Indians she could imagine. She noticed there were four horses. She looked around to see where the fourth Indian was but to no avail.

They were young men. Their faces were painted with black stripes and white circles. All had feathers in their hair. One of the warriors had earrings made of beads in both of his ears; another had what looked like a bear claw necklace. They conversed among themselves as she stood staring at them. Were they from Jumping Bull's tribe or were they from another band? She did not have the knowledge to tell the difference.

Discreetly, she reached into her pocket to hold onto her gun. Karen knew she had to keep it hidden from them. She wasn't sure she was in danger but something was telling her to be careful. To be extremely careful!

The Indian with the beads in his hair dismounted his horse and walked over to her. She quickly noted the knife on his belt, started to back away and was ready to run.

She turned around to run when he jumped and grabbed a fist full of her hair. He swung her around and twisted her hair around his fist and arm. In the bustle, Karen had let go of the gun. He had her pressed hard against his chest and body. The more she fought and kicked, the harder he pulled on her hair. He had her bound and helpless.

She could feel where the gun had fallen onto the ground underneath the skirt of her dress. She could and would be able to think of a way of getting herself out of this predicament.

Chest heaving, she forced herself to relax and as she did, so did the Indian. His lips were close to her neck and she could feel him breathing on her. He spoke quickly to the other Indians. Both men had already dismounted. The one with the bear claw necklace stood with his arms across his chest while the other walked over to her. They had wide grins on both of their faces.

Karen tried not to imagine what they had in mind. She knew. Karen could feel his member, his manhood, hard and ready against her bottom. He started to rub himself against her and kiss her neck. Karen squirmed and tried to get away from the hardness of him. He grinned at her and purred something in her ear. She may not have understood the dialect but his body told what was on his mind.

The other Indians reached for the bodice of her dress and pulled it wide open exposing her breasts to them. The one with the earrings spotted the gun immediately and grabbed it. Karen held her breath. The Indian took the gun, rubbed it on her private parts, and then slowly rubbed the gun up her abdomen to her breasts. He encircled her breasts and then, gently and slowly, up to her neck. He took the gun and slipped it in his loincloth. Before she had time to realize what was to be next, she was on the ground. Pummeling anything with in her reach, she screamed, punched and kicked.

"Hiya!" Jumping Bull yelled as he ran toward the group. "Hiya."

Oh, thank God. Jumping Bull, Karen thought. Oh, what wonderful timing. Somebody up there is watching over me.

Jumping Bull ran over to where they were and started yelling to the Indians. The three men let go of Karen immediately. As she was scrambling to her feet, she pictured herself pulling the man with the bear claw necklace by the hair. By sheer force of her will, he was yanked backwards by the hair. Karen closed her eyes and shook the vision from her mind. The Indian looked behind him and saw no one there. Puzzled, he reached up to rub the back of his head. Karen covered herself with her torn dress and buttoned what she could.

She watched as Jumping Bull spoke to the men. The Indian with the earrings reluctantly handed Karen's handgun back to her. They did not look very pleased with whatever Jumping Bull was telling them.

They spoke calmly and with respect to Jumping Bull as they walked over to their horses. The Indian with the bear claw necklace took the riderless horse and walked him over to Karen.

"Wanunhecun." He reached out to hand the reins to Karen. When she did not accept the gift from the Indian, he shook the reins and repeated, "Wanunhecun."

With her mouth wide open in astonishment, Karen looked at Jumping Bull unsure of what she should do.

"They Cheyenne warriors. They not harm you again. Now, they know you friend of Jumping Bull's." Jumping Bull told them more than that but Karen had no idea of what it was.

"What is 'Wanunhecun'?"

"That Indian's way of asking forgiveness. It mean mistake. Horse was peace offering. He no want bad luck to follow him because he harm you. I tell them you have great medicine. Important to make peace with you or bad luck follow warriors."

Karen laughed. "That's a terrible thing to tell him. Why in the world would you go and tell them something like that?"

"You have much power, little one. They can be used for good or bad."

Jumping Bull was successful in his hunt for food and asked the warriors to join them. As they cut up the rabbits Jumping Bull killed, the men spoke quietly among themselves. Jumping Bull was contemplating with the warrior who had the bear claw necklace as to why he had been picked for this honored position with the daughter of the Great Spirit.

He thanked the Great Spirit for the chance to prove himself worthy of the chance to do whatever He had in mind. Jumping Bull would be here for her, this woman Karen, as she calls herself, this spirit from the mountain.

After they finished with rabbits, Karen fixed her dress with the tools Jumping Bull had given her. She wished Bonnie were here to do it. She recalled Jumping Bull's words: "You have much power, little one. They can be used for good or bad." She was determined to never forget those words. It was a warning to her to be careful with what she thinks. She could seriously hurt someone if she was not careful.

Jumping Bull was a very wise man. He had a lot of spiritual and practical knowledge he would be able to teach her. It was exciting and scary to know that she had kinetic abilities, once she had control over them the possibilities could be endless. This kind of power in the wrong hands would be catastrophic.

Karen pictured the headboard with the Emblem of the Seven Gifts of the Holy Spirit. It was there as a reminder, she believed. It had to be there so whoever had the bed would use the powers with the Lord in mind at all times. These powers must be used with the gifts in mind, never to be abused. She felt she was beginning to sound as religious as Bonnie.

Obviously, there was something behind Bonnie's beliefs and she was right in the middle of it.

Jumping Bull watched Karen fumble with the dress. He was amused at her lack of capabilities to do womanly chores. She sewed his wounds with precision. Yet, when it came to life's necessities, she was unskilled.

He wondered why she was here and if she would tell him what the Great Spirit's plans were. He may never ask. It was not his place to question the Great Spirit. But he would ask if he had the chance. He decided to invite her to return with him. He would like to have a great feast in her honor to thank her for saving his life. He hoped she would stay for a while.

Karen enjoyed the silence. It was one of complete comfort. The peace and serenity she felt when she was in the past were overwhelming at times. There wasn't any necessity to hurry. There hadn't been any major stress except for the little episode with the Cheyenne. No need for clocks. Karen liked that. People at home were always in a hurry. Everywhere people were rushing, for what? She wondered. To save five minutes? Here, one just takes it as it comes.

Simplicity seemed to disappear in the modern world and the need to have all the luxury's life had to offer had taken over the world. The world she was raised in consisted of concrete building and paved streets. It seemed everything had to be the best and biggest, never being satisfied with what life had to offer.

Even she had fallen into the trap of material things. She had bought a huge home. Four bedrooms, three baths, formal living room, an office, a den, a family room … and the home was just for her. Why did she feel she had the need for such a large home? She rationalized that she needed a tax break, but couldn't she have done something else? She could have purchased sixty acres somewhere and had a small house built on the land. If she ever found the right man to marry, then they could add on to the house if it was needed. She shook her head in dissatisfaction with herself.

She did need a newer car though, especially if she acquired the job with the hospital. It wasn't the position she had originally applied for but she liked the idea of bringing back the traditional home visits. It was a new department and would interface with the hospital. The administrator emphasized that she wouldn't be required to be in the office every day.

She would be driving house to house and treating people in their homes, so they did not have to go to a doctor's office, just like her father did. Her father preferred house calls. He believed it was better for the patient.

Here, it is a different world. She silently watched the warriors standing near their horses preparing to leave. Karen realized she had much to learn. If Jumping Bull would be willing to teach her everything he could, she could survive in this time period without the need of anyone else's protection. Or he could possibly have someone else teach her. He may not have time for her, especially if he is a chief, like Bonnie believes.

After the farewells were made, Jumping Bull sat down beside her and waited for her to speak. He could see she had much to say.

"Jumping Bull, there is much for me to learn if I am going to continue to stay here in this unfamiliar land. I do not know how to take care of myself in the ways that you know. I already know how to hunt. My father taught me. But I do not know how to live off the land. I don't know what I'm not supposed to eat and I do not know how to shoot a bow and arrow. Nor do I know how to throw a knife. I would not survive without someone to protect me. I do not want the need for a protector. I want to do it myself."

Karen looked at him with hope that he would agree to help her. She waited in silence for his response. After a few moments he spoke.

"If what you say true, I help you. When I can. I have many good warriors and women in the village who help you. I have them help you. They also teach you ways of land, ways of Indian. How you have come this far in your life and not been taught the way to live as People do? You should have been prepared. You are the child of the Great Spirit. Did you not learn His lessons?"

Karen was puzzled by Jumping Bull's questions and unsure how to respond. She was well educated, but how could she explain the difference of her lack of knowledge he considers mandatory for survival, without making herself out to be an idiot? Books are one thing, surviving in the wilderness is another. She spoke cautiously, unsure of his knowledge of the way of the white man.

"Where I come from, there are not many trees and wildlife. One goes to a store for food and drink. You go to a store to buy clothing and anything else that you could possibly need. The buildings are made of concrete and steel, the streets are made of concrete as well. Where I am from, some of the buildings are two hundred and three hundred feet high." Karen reached up her arms to emphasize the height of the buildings, in comparison to the trees. She continued carefully.

"One does not use horses for transportation, they use large vehicles on wheels, called cars or trucks. They use fuel, called gasoline to make them go, and they are driven on these streets, what you call trails or paths, made of concrete. There are highways and expressways so you can go fast to wherever you want to go. There are hardly any dirt roads, usually one finds them in very remote areas of the country. It is a very different world."

Karen paused to see if there was a slight change in expression, but found none. She thought to herself that Indians would be proficient poker players. He sat silently waiting for her to continue.

"Hunting is a sport, it is something we do for fun and enjoyment. It is not normally a necessity to hunt for food. Even though my father taught me to eat what we hunted and not kill animals just for sport, not everyone does it that way." Karen paused and then continued.

"God, the Great Spirit teaches us humanity and has given us laws to live by. We are all children of God, of the Great Spirit. I am a normal person, just like you. I have just been chosen to come here and live this life to the best of my ability. I have been given many great powers that I do not yet know how to control. I do not always have these powers. I have knowledge of medicine because I studied it for many years. Those are the only powers that I am truly sure of. I can heal most people, cure some illnesses, and I do my best to try and help all people."

Karen prayed that he would at least understand some of what she had said. He listened with every sense of his being. He did not interrupt but let her finish her thoughts. She could see many questions rushing through his mind.

Jumping Bull nodded his head to acknowledge everything she said. He did not say a word in response to her explanations. Jumping Bull was not ready to ask Karen about her strange world. He wasn't sure if he really wanted to know. Jumping Bull reached into his bag and handed Karen the sunglasses.

"Don't you like them?"

Jumping Bull grunted. "I not hunt good with them blinding my eyes. Oiyokpasya. It makes sun dark. My horse return soon. It is good Cheyenne give you horse. I would like you to come with me when it time to leave. There many things we teach each other."

Jumping Bull handed her a piece of meat and they both ate in silence. After they were finished, Jumping Bull grabbed his bow and arrow and got up.

"Let us go," Jumping Bull said quietly.

Karen jumped up enthusiastically and shook off her dress as she followed Jumping Bull. They walked beside the pond toward the woods. Karen was about to get her first lesson in survival.

"Don't like dress, do you?" he laughed.

Chapter FIVE

Standing Deer was glad he finally spoke to Sitting Bull about his dreams, hoping Sitting Bull would understand what they meant. It was the haunting footprints that finally brought him to Sitting Bull's lodge. He wasn't sure if they were her prints when he first saw them.

Yet, Standing Deer kept having dreams about the woman. He could not get her off his mind. He kept dreaming the whole experience every night. Standing Deer would wake up trembling from the memory of how she had felt in his arms, longing for her arms to be around him. There was a magnetism he could not forget. Even now, riding next to Two Feathers on their way to where they found Jumping Bull's horse, he could still feel her body against his.

He could recall the sweet smell of her body, the soft touch of her hair, the urgent desire to want to make love to her, right then and there. Standing Deer closed his eyes slowly and seized the memory of how she had felt next to him. He took a deep breath allowing his mind to ravish itself. All sights and sounds escaped him. He could only think of Karen.

"Standing Deer, what world are you in?" Two Feathers shouted.

Startled out of his memories, Standing Deer looked blankly at Two Feathers.

"I asked you if you were feeling well."

"I'm fine. Why do you ask?"

"I have never seen you behave like this. Your mind is very far away. Are you sure nothing is bothering you, my friend?"

"It's that woman." Standing Deer breathed deeply. "She will not leave my mind. I just know they were her footprints. She must know what has happened to Jumping Bull. I can't explain it but I believe she will lead us to him."

Two Feathers arched one eyebrow but did not pursue questioning Standing Deer. He knew Standing Deer's dreams had a lot to do with his behavior in the last few days. It was obvious the woman was on Standing Deer's mind and not just because of Jumping Bull. He had never seen Standing Deer act so strangely. This woman must be something to look at if she has Standing Deer all flustered.

Two Feathers knew Standing Deer had not been with a woman since his wife died four years ago. As far as he knew, Standing Deer had not been interested in anyone and he definitely had plenty of choices among the unmarried women of the tribe. There were many that would be honored to be his wife.

Standing Deer and Two Feathers had been friends since boyhood. They learned together and hunted together. They even did the Sun Dance together. They both had the same amount of coups until Standing Deer's wife died of the white man's disease.

Standing Deer's boy died inside of her. Ever since, Standing Deer worked harder than anyone he could think of and received more coups than anyone else in the tribe did. Everyone knew it was Standing Deer's way of mourning his wife and child's death. Even still, Standing Deer was highly respected among their tribe.

Two Feathers and his own wife, Laughing Flower, stood by Standing Deer the whole time his wife was sick. They would take turns feeding her and caring for her. Laughing Flower even did all of the work that needed to be done in Standing Deer's lodge. After his wife's death, Laughing Flower continued to help Standing Deer until he growled at her one morning that he was not a puppy and did not need to be treated like one. The next day, Standing Deer had left his dead wife's horse in front of Two Feathers and Laughing Flower's tent. Even encircled by his deep sorrow, Standing Deer still had compassion in his heart.

Standing Deer was happy Sitting Bull had told him to take Two Feathers with him. They had been blood brothers since childhood. They were the best riding companions and warriors. Together, they were never defeated. Whatever Two Feathers was not strong at, Standing Deer was. Wherever Standing Deer was not strong, Two Feathers excelled.

Two Feathers had the biggest heart of gold ever in any man. As far as Two Feathers was concerned, there was no evil in a man. He was so idealistic, to a fault maybe. Though he was not a medicine man, he would find all sorts of injured creatures and bring them to his lodge to heal them. It seemed to Standing Deer that it hurt Two Feathers to see any animal in pain.

Standing Deer remembered how hard it was on Two Feathers the first time he had killed a man. It was a trapper. The crazy white man had tried to kill Two Feathers and he reacted exactly the way he was taught. Survival is a strong motivater. He was taught well, the way of the Lakota warrior. It was pure instinct to slash the man's throat.

Two Feathers had been shaken by it for days until Standing Deer was fed up with his moping around and finally told him that it was either his death or the trapper's. Which one would Two Feathers prefer it to be? Two Feathers found it hard to see evil in anyone. But that is what makes Two Feathers who he is.

Two Feathers had found the perfect mate. Laughing Flower was precious. Standing Deer smiled to himself. She was like a sister to him. Laughing Flower had a good sense of humor and a wonderful outlook on life. Her energy was abundant, like a child. Just don't get her mad or she'll kick you like one.

Two Feathers and Laughing Flower had listened with undivided attention when he had told them of his experience with Karen. She had teased Standing Deer and told him he had finally found someone as stubborn as himself. Laughing Flower said there would be much noise coming from his lodge once he found her again. Laughingly, she teased, that was of course if he was warrior enough to keep her in one place.

Standing Deer felt a tap on his arm and looked over to Two Feathers. Two Feathers nodded his head toward a clearing where Jumping Bull and the woman were getting ready to shoot a handgun. It appeared to them that the woman was showing Jumping Bull how to use the small gun that was in his hand.

Two Feathers let go of Long Horse Hair's reins and let her run to her master, Jumping Bull. Standing Deer and Two Feathers rode their horses slowly to the clearing. Two Feathers was zealously looking over Karen. In his opinion, as far as he could see, Karen was everything Standing Deer had described ... and more. She was beautiful. Standing Deer couldn't have described her better. Her hair, Two Feathers had never seen anything like it before! So many colors all shimmering and radiating from the reflection of the sun, as if the sun encircled her and shined from her being. He smiled at Standing Deer with complete understanding.

He watched Standing Deer's demeanor change right before his eyes. Two Feathers could see that Standing Deer's breath was coming faster as they got closer to the woman.

Standing Deer's eyes did not leave the woman, as if he was mesmerized. If it was possible, he sat taller and prouder on his horse. She was the woman for Standing Deer. The Great Spirit has indeed blessed him. He hoped the woman felt the same way about Standing Deer.

Jumping Bull looked up to see his horse galloping toward him and Karen. The reunion was a happy one for both master and his beloved animal. Not far behind the horse, Karen could see two Indians approaching them.

Was it him? She couldn't be certain with the sun shining in her eyes. She could not get a good glimpse of what they looked like. It looked just like him. That stature was unmistakable.

Karen took a deep breath. She could feel her heart palpitate in excitement. Hope was in her heart, she wanted to see him again and feel the things she felt while she had been in his arms. Oh my, she panicked, what if he is married? She hadn't thought of that before! He had to be married. Karen let out a heavy sigh. He's a grown man, at least around the age of thirty! He probably had six kids running around and possibly two wives. He did indeed appear to be an extremely sexy and strong man. Two wives probably wouldn't even slow him down. She couldn't fall in love with someone from the past. It would make life too complicated.

Jumping Bull noticed Karen sigh again with a look of sadness and disappointment on her face. He was puzzled by the change in her. Misunderstanding her reaction and sadness on her face, he promptly told her she did not have to worry. She was safe.

Karen watched as the two Indians dismounted off their horses. Jumping Bull was greeting them. They were having a lengthy conversation. It was all in Lakota and Karen had no idea what they were saying.

Karen was trying unsuccessfully to calm herself. It was him! His hair was braided to one side with a leather strap fastening it with a singular feather hanging across his chest. He wore nothing but a loincloth. Standing Deer's copper skin glistened from the heat of the sun.

Her heart was pounding so hard. She knew they would surely see it right through the stupid dress. She felt like pudding. Get rid of the childish school girl reaction, she reprimanded herself. Why was she like this with Standing Deer, she wondered. No one, not one person in her whole life had ever made her react this way. Look at yourself, she was yelling from within her mind. Her heart was racing a mile a minute, if she didn't slow her breathing down she would hyperventilate. Her palms were sweaty and her hands were shaking. She was more nervous than she had ever been in her lifetime.

Jumping Bull turned around to introduce the men to Karen. Two Feathers nodded his head and had a smile so wide that his whole entire face lit up when he smiled. She liked him immediately. The man was dressed in a loincloth as well. He had leather tied to both his lower arms, unlike Standing Deer who had only one on his left arm. She wondered if this smiling warrior was capable of shooting his bow and arrow with both hands.

Standing Deer gave her a lighthearted grin and told Jumping Bull they had already met. Jumping Bull looked at Standing Deer with raised eyebrows questioning his statement, but said nothing.

Jumping Bull turned to Karen and asked, "Do you have anything you want to bring with you?"

"Yes. My medical bag is in the cave." Karen started walking toward the cave entrance when out of the corner of her eye she saw the two Indians reactions. She smiled to herself and kept on walking.

Standing Deer looked at Two Feathers in surprise wondering what cave she was speaking about. Two Feathers spoke first.

"What cave?" he asked Jumping Bull.

"I will explain what I can on our way back home. And you, Standing Deer, can tell me about your experience with our little one."

There was much talking going back and forth between the four of them. She guessed Two Feathers did not know much English by the way he spoke it. He put many Lakota words in his sentences.

Karen was finally getting back to her normal self. Except when she would look at Standing Deer and catch him looking at her. She would direct her eyes somewhere else but she knew he had not looked away. There was such an incredible magnetism. Karen wondered if Standing Deer felt it as well.

Standing Deer was wondering the same thing. He liked the feel of the electrical pulse that was going back and forth. He was amused at her attempt to dress like other white woman. He could see she was not accustomed to wearing such clothing. He started chuckling to himself and caught himself before anyone could hear it. She looked so uncomfortable pulling the top of the dress up where it barely covered her breasts.

It was comical watching her try to straddle the horse with the long dress on. It took her three tries to get on the horse, with the dress fighting her the whole time. Finally, she just wrapped it around her arm and jumped up exposing those wonderful, muscular legs of hers. Then, she fought with the dress to tuck it under her legs. She succeeded on her own and was persistent, that was certain. She rode the horse well, too. All three of the Indians noticed that she rode like a man, not like a white woman.

As they rode northward, Karen could see the mountains to her left and the plains to her right. It was so breathtaking. The wilderness seemed hostile to her but the comfort of knowing she was with Indians that knew how to survive in this land kept her mind at ease.

They rode on until after dark and decided to camp overnight near a river. Standing Deer gave her a blanket to lie on while she slept. As she dozed off to sleep, she hoped that her leaving them would not make them think she was deserting them. How would they react when they saw she was gone? She could hear the three men talking quietly around the campfire as she fell asleep.

It seemed Jumping Bull was the only one who was not startled. He smiled at the two curious warriors and told them she would return in the morning. Then he lay down to go to sleep. Two Feathers and Standing Deer did not say anything to each other. They were too amazed by the sight to say anything.

Karen awoke at the campsite with the aroma of food teasing her. She opened her eyes slowly and saw Standing Deer squatting near the fire, staring at her. She smiled at him satisfied with the accomplishments she had made while the three Indians slept.

It was pure luck that her new job did not start for a month. She told the administrator she was going to take a three-week vacation and would call him when she returned. Then, she and Bonnie agreed to try out the canopy and see if it kept her in the past. She would be able to live with the Indians and experience this wilderness undisturbed. Karen was excited.

Bonnie kept saying she was jealous and couldn't wait for hunting season to start so she could go with Karen.

Standing Deer interrupted Karen's thoughts and asked quietly, "Where do you go?"

Karen thought out the answer very carefully. She wasn't sure how much Standing Deer would understand without it sounding like it was magic.

"I go to where I belong," Karen said slowly. "When I fall asleep here, I go to another place and when I fall asleep there, I come back here."

Standing Deer shook his head in confusion, "I do not understand."

"My friend Bonnie believes, God has chosen me," Karen corrected herself, "the Great Spirit has chosen me to do special things. My home is far from here, where I have work to do, with many people to help. And here ... there are important things that need to be done also. But I am not sure what the Great Spirit has in mind for me yet. I just know there is a reason why I have come to you and this land."

Karen hoped she had explained it without telling too much. Standing Deer at least nodded his head in acceptance. She could see by his reaction that he could not fully understand everything she had told him. But he was accepting what she had said. Karen believed that was all she could ask.

When Jumping Bull and Two Feathers arrived back to the little campsite everyone ate and headed out to the village. Jumping Bull told her it would not be a long ride.

A few hours later, as Karen was watching the horizon, Standing Deer touched her arm and pointed northward. She could not see anything but the high grass billowing in the wind. As they rode closer, she concentrated on where he had shown her to look. The village blended into the landscape so well that she could just barely see the lodges. If a person was not looking or did not know they were there, they probably wouldn't have seen the village. At least, not until they were right on top of it.

There was great excitement throughout the village as they entered. People were hustling and bustling around. One Indian yelled something to Jumping Bull, hopped on his horse and took off at a fast run.

Three women had run up to Standing Deer. There was a lot of confusion. Everyone was talking to the three Indians all at once.

A tiny woman, with a baby in her arms, came running up to Two Feathers and gave him a huge hug. Karen could see a lot of love shared between the two of them. She felt forgotten and overwhelmed by all of the confusion going on around them. She felt out of place and lonely. The feeling did not last long.

An elderly woman came out of the largest lodge in the village. The woman had a beauty and grace all her own. Walking up to Jumping Bull, she started speaking so fast Karen was surprised Jumping Bull could keep up with her. Her emotions and actions were filled with concern. Jumping Bull told her to stop and turned around toward Karen and said something in Lakota to the People that had surrounded the party of travelers. Instantly there was a roar of cheer and excitement.

Standing Deer helped her off the horse and the women came up to her and gave her hugs. The men kissed her on the forehead and told her, "Wopila eciya niye." Thank you.

Karen was stunned, but loved every moment. After the excitement died down, Jumping Bull's wife took her to their lodge. Within a few moments, another woman and Two Feather's wife came into the lodge with dresses. The dresses were exquisitely decorated. Karen admired openly the decorative handwork as she touched them and felt a softness that she knew took hours and hours of work to accomplish.

Karen looked over to Jumping Bull's wife and she nodded her head in approval. Then the woman started making washing motions around her body and hair. Karen nodded her head and told them yes, desperately.

The three women escorted her to a deserted area of water, handed her some soap, and turned around to give her privacy. The soap smelled like English lavender. Karen wondered what they had to trade to get it.

The bath was invigorating. She felt like a whole new person, completely refreshed from the long ride on the trail. Two Feathers' wife handed her one of the dresses and Karen put it on.

It was more comfortable than that long thing she had on earlier. The dress was fringed around the arms and bottom of the dress. The beadwork alone must have been tedious, taking long hours with careful loving hands. Thank God the dress went to the middle of her calf and not to the ground. This, she was used to. At least she could walk and not worry about falling on her face. She smiled and realized that Jumping Bull probably had something to do with it.

Two Feathers stood outside the lodge and called to the women to see if he could enter. When he came in he told Karen, "Good, waste. More better?" He honored her with his wonderful smile.

"Yes. Yes, thank you very much."

With his hands moving rapidly in Indian sign language, Two Feathers spoke slowly, "Jumping Bull kicicopi. Woyuonihan for you. Come."

Two Feathers walked out with the women following. Jumping Bull's wife grabbed Karen's arm and escorted her out to the center of the village.

Standing Deer walked up to her and gave her a mischievous smile, "You look wonderful, Karen. Maybe someday I can see you in that strange attire I saw you in, when we first met."

Blushing, Karen was brought over to be seated next to Jumping Bull. He was in a conversation with someone. Karen took the time to watch everything that was going on around her. The happiness in the camp was contagious. She could see everyone had been finishing all of the preparations for the feast while she had been with Jumping Bull's wife. Karen could feel a little bit of hostility around her, but it was expected. After all, she was a white woman.

Across the way, she could see Standing Deer surrounded by three women. They were the same women that had greeted him upon their arrival. They must be his wives, she deduced sadly.

She had already decided that falling in love with Standing Deer would be a tremendous mistake. It was just impossibility. She could not live in both worlds forever and it would not be fair to him or their children. She was determined to avoid Standing Deer at all cost. It was best.

Standing Deer was watching Karen and was impressed with her silence. He felt it would be easy to teach her their ways. His two sisters, Sunshine in the Morning and Little Fox, were questioning him persistently about the beautiful woman. They had decided Karen was perfect for him. Even their friend, Yellow Bird, was excited about the woman. He knew she had hoped to someday be his new wife.

Karen turned her gaze away from Standing Deer and watched two Indians approaching Jumping Bull. She was stunned to see the warrior with the bear-claw necklace. What was he doing here? The other Indian was in a breechcloth and had scares on his chest just like Standing Deer. There was something different about him. He walked with a presence. She could see by the Indians reactions in the camp that he was important. He was a good-looking man with distinguished features. She noticed he had many feathers in his hair. He bowed his head to Jumping Bull and spoke to him in Lakota.

The Indian with the bear-claw necklace recognized Karen immediately. She could feel his uneasiness and tension building up inside of him. He did not let anyone see it. She thought to herself that he would do well at poker, too. Karen nodded her head to greet him when Jumping Bull introduced Karen to the two Indians.

"This warrior Sitting Bull," pointing to the Indian with the many feathers. "You meet this warrior. He Gray Eagle. He from the Cheyenne and honored Dog Soldier. He has honor to carry Dog Rope and great warrior among his people."

Jumping Bull paused. "Sitting Bull great warrior in his people's eyes. He has many coups and from Hunkpapa tribe." Jumping Bull paused and looked at Sitting Bull with admiration in his eyes. Turning to Karen he whispered to her, "It custom you stand to greet, honor them."

Karen quickly stood. She did not want to offend anyone. She was unsure of their customs and prayed that instincts would pull her through. Karen looked from one Indian to the next.

Gray Eagle touched her hand and said something to her in the Lakota language. He smiled at her and then said, "Niye wopila eciya." Thank you, Jumping Bull translated for her.

She knew thank you. She had heard it enough when she arrived at the village. She returned his smile and said to Gray Eagle, "It is an honor to meet such a great and honored warrior of the People."

Aware that Gray Eagle did not want the white woman to know he understood her language, Sitting Bull turned to Gray

Eagle and translated what she had said. Gray Eagle nodded his head and walked over to the other warriors that were standing in a group watching the introductions. Karen kept silent. She was not sure if she was to speak first but she knew Sitting Bull had something to say to her.

After a few moments, Sitting Bull reached over to take her hands. He spoke slowly and quietly, as if to make sure everything he said would be as accurate as possible, without any misunderstandings.

"I thank you for saving the great Jumping Bull's life. It is an honor to meet someone with the great powers you possess. You will always be in my heart as an honored friend. It is a great deed you have done and we owe our livelihood to you. I honor you this day and make you my friend for life." Sitting Bull then kissed her on the forehead.

Karen waited a few moments, knowing now that it is the way of the People. She also spoke slowly, "It is an honor to meet the great Chief Sitting Bull. You have done many great accomplishments in the past and will continue to honor your People in the future."

Karen paused, and then continued, "I accept your friendship with honor and give you mine. I pray to the Great Spirit that I may never dishonor you or your People."

Sitting Bull waited a few moments then shook his head, "I am not chief. Jumping Bull is our chief."

Appalled at the error, Karen's eyes opened wide with astonishment. Oh dear, she thought. I have to be careful. Especially with the knowledge I have of their future.

Luckily, Jumping Bull laughed and told her not to worry about her mistake. He padded the seat next to him and told her to sit. The feast was about to begin.

There was dancing, music and laughter throughout the village. An abundance of every kind of food one could desire was placed before her.

Those who could speak some English came to Karen. They spoke to her of their pleasure that she had saved their great chief. Some of the Indian women who could not speak English grabbed her and taught her how to do some of the dances. The feast went on until nightfall when the children were rushed to bed and it was just the men left to themselves.

Standing Deer approached Karen as she was leaving to go to sleep in Jumping Bull's lodge. He asked her if she would return in the morning. He informed her that at first sunlight they would be preparing for the start of the Sun Dance ceremonies. Karen told him she hoped to return and backed away slowly.

Standing Deer had been on her mind most of the night. She had managed to avoid him ... until now.

Standing Deer took her hand. "Let us walk. It is a good night for a walk and I have not been able to spend time with you. It seems everyone wanted to be with the beautiful Karen."

Standing Deer and Karen walked quietly, hand in hand, through the woods toward the water. The singing of the night creatures and the pleasant coolness of the night surrounded them.

She looked up to the heavens and watched the stars twinkling high above. Karen felt one with the earth, Mother Earth as the Indians called it. She fully understood how they felt about this land. She couldn't get over the fact that there was a peacefulness and serenity that surrounded a person when they were here. It was wonderful.

She was fully aware that Standing Deer still held her hand. It felt so small inside of his. The warmth of his skin went through her like an electrical pulse. She could feel the surges going through her being. Karen felt like a thirteen year old experiencing her first love. She kept reminding herself that she should not be with him. Yet, she could not tear herself away.

Standing Deer stopped near the edge of the water. He had slowly and sensuously moved his hand up to touch her face lightly. He was awed by the halo of moonlight surrounding her hair, making it shimmer and shine like the many stars above him. Standing Deer looked into Karen's eyes and watched the gold inside of the brown twinkle like the gold rocks white men fought over. Ever so slowly and cautiously, he bent his head down to touch her lips.

Karen had taken a deep breath. She did not move. She did not want to move. With the first contact of their lips, she closed her eyes and allowed herself to be overwhelmed by his touch. It was pure electricity. She felt the heated pulsation sweep through her body and soul. As he pressed harder, she allowed herself to melt into him. Karen heard nothing but a roar penetrating through her, like a freight train out of control. They were alone in the world. All she could feel was the burning heat from his lips and the coolness of his body against hers. It was like fire and water. As Standing Deer pulled away slowly, she could still feel the tingling sensation on her lips.

The betrayal of her body surprised her. Never had she felt her body shake from a passionate kiss or any other kind of sexual encounter. It was as if she had never been kissed before. No one had ever left her feeling so aware of a gentle, sensuous kiss. A kiss that invaded all of her being. No one ever left her so satisfied. Yet, she felt the desperate heated desire for more. She breathed a sigh of ecstasy and realized she had been holding her breath the whole time.

They stood there, still in the passionate embrace that had left both of them breathless. Soon, the sounds of the world crept around them, slowly invaded their ears.

Karen was the first to break the embrace. She had felt an immediate loss from the separation. Her eyes started to swell with water from unbidden, uncontrollable tears. Sadness engulfed her. Haunting reality stopped her from going back into the comfort of his arms. She questioned herself for the first time in her life. How can something so beautiful be so undeniably wrong?

Karen looked up at Standing Deer and could see confusion on his handsome face. She shook her head in a sad attempt to erase the swirling of her emotions, to stop the resistant tingling of her lips.

"This is wrong," she whispered, choked with heartfelt grief. Disgusted with herself, Karen turned and walked slowly away from Standing Deer. To her, it was the hardest thing she had ever had to do in her life.

Standing Deer was stunned. Didn't she feel the same? What was wrong? Did he do something wrong? A sense of loss overwhelmed him. Fear of her loss surrounded him like a pack of wolves.

"Did I dishonor you?" he yelled to her retreating back.

Karen stopped in mid-stride. Very aware of the betrayal of her body, she turned slowly around to face Standing Deer. She shook her head no.

She could barely speak. Her voice croaked. "I dishonored myself," she said sadly.

Confused, Standing Deer watched as she walked away. His eyes did not leave her retreating back until she was no longer in his sight. He did not understand.

Chapter SIX

Karen's despondency continued through her day and into the night. When she returned to Jumping Bull's lodge, she couldn't shake the feeling of sadness over the loss of Standing Deer. An overwhelming loss, a loss that she would not be experiencing if she had possibly been anyone else. She kept asking herself repeatedly, why did he have to be married?

She looked around and found she was alone in Jumping Bull's lodge. She was glad no one was around. She needed more time for herself. Bonnie understood her feelings of confusion. Karen recalled the two of them discussing the fact that Indians sometimes took more than one wife. Bonnie explained it was acceptable to them and their religious beliefs. Her explanations didn't help ease Karen's feelings of pain. A man having more than one wife was not acceptable to her.

Outside the lodge, she could hear excitement and movement. She recalled Standing Deer saying the preparation of the Sun Dance ceremonies was going to start today. She stretched and prepared herself to go out into the new world God had given to her.

She stepped out into the sunlight and observed the changes made to the village. Karen saw Two Feather's wife wave her arms to get her attention.

"Karreen! Iho! Yau! Den u ye!" Come here. Two Feather's wife waved her arms dramatically to help Karen understand. She smiled at the attempt to pronounce her name.

As she walked over to the lodge, she was amazed at the quick changes throughout the village. The men were erecting an extremely large lodge. She noticed what appeared to be rafters inside, with poles leaning against them. There was some form of altar on the opposite side of what she thought was going to be the entrance. Next to the side of the lodge poles, she could see the covering for the lodge. All the men worked as a team, each seeming to know exactly what he was supposed to do.

She was watching the men meticulously doing their work and bumped into an elderly woman. The woman snapped at her in Lakota and spit at her feet.

Stunned by the offensiveness of the gesture, Karen looked at the woman and said, "Wanunhecun." Mistake. The elderly woman grunted at her and walked away.

Laughing Flower was aware of the confrontation and was impressed by the way Karen handled it. The old woman was a troublemaker.

When Karen arrived at the lodge, Laughing Flower pointed to herself and then to a flower. "Wah," flower. Then she started laughing and said, "Iha," laughing. She repeated the name together. "Wah Iha."

Karen nodded her head and smiled. It was the perfect name for the woman. She made an attempt to repeat it that made Laughing Flower frown. Laughing Flower repeated her name a couple more times before Karen could say it properly. Karen felt comfortable with the pronunciation. It seemed to her that some of the words were pronounced like French.

Laughing Flower proceeded to converse with an attempted form of sign language. She was easy-going and comfortable to be with. They worked together the rest of the day. Laughing Flower was patient as she taught and helped Karen learn the ways of the People. Laughing Flower enjoyed working with Karen. She worked hard and learned fast.

During the afternoon, Laughing Flower noticed Karen watching Standing Deer. He had been talking to his sisters and she noticed Karen had gotten a scowl on her face. Laughing Flower had touched her arm and raised her eyebrows in question. She couldn't understand how Standing Deer or his sisters could have possibly offended Karen.

Laughing Flower knew how Standing Deer felt about Karen, so she knew he wouldn't intentionally hurt or offend her. Karen hadn't met Standing Deer's sisters yet, so it couldn't be them. So what did Standing Deer do?

Laughing Flower took Karen's arm and started to walk her over to Standing Deer's lodge where the three of them stood talking. Karen pulled her arm away and said no. Laughing Flower was truly puzzled. She pointed to Standing Deer and his sisters. Standing Deer could speak the white man's tongue and he should surely be able to clear up any misunderstandings. Laughing Flower made another attempt to bring Karen over to Standing Deer's lodge.

"Iho." Come. She pointed at the sisters and raised two fingers, "Tanksitku, sha?"

Karen raised her hands in frustration and confusion. Emphatically, she shook her head and said no. Karen knew sha meant yes, but what did tanksitku mean?

Finally, Laughing Flower got the message and the day flew by. The next day went by quickly as well, and Karen had been able to avoid Standing Deer again.

Karen was tense from frustration. It had not been easy avoiding Standing Deer when his lodge was only three lodges from Jumping Bull's. Whenever she saw him approaching, she would hurry away in the opposite direction. She knew she couldn't continue to avoid him. She would have to tell him she was not interested in a man who was already married. Then, if he had any respect for her feelings, he would leave her alone.

The next day Karen awoke with enthusiasm. Today was going to be a good day. She would be able to experience the Sun Dance first hand. She was curious to see if the information she received from the internet was accurate.

It was also going to be the day Bonnie was going to hang the canopy up onto the bed. They were both curious to see if it would stop her from returning home. Hopefully, when Bonnie took the canopy down she would return home and not be stuck in this other world. They both knew Karen was taking a big chance experimenting with the unknown.

A high pitched, terrifying scream pierced the tranquillity within the lodge. Karen ran out of the lodge and found herself encircled by mass confusion. Across the village, near the water, Karen could see a woman holding a small child in her arms. Several people had surrounded the hysterical woman. Karen ran over to see what was happening.

She took one look at the small child and knew instantly. The child had gotten into the water and had been drowning. Her lungs had filled with water. For how long?

She reached over to feel for a pulse. There was a very slight pulse that told her there was still time. Karen reached to take the child out of the mother's arms and the woman started screaming hysterically again. The mother tried to hit Karen with her free hand.

Sitting Bull had been standing behind Karen and sternly spoke to the woman. Humbly, the mother handed the little girl over to Karen. Karen laid the child onto the ground and proceeded to perform CPR.

Everyone was watching in silence. Frantically, Karen worked harder and faster. Fear for the life of the child kept her going. She was having a hard time reviving the child. She was so small, Karen thought sadly.

After a few moments, Sitting Bull knelt down next to Karen and started pumping the tiny girl's chest the way Karen had been doing. Together they continued to work. Finally, with much relief, the child started to regurgitate the water. Karen turned the child over to aid the excretion of any excess water. The child started crying and the mother bent down and cradled her little girl in her arms.

Karen smiled at Sitting Bull. Tears of relief came from members of the tribe. Karen sat on the ground and watched silently, relieved that she ... they had succeeded.

Sitting Bull watched as the woman walked away with the child still cradled in her arms. He spoke to Karen quietly, "You have done well. I would appreciate it if you would teach me how to do that."

"Of course I will, if you wish, and anyone else who would like to learn." Karen replied.

Sitting Bull smiled at Karen. He needed to speak to her but it was not the time. It would have to be soon. He excused himself and Karen watched him walk over to Standing Deer. Karen stood up and walked over to Laughing Flower. They had a considerable amount of preparations to make before the ceremonies.

Standing Deer and Sitting Bull were discussing the council meeting the men had held earlier. Some of the warriors were against Karen watching the Sun Dance. A white man or woman should never be able to watch. Jumping Bull was adamant about Karen being there to observe such a sacred ceremony. Everyone did not agree until Jumping Bull told the counsel members that Karen was sent by the Great Spirit.

Jumping Bull told the warriors of the powers and great medicine Karen possessed.

This morning Karen had proved that to everyone.

Standing Deer spoke to Sitting Bull, wanting to join him when he spoke to Karen about the ceremony. After Standing Deer explained his mistake with Karen, Sitting Bull understood why he was concerned. Sitting Bull and Standing Deer spoke of Standing Deer's feelings for Karen. They agreed to speak with her immediately.

As they walked over to Two Feather's lodge, Sitting Bull reviewed in his mind everything Standing Deer had told him. He couldn't understand how Standing Deer would even think he was not a good enough warrior to be a good husband to the daughter of the Great Spirit.

Although Jumping Bull explained to the counsel meeting that Karen has denied she was the daughter of the Great Spirit, they believed she was sent by Him. Sitting Bull agreed and understood why Standing Deer needed to straighten out his actions from the other night. Then, he believed they could continue with their lives. He felt Karen would be honored to be the wife of such great warrior.

Sitting Bull called to Karen as they approached the lodge. Karen saw Standing Deer and approached cautiously. She believed that somehow Standing Deer had finagled Sitting Bull into talking to her.

Silently, Karen listened to Sitting Bull explain to her about the council meeting and their decision. She was surprised to learn that the white man was not allowed to watch the Sun Dance. She was also surprised at their decision to allow her to attend. After he finished explaining about the importance of the Sun Dance, he looked at Standing Deer and then at Karen and told them they needed to talk. He turned, leaving them alone. Karen tried to stop him but he shook his head and walked to Jumping Bull's lodge.

Heart pounding, Karen looked at Laughing Flower for assistance. Laughing Flower shrugged and continued tending to the baby. She thought, Fine, I have a piece of mind to give to him anyway. Determined, she placed both hands on her hips.

"Listen to me real good Standing Deer, because I'm not going to repeat myself." Karen looked at him with determination. "I will not lower myself and dishonor myself by getting involved with a married man. I don't care what the Indian beliefs are. I will not be subjected to such atrocities! I cannot, in anyway, understand how you could actually believe I would tolerate such disgusting behavior. The other night was a huge inexplicable mistake! I am disgusted with my own behavior. It was totally unacceptable. I allowed my emotions to control my behavior. I will not allow it to happen again."

Karen looked directly into Standing Deer eyes, and took a deep breath. "I will not be in this village long. I want you to stay away from me. Do not talk to me. Do not come near me. Just leave me alone!" She turned to walk toward Laughing Flower when he grabbed her arm.

"Now, wait a minute," he spoke through clenched teeth. His face was red with anger. A vein pulsed on his forehead.

Karen noticed Laughing Flower behind Standing Deer. Her mouth was wide open in astonishment. She did not know Laughing Flower was shocked that Karen would dishonor and humiliate Standing Deer by speaking to him with such dishonor in front of the whole village.

"I listened to you, now you listen to me." Anger reeked from Standing Deer. "I have no wives. I do not have a woman or women. Not all Indians have more than one wife. Where did you get the idea that I was married?" Standing Deer looked at her, in irritation, waiting for a response. When she did not answer, he continued.

"I did not mean to dishonor you the other night. If you had given me the chance, I would have done something to show you I was wrong." He leaned closer to her and growled, "Don't ever speak to me in that manner, in front of my People or anyone, again. I will leave you alone, if that is what you wish." He let go of her arm and crossed his arms. When she did not respond he walked away, satisfied with the look of surprise on her face.

Karen put her hand over her mouth as she stood dumbfounded, watching him walk away. He's not married? Then who are those women? If that was true, then they had a chance. Oh, no. No, no, no, she repeated to herself. It wouldn't work. They were from two very distinct, and virtually separate, worlds. How could it possibly work out for the two of them?

She turned and walked over to Jumping Bull's lodge She called, as was customary, before entering the lodge.

"I'm sorry to bother you," she said to Jumping Bull and Sitting Bull. "But can you tell me what tank ... tanksi ... tanksitku means?"

Immediately enlightened by the cause of Karen's behavior toward Standing Deer, Sitting Bull replied, "Sister, his younger sisters." Sitting Bull smiled to himself and shook his head.

Karen thanked Sitting Bull and left the lodge. She felt like a fool. She made an assumption and it developed into a very gross injustice toward Standing Deer. She still believed they could not pursue a relationship, but knew she owed him an apology. The ceremony would be beginning soon and everyone was absorbed in his or her final preparations. Her search for Standing Deer would have to wait.

Sitting Bull and Jumping Bull spoke to each other about the attraction they saw between Standing Deer and Karen. They concluded that the two of them were meant for each other. They both agreed it was a good match. Jumping Bull had told Sitting Bull it would be quite interesting to watch the two of them, with Karen fighting Standing Deer the whole way.

Jumping Bull was curious as to why Karen asked what sister meant. Sitting Bull laughed and told him he believed Karen thought Standing Deer was married. She did not know the women were Standing Deer's sisters. White women were very possessive when it came to their man. They did not want to share their man with anyone, especially another woman. Somehow, Karen must have gotten the impression that Standing Deer was married.

Jumping Bull laughed. He told his son he believed Standing Deer would have his hands full with that little one. The father and son finished their final preparations and exited the lodge to commence the sacred ceremony.

Karen stood to the side of Jumping Bull's lodge to watch, curious to see if the research she had read was accurate. There was a rhythmic beat of the drums that mimicked a heartbeat until Sitting Bull entered the center of the village to conduct the prayers and blessings.

Soon the dancing and music began again. Laughing Flower joined Karen with Standing Deer's sisters. The women took several moments to explain to Karen how to pronounce their names and what they meant. Sunshine in the Morning was adept at sign language. It wasn't too difficult for Karen to comprehend that Yellow Bird was their friend.

As usual, she had many questions. Karen pointed to a man who was unfamiliar to her sitting next to Jumping Bull. She also noticed that there were several men from other tribes joining in the ceremony. At this time Standing Deer had joined the women. Karen jumped at the opportunity and had made her apologies to him. The women discreetly left the two alone.

"He is Many Horses. He is from the Oglala Sioux. Many Horses is here to watch Crazy Horse attend the Sun Dance." He turned and pointed. "The young warrior right there dancing in the circle is Crazy Horse."

"There are many men here that I have never seen before. Is it common to have warriors from other tribes join in the ceremony?" Karen asked.

"Yes, we are all Sioux. Lakota, Nakota and Dakota tribes are here as well as the Cheyenne. Although we do not live in the same village, we join for the Sun Dance ceremonies. Over there is Sleeping Elk, and next to him is his brother Black Bear."

Standing Deer continued to point out to Karen the different warriors. Then he started to explain the ritual steps of the Sun Dance. Standing Deer explained how the young men had fasted before the performance of the ceremony. They danced and stared at the sun until they received their visions.

It would last hours. The young man's warrior society would dance, if they chose, to assist him in obtaining his vision. He pointed out the forks that would be used for the participants. Standing Deer explained to Karen that the fork would be thrust through the breast muscles of the dancers. Then, they would strain against it until they tore loose. Before they entered the ceremonial lodge, they must dance around and pretend to go inside four times. It was essential for them to do this in order for them to receive the supernatural aid that they needed.

Karen wanted to, but couldn't look away. She stood mesmerized as she watched the young warriors. She couldn't fathom why anyone would want to put themselves through such physical and mental torture. Appalled and disgusted, she wondered why they couldn't find another way. Maybe something a bit more civilized.

Several hours had passed and Karen lost all concept of time. One by one, the young warriors came out of the ceremonial lodge and collapsed into the arms of their friends. Karen noticed a murmuring going throughout the village. There was one young warrior left.

Standing Deer had been over with Two Feather's when Karen waved him over to her.

"He is younger than the others. Will they stop it?" she asked him.

"No. Besides, he is not that young. It would be Red Cloud's decision to stop it and he would not dishonor Crazy Horse. Crazy Horse is a strong warrior. He will do it," Standing Deer whispered.

Karen noticed more warriors going into the circle to dance. They wanted to encourage the brave warrior. All Karen could hear was the beat of the drums and the hushed murmur of the People.

Finally, Crazy Horse broke through. He collapsed into Red Cloud's arms. Standing nearby, Many Horses nodded his approval.

Instead of guiding Crazy Horse to his lodge, Red Cloud yelled out, "Where is the white woman from the mountains?"

Karen stood frozen, ears buzzing, stunned by the outburst. The village was silent, also stunned by the question. Standing Deer walked over to her and guided Karen over to Red Cloud. He was holding onto Crazy Horse, helping him stand on his feet.

Crazy Horse looked at her and then spoke quietly, gasping for breath. His eyes were filled with pain and anger. She could see he was in immense pain. His voice was hoarse as he spoke slowly, with the importance of a message he believed was from the Great Spirit.

Karen wondered what was so important that he had to tell her immediately. Why couldn't it have waited?

Crazy Horse had refused to learn and speak the white man's tongue. Standing Deer interpreted for them.

"These words are from the vision the Great Spirit has given me. You have come from a world beyond. Your powers are great. Use them wisely. Be careful of what you know. Life must continue, as it should be. Do not try to change anything. This I say to you. Learn the ways of the Indian and be there when you are needed."

Crazy Horse paused and closed his eyes, "Listen to me Spirit of the Mountain. Crazy Horse would never want to have to walk in your moccasins and know the things that you know."

Crazy Horse passed out and Red Cloud took him away to administer to the wounds Crazy Horse had received in the ceremony. The village was quiet until Jumping Bull yelled to continue the great celebration.

Karen was confused. How could Crazy Horse know such things? Was there something to this ceremony? What did Crazy Horse see in his vision? What does he know?

Chapter SEVEN

Karen told Standing Deer that she wanted to be alone. She decided to take a stroll along the same path Standing Deer had shown her the night they kissed.

So many confusing questions were going through her mind. Her analytical mind fought the mass confusion that peeked out through every corner. There were too many questions and no answers. Just theories, theories of supernatural powers. She had proof that they existed. With everything that has happened to her, she realized that supernatural powers have been around a long time and were here to stay.

How did Crazy Horse know what he did? Was there something to this ritual the Indians performed? What did he know? How was she going to deal with this? Everything he had said to her made her believe more and more of the wonders of how powerful these rituals could actually be.

She was amazed at the knowledge he had learned in the Sun Dance ceremony. How did he know she was from a different world? How did he get the information? Crazy Horse's genuine warning made her wary.

Be careful of what you know. Life must continue, as it should be. Words and warnings Crazy Horse believed were from the Great Spirit. *Do not try to change anything.* Would she? Could she? What would it do to the future if she did? What would it do to her future or the past? Or should the past be considered the present if she is living in it? She sighed and shook her head in confusion.

She wasn't sure what year it was, but knew thousands and thousands of Americans and hopeful immigrants would be coming to the western plains. The destruction of the great Indian Nation would be imminent, out of her control. Or would it?

What could she possibly do to change history? Probably quite a bit, she realized. She could warn them of the impending wars. They would be better prepared. It could save lives. Thousands of innocent people could be spared. Would it just prolong the inevitable? By warning them, would it make it worse and completely destroy the Indian Nation? She was better off leaving things as they were, as they are. At least, this way she knew where her worlds belonged.

Now, she understood why he wouldn't want to "walk in her moccasins." It was a cliche she heard for years but had never really expected it to actually happen to her.

Karen became so absorbed in her thoughts that she did not realize she had left the protection and confines of the village far behind. She continued walking, deep in thought, blind to everything about her. Karen was hearing the message from Crazy Horse repeating itself over and over in her mind.

She did not see the camp of the white traders hidden behind the brush. They saw her. A white woman that they decided was an Indian captive. Obviously, she was a very trusted whore or they wouldn't have let her wonder around outside of the village. She must be taking good care of their savage needs, they laughed among themselves. It certainly wouldn't make a difference if they took her and used her for a while. The Indians surely wouldn't care. She opened her legs wide and willingly for the savages. She would do the same for them.

One of the men slowly and quietly followed her. He waited for his chance and hit her over the head with a rock. He dragged her back to the camp like a sack of potatoes.

After a few moments, Karen became conscious. She was groggy and lightheaded with a searing pain in the back of her head. She felt a burning liquid being shoved down her throat. Groggily, she thought it tasted like whiskey. It was foul and burned her throat as it went down. Gagging, she tried pulling away but someone pulled on her hair and forced her mouth open. She had no choice but to swallow. The harsh liquid burned her throat and left her in a drunken daze. She was laid back onto the hard ground.

The ground felt as if it was moving. Oh God, I have the spins. It had to be whiskey they were forcing me to drink. They got me drunk! What are these people trying to do to me?

In answer to her question, Karen began feeling hands all over her body. They were touching her everywhere. So many hands. She became aware of two mouths sucking on her breasts. She tried to push them away but couldn't control her movements. Her arms felt so heavy. She had no control of her movements, no strength. Those men got her drunk! Helpless, she felt one of them enter her. Then, blessedly she passed out from the shock of absorbing so much liquor in her system in such a short time.

Karen felt nauseous. She ached everywhere. Every available place on her body had been used and abused. She realized that even her jaws hurt. Karen could feel the bile rise in her throat and knew she was going to get sick. She leaned over and regurgitated the contents of what was left in her stomach. Her head felt as if it was exploding.

Anger seized her and seemed to take a permanent hold. Those pigs! How dare they do this to her! Hatred and anger swallowed her. One of them spoke to her and asked her if she was ready for more fun. Bleary eyed, she turned to where the voice had come. Total, overwhelming, unadulterated anger enveloped her. She wanted to destroy these men. But first, Karen decided she would torture them. She would start with the one who had just spoken to her. Anger controlled her emotions and actions. Her kinetic abilities took control. She didn't consider that she was a doctor and was supposed to save lives. She wanted to punish them and punish them she would. She wanted them all dead.

Sitting on the ground holding herself up on shaky arms, Karen pictured herself choking the man who had spoken to her. In her mind, she pushed him against a tree and repeatedly banged his head against the trunk of the tree. Karen slowly turned her head and watched him trying to stop the invisible hands from choking him. In a panic, he tried to run away, yelling something about her being a witch. She laughed an unforgiving sick laugh. She didn't care. She wanted revenge. She wanted him in pain. She wanted all of them in unmistakable, torturous pain. She smiled as she sensed that their little camp was in a frenzy.

Suddenly, she heard a muted gurgling sound and a then a familiar voice. Distracted, she stopped torturing the trader and watched with complete satisfaction as Standing Deer killed the man. Controlled by hatred she felt elated with Standing Deer's rescue.

She was beginning to feel numb. Karen looked around and saw that Standing Deer had killed three other men. Four men who had defiled her and deserved to die.

Karen watched Standing Deer as he yanked his knife out of the chest of one of the traders. He stabbed the knife into the dirt and methodically cleaned the knife on the grass.

Karen felt as if she was watching him from a distance, as if she was in a dream. She started getting cold and everything around her seemed to slow itself in waves.

She was in shock. Standing Deer walked over to her slowly. He took her and held her in his arms waiting for the tears to come. He whispered softly to her and kissed her face. He held her as he would a hurt child.

"I ... I want ... to ... to take ... a bath," she barely whispered.

He walked her over to the water and tried to help her undress. Karen pulled away with such a ferocity of anger that he helplessly stepped away as he watched her struggle to take the torn dress off. Karen slowly immersed herself in the water. She felt the cool clear water gradually covering her body. Her body, that had been defiled, needed the coolness of the water. All she wanted to do was wash the disgrace and filth away. She kept submerging her head under the water. She repeatedly grabbed the gritty dirt and sand from the bottom and scrubbed her body with it.

Standing Deer watched silently. He was frustrated. His heart was breaking for her. If only he had followed her to make sure she was safe. When he realized that she had been gone too long, he started to follow the path she had taken. Being unfamiliar with the area and the village perimeters she must not have realized that she had left the confines of the village.

It never ceased to amaze him how white men treated other people. Didn't they know that all people should be treated with respect? It was becoming a vicious circle. White men raped and killed the Indian women, so the Indian raped and killed the white woman. Who cares who started it. When was it all going to stop?

He watched as she submerged herself repeatedly and came up with fistfuls of dirt and sand to cleanse her skin. Her motions of cleansing had started slow but as time continued her actions became quicker and more frantic. Standing Deer watched her as the frustration of the ordeal came out in Karen's actions. Her cleansing became harder and faster. Her skin was becoming raw from the scrubbing.

Standing Deer knew he had to stop her. He got up and went into the water. She resisted him with a viciousness that he believed was uncharacteristic of her personality. Her strength reached beyond as she fought him. With both fists she pummeled him until he fell back into the water. Sputtering he grabbed her from underneath and started carrying her to the shore.

She pounded his back in fury. "No, I have to get it off! I need to wash it all away. They were filthy. Lord only knows the last time they had a bath. Those men were probably diseased. I know damn well they didn't use protection." She ferociously rubbed herself.

Putting her down on the shore, he held her hands to her sides. With a strained tremulous voice she explained to Standing Deer, "I've never had unprotected sex. What if they had STDs? What if they got me pregnant? I believe abortions should be legal, but I can't have one. I don't believe that it is right for me."

Karen felt angry, frustrated and dirty. There were no tears yet. She still didn't feel remorse for the dead men. Perhaps she never would.

She was bleeding from the silt and had sand embedded in the cuts. Karen hadn't noticed. Standing Deer grabbed her hands with one of his and rinsed the sand out of her wounds with his free hand. She still hadn't looked at him.

"I need penicillin. Oh God! Bonnie's putting up the canopy tonight. I can't stay now. I need to go home. I have to get medication." Finally, the tears came.

Karen pounded the ground, racked with tears. She screamed hysterically, "I want to forget!"

As she cried, Standing Deer took her into his arms and rocked her. He stroked her hair, speaking to her in soft tones to calm her. She wasn't making any sense to him. STDs? Bonnie … canopy … pennies? What in the world could she be talking about? Why would she need the white man's money?

He walked her over to the edge of the water and put the dress on her. He was angry with himself and saddened as he watched her. She stood there looking defeated, like a beaten helpless child. He decided she would need Sitting Bull. Sitting Bull was the tribal chief medicine man. He would know what to do for her.

They started walking along the banks of the water. The silence was deafening. Standing Deer was worried for her mind. She just walked with her head down, blind to everything around her. After a time, without saying a word to Standing Deer, Karen stopped and sat down. Standing Deer sat next to her.

"I am not ready to go back to the village."

Standing Deer nodded his head and remained silent. He put his arm carefully around her and held her gently against the side of his chest. Karen closed her eyes feeling protected in his arms. She mumbled to him that she was tired. He laid back and Karen rested her head on his shoulders.

Chapter EIGHT

Bonnie let herself into the house with the key Karen had given her to use. She put the mail on the kitchen table and watered the plants Karen had scattered around the house. As she went from room to room, she tried to visualize the wonderful time Karen was having. She returned the pitcher to the sink and went into Karen's bedroom to hang the canopy on the bed. Karen told her the box would be on the chaise lounge.

"Oh!" Oh! He is a hunk, Bonnie thought. Oh goodness, Karen did him no justice at all in her description. What was he doing here and why is Karen back?

Bonnie touched her softly so she wouldn't startle her. When Karen opened her eyes, all she could see was the surprised and concerned expression on Bonnie's face. Bonnie excitedly pointed to Standing Deer. Puzzled, Karen turned around with wide eyes. There was Standing Deer laying next to her asleep in the bed.

All Karen could think was, oh my God now what am I going to do?

Karen and Bonnie silently tiptoed out of the room. They left Standing Deer asleep on the bed. He would probably awaken soon but she needed to talk to Bonnie as soon as possible.

"He is gorgeous! You're right, he is built like an Apollo. Are you sure you wouldn't want to be one of his wives?" Bonnie joked.

"Standing Deer isn't married," Karen said with an unusual dullness in her voice.

Squinting her eyes Bonnie asked, "What's wrong?" Bonnie noticed the change in Karen the minute she opened her mouth to speak.

"Let me have some coffee first. I also need you to go to the pharmacy for me. I can't leave him here and I can't take him with me." Karen sighed. She was glad Bonnie was a counselor. She really needed someone to talk to.

She quickly told the story from beginning to end, with Bonnie interrupting her as usual. Just then, she heard Standing Deer calling for her. Karen filled out a prescription for herself, gave Bonnie some money and sent her on her way. Standing Deer wasn't ready for Bonnie yet. She laughed to herself. Laughing Flower and Bonnie were very much alike.

Standing Deer was sitting up on the bed, eyes wide in astonishment. He was staring at the digital clock, watching the timer blinking. Now this was going to be an adventure. At least she had some idea of what to expect in his world but he had no concept of what he could expect from her world.

"Is this your world? Where am I?" he asked, curiously looking about the room.

"You are here," Karen said and laughed at the memory of their first encounter. Recalling that he had done the same to her, he laughed at her witticism.

Walking over to the closet, she pulled out a pair of shorts David had left behind. She handed them to Standing Deer and told him to put them on. She opened the bureau drawer and pulled out a T-shirt. He was twirling the shorts around in his hand, and looking at them with a puzzled look on his face. She explained to him to take his loincloth off and put the shorts on with the pockets to the front. She shut the door and left him to change.

When Standing Deer was finished, he walked over to the door and tried to open it. He traced his fingers along the crack before he pulled on the doorknob but nothing happened. He tried a few more times until he finally called for Karen.

Karen opened the door and explained to him that he needed to turn the knob in order for the door to open. The shorts fit him well. They just looked a little odd with his knife strategically placed at the waist.

"You have a strange world."

"Oh, you haven't seen anything yet."

As he followed Karen through the house to the kitchen, the different sights overwhelmed Standing Deer. He stopped and felt the roughness of the textured walls. They didn't bend or move when he touched them. Her lodge had strange walls with paintings surrounded by wood for decoration. Why didn't she just paint the pictures on the walls?

He felt the carpet underneath his feet and looked down. What kind of animal had it come from? He wiggled his toes. The fur didn't feel very soft on the feet. There were cloths on the walls throughout the lodge, stopping the light of the sun from coming into the lodge. When they arrived in the kitchen, he felt a cool breeze coming from the ceiling. He looked up and saw a shiny, square object with holes in it. Raising his hand up he could feel the cool air blowing against his palm.

"You must be very important in your world to have such a big lodge. Where is the rest of your family?"

Karen didn't respond right away. Instead, she handed him a cup of coffee and asked if he wanted to go outside on the patio.

Thank the Lord for privacy fences. As they went outside to the patio, she explained to him that she lived here alone. Her family lived out of state.

"What is out of state?" he asked curiously. There was a lot he could ask, if only he could do so without offending her.

"It's like a territory, only it all belongs to one country."

Standing Deer partially understood but as they reached the patio and he saw the pool, all other questions fled his mind for the time being. He walked over to the pool and submerged his hand in the water. He felt the coolness and wondered why she would keep her drinking water in such a strange and large enclosure. Didn't she live near a lake or stream? Where were the fish?

Standing Deer stood up and looked around the yard. It appeared as if someone had taken plants and placed them in an order. Nothing grew freely here. He didn't recognize any of the plants either. It seemed to be a pleasant piece of land except for the fact that they didn't let the plants grow where the hand of the Great Spirit placed them. He was puzzled. Here on this piece of land he couldn't see any plants she could use.

This piece of land surrounded her lodge like the white man's fort. It hid her land from the other strange lodges that he could see beyond her fort. Why would she want to be closed off from her own people? Did the white man in her world fear each other so much that they had to secure themselves behind wooden walls? Was her world so dangerous that she had to hide behind a barricade? No wonder the white man doesn't trust the Indian. How could they if they have to live like this? They can't trust their own people. How could they learn to trust something that is so strange and different to them?

Standing Deer jumped at the loud, unfamiliar screeching sound he heard from the sky. "Run!" His knife was in hand as he was dragging her to the door.

Why wasn't she reacting to this danger?

Karen wasn't paying attention to the jet overhead. She grabbed his arm and attempted to stop him from running into the house. She understood that it was pure instinct for him to react in the manner he did. She understood the anxiety and fears one felt when they are in an unknown situation.

"It's an airplane. It is used for transportation." Karen felt dismayed. She had a lot of explaining to do in the next several hours. She took a deep breath, looking toward the sky wondering how she got into this mess.

Karen realized she needed to explain some of this modern world to Standing Deer. He would at least be partially knowledgeable about this world, although he would not be here long. Just how much she should explain she was not certain.

She decided to start with the pool. "This is called a pool. It helps a person keep cool and refreshed. You don't drink from it. You swim in it."

He looked at the water and shook his head in a negative gesture. He understood what she had said but couldn't understand the necessity of needing one next to your lodge. But then, with the lodge surrounded by fort walls he was beginning to understand the necessity. Karen noticed his reaction but wasn't sure what was causing it.

"You use it for bathing only?"

Biting her lip, she realized that she wasn't explaining properly. "Maybe you should just ask me as many questions as you want. If I can I will answer you," Karen told him as she wondered if she wasn't walking into a Catch 22 situation.

Standing Deer was relieved to have her permission to pursue his questions. To the Lakota, it was rude to ask personal questions without the consent of the other person. So many questions, he wasn't sure where to start. Finally, he decided to start with the Karen's lodge and land. For about an hour, Karen diligently answered his questions. Bonnie returned just as he asked her if they could see more of the city.

Bonnie called to Karen as she walked through the house. She looked in the den first and then went straight to the back patio.

"Hello everyone. Standing Deer, it is a pleasure to meet you. I have heard a lot about you. My name is Bonnie." She looked to Karen and told her the package was on the kitchen table.

"So tell me, Standing Deer, what do you think of our world? Do you like it so far? Would you like to see more? Maybe you would like to stay for a few days? Or ... ?"

"Bonnie, stop! He's only been here an hour. I don't think it would be wise if he saw anything else. And, it certainly wouldn't be a good idea if he stayed for a few days!" Karen was irritated at Bonnie's typical burst of energy.

"Why not?" Bonnie was bubbling with her usual energy. "It would be great. Just imagine what it would be like for him to see all of this ... ."

"And imagine," Karen cut her off, "just imagine how he will have to deal with the overwhelming knowledge, the different technology. Wouldn't that be amazing?" Karen shook her head. Sometimes she wondered where Bonnie left her common sense.

Bonnie blinked, stunned by the sarcasm coming out of her friend's mouth.

"I don't think it would be wise if he saw anything else. And it certainly wouldn't be a good idea if he stayed for a few days."

"We could take him to all the sights. We are in Orlando. People travel from all over the world to come here. We could take him to the Seminole reservation."

"No! Are you crazy! We can't take him to the reservation. That's unfair! He should not see too much. He's not a guest from out of state, you know. How do you think he would react if he saw the reservation and how the Indians live now?" Karen shook her head angrily at Bonnie. What could she possibly be thinking?

"Excuse me," said Standing Deer. "You seem to be speaking as if I am not here. Do I not have a say in what is to be decided?"

"No," Karen replied.

"Yes, you do," Bonnie said. "Karen, don't you think you should get out of those clothes and put something on that is more up to date? Aren't you hot?"

Karen looked down at the torn deer skin dress and realized she wasn't hot. She had been so comfortable that she forgot she was still in the Indian mode of dress.

"I'll go change. I want to grab a bite to eat and take that medication anyway. Anyone else hungry?" Karen suggested sandwiches and all agreed. She went inside to change and make lunch to bring out to the patio.

As Karen was changing, she realized that Bonnie had manipulated the situation by changing the subject to her dress. She moved as quickly as humanly possible wondering why and what Bonnie was up to.

Standing Deer was alert and aware that the woman before him had managed to get the two of them alone. She was a striking woman. Her hair was a golden brown, cut short like a man's. Her brown eyes looked almost gold and flicked in the sun exaggerating the high energy and sincerity in the woman.

Bonnie jumped at the chance to speak to Standing Deer alone but he spoke first.

"Are you a medicine woman like Karen?"

"No, not really. I have a doctorate but it is in theology. That's the study of religion. I have my master's degree in psychology. I heal people's minds. Karen heals their bodies." She couldn't think of any other way to describe it to him. It was quite exciting for her to be here with this man from the past.

Uncomfortable with the ensuing silence, Bonnie asked a question she had been desperately wanting to ask. "So Standing Deer, you are not married?"

"No." It was not the way of the Lakota to speak of the dead. He understood she did not have the knowledge of the Lakota way and did not wish to explain why he did not have a woman.

"That's so great! I mean that you are not married. Karen is very interested in you. It really upset her when she thought you were married to those squaws."

Bonnie decided she was going to try to play matchmaker. She watched his face fill with anger and tension. Puzzled by his reaction she wondered what she had said to offend him.

"Did I offend you?" she asked, confused by his quick change in demeanor.

"Those squaws as you have described them, are my sisters and their friend. It is an insult to call an Indian woman a squaw."

"I'm so sorry! I didn't know. I won't make that mistake again." Bonnie was stunned. She had no idea that it was a derogatory term.

Standing Deer nodded his head in acceptance of her apology believing that it was sincere. Then he smiled, "You think Karen is interested in me? I have decided to marry her. Does she have a mate?"

Bonnie laughed. Oh, this is going to be a good adventure! Obviously, he was determined to be her husband.

"No. She doesn't have a mate. Marriage has always been a 'someday' with Karen. You will have a hard time convincing her that your marriage would work. She believes there will be a major conflict because you are from two separate worlds. I wish you all the luck you can get because she'll fight this love she feels for you as much as she can."

Karen came out with a platter of sandwiches. She did not miss the heads close together in conversation. She knew Bonnie well enough to know that she had something up her sleeve.

After they finished their sandwiches, Bonnie started talking about letting Standing Deer see the city.

"Karen, I agree Standing Deer shouldn't see the reservation. You're right. It would be confusing and possibly traumatic for him. But, I see no reason why you can't take him for a ride in the car and let him see some of the sights. Also, if it isn't inconvenient for Standing Deer, I don't see any harm in having him stay over night, at least one night." Bonnie looked at Karen and added, "Karen, it would be a good way to test the canopy."

Karen sighed. Hesitantly she looked over to Standing Deer. "What do you think, Standing Deer?"

"I would like to see your world. It will help me know you better. The ceremonies will continue without me, but I can not stay away for too long. Many Horses told us he saw white soldiers and Pawnee while they were traveling to the village," answered Standing Deer.

Karen sighed. She was out-voted. "All right. But only one night."

Bonnie was exalted. She only had two appointments this afternoon and she would be able to join them. She had loads of questions for Standing Deer. Bonnie started babbling about all the different places they could go when her beeper went off. She excused herself and went inside to get the telephone to make the call.

As she dialed the telephone, Standing Deer watched amazed as she stood and talked to no one he could see. What was that thing in her hand? Why was she talking to it?

Karen smiled. The telephone was such a common object. You never realized how wonderful modern luxuries were until you saw them through someone else's eyes. He was like a child discovering the world around him. She had to remind herself that this was a new world to him. She explained to Standing Deer about the telephone and its uses. She told him it was a common tool for communication and that nearly all homes had one or more.

Standing Deer felt overwhelmed. So much magic surrounding him and it seemed that Karen's world took it so casually. Was her world so large that she needed so much magic to survive?

Bonnie told Karen she had a minor crisis to take care of and she would try to get back as soon as possible. The two of them discussed Bonnie coming back to put the canopy up so Karen could stay with the Lakota. They agreed on the day and time.

Standing Deer noticed that they had been careful with their words. That appeared to be normal for Karen, but he believed it was difficult for Bonnie. Bonnie had said something about the future and Karen had reprimanded her. She told Bonnie to be careful on how she worded things. Karen emphasized that she would be returning to the present world, not the future or the past. Bonnie had apologized and looked over to Standing Deer to see if he noticed her slip of the tongue. He had, but Standing Deer was wise enough not to show it.

Their words confused him. What did they mean by returning to the present world? Or was it the past that they had said. The more they spoke with hidden meanings, the more he felt confused.

Standing Deer was relieved to see Bonnie leave. He liked her well enough, but he wanted to be alone with Karen. If Bonnie was right about Karen having feelings for him, he needed time to convince Karen that their love would survive between their two worlds.

Now that Standing Deer had seen Karen's world, he felt somewhat unsure of himself. With all this magic around her, why would she want to leave her world to be with him? What could he give her beside himself? She was accustomed to all this magic. Would his way of life be good enough? Standing Deer had a feeling there was a lot more magic. He had just not seen it yet. If she would be willing, how much would he be asking her to give up?

Karen thought it felt good to have Standing Deer here with her. It seemed so natural. The magnetism she had felt when she first met him was still very strong. Even as the two of them sat there in their own private thoughts, she could still feel the electricity pulsing between the two of them.

Maybe, it could work between the two of them. Would he want to give up his life on the prairie? He probably wouldn't have to. They could leave the canopy off the bed and she could put it away somewhere. They could live between the two worlds. Bea's parents did it. Their marriage survived. Bea's parents proved it was possible.

She shook her head, dismayed at her own thoughts. She was getting confused again. Karen wanted to be with Standing Deer for the rest of their lives. Oh, she groaned. It just wouldn't work. There's too much conflict between the whites and the Indians in his world. Karen felt like she was the rope in a fierce game of tug-of-war. What she greatly desired and what she felt were best were two very different things.

She decided this train of thought had to end. If fate had brought them together, she wouldn't be able to fight it anyway. Maybe she should just see what happens, one day at a time.

She decided to go for a swim. She stood up and asked Standing Deer if he would like to take a swim in the pool as well. He agreed and she excused herself to change into her bathing suit.

When Karen came out with her suit on and towels in her hand, Standing Deer stood up and pulled off the shorts and shirt. She took in a deep breath. Oh, what a magnificent body. Again, her heart raced and she feared he could see it pounding through her chest. She recalled how it felt to hold that massive body.

He stood exposed before her without a trace of discomfort. Karen felt the magnetism and experienced the electricity she had previously felt pulsating through her body. She watched him take his feathers out of his hair and put them on the table. Then, he turned around and went into the water. What she did not see was his grin and the look of satisfaction on Standing Deer's face.

Standing Deer knew she liked what she saw. He smiled. It was written all over her face. He thoroughly enjoyed her reaction. It pleased him greatly to see she was attracted to him. He swam to the deep end and called to her, "Are you coming in or are you just going to stand there watching me?"

Laughing, Karen put the towels down and dove into the deep end. The water was invigorating. Standing Deer was playful and knew how to have fun. The world around them seemed to disappear. It felt as if they were the only two in existence. The enjoyment of playing around in the pool with Standing Deer was such a pleasure for Karen. He didn't play emotional games. That's why she enjoyed his company so much. So far, Standing Deer was honest and down to earth. Karen really admired and respected that in a person.

She had forgotten that he was naked until they were in the shallow end of the pool. He had pulled her to him and kissed her. She could feel his nakedness against her belly. Her being was aflame with a fire burning with the desire she had felt before. The same burning desire she had felt with him and only with him. She felt herself beginning to succumb to their overwhelming need for each other when she recalled the traders. Karen went stone cold and pulled away.

He felt her instant withdrawal. "What is wrong?" Standing Deer was confused. One minute she was burning with desire for him and the next minute she was cold as the winter snows.

"Those traders, we can't. Besides, I don't have any protection. We can't make love yet. It wouldn't be safe. I'm not ready. This is going too fast for me."

Standing Deer shook his head in dismay. "A woman should never have to experience sex in such a violent manner. I'm sorry that your first time with a man had to be so cruel and disgusting. Let me show you what it is like for a man and woman to share their love properly. I want to make love with you and show you the tenderness and power that love can give two people." He spoke deeply, passionately and with true feelings.

"I wasn't a virgin Standing Deer. I have had sex before. I've never been raped. Those men have left a scar on me for life. It isn't safe for us to make love right now."

"Then why did you stop me before if you weren't a virgin? I thought I had offended you. I thought I had dishonored you." Standing Deer was perplexed.

"Well, I'm the type of person who likes to take things slow. I don't like to rush into relationships. It causes heartache. I rushed into a relationship before and I don't want to make the same mistake again. Please, you need to understand. With you, our worlds are so very far apart. We virtually come from two separate and distant lives. I don't know how we would be able to have a relationship with each other. Even though I desire to love you, it scares me because of the conflicts that our people have and will have."

Standing Deer pulled her into his arms. "If you are willing, we can make it work. You are a very strong woman. I cannot see you failing at anything."

"Well, I have. When I make mistakes, I make big mistakes. Besides, there are other reasons why we can't make love."

Standing Deer laughed. "So what are your other excuses?"

Indignant, she snapped. "They aren't excuses. They are legitimate reasons. I don't just jump into bed with anyone who comes along. I don't have a lot of experience like some women. I have never had unprotected sex until those men raped me. What if they gave me a disease? What if I'm pregnant? We can't have sex because of those men and because I don't want to take the chance of getting pregnant. We need to use protection. And most of all I am not ready. Don't push me."

"Forgive me. I should be more understanding of your feelings. What is this protection you are talking about?"

"It's called a condom." Karen explained. "You put it on your penis and it protects the man and woman from getting any possible diseases. It also stops the woman from getting pregnant."

"Well then," he laughed, "when you are ready. If that is what you desire, we will get some protection."

Standing Deer picked her up and threw her into the deep end of the pool. While they waited for Bonnie to return the two of them played in the pool, satisfied just to be with each other.

Chapter NINE

Bonnie called and said she would not be able to return but she would be able to get the canopy on the bed the day after tomorrow. Standing Deer and Karen decided to go for a ride in the car and see the sights.

When Karen showed him where the bathroom was and how to use it, the little shiny handle that made the water disappear entertained Standing Deer. Where did the water go? He tried lifting the bowl to see where it went but it appeared to be attached to the floor. He thought it was interesting how Karen's people relieved themselves. It was a strange and unusual device. He shrugged. One didn't have to leave the lodge to relieve themselves.

As they were entering the garage, Karen explained to him what a car was and why it was a necessary mode of transportation.

They hadn't left the housing division when, oddly enough, Standing Deer started moving around and looking underneath the seats and in the glove box. Karen warily looked at him out of the corners of her eyes.

"What are you doing?" Karen asked Standing Deer hesitantly.

"Where are the people?"

"What people? What are you talking about?"

"I hear voices singing. Do you have little people hidden in the car somewhere?"

"Voices? Oh, the radio!" She took so much for granted. "Right here," she pointed toward the radio/CD player. "You turn it on and off like this. You can change channels and pick different stations to listen to if you don't like what they are playing. It's another form of communication."

Karen smiled, "Except you can't talk back to it."

Standing Deer nodded his head and started fiddling with the buttons. He accidentally pushed the volume button to the highest setting. The car reverberated in sound. He seemed to jump four feet into the air. Astonished, his hands flew up in the air. "What? What happened?"

Karen laughed and adjusted the volume. "It's okay. That's called the volume control button. You turn it up or down, depending on how loud you want the music."

"You have a lot of magic in your world." It was all so very overwhelming for Standing Deer. There was too much magic. He wasn't sure he liked Karen's world.

Standing Deer started exploring other buttons. Some of the buttons he played with didn't appear to do anything. Trying to figure out what they did, he pushed the same buttons repeatedly. Karen cleared her throat as he moved her seat back and forth several times without realizing it. She told him to leave it alone. She couldn't drive properly with him playing with that button. Raising his eyebrows with laughter in his eyes, he played with the button as he watched her move back and forth.

Then, he found the button for the windows. With a huge smile on his face he watched the window … down, up, down, up, down, up, down, over and over again. He was like a two-year-old child discovering the world around him.

After he was tired of playing with the window, he found the switch for the trunk. Laughing, Karen pulled over to shut the trunk door. She couldn't stop laughing. People drove by looking at her as if she needed a straight jacket. It was so funny watching a grown man playing with those buttons like they were a new toy for him. She explained to him to leave that button alone, too.

Standing Deer hadn't been paying attention to what was outside of the car. He hadn't realized they'd arrived downtown until Karen told him. He gaped open-mouthed in astonishment. So many cars and so many people, he thought to himself.

"The buildings touch the clouds!" he said in amazement.

Standing Deer stared at all the people. "So many people! All different kinds of people from many different lands." He continued to look around in awe and pointed to a group of people. "I see your people have slaves here, too. The Lakota do not have slaves. They believe all people should be free."

"Slavery was abolished after the civil war. What makes you think we have slaves?" Karen asked, puzzled by his remarks.

"What is abolished?" Standing Deer asked.

"It means stopped, forbidden. It is no longer legal to buy, sell or own slaves."

"Then, why do your people still paint them black? Did the paint not wash off? When did you find out the war ended? The last I heard, your people were still fighting the Great White War. When we left the village, it had not ended yet."

"What do you mean? I don't understand your question about the slaves." Karen was even more puzzled than before. Hopefully, she could keep him distracted and avoid her slip about the war ending.

"The black people. The one's your people paint black, so you would know who the slaves are and who the free people are. If your people no longer have slaves because of the Great White War, then why do you still paint them black?"

How interesting. She could understand how the Indians would come to that conclusion. They paint themselves for war and hunting, etc. It was an interesting perception.

"I understand what you mean. We didn't paint them black. Many of their ancestors were taken from another country called Africa. That is their skin color. That is how they are. See how your skin is darker than mine?" She put her arm against his to show the comparison. Even with her tan, Karen's color was lighter than his.

Standing Deer nodded his head in understanding. He observed the assortment of the different types of people. As they drove around the lake, it was quiet as Standing Deer watched and absorbed everything that was happening.

"What is that they are riding on?" he inquired. His thirst for knowledge seemed to be as great as Karen's.

"Those are bicycles. They are used for transportation, recreation and exercise."

"A white soldier! Why is he here?" Standing Deer exclaimed and pointed to where he saw the man. He reached instinctively for his bow and arrow. Blowing out a breath, he remembered she had convinced him to leave it at her lodge.

Karen turned to see a city policeman on a horse. Karen decided they had seen enough of the city. She felt she was overwhelming Standing Deer. She needed to show him some of the farmland and orange groves.

"That is a policeman. He is here to protect the honest people from the dishonest people, like a dog soldier does. Let's get out of the city and go to the more pleasant areas of town."

Karen drove onto the east-west expressway and headed west. Standing Deer was ecstatic. He seemed so exhilarated from the speed of the car. He turned the volume up on the radio and made whooping noises. Now he reminded her of a teenager! Karen realized he had changed the radio to a rock station.

Standing Deer was moving his head and tapping his hand on his leg to the beat of the music. The song was unfamiliar to her. After the song was over, the DJ announced that it was Offspring.

"Did you like that song, Standing Deer?" Karen inquired.

"I didn't understand the words but the music was great!" Karen laughed. She didn't understand the words either.

He changed the radio station again and found country music. He decided to listen to that for a while. Then, he switched it to an oldie but goodies station and that's where he left it. He increased the volume of the radio to listen to a Beach Boy's song. It seemed Standing Deer had figured out the radio.

The rest of the day went by quickly for the two of them. Karen felt the more they spent time together, the more she realized how much she really liked and enjoyed his company. Though they were from two separate worlds, they had so much in common. Each moment seemed to bring Standing Deer more and more into her heart. The more they spoke of each other's feelings and dreams, the more she realized that he was the man for her.

By the end of the day, Karen knew in her heart that when it was safe she would want to make love with him. She explained to Standing Deer that she needed to go into the store and pick up a few things and she would be right out. Standing Deer waited patiently in the car while she ran into the drug store.

As Karen walked into the store, she did not see her ex-boyfriend. David was standing in line at the checkout counter. She picked up a basket and walked straight over to the prophylactics. As she was picking out a box, she heard an old familiar voice behind her.

"Well, I see you have not changed. Still so very practical. How come your boyfriend isn't buying those instead of you? You never bought them for me."

Karen turned to him in disgust. "Not out chasing ambulances today, David?"

"I'm not an ambulance chaser," he growled.

"No, of course not. You just wanted me to hand out your business cards to my patients in the emergency ward for you. But when I refused, you convinced your other girlfriend to do it for you. You know the one you were cheating on me with? Or did you just forget about her after she was fired for doing your dirty work? You realize that she can never be a nurse anywhere in this state because of you? You ruined her career to excel yours."

With his usual air of arrogance he retorted, "I didn't force her into doing it. And actually, I just got out of court. I won, as usual. So … ."

"That's because you won't take it to court unless you know you'll win."

David ignored her and took the box of condoms from Karen. Twirling them around in his hand, he smiled. "Plan on having fun tonight?"

"Go to hell, David," Karen said quietly and walked away, leaving him holding the box of prophylactics.

"Whoa! Straight-laced, 'goody two-shoes' Karen said a naughty word!" David laughed as she walked away to pick up some other necessities.

With anger, jealousy and resentment in his heart, David watched her walk away. Cautiously he started searching for a pin. He found a large button with a pin on the back. Carefully, he pulled out the wrapped condoms and methodically put holes in every single one. Then, he walked over to

Karen. He smiled to himself. He would pay her back for leaving him. And he would win her back, too.

David threw the box into the basket she was carrying. "Here, you forgot these. Have fun." Saluting, he turned and walked out the door.

Karen was fuming at David's arrogance. How could she have ever seen anything in him? She hurried into line. David knew what her car looked like. Hopefully, he would not go searching for it and find Standing Deer.

Great, all she needed was a confrontation between the two of them. He would humble David. That was certain. David had no idea what he was up against. Thank God, he didn't have his knife with him. She laughed. It would be nice to watch David lose for once.

Karen's car was easy to find and David approached Standing Deer.

Whoa, ho, ho, ho, he thought to himself. This is definitely out of character for Karen. He never knew Karen found men with dark hair attractive. She had always dated blondes as far as he knew. This man's hair was long and pitch black, too. Interesting, she always liked short hair on men.

Obviously, Karen was having a rebound from their relationship and this man was the product of that rebound.

"Hello. I'm an old, close friend of Karen's. Name's David." David reached his hand through the window to shake hands. Standing Deer just looked at it and silently looked at David, waiting for him to continue speaking.

David cleared his throat uncomfortable with the rejection of the handshake. He was unaccustomed to rejection from anyone. It just never happened. Everyone liked him.

"Why don't you come out of the car? It must be hot in there. Karen will be out in a few moments." David opened the door and Standing Deer got out of the car.

"So ... ," David cleared his throat again. This man made him uncomfortable. "How long have you known Karen?"

"I have not counted the days."

David thought to himself, days? She's only known him for days and she's planning on going to bed with him! She'll definitely be needing him now. Oh well, let her. There's still no competition between the two of them. He felt he was the better man compared to this loser boy she was seeing now.

This new beau of Karen's was quite tall, at least five inches taller than him, probably with some Native American blood in him, too. Not very talkative, either. He seemed to be quite stoic. Well, this relationship won't last.

"Well, aren't you the lucky one. You have known Karen for days and she is willing to go to bed with you. She dated me for well over six months before she went to bed with me. Don't get your hopes up too high on having her for long. I plan on winning her back."

Karen hurried out the door and saw David and Standing Deer talking by her car. David saw Karen coming up to the two of them and continued talking to Standing Deer.

"You may have her, now," David said quietly to Standing Deer. "But she will be my wife. Soon you will be out of her life and she will marry me." David turned and walked away.

Before David got into his car to drive away, he yelled to Karen, "Have fun, Karen!" Laughing, he drove off.

"What did he say to you?" Karen demanded.

"I do not like him. What he says does not matter. He is wrong and speaks like a foolish child."

Karen laughed. "Well, I see you figured him out pretty quickly. I wish I had. Let's go."

Karen thought, of all the people to see it had to be him. How in the world she had ever been mixed up in that relationship she'd never know. She recalled Bonnie had told her it was hormones.

When Karen saw the two of them together, there seemed to have been no comparison. Standing Deer had it all, compared to David. David was a scumbag, an ambulance-chasing lawyer. He was a two-faced liar. Standing Deer was honest and down to earth.

Standing Deer had killed men without remorse. David hadn't. She didn't feel remorse over the death of those traders either. He was from a different world. Survival of the fittest ... isn't that how it is supposed to be? She wasn't that blind to Standing Deer. Karen knew he could be a deadly, fierce warrior.

Even though she had only known Standing Deer for two weeks, she could see the major difference between the two men. This relationship with Standing Deer was moving too fast. She had only known him a short time, but it seemed like it had been forever. It seemed like they were meant to be.

Ever since the first time he touched her, nothing was the same. Nothing seemed the same. She could not get him off her mind. It was as if something out there was telling her they were to be together until the end of time.

Sometimes love turns out that way. Could it actually be happening to her? Could Standing Deer be her soul mate? He seemed to be so perfect for her, but ... how would she really know if he was the right one? She hadn't known him that long.

She hadn't even gone beyond the infatuation period, yet. They say ninety days. Infatuation lasts about ninety days.

Then you start seeing the real person. You see their faults and then you decide if you can live with them or not.

When she looked back on the past year, her life seemed to be incomplete without him. Something seemed to have always been missing. She was an independent, well-rounded person, yet it always felt as if something was missing, incomplete. Was Standing Deer the missing piece in her puzzle called life?

Karen shook her head. Why was she even considering these questions? She had not known him long enough. There were too many conflicts they had to encounter if they were to pursue this relationship. There was too much standing in their way. Then again, she smiled to herself, she always did enjoy a challenge.

Karen's train of thought was broken by the sound of the radio. She smiled to herself. Standing Deer turned up the volume. It appeared he liked The Beatles, too.

Standing Deer had briefly thought of his encounter with David. He decided the man was a child. That man was lying to himself if he thought Karen would marry him. She was the woman for Standing Deer.

When the pampered white man first approached him, Standing Deer took an instant dislike to him. There was something about the man that he didn't trust. He was too pleasant, at first. Too talkative, like he was hiding something. The white man appeared to be overconfident, like a child that feels as if they are indestructible.

Standing Deer shook his head in disgust. Her old friend David was not a strong enough man for Karen. That white man needed Karen for her strength. Standing Deer did not. He had his own inner strength. He did not need it from anyone else.

Standing Deer recalled the look of dislike on Karen's face when she had approached the two men. He smiled to himself, that white man didn't have a chance to win Karen's heart. He may be able to give Karen more magic from her world but he would not be able to give himself. It seemed to Standing Deer that the white man had nothing worth giving. At least Standing Deer had himself to give and it appeared that it was more than the other man had. Standing Deer believed Karen had enough of the white man's magic. She needed Standing Deer's love.

When they arrived home, Karen went into the kitchen to prepare dinner. Standing Deer followed her in and offered his help. She turned the offer down and told him to relax. As she reached around him to turn on the light, he softly touched her face.

"It was a good day, Karen," Standing Deer told her.

She smiled, "I really enjoyed myself, too. I hope the city didn't intimidate you or discourage you."

Standing Deer had watched Karen turn the light on and was surprised by the burst of light in the room. He flipped the switch back and forth and watched the light turn on and off.

"What is intimidate?" he asked as he was playing with the light switch. This was more interesting than the disappearing water from what Karen called a 'toilet.'

"It means threatened or to make you feel threatened by the extensiveness of something."

He continued to switch the light on and off, trying to figure out how it worked. "No, it did not make me feel threatened. We are all very small children in the eyes of the Great Spirit. It is just another world that He has given to His people. It is another world to learn about and discover."

Karen was just about to tell him to leave the light switch alone when he stopped. Standing Deer walked around Karen to the stovetop. He looked at the red coil underneath the pan.

He removed the pan from the element and put his hand over the top to feel the heat.

"What an odd fire. This is where you make you meals?"

"Yes, it's called a stove. That's an electric element. Don't touch it, it will burn you."

Standing Deer tilted his head and smiled, "If there is heat, there is usually fire. Where there is fire, one does not touch it unless one wants to be burned."

Karen felt foolish. Of course he had common sense. He would need plenty of it to survive in the wilderness.

"Sorry," she apologized.

The evening continued with Standing Deer discovering new toys to play with, each room bringing him closer and closer to Karen's world.

Karen grabbed the remote and turned on the news.

Standing Deer sat on the couch with eyes wide with astonishment.

He stood up and slowly, with caution walked to the television. He looked underneath it and behind it. He shook it, put his ear to it and tapped it lightly with his finger. Amazed, he looked at Karen.

"How do those tiny people get in there? Do they live in there?"

"No they don't live in there. It's called a television. It's like a picture, only it moves. They're people just like us only they're on the television."

Karen paused unsure if she should continue the explanation. "It's a bit complicated. I don't think you would really understand, but I'll explain it to you if you would like. Actually, I find it hard to understand."

"No, that is all right. I have seen too much magic today. I don't think I want to know how it all works." Standing Deer went and sat down next to Karen.

There was a small segment on the news about the senate and congress trying to pass a new bill taking some of the Native American Indian's privileges away. It would be breaking several treaties from the past.

"I see the white man does not keep his word in your world, either," Standing Deer said dryly.

"If I were you, I wouldn't worry too much about it. It'll cause too much of an uproar. There are so many Native American sympathizers across the United States that a bill like that would cause too many problems among the Americans. Unfortunately, sometimes not enough people speak up. They're just being politicians and are trying to get away with anything they can."

Karen paused. "You see, the politicians are making a big deal about the national deficit. They think that by cutting back on what they call unnecessary spending, it will help get rid of the deficit. Usually, they only make a big deal about the deficit during an election year."

"What is a deficit?" Standing Deer asked.

"It means debt. Our country owes people or the World Bank or whatever. We owe them money."

"You mean your world is poor? It no longer has any of the white man's money?"

Karen laughed, not at his question but at the reality of his question.

"No. Our country is not poor. Actually, we are one of the most profitable countries in the world. In my opinion, and quite a few people would disagree with me, the politicians don't want us to know what the country's assets are. They don't want the people of the United States to know how much they're worth."

Karen sighed, she tried to keep her political views to herself but it was so easy talking to Standing Deer. Maybe someday, as they grew closer together, they would have their political discussions. Now that would be an adventure, as Bonnie would say.

The news became a blur as Standing Deer cupped her face into his hands and leaned over to kiss her quickly and lightly on the lips. He looked deep into her eyes, penetrating his gaze into her being.

Kissing and caressing her neck Standing Deer whispered, "My beautiful Karen, where shall we sleep tonight?"

"You dear, will be sleeping in the spare bedroom. I will sleep on the fold-out couch in the den."

"Why can we not sleep together? I want to hold you all night. We can sleep together without making love. I want to make love to you only when you are ready." Standing Deer spoke with passion.

That would be nice. She leaned toward him and closed her eyes, wanting the kiss he was about to give her.

He smiled and touched his lips gently to hers. The rush of the electrical impulse was intense. They both could feel their bodies reaching for each other. Their desire was immense.

Standing Deer wanted to lose himself in Karen's arms. Not since his wife had he felt such a desire for a woman. He wanted to be with Karen for eternity. He could feel her energy and her soul. He wanted to be a part of it.

The intensity of the kisses grew stronger. His hands caressed Karen's body until she could only feel the heat from his touch. The more he kissed her, the more she wanted to kiss him back. She did not want to leave his embrace. This time she would not walk away. There was nothing wrong with just kissing.

Her heart pounded with desire. She felt him lifting her shirt. She arched her back as she felt his hot, moist mouth covering the nipple of her voluptuous breast. She ached for more as his lips went lower, slowly down to her waist. He tickled her belly button with a few flicks of his tongue.

Karen was overwhelmed with desire. A tiny voice inside said, "No, stop now before it is too late." She couldn't. She didn't want to.

Standing Deer played with her nipples as he caressed her with his tongue. Karen froze, the rape suddenly fresh in her mind. Instantly he felt her discomfort. Not wanting to upset her, he moved his way upward. He just wanted to simply please her any way he could.

As he continued to caress her breasts, she started relaxing again. Karen felt as if she was on fire. His hands were burning her flesh with desire. She could feel his burning fingers moving slowly ... slowly, down to her ... she moaned in pleasure.

Standing Deer felt her swelling with his fingertips. She was ready for him. Karen was moist and hot. Standing Deer had made her forget temporarily. He knew her desire for him was ultimate and she probably wouldn't stop him if he tried to enter her. He gave his word. He would keep it. He could feel her fighting it and knew when she had released her trust in him.

Was that moan from him or herself? As he stroked her gently, unfulfilled desires exploded from her being. She was burning, on fire. Time froze with the flames of desire engulfing her as her body started to explode in ecstasy.

Karen's thoughts ceased as time stood still. She felt a strange heated sensation, a burning. She groaned from the intensity and allowed Standing Deer to have what no one else had given her. She felt a pulse, an exertion from inner release as her body exploded and shuddered.

Her body shuddered uncontrollably. She gently returned exhausted from the intensity of the love. Standing Deer leaned his head on her chest. He could feel and hear her heart beat.

"My love," he said huskily.

Karen started laughing. It was silly but she was so happy she couldn't help it. She kissed him all over his face.

"Oh, that was oh so wonderful! I've never had an orgasm before. That was so ... so ... thank you. Never in my life have I experienced such intensity." Still out of breath, Karen continued. "You are wonderful, Standing Deer. Thank you."

Karen leaned back, still breathing heavily. Standing Deer smiled. He pleased her, that is all he wished for at this time.

It was there that they both awoke the next morning, entwined in each other's arms ... unknowingly wrapping themselves around and into each other's souls.

Chapter TEN

The only appointment Karen had was to go the doctor for her check-up. Luckily, the doctor had been able to fit her in his schedule. Then, she and Standing Deer could do anything they wanted before they returned to his village.

She knew Dr. Kindell well, but she also knew she could not explain to him why she feared having any sexually trans- mitted diseases. She knew herself enough to know she wasn't very good at lying and was afraid he would not believe her when she told him she had unprotected sex.

Karen told Dr. Kindell that it just happened in the heat of the moment. She explained to him that the next day she regretted it because she did not know the man well and prescribed some antibiotics for herself.

He was furious with her and reprimanded her severely for treating herself. He told her everything appeared normal but took several tests on her to be safe. Dr. Kindell continued pressing her with questions. Karen was relieved when the check-up was over and she could get out of there.

At times throughout the day, Standing Deer was like a child discovering a whole new world. Their friendship grew strong as each spoke of their own life styles and experiences. Karen could feel the bolt of electricity rush through her body each time he gently touched her arm or held her hand.

It was a form of friendship Karen was unaccustomed to having with a man. She would hear herself talking to him and be amazed at herself that she would speak to him of things that only she or her closest friends knew. Karen believed she could tell him almost anything and trust him enough to know he would never break that trust. Maybe someday she would be able to entrust him with her biggest secret, the truth behind their separate worlds.

Karen was pleased when Standing Deer spoke about the ways of his People. She was astonished and happy to hear that they never hit their children. The Indians from his tribe believed that it brought great shame and dishonor to your name if you ever hit any child in anger or for punishment. Everyone considered themselves parents to all the children in the camp and believed it was everyone's responsibility to teach the children to grow to be brave and honest adults. He explained that they all looked after each other, young and old.

Karen asked Standing Deer what they did to Indians who did hurt their children. He told her it just didn't happen. No one wanted to live a life with dishonor.

He spoke of a father from a different tribe that had been excessively beating his wife and children. The Indian was expelled from the life of the village and was told never to return. The wife was given the choice to stay or go, she chose to stay with the village.

"Your People have divorce?"

"What is divorce?"

Karen explained to him the meaning and concept of divorce.

"One discourages divorce, but it is not forbidden," he had told her emphatically. "It can also be a dishonor. Under rare and certain circumstances, it is accepted. A warrior never tells his wife to leave. He takes her for life. If he is unhappy with her then he takes another wife, if he so chooses. Taking another wife does not necessarily mean he is dissatisfied with the first wife either. If she is unhappy with him, she may leave." He shrugged, "But it just doesn't happen."

"Can a woman have more than one husband?"

"No."

"Why not? It doesn't seem fair. If a warrior can have more than one wife why can't the woman choose to have more than one warrior?"

Standing Deer laughed. "That is not the way. Besides, there are more women than men. You, my love, are trying to be difficult."

He bent and gave her a kiss that sent Karen reeling in pleasure. She wished he wouldn't do that, arousing her so deeply she couldn't concentrate when he was kissing her with such seeded passion.

"The Sioux believe a wife is his equal and should always be treated with the love and respect she deserves."

Karen was impressed with their beliefs regarding marriage and children. They were the ones that were considered savages but after listening to Standing Deer, were they really? Karen believed he would not be very impressed with her world if he knew about the divorce rate and all the abuse received by adults and children alike. She believed he would be disgusted with all the rapes, murders and robberies that happened daily. Iniquities that her world seemed to take for granted.

His life couldn't be that peaceful, could it? Karen wondered. It sounded almost like paradise. Could their village be that serene? She recalled the happiness and serenity she had felt when she was with the Lakota. Their village may be peaceful and serene but what about their warfare with other Indian tribes?

They fought, killed and stole from other tribes. What about the warfare with the whites? Karen spoke these concerns aloud.

"We are a peaceful people, we fight only when we are forced into it. We do not have warfare among ourselves. Our life-circles in the village most always remain at peace with each other."

"You fight and kill the Pawnee and other enemies. You steal their horses and anything you can from them in order to achieve coups. How can you say you are a peaceful people?"

"Doesn't your country award your people with honor for defeating an enemy? Do they not receive coups for conquering their enemies, stealing their possessions? Sioux does not war with Sioux. Americans kill Americans. We are not like your people who kill each other for land and the white man's money. I have seen how your people treat each other, your country will not live as long as the Sioux Nation if they do not find peace amongst themselves."

Her mouth dropped, she was furious. "How dare you! How can you say that when you war with your Indian enemies? Your people have fought the Pawnee for generations."

Standing Deer sighed. He did not want to argue with her. "The Scili, the Pawnee Nation is our enemy. We do not provoke war with them. We are not the same as the white man."

"You are still fighting among yourselves. Pawnee against Lakota is still Indian fighting Indian."

"Pawnee is not Lakota. We are not the same."

"You are the same! You're still Native American's fighting against Native American's."

"I do not know how to explain this to you. They are not the Sioux Nation. They are not of the People. You are putting the Nations together in one bowl. You can't do that."

Karen sighed. They were going in circles. "Standing Deer, some day you will have to join forces with all Indian Nations or your People will not survive."

Standing Deer saw the sadness in her eyes. "I will listen and heed your words for they are spoken with your heart."

He took her into his arms and gently kissed her lips. He was disarming her anger and she had no objection. Karen treasured every moment in his arms. She sighed. She knew that even if it was almost paradise, it wouldn't last for long. It saddened her to know that turmoil would soon surround and destroy the Indian lifestyle.

The time passed by quickly and before they both realized it, the day was over and they had returned to the Hunkpapa village.

"You must never speak of my world and what you have seen in it. It would not be wise," Karen whispered to Standing Deer as they left his lodge.

Shaking his head, Standing Deer laughed. "Little one, no one would believe me. They would think I had been drinking the white man's spirits."

The camp had the still quiet of early morning. The ceremonies had ended but there were many people from other bands still in the camp. Karen could see Crazy Horse and Red Cloud across the village. She would need to speak to him before he returned to his home.

"My friends!" Two Feathers called. Both Standing Deer and Karen watched Two Feathers approach with his customary smile on his face. Laughing Flower was not far behind.

After a short spell, the men went on their way and the two women started their chores. Karen was clumsily trying to soften an antelope hide when she was approached by Sitting Bull, Crazy Horse and Red Cloud.

"My father would like you to come to his lodge as soon as you can. He would like to speak to you before the big meeting of the chiefs," said Sitting Bull.

Karen immediately dropped what she was doing and walked over to Jumping Bull's lodge. As Sitting Bull opened the flap to let her inside, Karen felt an overwhelming sadness strike her hard in the face. Her heart jumped.

She looked into Jumping Bull's eyes as he sat quietly and knew that Crazy Horse told of his experience in the Sun Dance. But what and how much did Crazy Horse know?

Karen sat down where she was instructed and remained silent ... waiting, fearing what the questions could possibly be. She looked over at Crazy Horse. He looked so young, possibly fourteen or fifteen but he had to be older. He had the look of a man of age. She could see his eccentricities in him even now. She reflected, a quiet boy/man with the weight of the world on his shoulders.

His wavy hair was braided on one side with a feather tying it back. His eyes were a coal black, deep and sullen. It appeared as if he looked straight through you. His build was lean and solid as a rock. It seemed odd but his skin was light, like hers. She hadn't noticed that earlier. The tension laid like a thick blanket hovering over them. Crazy Horse stared at Karen with conflicting emotions of concern and anger.

She turned her gaze to the famous Red Cloud. He had a kind face. She could see in him that he could be a fierce warrior, if one crossed him. She smiled at him and knew she was proud to meet such a great and honorable man.

Jumping Bull cleared his throat and started speaking in Lakota. Sitting Bull, who had seated himself between Jumping Bull and Karen, spoke quietly in her ear and interpreted what was being said.

"We are here to find answers to puzzling questions that have arisen in the past few days. Crazy Horse has seen a great and tragic vision. He says you know what the future will be and you could save us but you can not. He says the Great Spirit will not allow Spirit of the Mountain to change what is to be. If you try, you will loose all of your powers that He has given you."

Jumping Bull raised his hands into the air. "He did not know where we had met and in the vision you were called Spirit of the Mountain. That will be your name from this day forward. Crazy Horse will speak now."

Karen turned her gaze to Crazy Horse. His head was down, his body so still that he appeared to be asleep. He inhaled a deep breath and stared with hard eyes directly at Karen. With resentment in his voice, he spoke quietly.

"I have already given you the message from the Great Spirit. There is no need to repeat it. Now, I have been advised to tell you my vision. I will tell you, only because you are the link to our future." Crazy Horse paused and was silent for a few moments as Sitting Bull repeated what he said in English.

"There are white men and black slaves in our Sacred Hills. They are digging for the shiny rocks that the white men feel is so important. They are destroying our Sacred Grounds looking for these silly rocks. There is war, with many dead white men and many dead brave and honorable warriors.

"I look to where the sun rises and I see many white people and families coming into our lands. They kill all our buffalo and we can not eat or live." Crazy Horse looked to Red Cloud. Red Cloud nodded his head in encouragement and Crazy Horse continued.

"I see clouds and smoke everywhere. I cannot see the sky. There are many, many white soldiers and they have come to destroy us. They have come to our village to kill us all. They want to kill the women and the children as well as our warriors. During the fighting, you are there in the middle of the camp. You are helping the wounded warriors. There is a white glow like a full moon surrounding you. I am ten feet from you and there is a white soldier on his horse racing toward you with his rifle aimed at your back. When I raise my rifle to shoot him I hear a whooshing sound like that of a thousand eagles flying over my head. The soldier's horse jumps up on his hind legs and knocks the white soldier onto the ground. The white soldier gets up and grabs his gun to shoot you when some unseen force pushes him down. The whooshing sound continues until I shoot the man." Crazy Horse shook his head in wonder, puzzled by the vision.

"You do not see what is happening. You are tending to a warrior and your eyes are turned away from the soldier. Women are grabbing you and taking you to wounded children and men alike for you to save them. The white glow, like a spirit, follows you. When the clouds and smoke are gone, you cry for the dead white men that are in our village." Crazy Horse cleared his throat before continuing, allowing Sitting Bull the time he needed to repeat his words.

"There is a white man in the village that is not dead and you go to him to try and save him. A warrior stops you and kills him. He tells you that we will take no captives. You walk away from the dead man and that is when I received the message for you from the Great Spirit." Crazy Horse looked at her with hardened, angry eyes.

"Why did you try to save the white man? Your skin is white. Do you choose to be with the Lakota now? Then in the future when you feel as if all is lost, turn your back on the Lakota to help the white man?"

Crazy Horse spit his questions in anger at Karen. "I trust no one who is white. Why would the Great Spirit choose a white skin to help save the great Lakota Nation?" Jumping Bull raised his hand and stopped the angry words coming out of Crazy Horse's mouth.

"Spirit of the Mountain, we are a peaceful People and do not want war with the white people. All we want to do is live on our land, raise our children with the freedom that our forefathers have given us, and teach them the ways of the Great Spirit. Will the white soldiers not stop until we are all dead? How many white people will come to our lands?" Jumping Bull asked quietly.

Karen's head was pounding for she was still absorbing everything Crazy Horse had said to her. She no longer wondered why Crazy Horse was said to be such an eccentric, withdrawn man. He had the gift of sight and knowledge and he was going to fight this all the way. Red Cloud, Sitting Bull and Jumping Bull waited patiently for her answer. Crazy Horse stared at her as if he knew what she was going to say before she said it. She could feel the anger brewing inside of him.

Karen spoke slowly and very cautiously; afraid she would say too much. "Even though I have the knowledge of what the future is supposed to be for your People, I cannot tell you what to do. I cannot tell you how to prevent the tragedies that will happen."

She paused, afraid to continue. Her heart was pounding in her ears. She wiped her sweaty hands on her dress.

"All I can tell you is to try your best for peace. Once the Civil War is over there isn't much anyone can do to stop the white immigrants from coming onto your land. There are thousands and thousands of whites that will be coming to this land to start new lives. Almost all of them will fear you and your ways. They do not understand the Indian way of life and have been told that you are uncivilized savages. They have been told you will kill them on sight and must defend themselves because you will hurt their wives and children."

Karen took a drink from her cup, trying to figure out how to word everything carefully. "Most of these people are poor and want to live in peace as you do and want to start a new life. If we could all live in peace and harmony, there would be no destruction."

Karen looked directly at Crazy Horse. "Not all whites are evil. Most are hard working, brave and honest."

"They will take what does not belong to them! You know there will be no peace!" Crazy Horse shouted at her.

"I can't deny what you say. Don't be angry with me because of what has happened. I can't change ... ." Immediately her anger and frustration had become dread. She had spoken in the past tense!

She looked around quickly and saw the astonishment in everyone's faces, everyone except for Crazy Horse, who could not understand English.

"Why do you speak as if this is the past?" Red Cloud questioned.

A sick feeling grew into a knot in Karen's stomach, her heart stuck in her throat. "I know too much. It is hard for me not to warn you of what is to be. I cannot tell you anything else."

There was a short silence when Jumping Bull dismissed Karen and Crazy Horse. The men prepared for their meeting with the other chiefs. There was much to discuss as there had been rumors that the Great White War was almost over and white men had been seen digging for the rocks in Paha Sapa, the Sacred Black Hills.

Karen was again, for the second time that day, relieved to be away from such scrutinizing questions.

Chapter ELEVEN

Karen had been waiting patiently for Standing Deer to return home. Almost everyone she knew in the village had been teaching her and helping her learn the language and the ways of the Lakota. Sunshine in the Morning and Laughing Flower had taught her how to prepare foods and medicines. Karen wasn't familiar with the plants but found the herb medicines to be quite effective. The only plant she seemed to recognize was the mint plant they used for their tea.

Their English was just barely comprehensible so they spoke to her in Lakota in order for her to learn the language as quickly as possible. Karen wanted to surprise Standing Deer when he returned.

Karen would listen to the elders as they told tales, teaching lessons and morals to the children. They would use sign language as they spoke so she could understand and comprehend the stories. Many of the stories sounded like the ones she had heard when she was younger. Many stories would have deep meaning and the children would listen hard with their hearts so they would not miss a word that was being spoken.

Living in the village and spending so much time with Sunshine in the Morning and Laughing Flower made her aware of how religious the Lakota were. They prayed each morning and at the end of each day. They would pray to the Great Spirit before a hunt, thank him for the kill and the chance to feed those who were hungry. They were grateful for everything He had given them and they never wavered in their thoughts. Everything was as He wanted it to be and one must accept His complete wisdom and do as He bid.

They had no need to put one day aside as a holy day to pray like the modern Christians. All days belonged to the Great Spirit. Everything they did, everything they felt belonged to the Great Spirit, and every day was owed to the Great Spirit. They found it strange when Karen informed them that her people chose one day a week to go to church and pray to God. They couldn't understand how her people could take just one day when all should be grateful to God each day; therefore, we should thank Him and praise Him always.

Always watching and learning, Karen noticed that when the warriors who hunted returned with a bountiful kill, if they had more than they needed, they would give the food to someone less fortunate. The People were careful in their generosity. It wasn't because they didn't want to give. They made sure their gifts never offended or made someone feel as if they weren't contributing their share. They took care of each other, young and old alike. Watching the way they lived increased Karen's spiritual beliefs in God. She felt it was ironic that she had to travel over a hundred years to find the inner peace she had been looking for all of her life.

She was quickly becoming a naturalist with a strong emotional attachment to God and everything He has given the Earth. The Lakota treated the Earth and all its creatures with a reverence. They were all gifts from the Great Spirit and must be treated with respect. One did not take any more than was needed.

On the morning of the warriors return, Karen and Sunshine in the Morning were filling their skins with water. Hearing the excitement from the village, they quickly ran to greet the men. Karen stood back as she watched Little Fox and Sunshine in the Morning hugging their brother. She scrutinized every square inch of his body to make sure he was unharmed and found herself becoming aroused by the sight before her eyes. As she looked up into Standing Deer's eyes, he could see the spark of her desire.

He walked over to her and kissed her gently, sending the now familiar surge of power through both of their bodies. Smiling, he looked into her eyes with enshrouded love.

"I hear you have kept everyone busy with your never-ending thirst for knowledge."

Huskily Karen said in Lakota, "Iyuskin kuwa, Tahina Nazinpi." I welcome you, Standing Deer.

Standing Deer's heart nearly burst with pride and happiness at her attempt of his language. Maybe winning Karen's love won't be as hard as Bonnie had said it would be.

The call came for the meeting. Standing Deer excused himself as the warriors entered Jumping Bull's lodge to inform their chief of what had conspired. Karen wasn't sure if she wanted to know. She was certain the law of the Lakota Nation had taken care of the gold-diggers.

After the evening meal, Standing Deer had asked Karen to walk with him. He was pensive and uncertain of how Karen would feel after he told her about the white men. He felt he needed to discuss it with her. They stopped in the privacy of the woods and Karen leaned against a tree anticipating and dreading the forthcoming conversation.

"I must tell you about the white men."

Karen nodded her head to encourage his words. She did not want to hear them, but understood that Standing Deer needed to speak with her to ease his conscience.

"Our intentions were to tell the white men to leave and never return, but they opened fire as they ran themselves into a corner. We had no choice but to defend ourselves and kill them. There was no honor there for it was pitiful. I do not believe we will be giving the white man any more chances." He sighed and looked at her with sadness and hoped that she would not hate him.

"You did what was necessary. It does not matter what their skin color was." She understood completely and hoped she would never be put in such a situation.

He approached her cautiously and swept her into his arms, his eyes flooding with the desire that was deep within him. He kissed her throat, face and lips, whispering seductively in her ear. "Wastehca."

Puzzled, Karen looked into his eyes. "Wastehca? I thought that meant delicious, as in good food?"

Nuzzling his face into her neck, then caressing her throat with his tongue, Standing Deer laughed. "It does my love, and your kisses taste sweet and delicious. I will never be able to have enough of you."

He grabbed her closer and seized her being, attacking her emotions with excitement caused by the touch of his hands and lips. The electric pulse surged through her with each touch of his lips as her body naturally leaned closer into his becoming one. They both felt the fires consume them and ignite a deep soaring passion.

Karen gave in to their desires and allowed herself to be swept away by the sweet rapture of his caresses. All conflicts were gone from her mind, she thought of only him and the pleasure and security she felt in his arms. They returned to Standing Deer's lodge after the long teasing sensuous walk by the water's edge. He had made Karen feel as if she was the most important person in the world. When they sat next to each other on the buffalo skin blanket, Karen's deerskin dress crept up to expose her muscular thighs.

Standing Deer could see her satin undergarment sensuously peeking out. Karen did not miss his reaction and watched with an inner satisfaction as his member grew hard and firm.

As she placed her hand on his thick, massive thigh, she leaned closer. Languorously, she reached over with her other hand and took his large hand into hers giving him a lingering, gentle kiss. She tasted the sweetness of his mouth. Licking her lips, she craved for more.

The electric impulse that she had avoided for so long was as strong as their first kiss. An emotional explosion of heat pounded and thrust through their bodies as they melted into one another's hot flesh. The kissing and caressing slowly became a heated passion experienced like no other.

"Do you have your protection that you feel is needed?" Standing Deer voice sounded husky with desire.

Karen nodded her head yes, wondering how she had gotten on her back. She was filled with fear, desire and excitement for the anticipation of their lovemaking.

With trembling hands, slowly and sensuously Standing Deer began to take off the deerskin dress. He slid his hands over her satiny skin and underneath her dress felt the silk and satin lingerie. Standing Deer inhaled a deep breath. In the dim light of dusk, each movement of Karen's body showed her shaped, muscular body under the translucent silk and satin lingerie.

He kissed her deeply and intensely as he carefully laid her down onto the buffalo skin blanket. Standing Deer felt as if he was going to go crazy with desire for her, wanting to submerge and bury himself in her silk- and satin-covered body. His hands trembled with desire as he began to remove the silky undergarment.

Underneath her lingerie, Standing Deer kissed and caressed her silky, smooth skin. He closed his eyes reveling in the feel of her skin on his hot lips and the lingerie against his rough hands as he slid it off and tossed it to the side. It was hard for him to tell the difference between the two. Her skin felt just as soft as her undergarment. His touch was a methodical and gentle caress as he cupped one of her voluptuous breasts in his hand and felt the nipple stand erect in his fingertips. Karen arched her back begging him to continue the overwhelming pulse of electric rapture.

He felt a rush of heat go through his lips as Karen moaned in pleasure and contentment. Slowly, Standing Deer placed his hot, moist lips onto her breasts and suckled them until her body stiffened from the heated desire she felt engulfing her very being. His hand moved across and down her flat, muscular stomach. She was ready. He closed his eyes and relished in the sweet, desirable scents of her body.

Standing Deer kissed her passionately and tasted the sweetness as Karen arched her back in overwhelming ecstasy. They were alone in this world of pleasure, as time stood still their two souls ever entwining for eternity.

Standing Deer could feel her body's tremors and quivers as she experienced the ecstasy of an orgasm. He held her tightly as her body trembled from the intensity of their lovemaking. Her heart raced. Her body felt as if it had weights holding her to the ground. She couldn't move and it felt wonderful. She smiled and lifted her arm slowly to hold him closer.

When her body started to allow itself to be commanded, Karen started to kiss and caress his nipples. Standing Deer found the feeling to be erotic as every part of his body seemed to be electrified by her caresses. Gradually and unsure of herself, she moved her way down to his engorged member.

She was more than happy to return and give any pleasure to him that she could. She wanted to excite and satisfy him as he did her, wanting to make him explode in sheer pleasure and ecstasy. Karen wanted to make him squirm with desire and have him reach a peak he had never experienced in his lifetime.

Cautiously and slowly she allowed her tongue to caress him. Karen felt self-conscious of her actions but it seemed to her that the slower she moved, the more intense it was for Standing Deer. The slower she caressed him with her mouth, the more his body bucked with pleasure. He moaned as he opened his eyes and watched her work her charms on him. Karen could see the fire of lust and desire flooding from his eyes, encouraging her to continue pleasuring him.

The intensity was too much, Standing Deer felt as if he was about to explode when he stopped her. He couldn't take anymore and needed to be deep inside of her, pounding and engulfed by her hot, soft body.

Karen leaned over and grabbed a package. Caressing his manhood, she opened it as he watched her with burning desire. Slowly, continuing with the intensity that neither had ever experienced, Karen slid the prophylactic on his engorged trembling member. It was almost all he could take.

"Now?" Standing Deer croaked breathlessly.

Karen nodded her head yes, afraid to speak, afraid no sound would come out of her mouth.

Standing Deer rolled on top of her and slowly entered her. He felt a tightness engulf him and the moist heat surround him as he entered her. It took all of his control not to explode as he felt the softness of her body wrap and squeeze his member.

An animal lust overcame the two of them as their bodies became entwined. Submerged in each other's soul, oblivious to all around them, the rhythm of their lovemaking continued. Standing Deer and Karen could no longer contain their passions, no longer wanted to.

At the peak of all their wondrous love, Standing Deer exploded deep inside of her, feeling her soft womanhood caressing him with her own pulsations. His body jerked from the impact of release as Karen received his love and clung onto him in seeded passion.

The two of them lay together in a passionate embrace for several minutes. Exhausted and completely satisfied, they were oblivious to the world around them, conscious only of each other. Possessively, they held each other, not wanting their private world destroyed by the hard realities of life.

Standing Deer kissed her face and neck, not ever wanting to let go of Karen, clinging to the continuous embrace.

"Waste celake," he murmured lovingly. I love you.

Karen, lost in his eyes, feeling the complete love of a man for the first time, whispered back to him, "Forever."

After a few moments, Standing Deer leaned up on one elbow and removed the condom. Unbeknownst to him, it was torn. He did not have the knowledge to look for damage and would not know what it would look like if it was damaged. He just knew it was what Karen desired and he would follow her wishes.

He stared into her eyes and caressed her face with his fingertips. He traced along her eyes and down her nose, looking at the freckles scattered about. Grabbing a handful of her soft curly hair, untangling it with his fingers, he watched it shimmer in the light. It still amazed him that she had so many different colors in her hair.

Karen watched him as he played with the separate strands of hair. She hadn't realized how light her hair was until she saw it lying next to his. His hair was as black as a raven's and intermingled with hers made an interesting contrast. It was tickling her chest and she could feel a slight velvety softness caressing her breasts. It stirred her to desire and she could feel the flame within her being as she reached up and pulled his sweet lips to hers.

"Did I not satisfy you, my love?"

"Oh yes, you did." Karen grinned and rolled him over onto his back. "But I think we might need more practice."

A husky laugh was her reply from Standing Deer as they again found themselves merging into each other's souls. Both knew their time together was precious, each moment cherished as if it might be their last. Karen had never felt so much love from any man. All these years she searched for such a love and now she had it deep in her soul. She had learned to have spiritual inner peace with God and found the love of a lifetime – everything she had always wanted.

She believed the conflicts that the Sioux Nation would face were going to cause friction between her and Standing Deer, as well as other members of the tribe. Why did she have to find the perfect love here, in the past? She didn't want to lose Standing Deer but how would she live with the constant conflict of their People?

Every private moment they could steal was enflamed in a passion that nothing could extinguish. Their two separate energies had become one and each strengthened the other.

Both avoided the knowledge that the time would come when a decision had to be made. Standing Deer did not care for Karen's world but he did not want to live without her. She had given herself and lived with him as a wife does and the members of his tribe, as well as himself, expected a marriage. She had not asked him to join her in her world and he was not going to ask to go with her. She must understand that in his world they live as man and wife. It is expected that they honor their marriage in a ceremony.

Her time with Standing Deer and the Lakota was passing quickly. One more night and her friend Bonnie would remove the canopy and she would have to return to the modern world. Could she do it without Standing Deer knowing he was now a complete part of her? Not wanting to imagine what it was like to be without him at her side, she avoided the nagging fears of what was to be.

How would she tell Standing Deer that they would not spend their last night together in each other's arms? Was she a fool to allow herself to fall in love when she knew it was wrong? She had allowed her heart to guide in her decision and it was going to hurt when she told him he could not be with her. It was going to tear her apart.

When Sitting Bull had approached her, she knew something was amiss. She knew how religious the Lakota were. What made her think that they would make an exception to the rule? With her mouth open in astonishment, she listened to his words.

"What! I have to what?!" She exclaimed, stunned by the seriousness in Sitting Bull's tone.

"You and Standing Deer have lived as man and wife. We have been patient because you are not completely familiar with the ways of our People. Standing Deer says that he has asked you to marry him and you said no. It is our way, you must marry."

Karen was furious. It was a shotgun wedding, only it was drastically reversed! No matter how much she argued with Sitting Bull, she was cornered and was to be married that day.

Sitting Bull knew she would be leaving soon but not for good. For every argument she gave him, he came back quickly with a better one. Now she knew why he became such a famous diplomat!

In a huff, completely defeated, she stomped off in the direction of Standing Deer's lodge. She was going to tell him a thing or two.

She was quickly sidetracked by Sunshine in the Morning and Little Fox. They were to prepare her for the ceremony and she was not allowed to see Standing Deer until the prayers began.

Chapter TWELVE

"Hiya. No. I will not be bullied into marriage. I do not want to commit myself to Standing Deer knowing that our happiness will be threatened every day. We will be living separate lives. A marriage cannot exist that way."

Karen looked at the dress spread out before her. It was Laughing Flower's wedding dress and it was beautiful. It was beaded intricately with rabbit fur sewn underneath the beads and along the sides. Next to the dress lay matching moccasins adorned in the same manner.

Sunshine in the Morning frowned. She didn't understand why Spirit of the Mountain was so furious. Didn't she love her brother? She should be honored to have such a good warrior for a husband. She watched as Karen stood in the middle of the lodge with her arms crossed, refusing to budge.

"He woniya tawa, len u wo ... lehan!" Jumping Bull's angry voice called to Karen. Spirit of the Mountain come here ... now.

Karen walked out of the lodge, determined not to waver from her refusal to marry. She did not want to anger him. He was like a father to her. Karen sighed when she saw the look of anger in his eyes. She knew then that she would do what he asked.

"You my adopted daughter. I grow to love you as my own child. You know most ways of Lakota. Do not dishonor yourself. You are not spoiled child and should not act like spoiled child." Taking both of her shoulders into his hands, he kissed her on the cheek, nodded his head and briskly turned her around as he walked her into the lodge. After a few moments, he left to prepare himself for the ceremony.

With a deep sigh, Karen allowed the two women to prepare her for the marriage ceremony with Standing Deer. Outside, she could hear the drums beating, alerting every one of the coming ritual.

Her stomach was in knots. Her hands were sweaty and shaking uncontrollably. What was Standing Deer doing? How did he feel, knowing that she had already told him she did not want to marry? Why was he allowing this to happen when he knew how she felt? She asked Little Fox and Sunshine in the Morning as they were helping her pull the dress over her head.

"He wishes to marry you. But even he has no choice, the law of the Lakota must be kept by all." Little Fox and Sunshine in the Morning replied.

After a few minutes that felt like eternity, Karen heard Jumping Bull call to enter. Little Fox and Sunshine in the Morning responded to his call.

Smiling, Little Fox spoke quietly to Karen. "It is time."

As Karen and Jumping Bull left the lodge, a silence swept through the village. All eyes were on the two of them as they walked slowly to the center of the village. Karen 's heart was pounding so hard that she felt as if all would hear.

Sitting Bull stood in the center of the village waiting patiently. He was impressively attired in full headdress and ritual ropes for the marriage ceremony. She recalled photographed pictures she had seen of him before she had met the man. They did him no justice. They failed to capture the real man, the love and pride he had for his People.

She inhaled deeply, trying to calm her nerves. She was honored to know him and felt privileged for the honor of having him marry her to Standing Deer.

Marry her! What in the world was she thinking? She couldn't marry him! There would be too many hardships. The marriage would fail miserably! She stopped suddenly and showed her fears as she looked at Jumping Bull, pleading silently to stop the madness. Jumping Bull wasn't blind to her fears and felt compassion, but refused to allow her to face shame. Besides, he knew they loved each other and belonged together.

He whispered to Karen. "It is meant to be."

Out of the corner of her eyes, she could see Standing Deer and Two Feathers approaching Sitting Bull. They would meet in the middle, thus connecting and combining their life-circles so they would become one. All thoughts of fear escaped her. This was the man she loved. Maybe, just maybe, love could prevail.

She heard the drums stop as Sitting Bull started reciting the prayers. In Lakota, he spoke first to the Great Spirit and then spoke of what was expected of them as a couple.

She understood some of the words but most of them she could not understand. It didn't matter. From the moment they joined each other in front of Sitting Bull, Karen was swept up and captured in the depth of Standing Deer's eyes. Her heart raced from the excitement of her marriage to the fear of defeat. Defeat never sat well with her. She would fight for their marriage to the day she died.

Tearing herself from the link of love with Standing Deer, she blinked, dazed as she looked over to Sitting Bull. Did he say something? She looked around and saw everyone staring at her, waiting.

Sitting Bull raised his eyebrow and repeated in Lakota, then in English. "Do you accept these vows?"

"Sha." Yes.

"Standing Deer, do you accept these vows?"

"Sha."

Sitting Bull continued with his prayers to the Great Spirit, asking for the union to be blessed and their future to be guided by Him.

The circle waited.

When Standing Deer didn't respond, Sitting Bull nudged him. "Come down to Mother Earth and seal your vows."

Smiles brightened both of their faces. As their lips touched, the fire surged. It penetrating their hearts and souls, etching a permanent flame of love and commitment that would burn forever.

A loud cheer filled the air and the celebration began with dancing and a multitude of food, ending late into the night.

Karen and Standing Deer were exhausted from the excitement of the day. As they entered his lodge, she teased him that he had tricked her into marrying him and never thought she would see the day when she would be involved personally in a shotgun wedding. He feigned injury to his heart and strode over to her in one sleek and graceful movement.

"Niye mitawa." You are mine.

With care, he removed the beads and feathers in her hair and loosened the curls to fall down upon her shoulders. He kissed and caressed her neck and shoulders and then with a surge of intense heat claimed his lips upon hers. They caressed with their hands and lips, each seeking to increase the feverish heat that was sweeping through their souls.

He untied her dress and let it drop to the floor. Surprised to find she had worn nothing of the white women's undergarments, he was pleased and disappointed. Pleased she would choose to dress in the way of the Indian and disappointed because he liked the soft touch of the lingerie. It gave him more to seek pleasure with.

A deep sensual laugh came from within as he placed his mouth on her breasts. They peaked quickly with his touch and gave him the satisfaction that she desired him as much as he had her. Karen was fumbling with his breeches and was frustrated when she could not relieve his member from the confines of them. Standing Deer chuckled again.

"Patience, my love, we have all night."

He proceeded to aid her in the disposal of his clothing and tortured her with his sweet caresses. She was soaring so high, the pleasure painfully sweet, no longer could she stand. Karen felt her knees weakening but Standing Deer's strong arm held her tight and securely. Tonight, she would fly with the stars into the heavens. He would make sure of it.

He kept that promise that he had made to himself. Both soared to the heavens, following a path that pulsed through the ever eternal beating of the universe. Karen wanted more, so much more and she wanted to give as much as she received. She briefly wondered why she had never felt this way before. She only felt this way when she was in Standing Deer's arms. And the thought was gone as quickly as it came. It didn't matter. Her mind was gone. There was nothing but Standing Deer as she felt his manhood push against her. She was with him. And she was in the heavens.

They moved sensually with the rhythm of the universe, their skin and beings on fire from the bursting flames of passion. Karen didn't know when it happened but somehow she was laying down, pulling on his hair. Shivering from the touches of his tongue, he was sensually attacking her. He was everywhere, touching … feeling … caressing.

The intense sensations of pleasure pulsed through her body and she tightened in the burst of an orgasm. She started to scream from the pleasure and Standing Deer thrust his mouth hard onto hers to stifle the sounds. He moved his throbbing manhood and rubbed it along side her inner thighs and along the peak of her womanhood. She ached to have him inside of her, eyes full of lust and desire.

She begged him, whimpering, "Please. Oh please, I want you inside me, deep inside me."

He smiled. "Not yet, I shall torture you with complete love so you will never forget me, no matter which world you are in."

He continued to pleasure her until she was again ready to scream. She was in a world unknown to her, as if a fever had consumed her. The only thing she wanted and cared about was to have him. Now.

With all her might, consumed by the fires surrounding and engulfing them, Karen turned Standing Deer and pushed him flat onto his back. She reached for his manhood and was placing it in her when he forced her to stop.

"No, not yet."

Karen growled in frustration, tears pouring down her face as Standing Deer quickly placed the condom on his throbbing member, unknowingly tearing it in his own frustration to hurry.

Karen begged, "Now, please Standing Deer, now."

Quickly he thrust deep inside of her and heard the sounds of satisfaction, the sounds of lust out of Karen's mouth, or was it his? He could not tell and did not care as he thrust deeper and deeper, lost in the heat of the moment … lost in the heavens.

Sweet surrender came swiftly for they were both peeked and high from the overwhelming sensations of the lovemaking. Collapsing from sheer exhaustion, their hearts were pounding. The sounds of the night creatures slowly came back to their senses, as if they were actually returning to earth.

Standing Deer heard her sniffle.

"Did I hurt you?"

"Oh, no. Heavens, no. I've just ... I've never ever had ... I've never felt this way before. I never knew it could be this beautiful."

"Then why do you cry?"

Karen laughed. "Because I'm happy. Because waste celake."
I love you.

Passionately, she kissed him and could feel his fire grow again. She laughed as she cupped his manhood in her hands and then stroked him until he was ready to pleasure her again with his love. Slowly this time, he planned to make love and cause her senses to reel again, but ever so slowly.

When he had taken her to another explosive paradise, they fell asleep in each other's arms. Tomorrow they would think of reality.

And tomorrow came too quickly.

Scouts spotted buffalo and half the village was preparing to leave. All that were going on the hunt must be prepared to leave by morning. Karen watched as the People readied themselves. It was an amazing sight. In few short hours more than half the village was ready to go.

The next day she bid farewell to Standing Deer, wondering when she would see him next. Only having two more days before she had to start her new job, she wondered what was deterring Bonnie. What if the canopy was not working the way they believed and she was stuck here in this world? She shook her head, too many questions, not enough answers, and she would find out soon enough.

Bonnie was in a frenzy. She needed to talk to Karen and had to get over to her house to take care of the canopy.

That son of a … that jerk of a husband had been cheating on her for years. Their argument last night finally brought the confession from his lips. Bonnie finding him with the woman was not just a one-time thing. Then he took her car, out of spite, and left his. Of course, it had no gas and she had to walk to the gas station the next morning.

It was bad enough that she had to wait an extra night to take care of the canopy. That was the fateful night she found her husband in their bed with that woman. Have they no shame?

He actually had the audacity to ask her what she was doing home. Then that woman made a smart remark about her being scatter-brained and maybe she couldn't remember where she should be. Never in her life had she ever attacked anyone with so much anger and vengeance. Her husband had to pull her off the woman and hold her against the wall while his mistress dressed herself and left.

Her world was destroyed and never had she felt so much hatred toward anyone.

She knew Karen was worried. She had to get there soon. Besides, she might as well stay at Karen's for a few days to calm herself down.

Reality set in the minute Karen awoke to the smell of brewing coffee. Standing Deer had been gone for the buffalo hunt but Karen had still felt as if she was in paradise. Now she was home and it was time to face the real world, her world. She smiled to herself, not that Standing Deer's world isn't real, and it would be nice if she actually was married to him. But she would never be able to accept that marriage ceremony as a real marriage. She performed the ceremony to appease Jumping Bull and his People and no other reason. She certainly couldn't be held to it, not in this world anyway.

She heard noises in the kitchen. Bonnie must be there waiting for her arrival. Stretching quickly, she jumped up and changed into modern clothing.

She had never expected to see Bonnie in such a state.

"What? What's wrong?"

Bonnie burst into tears and told her story as Karen cradled her closest friend in her arms. Bonnie and Kevin are getting a divorce? No way! They had the perfect marriage. What in the world was in his mind when he took that other woman into his arms?

"What am I to do?" Bonnie whimpered. "My life is over. I feel worthless. I'm so stupid and blind. How am I supposed to counsel married couples when I can't even keep my own husband out of someone else's bed?"

"Bonnie stop, you're being unreasonably cruel to yourself. You are far from stupid and blind. He was your husband. Trust comes with that love. Are you sure you want to divorce him?"

"Oh yes, I'm sure," she growled in anger. "I probably could forgive him if it was just a one time fling, but he's been seeing her for years, almost four years. My God Karen, he'd been with another woman for four years. I didn't even see it. Can I stay here for a while? I won't be in the way. I promise. And if I get on your nerves just tell me."

"Of course you can stay here. As long as you want or need to. Now let me get that cup of coffee I so desperately need."

They talked for a couple of hours before Bonnie had to rush off for an appointment. With Bonnie's help, Karen caught up on everything that had, of course, fallen behind in her absence. When Karen got to the part of the marriage ceremony and her attitude that it wasn't a real marriage, Bonnie was dismayed.

"What do you mean it's not a real marriage?"

"Well, how can you take a marriage seriously that supposedly happened over a hundred and thirty years ago, performed by a Lakota holy man and not in a church? Be serious, I love Standing Deer but marriage is out of the question. We've only known each other a month. I only did it to make Jumping Bull happy. It is their way and if I'm going to be living among them or in that time then I have to live by their rules. It was nice living in a fantasy temporarily. They're certainly not the rules that I have to live by here."

"You are just rationalizing. Karen, you are married under the eyes of God, regardless of what priest or religious ceremony was performed. You are Standing Deer's wife whether you like it or not. You'll just have to have a ceremony here in order for it to be accepted in this world."

"I don't think so, Bonnie." Karen was shocked and angry by her friend's attitude.

"You don't have a choice. You are married under the eyes of God. You are married to Standing Deer. Will he be coming to live here? Have you decided or have the two of you not even discussed it?"

"I don't know and we are not married." Karen spoke through clenched teeth.

Bonnie caught the familiar strain in Karen's voice. She knew it well. She was pushing Karen too hard, too fast. Quickly changing the subject, Bonnie brought up the subject of Karen's new job.

Relieved, Karen was more than happy to talk about something else.

Chapter THIRTEEN

Karen sighed. The past two months had been exhausting and ferocious. Her job had kept her considerably busier than she thought it would. Bonnie's life was in shambles and she hadn't seen Standing Deer in months. It seemed that just when he came back from the buffalo hunt, he was sent off to the Black Hills to do more fighting.

She had slept in the spare bedroom some of the time and intentionally missed him in between travels and realized now, how much he meant to her. Were they really married? She recalled her feelings after the ceremony. She had been so determined to make her marriage work. Then she came back to the modern world and it had seemed as if it had been a fantasy. She went as far as denying the marriage. A deep lump stuck in her throat. She missed him so much it hurt.

At the time, she was still angry with him for forcing her to marry. It had been easy avoiding the village but as time passed by, it was getting harder. Karen was determined. It was time to go back and settle their life and how they planned to live it. The time of uncertainty was over.

She looked around at the sterile environment of the hospital emergency room. In approximately six months, she would be here at this hospital as a patient having Standing Deer's baby. Frustrated, she wondered how she became pregnant, then laughed at herself. She knew how, but still wondered how it could have happened. They had been so careful.

She heard someone call her name and looked up as she watched David approached her. She groaned.

"David, please don't call me Karen at work." She looked around with a puzzled look on her face. "Why, I haven't heard an ambulance in the last few minutes. What are you doing here? Trying to hand out more business cards?"

David ignored the sarcasm, confidant that her tune would change soon. "Excuse me, Dr. Anderson, but I have a client in intensive care. I was leaving when I saw your beautiful face."

Karen looked into his eyes and wondered what he wanted from her. She watched his face light up as he gave her his best charming smile.

"Let's go for some coffee," he said with a grin from ear to ear. "Then you can tell me everything that has been happening and when the baby is due."

"W—what did you say?" A knot was quickly developing in her stomach.

"Didn't Bonnie tell you? I saw her the other day. I'm so excited for us. It's too bad your loser boyfriend hasn't been around for a few months. But that makes everything easier for us."

Us? Bonnie doesn't know. She couldn't know. I haven't told her. And what does he mean by us? Karen boiled inside as he continued to play his game. She was quickly jolted back to what he was saying by his mentioning marriage.

"What did you just say?"

"Karen, Dr. Anderson, pay attention. This is important. I know you too well. You would not be able to have an illegitimate child. It goes against everything that you believe in and all of your wonderful morals and principles."

Gently taking her arm, he guided her toward the doctor's break room. "You know I can't have kids. This would be perfect. We can get married and I will raise the little munchkin as my own. It would be wonderful. I'll make you the happiest person in the world."

David was beaming with excitement and Karen felt as if she was going to get sick. An undeniable alarm and warning light went off in her head.

"How did you know I was pregnant?"

With the ease of the typical lawyer she felt he was, he lied with compassion.

"Why darling, Bonnie told me."

Karen stopped in the middle of the hallway. "No, she didn't. I haven't told Bonnie. She's had enough problems of her own and doesn't need to be worrying about me. So David, tell me again. How did you know?"

"Don't you want to marry me and have this baby?" he asked her tenderly as he stroked the side of her arm. He reached up to trace the outside of her lips, getting uncomfortably close. "I love you. I want you to have this baby. That baby is mine. If it wasn't for me, you wouldn't be having it."

"What do you mean if it wasn't for you I wouldn't be having it? What did you do, David?" Karen was almost growling.

"Oh, baby. Darling, don't be mad. I did it for us. That man wasn't for you anyway, and I am. I couldn't give you a baby so I arranged it so he would give you what I couldn't. Now we can be together for the rest of our lives. I'll raise the child as my own, because I planned him. I planned the whole thing."

Karen breath was coming faster and faster. She was seething inside and about an inch from exploding right there in the middle of the hallway. She turned and walked quickly toward the break room again, knowing David would follow.

Karen turned on him as she quickly shut the door. "How?" she asked through clenched teeth.

He smiled and shrugged, "I put holes in the condoms. Okay? How else was I going to get you pregnant? You wouldn't have gotten pregnant voluntarily, but I knew you would have the baby once you discovered you were pregnant."

He watched the anger in her face and was irritated that the plan was backfiring. This wasn't going the way he had it planned at all. She was supposed to jump in his arms, be happy that he wanted her back, and wanted to raise the baby as his own. They were supposed to spend the rest of their lives together. He had to show her how much he really loved her. He made too many mistakes when he had her love the first time. He won't make those mistakes again. He was determined to prove to her that he could love her the way she deserved to be loved.

Karen had been pacing and stopped dead in her tracks. Abruptly, she turned and looked into his eyes. David saw the fire there that he always loved. Holding his breath, he prayed for an acceptance to his proposal. She would understand and the anger would disappear.

"You are a very sick man, David. Besides, you seemed to have forgotten another option that I had. Considering how successful you are as a lawyer, I'm surprised you missed something so obvious. I can't marry you David. I'm already married."

David stood flabbergasted with his mouth opening and closing. Stunned and feeling defeated, he watched her turn and walk away. Tears misted in his eyes as he realized that his one and only true love belonged to another man. He wanted to shout and deny what she had told him. Realizing he was in the middle of a hospital, he straightened his slumped shoulders, adjusted his tie and jacket, and watched her walk away.

A smile slowly came to his lips as he shrugged his shoulders and spoke quietly to himself. "No need to worry, a marriage under those circumstances and so quickly arranged would never last. I'll just wait until she divorces the loser. Then she'll belong to me."

Karen was furious. How convenient that she brought up the fact that she was married when she was denying it to Bonnie for the last few months. She realized that she had backtracked and quickly entered the doctor's break room. How dare he! That son of a, son of a ... that ... that ... "Bastard!" she screamed.

How could he be so stupid, inconsiderate and arrogant? That idiot has no idea what he has done! How dare he put holes in the prophylactics and intentionally get her pregnant? What kind of a warped mind did he have that even made him think she would marry him? Why had he been so sure of himself? Was she that easy for him to control?

She closed her eyes as her beeper went off stilling the anger temporarily. Her personal problems would have to wait. She walked to the telephone to continue with her day.

Oh, Standing Deer, it's been so long. I need you and miss you. How will you feel about the baby? Will you still love me and want me?

Standing Deer rode into the village with the band of warriors. Victory had been theirs but with many injuries. He looked over to his good friend, Two Feathers, fearing his injuries may be fatal. Standing Deer did not want to lose his life-long friend. Hopefully Sitting Bull or Spirit of the Mountain would be able to heal his wounds.

Searching the village, he tried to find Karen hoping she would be here and not in her magical world. A crowd had surrounded the warriors. He could hear the cries of the women, as if they were far away, his mind distracted in search of his wife.

Silently, he looked into Laughing Flower 's eyes and saw the sadness and fear of losing her love. Carefully and with complete caution to avoid the wounds, he picked up Two Feathers and carried the warrior into his lodge. Immediately he and Laughing Flower tended to his friend's wounds.

Guilt flushed throughout his inner being like a plague. If it hadn't been for him, Two Feathers would not have been injured. They had argued intensely. Two Feathers had told Standing Deer that he was not paying attention to what was going on around them and if he didn't be careful his foolish behavior would get them all killed.

Two Feathers scolded him as if he was a child and told him a five-year-old would be able to track him and find him. Standing Deer hadn't realized he had been so careless. His mind was on Spirit of the Mountain so much lately. Distraction out in the wilderness was a deadly mistake. He knew better than to allow his mind to wander.

He closed his eyes and remembered that fateful moment. They were squatting behind some bushes, watching and waiting for the white men to show themselves. Two Feathers was talking to him, never raising his voice to his good friend. If Standing Deer had been paying attention to his tone of voice, he would have realized that there was concern and not criticism.

Standing Deer accused Two Feathers of not being a true friend. Anger had controlled his actions. Like a fool, he exposed himself as he went to move away from Two Feathers words and accusations. Immediately, Two Feathers realized what he had done and jumped on Standing Deer to pull him down. Two Feathers took the bullet that was aimed for Standing Deer.

Standing Deer prayed to the Great Spirit, asking him to keep his friend alive and not die because of his foolishness. He looked over to Laughing Flower and asked her forgiveness. Laughing Flower watched Standing Deer's expressions of pain as he spoke to her of how Two Feathers had become injured.

"Two Feathers will not blame you. You must forgive yourself. Standing Deer, you are his blood brother. He will always love you in that way."

Standing Deer nodded his head in acceptance. It seemed to help, just hearing the words.

"You have not asked about Spirit of the Mountain. She is on your mind, as well."

Standing Deer frowned and nodded his head again. "Yes, she is in my thoughts. It seems I cannot think of anything else."

"What bothers you, my friend?"

"I wonder if she hates me for forcing her to marry me. Maybe I should have waited until she was willing."

"It is our way. You were living as man and wife already. You did not force her into anything."

"It is not her way. We did not consider Spirit of the Mountain's feelings on the matter." Standing Deer sighed.

"She loves you. She must live by our laws if she is to live with us. And you shall live by her laws, if you are to live in her world."

"Spirit of the Mountain does not want me in her world. She has told me that much."

Laughing Flower was confused. It didn't make sense. Why wouldn't she want her husband with her? She recalled the last few months and the time Spirit of the Mountain was in the village. Spirit of the Mountain had watched constantly for Standing Deer's arrival, never letting her eyes stray from the entrance of the camp for long.

She could see Standing Deer's heart ached to be with his wife. Was Spirit of the Mountain still fighting her love for Standing Deer? Their world couldn't be that different to make it impossible to be together as man and wife. Could it? She, like everyone else, was very curious about Spirit of the Mountain's world.

"Is her world that different from ours, Standing Deer?"

Standing Deer smiled and recalled his adventure in the land Spirit of the Mountain called Florida. This Florida was a complicated world. It will cause problems in their life-circle. But if Spirit of the Mountain was willing, they could make their lives together happy and prosperous. It had been overwhelming at the time. Yet he would enjoy being there again as long as it wasn't a permanent situation.

"Yes, it is very different. I cannot speak of her world but I can tell you that it has as much magic as there are stars."

Her eyes widened in wonder. She was amazed at the description of so much magic. How could one live with so much magic? No wonder Spirit of the Mountain was so powerful. She recalled a time when she had accidentally seen Spirit of the Mountain moving arrows up and down in the air by just pointing at them. She recalled how much it scared her. This woman had much power if she could move objects without touching them.

An emptiness filled Standing Deer. A sadness overwhelmed him as he looked at his friend dying on the buffalo mat and ached for his arms to hold his wife.

Sitting Bull called out and entered the lodge with his medicine bag in hand. Standing Deer stood and allowed Sitting Bull to take his place. He watched silently, as Sitting Bull tended to the wounds of his blood brother. After a length of time, he completed his task and there was nothing to do but wait. Both Sitting Bull and Standing Deer left the lodge together. There was much to do and a meeting had been called.

Sitting Bull looked over to Standing Deer and smiled. "I have good news for you my friend. Your wife will be arriving soon."

Puzzled, Standing Deer watched the entrance of the village for Spirit of the Mountain's arrival. When he saw no one, he turned to question Sitting Bull and saw the laughter in his eyes.

"It seems that when she has been gone from our village for any length of time, she goes to her cave that Jumping Bull spoke of. Her horse leaves the camp to bring her to us. If you go look for yourself, you will see that it has left the grazing grounds."

Standing Deer was far from surprised. He had seen Spirit of the Mountain disappear into thin air, calling a horse to come and get her was minor magic.

Karen was tired of seeing the vast prairie land before her eyes. When, she wondered, was she going to find Yankton? It was supposed to be the capital of Dakota Territory during this time. Yankton was where she had to find out how she was to buy land in the Dakota Territory.

She laughed as she recalled accusing the first dealer she spoke to of selling her fake money. How was she supposed to know they actually had three dollar and seven dollar bills in those days ... these days? Oh, whatever! She signed heavily. She wasn't sure how to think sometimes. Was it past or present? If you are living in the past, was it considered present? She shook her head in dismay. It was easier to think that a three dollar bill actually existed.

She had more gold in her satchel than cash but the cash she studied the night before she arrived back in the Dakota Territory. The gold she had taken from the Black Hills. She knew it was wrong to take it. She didn't do any actual digging. Gold rocks were just laying there for her to take. It must be kept secret from Standing Deer and his People. Lord knows how they would react if they knew where she had gotten it. How would the Lakota feel about her taking anything from the Sacred Hills? She doubted they would be happy about it in the least bit.

The three dollar bill was unusual to say the least. It had a maiden sitting on a pile of coins with what appeared to be a spear in her hand. Behind her on the left was a picture of George Washington. To the right and just a bit behind the maiden was a plaque. An eagle stood on the plaque with its wings spread wide. The large three in the middle of the bill made it quite easy to identify as a three dollar bill. The remaining three corners had the number three in them as well. The scrollwork on the bills was so intricate it was hard to believe they were capable of printing that kind of detail so long ago.

She wasn't sure if the seven dollar bills were confederate money or not. The dealer said that they weren't. She was hesitant to buy them since a bank in Virginia issued them in 1861. The center of these bills has horses playing in a field near a creek. Behind them is a drawing of a train. In each corner, a seven was encircled by scrollwork that the dealer said had been machine engraved.

Karen laughed aloud, happy with the money she had bought but nervous about the way she had taken the gold. It would make things easier and her plans should now fall into place. Now that there is a baby involved, it was that much more important that she purchase land in this wilderness.

Her son or daughter would be raised in the modern world. She would not allow the death and devastation of the Lakota Nation to hurt the child. She would try her best to preserve anything she could for the Lakota.

Karen caressed her stomach. When he or she becomes an adult, she knew she would have to let him choose their own path. In the meantime, she will not allow the chance of the child's life to be destroyed by greedy and selfish white men.

As she followed the river southward, Karen finally arrived in the settlement of Yankton. Although it appeared to be what they would call a thriving river port, it was out in the middle of nowhere! She was expecting some kind of warning that a town was nearby but it just appeared as if it was a mirage. She looked around at the log buildings and wooden structures and realized she was seeing the real thing. This wasn't a restoration and re-creation of an old western town. This was an old western town!

It wasn't difficult to find the bank. Once finished with that business, he sent her in the direction of the mayor's office with an application for a land grant in her hand. It appeared her timing was perfect. A Mr. Leavenworth was in town visiting the mayor at this very moment. He was the one who signed the land grants. She wouldn't have to spend a dime!

Karen wondered if it was the same Leavenworth that she had read about in history. She searched her memory but couldn't quite recall. She rode past a hotel and decided to get a room.

A young boy was passing by and she inquired about where to keep her horse. "Young man, could you tell me where I can bring my horse to be taken care of properly?"

The boy, about twelve years, had golden blonde hair pulled back into a ponytail. His eyes were a watery blue with dark circles underneath, showing he had not gotten much sleep lately.

He shoved his hands into his pockets and shuffled his feet. "Why ma'am," he drawled. "Rat down thar at Mr. Sam's." He pointed with his nose. "I can take it far ya."

Thanking him, she pressed a coin in his hand bidding him to do well. She asked that he return her horse to her first thing in the morning. His eyes doubled in size when he saw the coin.

"Thank ya ma'am. Thank ya. I make sure ya harse is tooken real good care of. Good as gold, I's shores will."

She watched as he took the horse and smiled as she entered the hotel. She obviously gave him much more than he expected. No harm done. He'll make sure the horse is taken "real good care of, good as gold."

After she paid for her room, she requested a bath and thanked God she had been smart enough to pack one of those long gowns. Quick as humanly possible, she was bathed and dressed looking like the grandest southern belle ever to set foot in the west.

It was well worth the effort. Mr. Leavenworth was talkative and became excited when Karen inquired if he was related to the Leavenworth family from Fort Leavenworth. Proud of his heritage, he stuck out his chest and said Col. Henry Leavenworth was his grandfather.

He was more than happy to grant her one thousand acres instead of the customary five hundred. In his mind, she was a Southerner trying to start a new life now that the North had destroyed her land. Inviting her to dine with him, she could not refuse his offer. Thankfully, Mr. Leavenworth was a Southern sympathizer. He had been quite generous with the land grant.

Morning came quickly and she was on her way. The plans were now in motion.

Chapter FOURTEEN

Standing Deer couldn't wait another week. Something was wrong. He could feel it in his bones. Sitting Bull had said she would arrive soon but a week had passed. Even he had been watching the entrance to the village and worrying. Two Feathers was still deathly ill. Perhaps, Karen would be able to save him. He had to find her.

Standing Deer headed toward the cave near the hot springs. He had to be cautious now that the Great White War was over. There were many white men and black men going throughout their lands. If any of these white men harmed Spirit of the Mountain then he would have their scalps. If they harmed her in anyway, he might even use methods from the Scili and use them for torture and human sacrifice.

Days later, he retracted his steps forever searching for a sign of the woman he loved. Spying a lone traveler, he recognized the stance of the man on the horse. It was John Colby, Little Fox's husband.

John had recently returned home. Now that he was back, Sunshine in the Morning was once again in Standing Deer's lodge. While John was fighting in the white man's war, Sunshine in the Morning stayed with her sister to keep her company and help the time go by quickly.

John approached Standing Deer. He had also been out searching for the white woman who had married Standing Deer. The whole village was in love with her. Curiosity had gotten the best of him. This woman had to be something else if she had these heathens thinking she was some kind of child of God. What did she do, tell them she is the sister of Jesus? He'd get down to the bottom of it all. No wench was going to play witch with him. He knew how to tame a woman.

The two men rode silently to the village, each deep in their own thoughts. As they entered the village, a young brave yelled to Standing Deer.

"She is here, Spirit of the Mountain has arrived!"

Standing Deer dismounted from his horse and ran, with John Colby at his heels, to the center of the village where a group of people had gathered. He picked up Spirit of the Mountain and swung her around before he gave her a kiss that sent them both to the heavens.

John stood by patiently waiting while Little Fox stood next to him in silence. This Spirit of the Mountain was indeed very beautiful and she had the People in the palm of her hands. It would be his pleasure to humble the wench in front of these naive and ignorant Indians. He noticed standing next to Spirit of the Mountain was another exquisite looking creature. He wondered where this white woman came from as well, and if she supposedly had magical powers from the Great Spirit.

Standing Deer looked over to John Colby and called him over to introduce Spirit of the Mountain and her friend, Bonnie.

Karen watched silently as a young man in a confederate uniform limped slowly over to greet her. His eyes were a steel gray and his dark brown curly hair stuck out from under his hat. The man was very thin, tall and looked quite sickly ... definitely war-worn. The young man had a distinctive frown curling around his eyes with a flash of sparkling insanity. She felt an instantaneous dislike of him the minute she looked into his face.

"John Colby has recently returned from the Great White War. He fought for freedom. He has returned a great and honorable warrior."

Karen raised her eyebrow. "It is a pleasure to meet you, Mr. Colby. How long were you in battle?"

Karen cleared her throat as she saw Bonnie's mouth open wide in astonishment, and then quickly clamp shut.

"I've been gone for over two years and am very glad to be back with my Sioux family," responded Colby as he roughly pulled Little Fox into his embrace.

Karen noticed immediately that something was seriously wrong. Little Fox had never mentioned a husband and she did not look pleased that Colby had arrived safely back to the village. She was stiff with tension. Perhaps Little Fox had thought her husband was dead. The Lakota do not speak of their dead, out of respect for their souls. She had thought Little Fox was interested in Sleeping Elk.

"I'm sure you are, perhaps during the meal you could entertain us with some of your stories of the war."

"I would be delighted. Now, if you will excuse me, I would like to spend some time with Little Fox."

Karen watched as he walked away, wondering why she didn't trust the man. A few feet to her right stood Crazy Horse and Sleeping Elk, watching with obvious anger in their eyes. Anyone could see trouble brewing.

Sitting Bull and Standing Deer took the opportunity to whisk Karen away and bring her to Two Feathers. Sitting Bull's work on Two Feathers was meticulous. No one could have done a better job under the circumstances.

As she checked his wound, she realized how much blood he had lost and felt helpless. There was no way he could get a transfusion but she could give him vitamins and iron pills.

Her hands were tied, all she could do was pray. She instructed Sitting Bull and Laughing Flower on how often to give the pills and then solemnly left the lodge.

After their meals most of the village went about their business, few stayed to listen to the stories of the white soldier. Karen saw Crazy Horse and Sleeping Elk across the village close enough to hear, ever watchful but keeping a safe distance. Karen and Bonnie seized the opportunity to approach the group.

"That was a rough one. By capturing Vicksburg, Grant was able to have complete control of the Mississippi. After that Bragg made a lot of mistakes in the war and was pushed back over to Chattanooga." Colby looked around at the faces of the people around him and continued with his war stories.

"After Bragg was defeated, Johnston took over the command. Because he needed time to strengthen his troops, Johnston stayed at Dalton. While Johnston was in Dalton, Sherman captured Atlanta but the Confederates escaped.

Johnston's command was taken over by Hood, who was forced to evacuate Dalton. We made our way around for a few months until we were delayed because of supplies, that was in Florence. The last battle I was in was the one where my legs were injured, that was in December past. We were in Nashville waiting on troops from Texas when Thomas defeated Hood's troops in a bloody ruthless battle. Hood managed to escape over to Tennessee. I was injured and in an army hospital. The next thing I know, the war is over."

Colby looked up to see Karen intently watching him. She noticed he had been careful not to let the Lakota know whose command he actually fought under. He spoke of the war as if he watched it from behind the scenes, as a spectator.

"You fought for the North, Mr. Colby?" Karen inquired. "I detect an accent that's a bit familiar."

John drawled in a thick southern accent, "I fought for freedom of choice, madam."

"If you fought for freedom, Mr. Colby, then why do you wear the Confederate uniform?"

The village was silent. Listening to the conversation, not knowing what to expect, they were surprised by the tone in Spirit of the Mountain's voice. Standing Deer took a step back to listen to the conversation when Crazy Horse took Bonnie's arm and moved her behind him, placing himself next to Spirit of the Mountain.

Crazy Horse never liked the white man that Little Fox married but he could never put his finger on why. He watched Colby's expressions of anger cross his face and knew Colby did not hide his dislike of Spirit of the Mountain's questions.

"I told you, I fought for freedom ... of choice."

"Why did it take you so long to return to the Lakota if the war was over for you last December, it's now October ... almost November, isn't it? And Mr. Colby, who's freedom of choice did you fight for. Certainly not the black man's or the Indian's. If you fought with the Confederate army then you fought for slavery and succession. You did not fight for freedom ... of choice, as you say."

"Being a woman, I will acknowledge that you do not have the capacity or the ability to understand the degrees of warfare. I do not believe you understand or comprehend what the war was truly about. The southern states wanted the freedom of choice. Standing Deer, do you not have control over your wife?"

Standing Deer's eyes blazed with anger. "My wife is my equal and may speak her mind."

"But I do know what I am talking about. I completely understand what the Civil War was all about. I know exactly what the South was fighting for. You sir, failed to specify which side you fought for and who's commands were under which officers." Karen paused and looked around.

"History states that Grant took control over Vicksburg. He fought for the North, the Federal or the Union army, whichever you prefer to call them. Bragg and Johnston both fought for the Confederate armies. Sherman did indeed capture Atlanta but he fought for the Union.

"Thomas, under Sherman's command, was left behind to fight Hood, and Thomas was the one to defeat your Confederate troops in December."

She smiled and crossed her arms while she tapped her foot. She was more than willing to play devil's advocate. History had always been one of her favorite subjects in school.

"You fought for the Confederate side. You fought for slavery and succession. Mr. Colby, you have deceived these good people into believing that you fought for freedom."

Colby stood up in anger, grabbed Little Fox and pulled her to her feet. "I see you are a Northern sympathizer. You are a traitor to our Southern heritage, as well as a deceitful wench. You may have the Indians fooled with your witchcraft and sorcery but you have not fooled me."

Karen looked around and watched the curious stares from her friends. Now was not the time or the place to pursue this disagreement. She hadn't noticed until then, but Crazy Horse had placed his hand on her shoulder. It was a sign for all to see that he would back her up, if he was needed.

"No man regardless of the color of his skin should be a slave to anyone. Believe what you wish about me, but I wonder whose side you will choose when the white man comes to conquer the Sioux territory. Where will your heart lie then, Mr. Colby?"

"You are a stupid wench. The white man will not come here, you have these peaceful people worried unnecessarily." Red-faced from anger, Colby hissed at her and spit on the ground.

Abruptly he grabbed Little Fox's arm and walked away. Crazy Horse whispered to Spirit of the Mountain, "You have made an enemy today."

Karen looked at Crazy Horse and gave him a half-hearted smile as he spoke in hushed tones with Standing Deer. She didn't truly believe John Colby was wrong in fighting for what he believed. She just didn't agree with slavery or his deception. She found it hard to believe that he would fight for slavery when he knew how much the Lakota believed in freedom. They did not believe in slavery. They believed no man or creature, big or small, should be a slave.

Did Colby know that they had taken Indians from all different tribes and used them for slaves as well as the blacks? He had to know. His family probably owned slaves.

Colby led them to believe that he fought for freedom, conveniently omitting to explain to the Lakota whose side he had fought for. He was a man that will show his true colors soon enough. Hopefully no one will be hurt. Karen would have to watch out for this man. Crazy Horse warned her wisely. She had indeed made an enemy today.

Bonnie shook Karen's arm. "Oh Karen, why did you intentionally bait him? This is so exciting! Who was the Indian standing next to Mr. Colby and who was next to you?"

Bonnie was so excited her eyes rushed around the village in a frenzy trying to absorb everything all at once. As usual she was spouting out so many questions it made Karen's head spin.

"Slow down. You will learn more if you stay silent. Silence is a virtue in the eyes of the Lakota. You must use patience. If you start talking when it is not your turn, you will offend someone.

The Lakota believe that silence is the complete balance of the mind, body and soul. It is a cornerstone of their being."

"Who's that talking to Standing Deer?"

"Tashunca Uitco, Crazy Horse. "

Bonnie's eyes grew as large as golf balls. "THE Crazy Horse?!" Her eyes darting quickly to where Standing Deer and Crazy Horse stood talking. "That's the infamous Crazy Horse? Why he's just a boy! He's the one who is determined to hate and destroy all white men?"

"Hush Bonnie, some of these people understand English. Crazy Horse is already considered a man in his people's eyes. He's older than he looks. This is 1865. He does not become chief until later. It will take him years to learn the war techniques that will make him the famous man he was … is … oh, you know what I mean."

Bonnie was staring at Crazy Horse. "So what is he really like? Is he like the way history has described him?"

"Bonnie, history describes a man in his late twenties and older. He is still growing into what he will be." She noticed discouraged feelings and sighed.

"Some of the things they wrote about him are true. He is not a guiltless, uncaring savage. Crazy Horse is an extremely intelligent person with a big, generous heart. He will change some when he goes to war. Remember that he goes to war to defend his family and country. What man has not changed because of war? This is his home. He will not want it taken away from him and neither will the rest of the Sioux Indians."

Karen started walking toward Standing Deer's tent. "The Lakota are purely family-oriented. You will soon be very impressed by their attitudes toward family and friends. Keep your eyes open and your mouth closed. Do not speak unless spoken to. Otherwise, you may offend them. Your personality is a little bit more outgoing than they are accustomed to. Be careful. The Lakota believe that when a person talks too much, they have nothing to say."

"I know. I talk too much and the Indian's don't care for it. Whose lodge is that?" She pointed to the largest one in the village.

"That's Jumping Bull's and next to his lodge is Sitting Bull's. This is Standing Deer's lodge."

"It isn't far from Sitting Bull's at all. It's just one lodge away. Does that mean Standing Deer is important in the village, also?" Bonnie inquired.

Karen nodded her head. "He is highly respected among his people. Standing Deer has accomplished many coups and is a member of the Strong Heart Warrior Society."

"What is ... ?"

"Bonnie, please. Let's just go sit inside and relax for a while. We'll have some tea or coffee. There's plenty of time to answer questions and a lot of them will be answered if you watch the people and everything else that is around you."

Hours passed as they spoke about the Lakota and Karen's pregnancy. While they waited for Standing Deer, there were several interruptions from women and men coming to the lodge to welcome her back. Bonnie was amazed at how quickly Karen had learned the language.

Karen laughed when Bonnie commented on her accomplishment. I have the vocabulary of a child and I still pronounce some words incorrectly, but the People are very patient."

Standing Deer entered the lodge and spoke of how he would like to take Bonnie and Karen out for a ride the next day. He felt Bonnie should see the prairie and all of the Great Spirit's wonders.

Bonnie offered to leave so the two could be alone, but Standing Deer replied that he would like to take Karen for a walk along the river.

Smiling, the two left the lodge. It felt good to be together. There had been too much lost time. There was much to discuss. Karen wasn't sure where to begin. She believed Standing Deer was waiting for her to begin speaking first.

Standing Deer watched her silently. He could see there was much weighing on her mind and it was not the deceiving Colby. They would have to keep their eyes on Colby. He had deceived them greatly, leading them to believe that he fought for the freedom of people.

Karen inhaled deeply, "Standing Deer, I guess the best way to tell you is to come right out and say it. I'm ihlusaka." Pregnant.

Standing Deer howled in joy, picked her up and swirled her around. He hugged her so tight she could just barely breathe. He was ecstatic. Oh, the Great Spirit had blessed them with a child. How thankful he was to Him.

"Please stop. This wasn't supposed to happen. That's why I insisted that we use the prophylactics. David did it. He ... ."

"What?" Standing Deer roared. "David got you pregnant?"

"This isn't coming out right! Listen, please. David had taken the prophylactics and put holes in all of them so I would conceive. He did it intentionally. David claims he loves me and believed that if I got pregnant by you that you would desert me. Then he would marry me and raise the child as his own."

"That is stupid. That is the last thing a person should do if you truly love them."

"Marry them?" Karen asked with a twinkle in her eyes.

"No," he laughed. "Get them pregnant on purpose with someone else's child!" He turned and looked at her and saw she had been teasing. He smiled and gave her a hug.

"Well, what shall we do? We needed to decide how to live anyway. Now we just include our child in the plans."

"Actually ... ," Karen hesitated. It was going to be hard to tell him. "It is a harder decision because of the child. If it was just the two of us, it would be different. We probably could have worked out the difference in our two worlds. With a child, it's too complicated. The child cannot be raised with two separated lives. The child will have to be raised in one world only."

Standing Deer nodded in approval. "There are plenty of women in the village to help raise the child when you are not here. All will love the child as if it was their own."

"No! That is not what I meant! The child will live in my world. It will be safer and he will receive the proper education."

"He is Lakota and will be raised as a Lakota. My word is final. He must learn to live as one with the Earth. He needs to learn the ways of the Great Spirit and what is expected of him as a warrior. He must learn to wanase, hunt buffalo.

"What if it is a girl? Besides, neither one of them is going to be raised as a warrior. The child will be raised in my world and you can't stop it!"

Karen turned to walk away when Standing Deer grabbed her arm.

"Mitawin, niye namlasva!" My wife, you break the heart!

Tears streaming down her face, she yanked her arm out of his grip. Karen replied with determination that would move a mountain. "I will not allow the child to live two separate lives. If you choose to help raise your child in my world, that is agreeable. If you insist that the child live in yours, you will never see the child again,"

With that said she abruptly walked away. Bonnie was already half asleep when she arrived back at the lodge. Karen laid on Standing Deer's mat. She could smell his manly odor as she tossed and turned restlessly. Arguing with him was futile, regardless of how much she felt she was right. It was a long time before sleep claimed her.

The next day at the river, Karen and Bonnie had heard rumors that Sleeping Elk had called out Colby to kicie conape, fight to the death. Colby was nowhere to be found. As far as the Lakota were concerned, Colby was dead along with his woyuonihan, his honor.

As the women approached Standing Deer's lodge, they saw he was ready and waiting. He had not forgotten his promise to Bonnie to take her to see the prairie lands.

They rode along the river for about an hour and proceeded toward the prairies. Bonnie was amazed to see the abundance of golden colored prairie dogs. She spotted an osprey as Standing Deer was pointing out some black-footed ferrets scurrying around one of the prairie dog nests.

Standing Deer explained to Bonnie how the prairie dogs were much like any other creature on earth. They lived in colonies, living in the underground, using the earth as their homes, for protection against predators and the elements.

As they approached the animals, Bonnie heard a high-pitched chirping sound that seemed to be a form of communication that danger may be approaching. They watched and listened as the sounds became louder. The pitch increased higher as the three moved closer to their nests. Bonnie stared, amazed as the creatures dove into their homes and peaked their heads out to watch the three intruders go by on their horses.

Standing Deer explained to Bonnie how snakes and badgers hunt the prairie dogs and how the circle of life includes all of the Great Spirit's creatures. He told them how black widow spiders will live near the entrance of the burrowed homes and one must be extremely careful if they upset a nest.

As they rode on, Bonnie saw and understood why Karen loved the Dakota Territory so much. It would be easy to live here for the rest of her life. But that was her, not Karen.

Not many words had passed between Standing Deer and Karen. Uncomfortable because of the unnatural silence, Bonnie had started talking about the land Karen had been granted and how she had applied for a job on the Lakota reservation in South Dakota. By Karen and Standing Deer's reactions, Bonnie had realized too late that Karen had not told him yet. With dread, she quickly clamped her mouth shut as tight as possible.

The last twenty minutes back to the village passed in dead silence.

Chapter FIFTEEN

When John Colby finally reached the Black Hills, he was still blind with fury. Thank God those heathens didn't chase after him. That wench Karen ruined years of planning. If she had just minded her own business, he could have stayed with the Indians until he had enough gold to live the rest of his life in luxury.

Colby shook his head in disgust. His plans started going wrong with the loss of the Civil War. They had to win that war, how would he be able to own the biggest plantation in all of Georgia without slaves? Now he would have to pay people to work for him. Instead of having the protection of the Sioux, now he would have to mine for the gold and watch his back, all because of that high and mighty wench.

He'd get his gold. Then, he'd get the wench. She'd pay if it's the last thing he does in life. He'd make her pay.

Standing Deer entered the lodge with the fury of a bull. Bonnie quickly excused herself and ran out the door.

"Why did you buy land?" he growled.

"I didn't buy land, they gave me a grant for it. I own the land but it didn't cost me anything."

"It is not our way. We cannot sell or own the land the Great Spirit has given us. No one can. It is not their right. It belongs to all, not just one person."

"I did it to help. It was the only way I knew how without interfering with the future," Karen explained.

"It is not our way!"

"Your way will change. This was the only solution I could come up with at the time."

Standing Deer was frustrated. He knew deep in his heart that she was right. Even though he didn't like it, for the time being he was going to have to accept it.

"We have more important things to discuss."

Standing Deer raised his eyebrows in question. "What?"

"The baby. We seem to disagree on what is best for our relationship and this child's upbringing."

"But we do agree to a point." Standing Deer poured himself a cup of tea and offered some to Karen. "A child must be with both parents. Do you disagree with that?"

"No. That is very important."

"And you also agree that a child should receive the benefits of what both parents can teach the child."

"Yes, of course."

"Then our disagreement yesterday was unnecessary, The child will live in both worlds."

"No."

Standing Deer sighed. "My love, you just agreed what was best for the child and now you say no."

"Standing Deer, please understand. Our life is complicated enough for us as it is, living in two separate worlds. If it was just the two of us, then we could probably make it work but with a child it would be too difficult. The child can learn from you without living in the village. I cannot allow the child to live in two separate worlds. It would be too confusing and frustrating."

"I will not be able to teach him the ways of the Lakota in your world of concrete buildings!"

"I agree, wholeheartedly. That is why I have applied for a job at the Pine Ridge Reservation."

"The Pine Ridge Reservation? But you are happy with the job you have now. Why change?"

"For you and the child. We will be living on Sioux land and you can teach him everything he needs to know. The only difference is that it will be in my world and not yours."

"Why bother to leave the work that you love? You will be taking a chance that you will not be happy with the new job. How can he learn the ways of the Lakota on a reservation?"

"It's safer! I will not have my child's life taken away by some greedy white man who wants to hunt for gold."

"I will not live on a reservation and I will not allow my child to live on one. The Lakota are free and it must stay that way."

Karen lifted both hands and started rubbing her temples. This conversation was heading for a brick wall.

"Then we will live near the reservation."

"No. What you plan is unnecessary. The child can learn both worlds without living in or near a reservation. I do not want our child living near those pathetic people who gave up their freedom."

"They are not pathetic! Maybe you could find a way to help them if you feel there is such a great need!"

"No. They made their choice. My child will learn the ways of the Lakota as I did."

She growled in frustration. "What do you mean they made their choice? They didn't have a choice. No, Standing Deer. No, plain and simple. I will not allow my child to be raised in a world where the only future is death and destruction."

Karen pushed herself up and turned to Standing Deer before leaving the lodge. "You have no choice, Standing Deer. The child will not live in this world."

Karen found Bonnie with Laughed Flower and Two Feathers. He was recuperating slower than she had hoped but he would live. Karen tried to find Standing Deer but he was nowhere around. It was a tearful good-bye with Sitting Bull and Jumping Bull. They didn't want to believe that she would not be returning.

As they left the village, Karen turned and waved a last good-bye before they headed toward the cave where she first came to this land. She noticed that Standing Deer's horse was missing and hoped that he would not try to stop her. What she didn't see was the lone warrior in the woods, silently watching them leave with tears in his eyes.

Karen was driving in a rental car down State Highway 240, the Badlands Loop. The correspondence between her and James Black Elk took months before an interview was finally set up, red tape, red tape and more red tape. With the baby being due in a month, she was lucky her doctor had approved the plane trip.

She needed the drive through the scenic route of the Badlands. For the last few months Bonnie had nagged her to no end about how wrong she was about her decision with Standing Deer. Her nagging caused doubts to flourish in her mind. Maybe being so close to his land she would be able to think more clearly. She needed to be as near to him as she could. Her heart ached with the pain of a lost love.

Karen still believed her decision was the best for the child. But Bonnie's constant nagging made her question herself. Was she being the inconsiderate, cold and callous person Bonnie accused her of? Was she really rejecting the one and only true love that can only be found deep in the soul? Her mind raged in it's own personal war.

Karen decided to play tourist. She was here for the first time and she was going to see Mt. Rushmore and the Crazy Horse Monument while she could.

Driving on 16-A, Karen could see through the trees and got a quick glimpse of the monument. When she finally reached the sight, she stood in awe and stared at the sixty foot faces. Realizing time was getting away from her, she started toward the Crazy Horse Monument before she checked into her hotel in Keystone.

She hadn't known they were creating a monument for Crazy Horse until she became involved with the Lakota. When she arrived at the unfinished monument, Karen learned that the sculptor Ziolkowski had started carving Crazy Horse somewhere around 1947.

The Lakota Chief Henry Standing Bear had wanted all people to know that the Native Americans also had great heroes. His requested project was accepted. The monument is still being sculpted, even after the death of Ziolkowski. His wife and family have kept it going. The Crazy Horse Monument will be the largest known statue in the world. When it is finished its size is estimated to be five hundred thirty-one feet high and six hundred forty-one feet long.

Karen felt strange and awkward. To know Crazy Horse personally as she does and to see his face carved in stone was eerie. Chills went up her spine.

There was a slight wonder as to why Red Cloud or Sitting Bull had not been chosen, but she dismissed the question as quickly as it came. All were great heroes to the Sioux Nation. She was sure it was hard to choose one to represent them all.

The night went by quickly. She had the best sleep she could recall in months. As she headed south and turned onto the lone road heading for the reservation, Karen felt a presence. She could hear drums beating and the sounds of a familiar Lakota ritual song. She looked around and could see no one. She could not shake the feeling that she was being watched. The song stayed in her mind as she drove on.

Karen saw buildings that weren't suitable for people to live in, yet she watched children playing in the yards. This is awful, she thought to herself. Karen felt as if she was in a Third World project.

Relieved, she saw the building she was looking for as she slowly pulled the car up to the side and placed it carefully in park. Awkward with her added weight, she slowly exited the car. She noticed two teenagers leaning against the building. They silently watched her brush her hair.

As she walked up the steps, she noticed the scarves sticking out of their pockets; both were blue. She wondered if the stories were true that gangs were now among the reservations. As she looked into their faces, she noticed that both boys stood looking stunned, with their mouths wide open.

The taller one whispered something to the other boy and he took off running. With the look of shock still on his face, he opened the door for her and let her in. Then he turned and ran in the same direction as the other boy.

Puzzled, Karen shook her head. Their reaction to her was quite strange. As she entered the building, she looked around at the various pictures on the wall. There was a quiet conversation going on between the woman behind the desk and a gentleman who was leaning over her reading a paper.

They both looked up at the same time and both stared at her in the same manner as the young boys.

"Hello," Karen said as she put her hand out to shake theirs, "I'm ... ."

The woman jumped up, "Yes, yes, we know who you are. I'll tell him you're here." She ran to a closed door and proceeded to run into it. She turned to Karen, apologized, and then entered the other room.

Karen heard muffled voices as she nodded a hello to the gentleman who stood staring at her without saying a word. She wondered what was wrong with these people. Why are they looking at her in such a strange way?

The woman came out, escorted her into the other room, and shut the door behind her. The man's head was bent down reading some papers. She took the time to glance at the pictures on the walls. There were many pictures of Indians and villages showing the old ways of life. She saw a quite pleasant picture of Red Cloud laughing. As she looked at the picture behind the desk, she realized it was a picture of Sitting Bull, with a woman standing near him in the background. She squinted her eyes to get a better look, when she recognized the woman.

She closed her eyes and inhaled a deep breath. Oh, no ... .

The man looked up from his work. He showed no sign of any kind of reaction as the others had given her. Slowly he rose from the desk and just as slowly walked over to her. He touched Karen's shoulder with both his hands and whispered ...

"He Woniya." Spirit of the Mountain.

A Sioux Prayer

Oh Great Spirit,

You have shown me a vision that saddens my heart ... .

Bless me with the sight of an eagle, the cunning of a fox, the strength of a buffalo, and the wisdom of the wind, so I may defeat my enemy that wants to destroy what you have given your People.

Guide me to teach the young ones your ways, so they will follow the right path ... even when they are told it is wrong.

Help me open their arms to your love, so they will not fall pray to the evils of our enemies.

Help me open their arms to your love, so they will not fall pray to the evils of our enemies.

Thank you, Great Spirit, for the life you have given me. I pray that I return your gift of life with honor and love when it is my time to be with you for all eternity.

Home of the Braves

PART TWO

Pamela Ackerson

IMPORTANT DATES

1866: General William Tecumseh Sherman issues statement that if you kill the buffalo, you kill the Indians. General Philip Sheridan commands the American forces to bring peace to the lands by exterminating the buffalo.

IDAHO TERRITORY: Chief Red Cloud defends land given to them by a treaty by attacking a wagon train bringing supplies to Fort Kearny. Captain William Fetterman led the battle against the Sioux chief. Eighty soldiers were killed.

1867: The first white settlers arrive in Cheyenne, Wyoming.

1868: A treaty was signed between Chief Red Cloud and General Sherman at Fort Laramie, Wyoming Territory ending the battles along the Bozeman Trail. Under the treaty, part of northern Wyoming and land in the Dakotas were retained by the Sioux.

BATTLE OF WASHITA: Lieutenant Colonel George A. Custer attacked a winter camp of Arapaho and Cheyenne Indians led by Chief Black Kettle. The cavalrymen killed more than one hundred men, women and children in the Indian village. Lieutenant Colonel Custer attacked the camp under General Sherman's orders.

1869: General Philip Sheridan is quoted as saying: "The only good Indian is a dead Indian."

1871: The Indian Appropriation Bill was passed. Under the new Bill, each Indian will be considered individually. The Bill was passed to alleviate the confusion of the signing of treaties between individual Chiefs. The issue of sovereignty is a difficult one for the Indian Nations. If one Chief signs a treaty, the authority covers his village only. It does not apply to the entire Indian Nation. The Bill also gives the American government the right to enlarge or shrink the treaty lands and reservations by executive order.

1874: Lieutenant Colonel Custer announced the discovery of gold in the Black Hills, Dakota Territory. Lieutenant General Philip Sheridan issued orders to Custer to find a practical route to Fort Laramie. Prospectors have been digging illegally on the Sioux land. The agreed Treaty of 1868 does not allow non-government whites to be allowed in the Black Hills, which the Indians consider to be sacred land.

1875: Conflict between prospectors and Sioux Indians increase in the Dakota Territory. The armed forces stationed in the area to enforce the Treaty of 1868 have disregarded the illegal infiltration of the sacred Black Hills. A meeting was requested by the American government to allow legal access to the area. The Indians refused access to the sacred lands. Chief Red Cloud and many others pledged to continue protecting their land.

Chapter SIXTEEN

Jennifer Standing Deer held her breath as she slipped silently through the hall. Her hands and fingers shaking as she cautiously felt her way along the coarse textured wall. The house was in a cave-like darkness that was pitch black. Her eyes not seeing where she placed her trembling hands, Jennifer guided herself with instinct.

No lights were on and she feared using one. She didn't want to wake her brother or their nanny. They would stop her from doing "the forbidden."

As she crept silently down the hall, a night-light glowed eerily from her nanny's bedroom. Holding her breath, she peaked through the slight opening of the nanny's bedroom to make sure she was soundly asleep. Satisfied, she crept silently forward.

Smiling, Jennifer continued slowly and methodically toward her parent's bedroom. She would be safe there. She would go to sleep, find her parents and have them explain that horrid dream. She can still hear the echoes of the scream that woke her in a cold sweat; her mother's screams, and she was scared.

The dream was a forewarning. It had to be. She was convinced of it. Jennifer had heard too many stories of dreams guiding you to give warning. Some people didn't listen and regretted it. Well, she was going to listen to this dream and she was going to find her parents.

At nine, Jennifer was smaller than most of her classmates. Her skin was a golden copper like most Native Americans but her hair stuck out like an injured thumb. She had her mother's hair, long and colorful, very colorful. Jennifer wrinkled her nose in disgust. Its beauty awed people. Even the kids in her class would constantly be trying to touch it. She had wished so many times for it to be jet black and straight, like her father's.

Finally, her fingertips felt the roughness of the door she was seeking. Grasping for the doorknob, she quietly opened her parent's bedroom door. Closing it quietly behind her, she leaned against the door waiting for her heart to slow.

Moonlight danced through the open windows. The wind was restless and found its way through the room. Jennifer felt a chill go up her spine. Why did this feel so ominous?

She shook her head to try to shake the feeling. She was just nervous and jittery because her parents had forbidden her to sleep on the bed without them. Jennifer eyed the ornamental mystical bed with caution. She had to do this. It would transport her to the past ... to her parents. That is where she needed to be right now. She needed to be in their arms ... in the comfort and security of their embrace.

She had to relax as she crept silently toward the bed. Otherwise she would be too nervous to fall asleep and then the bed wouldn't take her to her parents. Jennifer lay with one arm under her head and the other touching one of the angels that had been carved onto the wooden headboard. Slowly, she relaxed and fell to sleep.

Something rough and hard was scratching her back. Jennifer turned in her sleep to avoid the uncomfortable feeling and slid to the ground. Staring at the ground in a groggy sleep that only a child knows. She stared without comprehension. Slowly her mind awoke and she smiled. It worked. She was here. Now she just had to find her parents.

Jennifer heard yelling. Men and women were yelling. She cocked her head sideways and tried to comprehend what they were saying. She had expected to hear the Lakota language, but what she heard was English.

Kill the bitch. Is that what they were saying? No, no it was kill the witch. Witch? Crawling on the ground so she would not be seen, she slowly made her way to where the sounds were coming from.

Staying completely hidden behind some bushes, she parted the leaves to watch the scene. What she saw was horrifying. A large group of people dressed like pilgrims were standing near the fence, arms raised in anger, hands fisted. Shouting. Jennifer saw fear and terror in their eyes.

Two men and a woman were standing near the entrance to a small, well-built cabin. The woman's face looked bloodless. Terror reeked through her eyes, piercing the men and the crowd near the fence.

One of the men standing next to the woman at the door spoke loudly enough to be heard over the yelling. There was an eerie silence once the words were spoken.

"Thou have been accused of witchery. Thou have fooled thy people with thy doctoring. All are appalled that thou have used witchery to help these God-fearing souls."

"Nay, good sir. 'Tis not witchery. 'Tis a God-fearing Christian thou hast accused."

"Thou cannot use the trickery of the devil whom thou worship to fool us now. Stand before thy people whom thou have tricked and be tested for witchery."

"Forsooth ... thy not a witch. 'Tis Master Stevens who has accused this Christian woman. 'Twas by and by a refusal to bed him. 'Tis what thy received from thy friends and neighbors ... for being a God-fearing Christian? Nay, 'tis not right and just!"

The woman called to the crowd that had formed around the fence.

"All of thee know Master Stevens! All know Master Stevens is not an honest man but has bedded many a woman and left some with child. Because Master Stevens is wealthy and has much influence over thy prosperity ... thou do as Master Stevens bids!"

"Hush woman, stop thy devilish words!"

"Nay, thou knows thy speak the truth!"

"Stand and be pricked!" he yelled.

The crowd cheered as the man who had stayed silent reached forward. Jennifer could not see what he was doing. She held her breath and squinted, straining to see what was happening.

"'Tis no blood on thy needle!" the man yelled triumphantly.

An angry roar and then chanting came from the crowd.

"Kill the witch ... ."

"Nay!" the woman yelled. Her cries of denial were crushed by the roar of the crowd.

They dragged the struggling woman out of the yard and down the road. Jennifer scrambled to her feet. Her muscles were aching from bending in a crouch for so long. Staying hidden she followed the crowd, her parents temporarily forgotten.

She heard the woman yelling, "Nay ... nay. Master Stevens just wants thy land. 'Tis why thee tried to bed this Christian woman. To get thee with child so thy would leave in shame. Nay, nay ... ."

They brought the woman to an open area of the township. There Jennifer hid behind a water barrel, wiping the uncontrollable tears that were flooding her eyes and blinding her sight. She watched in shock as they tied the woman to a wooden pole, and threw wood chips and dried straw around the bottom, covering her feet.

The woman yelled, "Thou will give thee no trial?"

As if in ceremony, a man approached the woman with a burning broom. Jennifer would have laughed at the pomposity of it all if she had been watching a movie. But this wasn't a movie and it was happening. A sick drama unfolding before her very eyes. Jennifer's ears were buzzing and her stomach was churning as she watched the man parade as if in ceremony around the unfortunate woman.

With the dramatic swoop of a Shakespearean actor, he touched the straw with the burning broom. The flames burst upward. Jennifer stared in horror and shock, not able to look away, yet begging herself to stop watching. The crowd went wild with excitement and cheers. There were probably over a hundred people cheering for the death of this innocent woman! Jennifer could smell the acrid smoke fill the air. She was going to get sick.

Jennifer ran through the township and into the woods. She believed no one saw her because they were distracted by the horror she was running away from. They all were watching the horrid show. She ran until she could run no longer. Collapsing on the ground she pounded her fists into the dirt and cried. She cried until it hurt to cry and then cried more.

Twenty feet ahead of her the boy hid behind the tree and watched. He wanted to reach out to her and give her comfort but was wary. With patience, he waited. She was dressed as an Indian maiden, in a deer skin dress and hair braided with rawhide ties fastened at the bottom. His eyes widened in astonishment. Her hair! It had every color of autumn leaves in it. It was as if Mother Earth had personally painted her hair.

He watched her look around. Her skin was copper colored like his. Her eyes were a dark brown, almost black. They were startling to observe and stood out because of the lightness of her hair. It was a unique combination. She was pretty for a child. When she grew up she would have many warriors wanting to be her husband.

They both jerked up, alerted at the sound of branches breaking. He watched as terror filled her eyes. She jumped to her feet as she grabbed a knife that had been hidden under her dress and ran as fast as she could. She ran blindly forgetting all that had been taught to her.

He reached out and grabbed her, dragging her down into the brush with his hand over her mouth. Jennifer turned her face to see her abductor and was partially relieved that it was not one of those pilgrim people.

Two men came into sight as the two watched in silence.

"Thy knows thy saw a child head this way," the tall man said to the thin short one.

"Nay, the child went down the other path. Thy will go there."

Both men turned and walked back the way they came.

The boy released his grip over Jennifer's mouth and waist. Jennifer pointed in the direction of the township.

"You should have seen what they did back there! I have never seen anything so barbaric in my life." She spoke in Lakota.

The boy looked at her with a puzzled expression. What language was she speaking? It certainly wasn't the white man's tongue.

Jennifer tried a different dialect, asking if he understood her. Then she spoke Cheyenne. Again she tried, in English. He shook his head no, though he did recognize the white man's tongue.

"I do not understand you," he said in the Narragansett tongue. Jennifer looked at him blankly.

"Come," he said.

Jennifer followed him through the woods for well over two hours. Deeper and deeper into the warm embrace of the woods until they reached a small campsite.

Two men stood and looked at the girl dressed as an Indian maiden.

"You were supposed to be hunting game," they teased.

The boy rolled his eyes, groaning, and knew their humor wouldn't release him from their teasing for many weeks.

"She does not understand our tongue. There was much noise coming from the white man's village. They have frightened her somehow and came looking for her. We hid in the brush."

The taller man with the high cheekbones offered her a blanket to sit on. The other man offered her some food to eat. The taller man signed to her asking if the white villagers had harmed her.

Excited that he could sign, Jennifer answered him back and explained what she had seen. He introduced himself as White Bone, his elder son was Running Antelope, and the boy who found her was Little Wolf. Jennifer told them to call her Prairie Flower, for that was her Indian name. They asked what tribe she belonged and was stunned when she said she was Lakota, Sioux. They did not question her more and she was relieved. How would she be able to explain it?

Night came quickly and they provided her with blankets to sleep. As she fell to a restless sleep, she prayed she would arrive home before her parents awoke.

Luck was on her side. She awoke and quickly scurried to her bedroom as silently as possible. How very odd that she had not gone to the Lakota. Would she go back to that land again if she were to try it again? Would she see Little Wolf and his brother and father ever again? Jennifer had many, many questions to ask her parents. The worst part of it all was she could not even tell her parents!

Chapter SEVENTEEN

The two bodies lay in each other's arm, entwined in their never-ending love, forever imbedded in their souls. The early morning sun welcomed them with a cheer each wished were in their heart. A breeze caressed their naked bodies stirring them to a lazy awakening.

Their love had never dwindled. Each day growing stronger as their fears had increased in the opposite fold on their lives. The war in Standing Deer's land put anger in his heart and pain in hers. Each day brought the destruction of his world closer and closer. They had loved for eleven years now and had borne two beautiful children.

Karen's eyes flicked open and met her man's eyes with a matched love. He inhaled her beautiful scent, caressed her hair that was luscious and thick. There were streaks of gray now sprouting, shimmering among the gold and amber highlights. Standing Deer frowned as he saw the slight circles underneath her eyes. The time-travel was starting to weary her or maybe it was the knowledge of what was going to happen and the frustration of not being able to do anything about it.

She was one pebble in an ocean of fury. She could not stop this storm any more than he could. It was a prophecy in the making. All knew that the prophecy said they would become a powerful Nation and all knew the prophecy said the Nation would fall.

Hopefully it would not exhaust their love. Standing Deer kissed her gently on the lips. Not wanting to leave the comfort and warmth of the bed, with a sigh he slowly got out of bed to shower and prepare for work.

It amazed him how diversified he had become over the years. Within hours he would go from an Indian warrior on the warpath, to a Native American teaching children in a cement building with all the modern technology available at his fingertips.

Karen felt the emptiness when he left the bed. The warmth of his love still radiated in her heart and soul. It was already June and in a month the children would be out of school and with them in the land of the Lakota. She sighed. One month was all she had to prepare herself for the Battle of Rosebud and then the impending Battle at Little Big Horn.

She must continue to try to convince him that the children stay here in her world and not be there during the fiercest wars of the Sioux Nations. He had refused to concede and she must make him listen.

As she dressed herself to go to the clinic, she started an argument that she knew was unavoidable but had to continue until he gave in.

The day had been uneventful except for the disagreement she had forced upon her love that morning. Waiting for Standing Deer to come home from work, Karen gazed out the back door of her home. Peace and serenity were hers among the vast wide-open plains. Today she sought inner peace. Her beloved Standing Deer would be returning soon and she knew her inner turmoil must be thrown to the winds before they returned to his time.

The prairie was being tickled by a slight wind. The musical sounds of various animals were singing in her ears. The azure sky above was empty, cloudless and without birds. Despondency flooded her. What was she thinking? She wanted to run away from the past, Standing Deer's impending future. She wanted to move back to Florida. It didn't matter where, Titusville, Lakeland, or Holopaw. They could buy a good piece of land in Holopaw and Standing Deer could hunt on it and do whatever he wished.

She couldn't time-travel anymore. She covered her face in shame, pushing back the tears that were ready to explode out of her. She needed to find the energy to face what was to be. Could she, knowing the outcome?

Living through the Indian Wars had torn her apart, was still tearing her apart. Every day for over ten years she has had to watch her beautiful Standing Deer leave their lodge to war on the soldiers, afraid that he would not return. Death surrounded them every day. Their love strengthened, although there were nights when she clung onto to him like a baby in fear of his loss. She held her head high and had to believe he would return. He had so far.

But now, the Battle of Rosebud will be happening in a few weeks and then Little Big Horn. None of it could she prevent. None of it could be avoided. God had given her these paranormal gifts and yet she couldn't use any of them. She could use them to protect herself but not change what will be happening to the People. What good was it for Him to send her to the past if she had to watch them all die slowly and painfully? Why did He send her if she could not change it for the better? She hadn't any right to question His judgment. She needed a sign, some guidance and encouragement.

This morning she had spoken with her love about leaving the reservation and moving back to Florida. Karen had told him she didn't want to time-travel anymore. It had angered Standing Deer. He had been working with many of the teenagers, teaching them the old ways. So many of the People were looking to be a part of the People but did not know where to go. Many did not know the old ways and Standing Deer was showing them. He yelled at her to see the commercialism that has swept the Indian way to oblivion. His People were lost and he was trying to help them. Now that he had come this far she wanted to leave? She was asking him to avoid the impending battles. Did she forget who he was or did she ever really know him?

He told her she was being a coward. She was trying to run away from the past, run away from his future. There was nothing wrong with this modern reservation that couldn't be changed. It was her and she needed to seek guidance with the Great Spirit and Mother Earth.

Karen's anger flared. It was his accuracy that angered her. Yet, she wasn't willing to admit it. She stated she was tired of the prejudice and the reactions of some emergency patients when they saw she was a white woman. It offended her when some insisted on leaving. They did not want to be treated by a white. Nor did they want the white man's medicine because they believed it would kill them. She was tired of the prejudice. There was more prejudice she had to face here in the present than she did in his world in the past. His People accepted her better in his world than they do now.

He accused her of looking for excuses. She was and she knew it. Why did Standing Deer have to be so accurate? He told her to pray. He was right.

Their circle of life has spun so many turns. Was she following the right path? "Two roads diverged in a yellow wood ... ."

Where is her place on the path of life? Where is her circle of life supposed to be? She didn't want to capitulate. She didn't want to grovel in pain. What happened to soaring with her eagles? The sky was bright and endless. Where were the eagle guides to help her follow her life paths?

"Help me to believe!" she whispered to the heavens. "God, give me strength to face the path of tragedy that I know is ahead of me."

A familiar high-pitched screech broke her thoughts. Seeking the sound, she looked up into the azure sky and saw two eagles circling above her house. A smile touched her lips and tears came to her eyes as she stared open-eyed at her animal guides.

God speaks in mysterious ways. Just when she was ready to give up, He sent these magnificent birds to call on her. Their white heads reflected off the sun as they floated above her, descending and circling closer to her. Their wingspan was enormous compared to any other bird. They were so close she could see the golden yellow of their beaks.

Karen stepped out of the doorway to the center of the yard. Closer and closer, the eagles came to her. She raised her hands up in triumph, her body trembling in excitement. She could feel her heart thumping to the beat of the bird's wings. Keeping her arms open and falling to her knees, she accepted the sign as the one she should follow. She knew she would now find the strength to continue with the time-travel. This was her path. She did not understand why. It was what He wanted.

Both magnificent birds swooped down before their flight took them upward again. She could hear the whoosh of their wings, the soft rustle of their feathers. She felt the air stir her face and hair from the power of their winged flight. Karen watched mesmerized as both left the area. Higher they went until they were black dots in the sky and then no longer seen.

It had been eleven years since the fateful day when her life was abruptly changed. From the moment she arrived in the past, her life had been spun intricately for a new purpose. When it first happened, she knew something had been different. She laughed to herself, recalling that she had kept thinking it was all a dream.

Karen could feel there was more than just what she saw as a dream. She tried to deny it but found there was more for her to see. She had learned and evolved so much it amazed her to see it was all an endless circle.

Inner peace is the goal of all humans. If they would just open their eyes they would see more than could ever been seen. They could accomplish more than they ever dreamed possible. The Lakota showed her the path to inner peace. They taught her to accept life, never to take more than she could give. She always had faith and hope and by learning the Indian way, it had just strengthened her more.

Some of her modern colleagues didn't take her seriously. They ridiculed her behind her back because she combined her medicinal herb knowledge with modern medical technology. What and whom did it hurt? Any true modern herbalist can prove that plants are used for modern medications.

By accepting their lessons she had reached the stars. Life was an adventure and she learned to grasp onto it with heart and spirit. To interfere with His plans would be a travesty.

Enlightened, she knew she was there in Standing Deer's world for a much more important quest. It was a quest to combine the worlds. Join the People so that they may become one great Nation in the future. Standing Deer was here in her world to do the same. Why had it taken her so long to understand this?

She had accomplished much while she had lived with the Lakota. They had learned from each other and it strengthened all of them. All grew from the experiences. She would be ready for the battles and she would be a backbone for the People. The eagles had been a sign. She would follow their lead. Smiling she went into the house happy with the peace and serenity she had found.

Standing Deer had seen his beloved wife speaking with the spirits. He sat at the table waiting for her return. As he watched her approach the doorway, he could see she had found what she had been searching for. It gladdened his heart. It troubled him to see her in such inner turmoil. He knew what his People were facing and would be there as a warrior. Had she decided to stand by him?

"My love?" he inquired quietly. "Spirit of the Mountain, did you find what you were seeking?"

Karen surrendered herself into his arms. Tears trickled down her face.

"I know what I must do, but I still believe the children do not need to be involved. They could accomplish more in this world. The legend of the Rainbow People has come upon us. They can follow our lead to combine the nations as one. They should not have to experience the wars of our peoples. It isn't necessary."

"You will be there?"

"Yes, my love I will stand beside you and our People, for I believe I am a part of them. They are my family as well."

Standing Deer conceded, "I can agree that the children should stay here. But right now I want to hold you."

He lightly touched her neck with his lips and sent a hot, searing shivering pulse through her being. Karen smiled. It was always like this with him, even after all these years.

"My love … ," Standing Deer's voice was thick.

Standing Deer continued kissing her as he unbuttoned her blouse and caressed her shoulder with his lips.

" … we can stay … "

He took her breast in his hand and twirled his fingers around the nipple until she ached for his mouth to be upon it.

"… in your world … "

He nibbled scrumptiously as he started to tease her. Picking her up to carry her into the bedroom he kissed her lips with an intensity that sent her in waves of passion, knowing the outcome.

" … after the battles are over."

He laid her upon the bed and masterfully raised himself above her.

Karen's eyes were barely open as she caressed his muscular, massive body. "After Little Big Horn is over … "

He leaned down and kissed the sensitive area between her thighs.

" … we will live in your world."

Karen's body tensed and tightened against the hot touch of his lips.

"The children aren't here," he added with a sparkle in his eyes. "I want to surrender myself to your love. The rush of the day has ended. Let's take this moment for ourselves. It is enough for this warrior to be with you and let worries be put aside for a while … ."

Their love covered them like a warm winter blanket, each holding their desires with open hearts. Standing Deer kissed her lightly and trailed his lips along her slim neck. Karen felt the heat of desire surge and conquer her body and soul. She reached up and clasped her hands around his neck, receiving his kiss and returning it with the same fervor.

A door slammed somewhere in the distance.

"Hi, Mom, Dad! We're home!" Jennifer and Matthew called as they entered the house.

Two deep sighs burst out of their passion swollen mouths. Both groaned in unison.

"Oh well, it was a wonderful thought. Hold onto it till later. Okay?"

"Believe me, I will," Standing Deer replied huskily.

Chapter EIGHTEEN

Returning to the past, Karen had been praying for strength. It had been two days since she had left her beloved Standing Deer at the ranch. He was riding north to Rosebud; she to the Standing Rock Agency, in disguise. Time was slipping by too quickly. By Friday she should be in his arms again.

It had taken her years to figure out how to control the time-travel. All she had to do was decide where she wanted to go before she fell asleep and she would arrive there. Spirit of the Mountain found that if she didn't do that she ended up being at the cave in the Black Hills where she had met Jumping Bull. Then she would have to wait for her horse to arrive so she could find the village. The waterfall there was one of the most beautiful she had ever seen. She fell in love with it from the very beginning.

So much needed to be done. Hopefully she wouldn't run out of time. She may not be able to change the future (or the past however one would look at it) but she could avoid potential problems. This is why she chose to hide the buffalo. This is why she was heading to the Standing Rock Agency.

It was hot and humid as she and the caravan rode through the boundaries of the Standing Rock Agency. There was a hushed silence that swept among the Indians. She knew the Indians on the reservation called her the "man who brings death." Red Cloud was the only one who knew who she really was. She sighed. So many lies have been told about Red

Cloud. If the Indians only knew how much he was really helping them, they wouldn't feel as if he had betrayed them.

The men, women and children stood behind Red Cloud as the caravan of eight empty horses and two wagons pulled up in front of the agency office. The wagons were full of blankets, clothing, medicinal herbs, and foods that the Indians preferred but the agency men wouldn't touch. Live cattle were brought for them to butcher when they saw fit.

She knew the Indians would never see the beef for themselves, which is why she hid the food underneath the clothing and blankets.

Dressed in men's clothing, a large hat strategically placed on her head so as not to show her hair or her full face, she rode next to Two Horns who did all of the speaking. She did not know the names of the agency men and preferred it that way. Besides, if they heard her speak they would know she was not a man.

When she started taking Indians from the agency two years ago, it wasn't hard for her to convince the agency men to take the gold and supplies in return for her "use" of the troublesome warriors. These troublesome warriors would work on the cattle ranch as punishment for their misbehavior.

Spirit of the Mountain grinned. She had taught Two Horns to quote certain parts of the constitution and she had it made. It was so easy to twist the laws to the advantage of the ranch and the agency.

Two Horns quoted the thirteenth amendment and stressed the servitude of the Indians on the ranch as a punishment for their crimes. Since there wasn't a judicial system available, he queried, shouldn't the officers of the agency be able to make a decision like that? She almost laughed aloud. It worked all too well.

The agency didn't care that they wanted the wives and children as well. It just fattened their pockets that much more. She stood a short distance from the shackled warriors that had been brought to her for inspection while the agency officers instructed men to empty the wagons and corral the cows.

She signed to Two Horns that she wanted more men to take with them. This was most likely the last time she would be able to take warriors from the reservation and she wanted as many as she could get.

After he spoke with the two officers of the agency he explained to her that there would be no volunteers, she should know that. He had been told there were five warriors locked up that the officers did not want taken because they were too hotheaded and uncivilized. She whispered to him to get those warriors ... regardless of the cost.

The price for the "use" of the Indians was tripled. Shielded by her enormous hat no one but Two Horns saw the fury lashing out of her eyes. Without hesitation, she handed the sack of gold to Two Horns.

As she watched, she had to contain her fury when the five warriors were brought to her line up ... more accurately dragged out. She inspected their bruised and beaten bodies. They stood in front of her with as much pride and courage as any man could. Thank God she had been with the Indians long enough to learn to restrain her anger.

Without looking directly at any of the warriors she was taking, she nodded her head in approval. The five manacled warriors were dragged and shoved into one wagon. The others were reluctant but had not caused much commotion. Their meager belongings were placed on the horses with the wives and children who would follow behind on foot.

She signed to Red Cloud that she wished the Great Spirit to be with him always and told him that this may be the last time they would see each other. She thanked him for his friendship and made a final good-bye as the caravan of "prisoners" made its way out of the confines of the agency.

The two days ride to the ranch was disconsolate and arduous. Spirit of the Mountain could feel the hateful stares from the Indians. When they arrived at the ranch they would know the truth soon enough.

As they reached the property line, she waited in anticipation for the approach of the men that chose to stay on the ranch to help her. She could feel they were watched and knew the warriors in the wagon felt it also. She could see their attention augmenting as they watched the horizon.

Three warriors were seen from a distance approaching quickly on their ponies. She knew immediately something was amiss by the speed in which the caravan was approached.

Squawking Bird quickly spoke in Lakota. Two soldiers were killed escorting a family through her ranch but the warriors had been forced into defending themselves. The warriors knew there was no warring allowed on the property but they had fired in self-defense. The warriors who shot the soldiers were waiting for her at the house. All of the extra men had been alerted and were on guard scouting for more soldiers and wagons.

When they arrived at the house, the women and children who lived on the ranch swarmed around the wagons and newly arrived families. Excitement filled the air and she could feel the new members relaxing with each hearty welcome. Curious and puzzled about the surroundings they stood quietly and no longer struggled.

The shackles were being removed as she entered the house. She could here murmurs of explanations and encouragement to the new arrivals. The newcomers would be shown where to bathe and be deloused. It seemed there was an enormous problem of lice among the reservations. Such a shame, it was rare to find children or adults in an Indian village with lice but the reservations crawled with them and were found everywhere.

By the time they were fed, Karen would be ready to speak with them. So far they had not even heard her voice and still did not know who she was.

Karen entered the living room where Little Eagle and Red Bird waited. They were sitting on the buffalo hide rug like two children waiting to be reprimanded. They had not been on the ranch long and still didn't quite believe they were not captives.

She looked at the comfortable furnishings in the room, shook her head and sat on the floor next to them. The Indians rarely used the furniture, always preferring the floor.

"Tell me what happened?" Spirit of the Mountain asked quietly.

In their village, it would have been a coup; here they knew it would cause trouble. Worried about the killings of the two soldiers and what it could mean, the young warriors were more afraid of Spirit of the Mountain's reaction than the fact that they killed two soldiers. They knew if more soldiers came, the plans of the ranch would be ruined and Spirit of the Mountain would be furious.

Red Bird spoke for the two of them.

"We were bringing stray cattle from the east side of the ranch when we saw the soldiers and the wagon. They were maybe a hundred feet from us when all of this happened. We did not have rifles with us. We were not expecting to need them. We did have our bows and arrows," Red Bird stopped for a moment.

"We gave them the sign of peace but they did not listen. One of the soldiers lifted his rifle to shoot and the other pulled a handgun out of his belt. The man with the handgun missed me and we shot them both with our arrows before the man with the rifle could shoot. The bullet from the handgun hit one of the cattle. Little Eagle approached the wagon and spoke to them in English. He told them we would escort them through your property but we could offer no protection beyond the property line."

"Did they see any buffalo? Did they see the house?"

"No, they did not see the house," Little Eagle replied. "We also gave them dried meat and berries to take with them. They said they were going to Deadwood. We warned them that it was not safe for them to go there and they were better off heading west to California."

"Did they listen?"

Both men nodded yes. "It appears that way. We told them the best route to travel and the safest way. That is the direction we saw them travel," Little Eagle answered.

"What did you do with the soldiers?"

"We looked for papers to find out who they were but there was nothing, so we buried them. We are sorry if this has caused you trouble."

"And the guns?"

Both men pointed to the corner.

"You may keep the rifles for yourselves. Don't worry about the soldiers. They may have been renegades. It doesn't make sense that they wouldn't have any identification papers with them. Our biggest concern is to keep those buffalo hidden so the white hunters do not exterminate them."

Spirit of the Mountain stood up and smiled at both warriors. They were young and strong. Their choice to stay and work for her cause surprised and pleased her. They have both worked hard since they had arrived.

"Go and count your coups, you deserve them. I'm going to get myself cleaned up for the new arrivals. Thank you both."

With a whoop and a cheer, both men nodded their heads. As they left the room she turned to the bookcase and pulled on it to expose a hidden door to where they lived inside the cave home.

Smiling she recalled the day Standing Deer had brought home an old Mother Earth News magazine showing a picture of a rock sheltered home. They had already found the hidden valley for the buffalo and were trying to figure how they would be able to house so many Indians. His idea to build a house covering the cave opening was superb. If anyone did find the house, they would never realize that there were over a hundred Indians living in the shelter of the cave.

He had gotten the idea for hidden doors in one of the gothic books he had read. All of the rooms that lay against the cave have hidden doorways. It was amazing and ingenious.

There were three natural hot springs in the cave. She looked forward to a leisurely bath. The women would keep the newcomers from the water hole nearest the house so she could bathe. Normally all three water holes were available to everyone but the newcomers had not been oriented to her cause yet. This one was smaller than the others, about six feet wide and ten feet long. The steam rising from the water was a beacon for relief after a long and miserable journey.

Spirit of the Mountain entered the pool and felt the smooth stone under her feet. The pool had a slow even decline toward the center. The shallowest part of the hole was about three feet deep. The deepest was in the center and was about five feet deep. Submerging herself under the water, she felt the heat surge through her and snatch the tension as it lifted away.

Closing her eyes, she recalled the last time she had been in this particular pool. Standing Deer had been with her and all were sleeping. It was glorious, as he had made love to her. She sighed. Soon she would be in her love's arms again, and she would show him how much she missed him.

Reluctantly she left the water, wanting to read the financial reports before she spoke with the newcomers. Delving into the figures for the ranch, she smiled. She had made an excellent choice with Two Horns. He was good with figures and led the warriors with a fairness that made anyone proud to work for him.

She was pleased to see there were forty-seven new buffalo calves, ten more than last time. If they keep reproducing at that rate, we'll have to find another valley for them. It was working well.

Two Horns interrupted her train of thought when he alerted her that the newcomers were ready for her in the living area of the house. She followed him through the hidden door that entered the kitchen area. He informed her on how the new warriors and their families had responded to the new captivity. It wasn't encouraging. They smiled at each other. That would change. She had an ace in her pocket.

Crazy Horse stood outside the double doors of the living room out of sight of the newcomers. He greeted her with a silent kiss on the cheek and the three of them entered the room together, with her in the middle.

A hush slammed through the room and all eyes went to Crazy Horse and then to Spirit of the Mountain. Four of the warriors recognized her immediately, all recognized Crazy Horse.

She nodded to Crazy Horse to begin.

He smiled at her and turned to survey the group. Opening his arms to the people in front of him, he spoke with compassion.

"Welcome. What is said here today must never leave your lips. I ask you to protect with your life what you are about to learn."

Each man stayed silent as Crazy Horse explained how the ranch had been started and where the buffalo were hidden. He explained that all the People knew the whites were killing the buffalo and this was their way of salvaging what they could. The buffalo would never become extinct as long as this valley was protected. This way, knowing the life blood was protected, they could fight the white man and not worry that their descendants would starve and die off. The ways of the People could be protected to the best of their ability.

The warriors had a choice. They could stay and protect the land where the buffalo was hidden under the pretense that they were "cowhands" or they could join the tribes that still freely roamed. If they chose to join the tribes, they could never return to the reservation ... for the agency would be told that they were dead. They could however, return here to live if they so chose.

If the agency found out what was happening, the ranch would be destroyed, the buffalo killed and Spirit of the Mountain could possibly be hung as a traitor. She has deceived the agency and they would not take it kindly.

He explained to the warriors that he would be leaving in the morning with Spirit of the Mountain and any warrior who wished may leave with them. They would travel at first light.

When Crazy Horse finished speaking, questions were asked and it seemed most of the warriors were comfortable with what they had been told. They were excited that Crazy Horse and Spirit of the Mountain had calculated such a unique idea.

Two Horns asked if they would like a tour. All agreed. As they left, the warriors clasped Crazy Horse and kissed Spirit of the Mountain on the forehead. Crazy Horse stayed behind with Spirit of the Mountain so they could speak privately.

Two Horns explained that the ranch was one of the largest in the area. Buffalo were found on the property along with antelope and other meat animals the Indians needed for survival. Those buffalo and other animals were allowed to be hunted and were used for the people living on the ranch. He stressed that the buffalo in the valley were to be guarded and not hunted.

Housing for the ranch hands was strategically placed against the hill with the stables to the right within quick reach. He pointed out where the hidden path was that led to the hidden valley that contained the buffalo.

For those who would be interested in staying, Two Horns explained where the ranch supplies were kept and how the schedule was made so that all could spend time with their families.

Two Horns showed the newcomers where they could sleep while they worked the ranch. Explaining that there may come a time when trouble hit the ranch, he also showed them where a tunnel was being built that led to the main house. Though most of the families stayed in the cave, he explained there was a tunnel from the family homes to the main house that was already in use.

To the left of the main house were the homes for the families. They were large enough to hold the wives and children of the ranch hands with a large garden off to the left side. The women tended the herbs and vegetables that were grown to supply the large group living on the ranch. It was a communal setting and most did not find it hard to adapt.

Later that evening there was a celebration for the new arrivals. A feast had been prepared to welcome them to their new life. All were encouraging and reassuring, both those who chose to follow the warpath and those who chose to stay.

Chapter NINETEEN

The day was already hot. The sky was a clear blue with no clouds in sight. The wind stirred across the prairie relieving some of the heat. A unique and spurious peacefulness surrounded the Pine Ridge Reservation.

James Black Elk paced back and forth anxiously in Karen's office waiting for her to arrive. His clothing was disheveled, his normally well groomed, gray streaked hair was in disarray. Worry lines were etched in his normally passive and peaceful face. He anxiously twisted his Stetson hat in his hands, a gift from her.

It had been a long and lugubrious night. He was tired. Fear had kept him going. That particular adrenaline was keeping him going even though he wanted to go back to sleep and wake up from a nightmare that wasn't real. But this was real and it was happening. It was happening to his brother. His younger brother had been so energetic and full of life.

He believed Karen would be able help him. If anyone could, it was her. She was the only one he could trust with his brother's life.

Jim stared at the numerous pictures and paintings of the mountains, prairies and eagles. Although it was just a hobby, Karen was an excellent photographer. She could find the most precious moments with her camera's eye. His favorites were the photographs of the eagles. There were pictures of eagles in flight, eagles perched on trees and diving toward the water for food. She even had one of them mating. He grinned. To even possibly have the chance to see them mating was amazing. To have the luck to catch it on film was even more so. It amazed him how she managed that one, but only she would have that kind of luck.

A smile slowly broke through on his drawn and sullen face. Karen's Indian name, Spirit of the Mountain, suited her well. Her spirit was part of the land, a land and country that she loved with her heart and soul. She was a beautiful woman inside and out. He had much respect and high regards for her as well as her husband. Paul Standing Deer was a lucky man. They were the perfect couple. The Great Spirit definitely had something to do with that relationship. They were blessed.

He sat on one of the chairs against the wall and looked at his dirty clothes. He saw his brother John's blood on his jeans and shirt. Again, he stood up to pace. It helped him think, sometimes. This time it was working too well. He didn't want to think.

His brother ... they had to get his brother here. Would Karen be able to help get him here? She had to. It was his brother's life they would be saving.

When was Standing Deer coming back? He had been only gone for a few weeks when the gangs started fighting each other again and the elders of the reservation started bickering. He felt like he was in the middle of a civil war.

He shook his head. He was in the middle of a civil war.

Gambling profits were causing all sorts of disagreements among the elders. He didn't have proof but believed some tribal leaders were lining their pockets with casino profits, voting out and yanking the rights of anyone who challenged them. Greed had taken over.

Tribal memberships were increasing since they lowered the requirements of bloodline and it was causing dissension among those that wanted to keep control. At first, it worked out well.

Now, he was watching the tribe stray from the ways of the People. New Agers argued with traditionalists and the young argued with old. Prejudice was rampant among the People. They were destroying themselves. Why couldn't they see it?

Don't they understand what is to be happening soon? The People need to unite, not divide. The white buffalo had been born years ago and has since changed its colors, just as it was prophesied. The time is now for the People to become one. Was there someone or something trying to keep the People from uniting?

Even his brother was on his way back to the reservation. After all these years he was returning to help work on the unification of the People. His brother, who rejected all of reservation life, came back to help the People.

Now, he was in a coma and lay dying in a hospital in Rosebud from a car accident. Could it have been a set up? Would it be safe to transfer him here so Karen could attend him?

James Black Elk had reached the point where there was no one to trust. No one but Karen to trust.

Karen's morning started out with another one of her ferocious headaches. She didn't bother to take her braid out and brush her hair. The only thing on her mind was that she felt Bonnie was becoming obsessed.

The bed was getting to be a problem. For the first time in ten years, Karen actually wished she had never purchased the mystical magical bed. She should never have allowed Bonnie to time-travel with her. It was causing problems. Those problems were going to get worse.

She and Bonnie had been the closest of friends since college, almost fifteen years ago. Now she could feel a major disagreement coming soon. The kind that ruins friendships.

Bonnie has become completely prejudiced and hateful toward "the white people," as she calls them. She is becoming a radical. Why hadn't Karen seen this coming sooner? She wanted to control and change history. It's the first of June and the battle of Rosebud and Little Big Horn will be in full swing come July. Bonnie wants to manipulate and change all of that. She wants to warn the tribes and unite them, so they can attack and annihilate. She wants to make sure they know everything that will be happening so they will not end up dead or dying on some reservation. The last time they spoke Bonnie said she would stay quiet. Karen had a sick feeling she had been lying.

She would have to stop Bonnie any way she could. It was not in their hands to change the future and play God. She was specifically told not to interfere with the future. An Indian ... one of the most respected Indians that ever lived ... told her. Crazy Horse gave her the message from one of his visions during the Sun Dance and she was going to live by that promise.

Karen squeezed her eyes shut before she opened the door to her office, wishing for the weight of the past to be off her shoulders and left to God like it should be.

She opened the door and was stunned by the man standing before her. She did not expect to see her good friend with blood on his clothes and pale as a ghost. James Black Elk walked over to her with pain shooting from his eyes.

"What happened to you?"

"Not me, my brother John. He's in a coma in the hospital in Rosebud. He was in a bad accident involving a rig. The driver of the rig claims he swerved in front of him for no apparent reason." James Black Elk started pacing again.

"They said he was lucky to be alive. Then they told me they didn't think he would make it and if he did the chances would be that he would have to be on life support for the rest of his life."

Taking a deep breath, he continued, "All I know is that I want him here at this hospital so you can take care of him. Can you get him transferred here so you can take care of him? I don't want anyone else doing it. I think it was a set up. Why would he intentionally pull out in front of a rig? I think they didn't want him coming back to the reservation to help unite us. I know ... ."

"Slow down." Karen put her hands over her face and rubbed her eyes. "The doctors will not have anything to do with this reservation conflict. Your brother will be in good hands."

"What if someone sneaks in the room to do something to him? If he is here we can watch him better."

Karen stared blankly at Jim's clenched fists. He sounded paranoid but she didn't really doubt his suspicions either. It's uncanny. Her life with Standing Deer and the tribes in the Sioux territories were uniting as one. Here in the present they should be uniting as well. They're practically split in half. Karen walked over to him and gave him a hug.

Walking to her desk, she leaned casually against it. "I'll tell you what I'll do. I'll call the hospital and find out what I can. Okay? You go home and clean up and get some rest ... ."

"No, I want you to call now."

Karen looked at her good friend and sighed, "Who's the doctor? And please remember that I may not get your brother immediately. We may have a long wait for the doctor to return my call."

Jim handed her some papers with the information about his brother. Karen buzzed her secretary and had her call the hospital to connect with Dr. Martin.

While he waited, Karen explained to Jim that depending on his brother's injuries, he might not be able to be moved for a while. "According to the papers, he has had some very serious traumatic injuries. The hospital is better suited for those types of traumas. Rosebud is a reputable hospital and he really shouldn't be too worried. The doctors there are highly recommended and very competent. It was also quite unusual and irregular to have another doctor from a different health system to request a patient's transfer. He is not my patient."

He argued with her that he was requesting the transfer because he preferred that Karen attend to his brother John's needs.

As Karen read the papers and saw there was trauma to the head and internal bleeding that they were trying to locate. Neck injury, hip, back … .

She explained the doctor probably might not be able to call her immediately so he might as well go home and take care of things there. She stressed that he needed to take care of himself as well. Right before he left she promised to call as soon as she heard from the doctor.

A few hours later, Dr. Martin returned her call. Jim's brother John was very close to non-recovery. The doctor was amazed that John was still breathing when he was brought to the Trauma Center. He had massive head injuries with brain swelling. They had to jump-start him a couple of times and couldn't operate yet. His blood pressure is slowly rising to a normal status. His lungs are working fine. His heartbeat is irregular. The internal bleeding has slowed by not enough to avoid surgery. Karen explained that she did not think it was wise to request a transfer at this time. She would speak with Jim Black Elk and again explain to him the repercussions of moving his brother at this time.

Dr. Martin understood why Jim wanted his brother John moved but said he needs to understand that his brother is lucky to be alive. God's wish and the fact that John was obviously a fighter are the only reasons Dr. Martin could come up with to explain why the young man was still alive.

He also explained that he had told Jim to notify the relatives because they didn't think John would make it.

Karen winced. That was, in her opinion, one of the hardest parts of the job. She had not wanted to be put in such a precarious position but she would do it for Jim. Diplomatically, she asked Dr. Martin that if John recovered, when would it be safe to move him since Jim was so insistent on it. She already knew the answer.

The doctor sighed. He just didn't know.

After she hung up with Dr. Martin, Karen rubbed her temples. She was getting a ferocious headache again. She reached for the telephone and called Jim Black Elk. He was not happy with the results of her conference with Dr. Martin. Every time she gave him a reason why his brother John should not be moved, he came up with another reason why he should be moved. Frustrated, Karen cruelly stated that if Jim insisted on moving his brother, it would kill him.

Karen wanted to throttle herself when she heard the cries and despair of her closest friend. She should have done this in person. How could she have been so callous with someone who was so dear to her?

She wondered, would there ever be peace again?

Chapter TWENTY

The two children spoke quietly in Matthew's room while Charlene, their nanny, was cleaning the kitchen. She was a plump woman in her sixties and thoroughly enjoyed living with the Standing Deer family. If it weren't for James Black Elk, she would probably be sitting at home alone looking for anything to occupy herself.

She had been with them for ten years. It didn't take much convincing on Jim's part to talk her into renting out her house and moving in with Karen and Paul Standing Deer. She knew what happened at night when they fell asleep. At her age nothing surprised her, especially when it involved the Spirits.

She smiled at her good fortune as she started to mop the floor. The children were wonderful, easy going and well behaved. She never had a problem with either one of them. Charlene never had to worry about them sneaking around or being dishonest. She sighed. They were such a pleasure.

She listened to the music filtering from Matthew's bedroom and started singing along. They were listening to the Lion King soundtrack again. Charlene knew it by heart and should, she had heard it enough.

She was worried about their parents. Karen seemed to be having an inner conflict with herself. It was understandable, Charlene declared to herself. She would not want Karen's responsibilities.

Matthew sat on the floor staring at his sister, eyes wide in astonishment. Mom and Dad would be furious if they found out. He was excited and curious.

"You did what?" he asked as he bounced up and down in anticipation of her tale.

"What happened?"

"Oh Matt, it was awful. They burned someone they accused of being a witch."

Jennifer closed her eyes trying to will the vivid picture to disappear forever. She repressed the tears that were threatening to burst out of her.

"I wanted to find Mom and Dad. I had a really scary dream and I just wanted to find Mom and Dad!"

"Geezimo, Jen. How come it didn't work?"

"I don't know. I think I ended up in another time, like when they did the Salem witch-hunts. I don't know. I just know it was awful."

Jennifer shivered, recalling the man dancing around the woman who had been tied to the pole. "I read a book from the library at school. It said the witchcraft hysteria started in 1692. They talked funny."

"What do you mean?" Matthew asked.

"You know, like Shakespeare. 'Thee, thy, nay.' It was weird."

Matthew laughed, "Tell me what else. Come on ... ."

"I met some Native Americans. One of them helped me hide from the men who followed me."

"Oh cool! Okay, start from the beginning," Matthew commanded.

Jen told her story from beginning to end. Matthew sat mesmerized, listening to her adventure.

He jumped up in excitement and started staring out the window, "Hey Jen, where do you think I would go? I want to try it."

Jennifer's eyes widened in fear. Running over to the window where her brother stood, she grabbed both of his shoulders and shook him.

"Are you crazy? You can't do that. It might be too dangerous. I'm never going to do it again unless I'm with Mom or Dad."

"Stop," he growled. He stared at her with his lip stuck out and frowned. "You did it! Why can't I?"

"No. Don't you dare try it."

Matthew shrugged and then smiled, "You can't stop me. Because if you do try then you'll have to tell Mom and Dad what you did."

Jennifer pushed her brother and stomped out of his room. Stupid! Stupid, stupid, stupid ... why in the world did she tell him? Now he was going to go into the past. Jennifer groaned as she threw herself onto her bed. She didn't hear her mother call out hello when she came home. She was too lost in her own thoughts to hear anything around her.

Karen kicked her shoes off and lay down on the chaise lounge in the screened porch. Something was going on with her kids and she couldn't put her figure on it. Both of them stayed in their respective rooms when she came home. That in itself was strange. When she peeked her head in the doors, they were both distant. Not normal, she sighed. When she questioned them, they said nothing was wrong. She sighed. Something has happened. She just didn't know what it was. Yet!

When she questioned Charlene, she said nothing out of the ordinary had happened. Yet, Karen felt something and she didn't like it. The kids were distracted by something. She would mention it to Standing Deer. Maybe he could figure it out.

She was tired. Karen wasn't just physically tired but emotionally tired as well. She had too many worries on her mind. Now she had one more. What was going on with her children? She had been blessed. Her children were happy and well behaved. That is why she knew something was going on. It was written all over their little angelic faces. She laughed.

Karen waited patiently for Standing Deer to come home from work. She loved Paul Standing Deer with all her heart. He was of her heart and soul. She was relieved that he had agreed to stop going into the past. They just had to make it through the month of July. Several more weeks and it will be over. Then they could live a normal life.

She would also have to speak with Bonnie. Give her the option of staying in the past or returning to the modern world. She shook her head at the thought of Bonnie. She had changed so very much. They used to be so close and now ... now there was anger and resentment between them. If Karen's suspicions were correct there could be a very serious argument coming up between them.

Bonnie had chosen to stay in the past with Two Feathers but she may change her mind when she discovers Karen and Standing Deer's plans. Karen was looking forward to the conclusion of the Little Big Horn Battle.

Life wouldn't be perfect, she was not that much of an idealist. At least she and Standing Deer could concentrate on just the modern world. They can't change the past but they could still do something about the future.

She knew what she needed to do but it didn't stop her from being tired of living two conflicting lives. She didn't want to time-travel anymore. She was overwhelmed by the reservation garbage that was going on around her now and by the war between the soldiers in the past.

Karen felt herself getting depressed with the thought of the conflicts in this modern world as well. Some of these people have been her friends for the last ten years and are now turning their back on her. It's almost like the reservation is going to have its own civil war.

Maybe she should talk to Standing Deer again about moving back to Florida now instead of waiting until the end of July. They could live a peaceful quiet life without time-travel. Just living the rest of their lives together undisturbed by the past. Karen sighed. To her own ears she sounded like she was running away from her problems. That was not like her.

No, she was not like that. Even if she would run away from her problems, she couldn't leave yet. She needed to help Jim with his brother. She couldn't desert him now when he needed her. He had never asked anything from her before. She was not about to let him down now.

When his brother was well and the reservation problems were settled, they could go back to Florida. Jim has always been there for her. When her world was falling apart, he was there. When life was too hard to face without Standing Deer, he guided her to the right path, to the life circle that was meant for her. He knew her life circle was to be with Standing Deer. Jim saw it immediately. He knew they belonged together and guided her back to him. Jim encouraged her to hang on to the love she and Standing Deer shared.

Now there wasn't anything she wouldn't do for Standing Deer. She would die for him if it meant that he would live on. Karen never thought there was ever a time she would find a love like that. She had not forgotten what it was like before they had met. She hadn't forgotten how she was before.

She had been content with her life then but knew something was missing. She fought her love for him all the way. Six months after Matthew was born she arrived back in Sitting Bull's village. Then of course, Sitting Bull had his say as well. She laughed, recalling how he had diplomatically told her that she was being unreasonable. She was going to miss him. She was going to miss all of them.

Yes, she was lucky to have such cherished friends. If it hadn't been for them, would she have gone back? Probably, she surmised, but it would have been a longer separation. She was definitely stubborn.

She couldn't imagine her life without Standing Deer. It was all written in the web of life. She thanked the Creator every day for her blessings.

Chapter TWENTY-ONE

The village at Rosebud was quiet except for a few early risers who were starting their day with relish. Spirit of the Mountain opened her eyes and looked at her love. Their arms and legs entwined around each other as always.

He was magnificent. His hair had slivers of gray now shining around the crown of his forehead. To her eyes, it had done nothing but make him that much more attractive.

Even after more than ten years of marriage, the feel of Standing Deer's body still excited her. She could feel her heartbeat increase and her body awaken to the thrills of anticipation. Early mornings in their lodge always welcomed them together as one. The anticipation of making love with him spiraled her into another world, a world of eternal bliss. His touch was an electric shock wave pulsating and plummeting her into that realm.

Spirit of the Mountain felt his strong massive body underneath her fingertips as she caressed his chest working her way down, waking him slowly as she stroked his manhood.

Standing Deer opened his eyes and smiled at his wife. They would never tire of each other. He saw a mix of mischief and alacrity in her hooded eyes. Whispering that he loved her, Standing Deer kissed her sweet lips. Trailing his fingers up and down the back of her spine, he kissed her neck and worked his way around her sweet voluptuous body. Every caress he gave to her she returned with passion.

A flute was being played softly somewhere in the village. The background music was ecliptic to their lovemaking. They were floating along with the sounds of the music as the sweet melody swept the village.

Standing Deer's hot lips enveloped her as the music swelled around their lodge. Someone in the village joined the lone flute player with their drums, unknowingly adding to the music of their love. Standing Deer and Spirit of the Mountain's heartbeats matched each rhythmic pound of the drum, beating as their souls combined together to join as one.

Their bodies trembled in time with the rhythm of the music. Their hands moved in harmony, sending shock waves surging through each other.

Spirit of the Mountain could feel her body languorously floating upward to the heavens. She could feel nothing and everything. There was an emptiness that they filled. The earth below them breathed on as they reached a plateau of ultimate passion. They rose together with their bodies entwined eternally. Their souls played and danced together like butterflies reaching a spiritual plane in the heavens among the spirits.

Caressing and turning in a slow methodical dance … the two souls ultimately alighting and joining their eternal life forces.

The power of their love was forever joined as one.

Slowly the two eternal souls came back to the earth rejoining their bodies. A silent sigh filled the lodge.

As Standing Deer and Spirit of the Mountain lay in each other's arms, the sounds of wildlife and the village gradually came back to their ears.

The music they had heard earlier still playing in the background. The straight song was powerful, enlightening their lovemaking and passion. The emotions in the straight songs played by the men in the village had carried them beyond anything either one had ever experienced.

Standing Deer pushed the damp strands of hair away from Spirit of the Mountain's face. She, as well as he, was flushed from their lovemaking.

The Spirits had blessed him again. Standing Deer huskily spoke in a quiet voice, afraid to disturb the Spirits that had just blessed him and his wife. "Canhiya." Love of my heart.

"Never did I think I could feel the way I do right now."

He leaned over and softly kissed her lips.

Spirit of the Mountain gave him a soft laugh that tickled his heart. "I'm still shaking ... ," she whispered to him.

"Pray there is no emergency for I fear I could not get up and walk," laughed Standing Deer.

They held each other until they couldn't avoid the sounds of life outside of their lodge any longer. It would be a busy day.

Spirit of the Mountain was finishing a shield of animal bones for Standing Deer. It wasn't made in the normal round shape. She was making it in an upside down U. It would be wide enough to rest atop his horse and lean against him if Standing Deer needed both hands. Or, if he were standing, his legs would be protected. Once the bones were set in place she would attach a buffalo hide over the top to make it stronger. Beside her was an assortment of arrowheads and shafts that she would be preparing for herself and Standing Deer.

The heat was unbearable for a June morning but she would persist. She may not be able to change what was going to happen next month but she could surely protect her man as much as possible.

There was going to be a meeting tonight of the warriors and elders. Standing Deer would be late returning to the lodge. She would be returning to the modern world without him. Spirit of the Mountain spoke with him about staying in the modern world for a few days so she could help James Black Elk. He agreed with her. It was their turn to help repay their friendship to their brother.

Bonnie, Sings to the Wind, called and entered into the lodge. Spirit of the Mountain watched her old friend with a smile on her lips. Sings to the Wind's belly was swollen with child. She never looked healthier in her life, but her face was troubled. She poured herself a cup of coffee.

"We have to talk," Sings to the Wind said in Lakota.

A sick feeling lay suddenly heavy in her stomach. Spirit of the Mountain nodded her head in agreement.

"I see you are making a war shield and some arrows for Standing Deer."

"Yes, my hands are tied and I cannot change what is to come next month. But I can help him as much as possible."

"No one dies at the Rosebud battle, but sixty-six die at Little Big Horn. That is a different story. That is what I came to speak to you about," Bonnie said with a touch of arrogance.

Spirit of the Mountain stretched the buffalo hide across the new shield and waited impatiently for her friend to continue speaking.

"I have spoken to Sitting Bull and have told him of the coming battles, where the soldiers will be coming from, their battle strategy ... ."

"What?"

"I have warned our People of the impending battles and everything I know of what is to be."

"NO! Do you know what you have done? By doing that you have changed history. You have no right," Spirit of the Mountain had switched to English and was seething with anger. Her breath and heartbeat were pounding faster and increasing with fear.

"Sitting Bull will be warning the other tribes. They will be meeting tonight and the next few nights to make battle plans. They will join together. We will not be destroyed. The white soldiers will never get to the village. The warriors will attack before the white soldiers can reach us. I will not sit here and watch our Nation be destroyed. If I can save their lives ... ."

"You cannot play God. Who do you think you are?"

"I am the one who will make a difference for my People ... ."

"Your People? Excuse me. I thought you were an American. 'Just plain American,' isn't that what you have always said?"

"Don't give me that bull, Karen. I am not playing God! You are. You know what is going to happen and you are going to sit there as if on a throne and let it happen. I will not. If I can stop it, I will."

"You can't stop it! Because of this, you may have changed everything. What if it is worse because the warriors now seek the white soldiers? Don't you think the government's wrath will make it ten times worse?"

"I was brought to the past for a reason. I will not allow ... ."

"You will not allow? You were brought here because I allowed it. I brought you to the past. It was my choice to allow you to sleep on the bed and go to this world. You have no right to change the past!"

"I do have the right!" Sings to the Wind yelled in anger.

"You claim you want to do something to help the Indian. Why didn't you go to DC and lobby for Indian rights here in this world? Why haven't you gone to President Grant and pushed for the Indian's rights? If you are so worried about the Indian, why don't you do something about our world? Pine

Ridge is one of the poorest areas in the nation. Why don't you do something about that? Well, Bonnie?"

When there was no response, Spirit of the Mountain continued. "The Bureau of Indian Affairs is having serious problems. Instead of hiding in the past, why don't you do something about that? Peltier is still in jail. Why don't you do something about that? I could keep going, if you insist. Bonnie, why don't you do something that will change our world and the future, make things better for the Indian Nation in the modern world?"

"I have. By doing what I have done, it will change the future. For the better."

"I was warned not to change the past ... the future. It was meant to be," said Spirit of the Mountain.

Sings to the Wind growled. "I was not warned. So this was also meant to be."

"No, Bonnie. You have made things worse. Now the white soldiers will be on an even bigger rampage."

"You are a coward, Karen. You just didn't have the courage to change the past and I did."

"Get out!" Spirit of the Mountain yelled and pointed to the lodge's opening.

Bonnie blinked in surprise.

"Bonnie, get out of my home. Now!"

Bonnie stomped out of the lodge. Standing about ten feet away, discretely waiting for the argument to end was Crazy Horse. He had unintentionally heard much of the conversation. They had started out speaking in Lakota and ended the argument in the white man's tongue. He may refuse to speak the white man's tongue but he had learned enough words to know some of what was being said between the two friends.

Crazy Horse could not help hearing their angered words. He tried to block it out of his ears and mind. Their words were loud and full of anger. If he hadn't needed to speak with Spirit of the Mountain, he would have left when he realized they were arguing.

Sings to the Wind spotted Crazy Horse immediately and waddled up to him. As she spoke, she rubbed her swollen belly. Crazy Horse looked at her swollen belly and smiled at Two Feathers and Sings to the Wind's blessing.

"Speak with her. She must understand."

Chills went down his spine. A cold feeling of a forewarning swept through Crazy Horse. Sings to the Wind watched as Crazy Horse entered Spirit of the Mountain and Standing Deer's lodge.

Crazy Horse called and entered the lodge. Spirit of the Mountain jumped up and hugged her good friend. He was plainly dressed as always. The waves in his hair were more abundant because of the humidity. He had given up on straightening it years ago. It was a useless battle once moisture hit the air.

"Oh Crazy Horse, I believe the People are in serious trouble. Sings to the Wind told Sitting Bull what is to happen in the next month. She has told him of the future. What am I to do?"

"There is nothing you can do," Crazy Horse replied sadly.

Spirit of the Mountain poured him some coffee and they both sat down.

"I have a gift for you but tell me first what bothers you."

Spirit of the Mountain repeated their conversation to Crazy Horse. He was silent until she was finished.

"We already know where the soldiers were and have been. We have scouts out all the time now and they are watching them. Do not let it worry you. It appears that the only thing she has done is told us when. Do not fret too much. I don't think it will change history. What is to be will happen anyway, no matter what type of preparation we may have."

"Crazy Horse, you of all people know that I was warned to be careful of what I knew. 'Life must continue, as it should be.' Isn't that what you said? You told me that the Creator didn't want me to change anything. The Creator wanted me to learn the ways of the Indian and be there when I was needed. What am I supposed to do now?"

"This will happen in the Moon of Red Cherries (July)? You have a month to prepare to be there when the People need you. That is the will of the Creator."

Spirit of the Mountain nodded her head and smiled. She leaned over and gave Crazy Horse a hug and a kiss on his cheek. "You always make me feel better."

"I do not think you are a coward. This I prove to you by giving you a gift."

Crazy Horse unwrapped the deerskin package that he had put aside. It was a beautiful pipe. Spirit of the Mountain caressed the pipe with love, respect and admiration.

The four quarters of the universe were represented by four ribbons hung on the stem. The white ribbon represented the north, symbolizing the white cleansing wind. A yellow ribbon, signifying the summer and the power to grow, represented the south. The black ribbon was for the west where the thunder beings live to send rain, and the red ribbon represented the east where the sun rises and the morning star lives to give wisdom.

She stroked the eagle feather representing the Creator, who is a father to us all, knowing it also meant men should rise as high as the eagles. The mouthpiece was made of buffalo hide, it representing the earth.

As she admired the pipe and the love it was made with, Spirit of the Mountain once again understood how very religious the People were. The pipe was holy because it meant all of those things. The Creator was a father, the earth a mother and all living things their children. The earth was a mother to all the plants and animals. Isn't that also what Jesus taught? To honor all God had given us?

"You honor me with your gift, Crazy Horse. I thank you with my heart and soul for you have indeed blessed me. Hetchetu aloh." It is so indeed.

Chapter Twenty-Two

Karen had been gone from the Rosebud village for three days now. She missed Standing Deer with all her heart. The time away from the village and its impending tragedy had not helped her.

She knew what needed to be done and didn't understand why she was trying to avoid it. Karen didn't want to time-travel tonight. She would miss Standing Deer being in her arms. To have one more peaceful night, with no one to pressure her about the coming battles, would be a pleasure.

One more night turned into two and then three. More than a week had passed before Karen realized how quickly time had flown. She acknowledged that she couldn't stay away any longer. It was time. The children were missing their father and they noticed she was getting more irritable instead of better. It was a very rare occasion that she and Standing Deer be separated like this.

Karen felt annoyed with herself. Avoiding problems was not in her personality. She was avoiding conflict, yes. Maybe that was why she didn't want to return to the village. There is going to be a huge conflict coming within the next month. Avoiding the inevitable would not improve the circumstances. It would only make them worse. She was now ready to face them. Face them all with as much panache as she can muster.

Speaking with Bonnie was utmost on her mind. She needed to salvage their friendship, but she found it hard to accept what Bonnie had done. But, there wasn't anything that could be done about it now. There were going to be some serious consequences. She believed her friend's heart may have been sincere – her common sense wasn't. What were the ramifications going to be? Maybe, prayerfully, it would be better in the future. Dread engulfed her – somehow, she knew it would not.

Bonnie wanted to have her baby in the modern world, with all the benefits that go with it. She wasn't going to take a chance and lose the baby in the past. Karen had to get herself ready to help her alienated friend with that as well. The baby was due in mid-July.

Sighing, she had to shake this build up of resentment she felt toward her friend. Karen laughed. How ironic that Bonnie sang praises for her life in the past, yet wouldn't give birth anywhere but in a modern facility. Her baby would arrive right before the destruction of the Lakota Nation.

The battles may have been won but it was the end of their lives as they knew it. Tears came to her eyes. It was hard enough to know what was going to happen to these wonderful People, her People. To have to watch it happen ... and see it happen ... was deplorable. It was too depressing to think about. She needed to shake these foreboding thoughts now. Surely she could reconstruct a positive attitude in her heart and mind.

Standing Deer and her children were her strength and love. Thinking of them made her feel peaceful and loved. Karen smiled in anticipation of seeing her husband. She closed her eyes, capturing the memory of holding him and feeling his strong arms around her. She ached for his sweet passion. Together they were a powerful force and could survive anything.

Standing Deer was worried. Spirit of the Mountain had said she would only be gone for a few days. She's been gone for six days. He knew she had been quite upset with Sings to the Wind. This was the first time she had stayed away for so long in her world without him since returning to him ten years ago. Maybe something was going on at the reservation in her world and she was unable to leave. There could be serious problems with Jim's brother John or maybe she had an accident. Maybe ... maybe ... maybe. If he didn't hear from her soon he would go crazy.

There wasn't any way to get in touch with her. He wished he had a telephone. That would be interesting, if it worked. Any other time he cursed telephones. They were more of an inconvenience to him than anything else. Standing Deer thought he could sure use one now. In spite of his anguish, he laughed at the absurdity of a telephone being in the village, in his world. Standing Deer was frustrated. There wasn't any possible way to reach her.

Spirit of the Mountain needed to be here. He needed her in his arms, needed to know she was safe. He wanted to love her with his body, heart and soul. He wanted her to be here. His family needed to be here for the celebration of the Sun Dance. They had promised the children that they could be here. It was going to be the greatest Sun Dance of all.

The council of the tribal leaders resolved to have the Sun Dance earlier than planned. They believed it might possibly be the last one for many years. It would be a long time before it would be done again. Everyone knew it. They just didn't want to admit it.

He knew it would be the last. It was outlawed in her world, their future. Then he smiled. At least, as far as her world knew, it wasn't celebrated.

All of the great warriors and leaders have arrived and were still arriving on the Rosebud for the Sun Dance gathering. They gathered for the last celebration of the old way of life.

Low Dog, Two Moons, Touch the Clouds, Little Big Man, Rain in the Face, Gall and Crazy Horse had all arrived with their bands and nations eager to celebrate one of the greatest ceremonies of their People.

Thousands were coming in from the north and all of them with virulent anger because of the continued invasion of their sacred grounds in the Paha Sapa, the Black Hills.

As Sitting Bull strode back from the river, he watched Standing Deer with the other warriors as they finished working with the branches and vines that created and constructed the arbor. He could tell that his friend's mind was not on the work before him. It was obvious something was amiss.

This was not like Spirit of the Mountain. He was worried about her as well. She could not miss this sacred ceremony. Sitting Bull wondered where she could be and what had happened to cause her to not be here.

Looking around the growing village, he took a deep breath relishing in the sweet smell of the valley and various foods cooking on the fires surrounding him. A breeze swept his wet hair. The sky was a bright azure dotted with billowing clouds. Eagles were in flight above the village, singing their song of life. The cool morning air circled and refreshed the vast camp. It was a good day.

It was exhilarating to look upon the Valley of Rosebud. His heart quickened as his eyes surveyed the largest gathering he had ever seen in his lifetime. There were many lodges. The valley was wide and flat, yet Sitting Bull could not see all the camps. The village formed a magnanimous circle with the Rosebud River flowing through the center of the camp.

Many of the Indian Nations had answered his call for the Sun Dance. From the Sioux Nation alone there were over eight thousand people with more than fifteen hundred lodges and wickiups. Sitting Bull smiled. There had to be at least three thousand of the best and strongest Sioux warriors that were ever put upon this earth. They had never been so amalgamated as they were now.

The excitement of the approaching Sun Dance sparked the air. His spirit as well as those in the village was strong. Never had the Sioux, Cheyenne and Arapaho been so unified and powerful as they were this day.

The buffalo were plentiful. The momentous hunt the day before was a success and a blessing from the Creator. The Great Spirit had blessed His people with the abundance of spiritual strength and the abundant flood of buffalo to seal them.

Sitting Bull entered his lodge. The warriors had finished with the arbor and it was time for him to dress in his holy regalia. As he picked up each garment, a prayer was spoken to the Great Spirit. He was a Holy Man, a Chief, a husband and father. He would be none of these if it had not been the will of the Great Spirit. His prayers filled the lodge with each breath he took. Once he was done, Sitting Bull picked up the Sun Dance Peace Pipe. It was simple and unadorned, as it should be.

The sound of flutes danced in the air. Soon they would be silenced and he would hear the beating of the drums, the heartbeat of Mother Earth calling to him to begin the celebration. As Sitting Bull exited his lodge with his wife behind him, he watched as the warriors who had been chosen to play the drums of Mother Earth enter the sacred circle.

Moments later Sitting Bull took a slow, deep breath and looked to the heavens. He methodically and ceremoniously raised the Peace Pipe to the heavens and chanted a prayer to the Great Spirit. Again he raised the Pipe, chanted another prayer to the four corners of the earth. A song came from his lips for all that would be honored in the great Sun Dance Ceremony.

The drums began their slow rhythmic heartbeat.

The vast opening of the arbor faced the east. Wiwanyag wachipi had begun and would purify the People and give them power and subsistence.

A strong and solid cottonwood was chosen to stand in the heart of the dancing circle. Among the voices of Mother Earth, the People came to the holy tree singing their sacred songs. Those blessed by the Creator with life growing in their womb danced around the tree celebrating the gift they had been given. Each one thanked and praised the Creator.

With their dancing complete, White Feather was the honored brave chosen to strike the tree. When he was done counting coups, he distributed gifts to those who were in need. As was the way, for every coup he counted, a gift was given. White Feather was a generous, unpretentious brave and he distributed many gifts among the People.

Gathered around the holy tree, a group of specially chosen unmarried girls circled the tree. They too danced and sang their praises to the Creator. It was their given honor to chop down the tree with their own personal axes.

Sitting Bull and the other Chiefs, accompanied by their sons, carried the Sacred Tree back to the village. Four times the warriors stopped, singing thanks and praise. Each stop representing the four seasons of the year.

When they arrived back at the village, the Sacred Tree was carefully placed in the center of the arbor. The warriors backed away joining the circle that had gathered around the arbor.

Standing Deer stood and watched as the sacred drums of Mother Earth continued. The warriors on horseback waited patiently for the signal from Sitting Bull. Once the tree had been placed in the heart of the arbor, the People waited in silence. The rumbling of the drum was invariably present.

Not a word was spoken as anticipation and excitement filled the air. All eyes watched Sitting Bull raise his hand. With a graceful swish, he dropped his hand.

At his signal, the mounted warriors started the rush. Each warrior wanted to be the first to touch the Sacred Tree. The warriors shouted and fought their way to the center of the arbor using every available resource to throw each other off the horses. It was a mock battle to reach a coup. It is believed that the one who touched the Sacred Tree first would be successful in battle and not be killed in the coming year.

The Sacred Tree was planted in the center of the arbor. The holy men danced and sang their sacred songs and vows.

Lt. George Armstrong Custer watched as the procession of just under thirteen hundred army soldiers and two hundred civilians approached the camp where he had chosen to rest. He scanned the great army with pride. A deep sigh of contentment eased out of his mouth as he watched the American flag with its glorious Stars and Stripes wave in the wind. Another exaltation of pride left his lips as he also watched the Seventh Cavalry flag with its eagle symbol wave honorably beside the great Stars and Stripes.

Riding up to the hilltop for a better view, Custer could see the forces of the united Sixth Infantry, the Seventeenth Infantry and his own Seventh. It was a breath-taking inspiration to see these great and brave men together. It was history in the making and he would be at the height of it all. A smirk curled his lips as he thought of the coming battle. From what the scouts had found, and apprised him of, it would be an easy fight.

He was determined to earn his title of General again. He would destroy the rebellious Indians and be on his way to Washington for a career of a lifetime. It would be his dream come true, the ultimate goal. He would be President George Armstrong Custer.

He had to prove himself to Grant. He had tried to avoid testifying in Congress. He knew it was his duty as an American citizen to speak out about the fraud in the government. It had been shameful the way the traders had cheated the Indians and his troopers. Custer frowned. They called it hearsay. It didn't do an ounce of good. The tribes continued to receive little rations and rotten food. His soldiers were forced to buy this food and pay ridiculous prices.

Custer shook his head, recalling the charges against him concerning insubordination. The whole situation still made him angry. He hadn't lost one man in that battle. The accusations were ridiculous. He was a soldier and soldiers do what they have to do to succeed for their country. He should never have been reprimanded for those actions. They claimed his refusal to obey orders imperiled the lives of the soldiers he had lead into battle. Custer shook his head. They are soldiers and soldiers put their life on the line. It was all part of the process. This was their country and they fought for it with pride. He fought to win and used any means he could to do it.

That was exactly what he was going to do now.

On the third day of the Sun Dance celebration, the mothers of the united bands brought their infant children and laid them under the Sacred Tree. They prayed to the Creator that their sons would grow to be warriors, brave and true. They sang prayers for their daughters so they would grow to be strong women and mother their own children to follow the path given to them by the Creator.

The braves and warriors who chose to participate in the Sun Dance were in the sweat lodges fasting and purifying themselves. They prayed and meditated to reach their goals on the following day, the last day of the celebration.

With the seriousness of the ceremony also came a happiness that danced in the air. Games and practical jokes were played among the People as well as much feasting and dancing. The children of the villages enjoyed themselves as well. The ceremonies gave them the freedom to play tricks and jokes on the adults.

Speaking quietly with each other, Sings to the Wind and Sunshine in the Morning were carrying bladder bags back from the river. Out of the corner of theirs eyes they saw the young Black Elk and a few of his friends running toward them. Smiling with a twinkle in both of their eyes, they knew a trick would soon be coming their way. Sunshine in the Morning feigned a slight yell and jumped as their arrows pierced the bladder bags spraying water everywhere. Sings to the Wind feigned a yell of anger as the boys ran off laughing.

Sitting Bull and Crazy Horse watched in amusement at the comical conspiracies of the children and adults. Later, when the day had reached a quiet atmosphere, they watched the young boys sit in a circle playing one of their games of skill.

"Look over there, Sitting Bull. Near your lodge," Crazy Horse whispered.

Sitting Bull watched with amusement and curiosity in his eyes. Sunshine in the Morning and Sings to the Wind were sneaking closer to the huddled boys near the front of his lodge. He and Crazy Horse chuckled when they saw the popguns the women had made out of ash boughs. The women waited patiently for the children to be absorbed in their game.

The group of boys jumped simultaneously at the sound of the pops, all throwing their arms up into the air as if it had been rehearsed. Laughter filled the air for this was a trick the youngsters usually played on the adults. The fact that an adult had retaliated in the same manner made it that much funnier.

Leaning back in his chair, Custer watched the army camp in silence. He was surrounded by the sounds of horses, mules and laughter. The men were excited and hankering to beat the Sioux. The scouts had told him earlier that this would be an easy fight. Colonel Gibbons would be joining him with his cavalry and infantry. General Crook would join him with thirteen hundred more men. It would be a clean sweep, an enormous annihilation that would give him fame for the rest of his life.

George Custer reached for his tea. Never would he touch the evil spirits of alcohol. He didn't like the loss of control and never would. He had always striven to be in control of everything he did and everyone around him whether they liked it or not.

Besides, if he lost control, how could he care for his men, his Seventh? This was his life and these men were his extended family. The Seventh Calvary depended on him and the welfare of his men always came first. He had been given this chance to defeat the Sioux because he was the best. Grant was depending on him to move the Indians to the reservations and he would not fail him, or his country.

Standing Deer stood watching as the fourth and last day of the Sun Dance was beginning. Spirit of the Mountain and the children should be here. What could possibly be going on in her world that would stop her from being with him?

As the majestic sun rose, colors painted the sky that would make an artist blush with excitement. The sun lit the sky as no other day that he had seen. This day would be one to remember for eternity. It will be written in the winds of time to be passed on through the ages.

There were hundreds of warriors who would be taking part in the Sun Dance this day. Many warriors were participating for the first time … and all for the last. Standing Deer had chosen not to participate. He would be dancing among the participants giving them his support through his spirit.

The holy men approached the heart of the arbor. The People danced around the Sacred Tree as the warriors who had purified themselves in the sweat lodges stood in the center of the village in front of the People. Once the men were painted, each lay down under the Sacred Tree and waited their turn for the holy men to cut holes in their chests. The holy men pushed and impelled the strips of rawhide through the skin and attached the strips to the Sacred Tree.

The drums sang to the heartbeat of Mother Earth as the warriors danced to the beat. They would dance until they could no longer move or their flesh would tear and rip loose from the rawhide strips.

Sitting Bull and his adopted brother Jumping Bull sat against the Sacred Tree while the warriors danced and stared into the sun. Both warriors sang songs of prayers and praise to the Creator. Jumping Bull chanted and cut one hundred pieces of flesh from Sitting Bull's arms. When Jumping Bull concluded the ritual, Sitting Bull stood and joined the circle of warriors, singing and dancing amongst them.

Much time went by as the villagers danced and sang, joyous in this Sacred Ceremony. Sitting Bull stood at the edge of the arbor. Staring into the azure sky, his eyes watched the bright clouds billowing down encircling him with a vision. His eyes pierced through the clouds. White soldiers were riding on horseback, attacking a village. The soldiers were everywhere. They were surrounding the village and his People.

It was a familiar place but not the campsite that they were now staying. Squinting, he looked below the outline of the sun. Sitting Bull concentrated and stared harder as he tried to identify where this vision was occurring.

Sitting Bull watched as the soldiers fell headfirst. It was as if a wild rainstorm was flooding his village. A deafening rumbling sound filled his ears as loud as the pounding of thousands of buffalo stampeding. The ground below him felt as if it was shaking. His heart beat fiercely. His breath was short and quick.

The dead white soldiers lay before him on the ground. Sitting Bull heard a voice.

"So many innumerable times you have asked for peace. The Lakota have asked only for peace and to live on their land as they have always since time began. They ask to live as they choose, where they choose, and to live free. You have not been heard because the Washita does not listen. They do not hear. The white soldiers do not listen. The washitu do not possess ears. For this ... they will die in battle."

Chapter TWENTY-THREE

On the afternoon of the sixteenth of June, Young Sky of the Hunkpapa tribe raced into the vast village yelling a warning of white soldiers. Expeditiously the message was spread through the village. A soldier camp was found with over one thousand white soldiers. It had been located approximately twenty miles south of the Rosebud. The One with the Red Beard, General George Crook, had been seen moving about the soldier's camp.

A council was called and unanimously decided that Crazy Horse would lead this battle. Volunteers had gathered around and joined Crazy Horse with his great warriors. United as one they sat around the fire in the heart of the camp and planned the coming battle. In the early morning, the Lakota as well as the Cheyenne and Arapaho would strike the soldier's camp. Tonight they would prepare themselves for battle.

The news of the approaching battle flew through the camp. In a quandary, Sings to the Wind ran to Standing Deer as quickly as her swollen belly would allow. She watched as he brushed down his favorite horse.

"Standing Deer, this isn't supposed to be happening! Not now! It's not supposed to happen for two more weeks. I was hoping that it wouldn't be happening at all. I thought history would have been changed when they had the Sun Dance early. I heard it was Crook they found."

Standing Deer looked to the east where the sun would be rising over the horizon. He may die this day and never see his beloved wife and children again. History will be rewritten and what will the outcome be? Could it change so much that all of what he loves in Spirit of the Mountain's world be destroyed? Would his world be destroyed?

Without looking at Sings to the Wind, he continued brushing down his horse and preparing the mare for battle.

"Standing Deer?" Sings to the Wind whispered.

"Yes, it is Crook. Amazing what happens when you choose to play God."

"No, you don't understand. I wasn't trying to play God," Sings to the Wind whined. "I just wanted it to be better for the Sioux, for my People."

Seething with anger, Standing Deer grabbed the reigns and started to walk away.

Turning, he whispered, "I want what is best for my People as well. We should not make decisions that are for the Creator only. It was not your place to decide who would live and not live. It was not your place to decide what will happen to the thousands of ancestors that will be born or not be born after we have gone from this world. You forget, my old friend, that there are two worlds that you should have considered."

The crisp morning air chilled the lodge. Embers glowed from the dying fire of the night before while Standing Deer languorously awoke. Subconsciously he reached over to hug and hold Spirit of the Mountain in his arms. With a deep painful sigh, he realized she had not yet returned to him.

Reaching for a log, he unceremoniously dropped it on the embers. Eyes half open he put a bowl with yesterday's coffee next to the flame. Pouring water into another bowl, he used that to splash water on his face and clean his teeth, wishing he had electricity and modern plumbing.

Drinking the now hot coffee from his ceramic cup, he relished in the taste of the bitter black caffeine. A fresh brewed pot of coffee would be wonderful. Laughing aloud, Standing Deer realized his thoughts sounded like the men and women from Spirit's world. Yes, he was indeed being spoiled by the luxuries of her world. He had the best of both worlds.

"Pilamaya wichoni." I am thankful for my life.

Two Feathers came in, grabbed a cup of coffee and sat down beside his friend. The two sat in silence until it was time to prepare each other for the coming battle.

For many years since becoming warriors, the two men painted each other before battles. They were the closest of friends, brothers as it should be.

Two Feathers painted Standing Deer with the customary yellow, black and red. Starting with Standing Deer's face, he worked his way down to the feet.

When that was done, Two Feathers stood back and studied his artistry. Half of Standing Deer's face was painted black, the other red. Black circles covered his chest and back. Two Feathers had painted bright yellow lightning bolts shadowed with red on his friend's arms, legs, hands and feet. Standing Deer's red sash was tied deftly to his loincloth.

Two Feathers preferred nothing on his face until after the conclusion of the battle. Standing Deer painted two large yellow wings on his friend's back. Black circles and squares were painted upon his chest, surrounded by lightning bolts as well.

Standing Deer grabbed his new shield and put on his war bonnet. The two warriors stood in their loincloths facing each other admiring the work on their now hidden copper flesh. Nodding silently, they left the lodge.

Sings to the Wind watched Two Feathers put his antelope horns on his head. She smiled at him thinking surely these ignorant white soldiers would take one look at her brave, fearless and spirited husband and run in the other direction.

"Wastelaka niye, Two Feathers." I love you.

Atop his horse, Two Feathers eyes caressed his pregnant wife. "Wastelaka."

Sings to the Wind stayed in front of the lodge. She did not turn her back until all the warriors going into battle had left the camp. Her feet seemed glued to the ground; she was feeling timorous by what she had done.

Standing Deer joined Gall as he finished saying goodbye to his young wife and children. Together they waited patiently on horseback near Crazy Horse's lodge. They watched as he concluded his pre-battle ritual. Dressed in a loincloth only, Crazy Horse knelt down in a trance-like manner and spread dirt upon himself. A pebble, the charm given to him many years ago, was tied securely behind his right eye. Crazy Horse always fought unadorned.

Sitting Bull approached the two men. He looked upon Standing Deer and saw that he was painted fiercely with his impressive war bonnet sitting atop his head. The baby-faced Gall didn't look so childlike on this crisp early morning. He was painted in all manners with buffalo horns adorning his headgear. The two were strong warriors; together they would strike fear in any enemy.

"Fight hard my brothers, fight strong. Remember and remind the other brave warriors not to take the spoils of this battle. If they do ... it will be a curse to this great Nation."

Both men nodded and Crazy Horse joined them. Sitting Bull said a quick prayer for a successful battle and the braves rode off to join the rest of the warriors.

General George Crook had been searching fecklessly for the Sioux and Cheyenne. With over one thousand soldiers and half a dozen Crow scouts, he had been moving prudently northward hunting for the camps.

Seated in front of his tent, he watched as some of the early risers prepared themselves to strike camp. As he drank his first cup of chicory coffee on this fine clear morning, he wondered how the extravagant Custer, Gibbons and Terry were fairing in their search.

The distant sound of pounding hoofs broke his reverie.

General Crook slowly turned toward the sound and heard the bugle warning of the attack just as he saw the dry dust being kicked in the air from the warriors' horses.

With the speed of well-trained and skilled soldiers, his troops mounted quickly, half-dressed, adrenaline pumping and now fully awake. Crook's officers were shouting orders, instantly aware of the infamous frontal attack.

Crazy Horse instructed his feral warriors to come charging out of the bluffs and harsh rugged hills for a full frontal attack. Barking orders, Crook watched his regiment form ranks in three directions. Chaos and disarray encompassed the soldier's camp.

The approach and attack of the Lakota and Cheyenne warriors began pummeling his men. Crook squinted to see through the dry dust that was being kicked in the air, making it impossible for the General to see clearly.

The thundering of hundreds of hoofs pounded in his ears. The ear piercing cries of the Indians were cutting through the air. The dust-filled air gagged his men as they watched the approaching throng of warriors coming in waves making the battle and its men appear ghostly.

"Level out and aim for the horses!" Crook yelled.

The shrieking of wounded horses and men was deafening. The warriors kept attacking in waves like a beach being pounded by the surf in the midst of a hurricane.

The ferocity of the warriors unnerved the best of his men. It was impossible to keep them organized. Crook and his officers were shaken. The Indians didn't fight like they were supposed to fight.

His horse had been lost in the confusion. Crook ran back and forth among the men and officers in the camp continuing to shout orders as the waves of warriors came down upon them. He knew then that they would have to break up and fight whichever way they could.

It was a skirmish like Crook had never experienced. Crazy Horse and his strong warriors battered his regiment with conflagration. It was as if Satan and his cohorts had attacked in full regalia. The warriors had full war paint on themselves and their horses. The war bonnets of the warriors were regal and adorned with the horns of steers and buffalo.

It was terrifying even for the most experienced of soldiers. Waves of warriors kept pounding at Crook's soldiers. Crook watched and saw the terror that had filled his men's hearts in their eyes, and mirrored back to him, knowing they saw the same in his. He felt his heart stick solidly in his throat, yet he would stay strong and composed for his men for their lives depended on it.

The intrepid warriors charged expeditiously with lances and knives. The warriors' arrows cut through the air silently striking his men with precision. Crook watched from a distance in frustration, as one warrior knocked a soldier from his horse. The warrior quickly dismounted and killed him, cutting off the soldier's right arm and carrying it away.

Standing Deer balanced the shield Spirit of the Mountain had made him against his chest. It leaned strategically against his body and his horse the way she had planned and envisioned it. As he sent his arrows alight, fighting with pugnacious abandon, Standing Deer heard and felt the fear and anger that was surrounding him.

He knew in his heart he would fight to the death to protect this world and this way of life. And he would die for his country, his land that was also his wife's world. Standing Deer would die fighting for that world and everything it meant, too. He was Hunkpapa and American and proud to be both. It was an interesting thought, one he would have to concentrate on at a more opportune time. Right now any thought or distraction from the battle could be deadly.

A bullet whizzed by his ear and Standing Deer turned to face his assailant. Another crushed into his shield and yet another. Before either of the two men could shoot again they were lifeless, each an arrow in their throats. Anger, hatred and revenge filled his heart and soul.

With a sense of pleasure and accomplishment, Standing Deer leapt down off his horse and scalped both men, throwing their scalps onto the ground next to his horse. They were souvenirs he would not keep.

The lethal fighting continued through the day. The battlefield sizzled and charged like an electrical storm. Crook and his officers had given up on keeping their soldiers organized. It was impossible to fight the warriors in standard battle form.

The soldiers had been disconcerted by the ferocity of the full frontal attack. Crook finally had ordered his men to fight in random and isolated skirmishes and knew that was the only way they would survive.

The battle raged on until nightfall when both sides withdrew taking their wounded and dead with them.

Crook stood mesmerized and stunned as the chaos unraveled before his eyes. He watched the dark shadows of the warriors grabbing their dead and wounded as they raced northward into the hills. The futility of the battle weighed heavy upon his shoulders. His men had fought with bravery that anyone would be proud of. There wasn't one soldier who displayed any form of dishonor and shame.

The feral battle left Crook and his soldiers beaten and bitter. General George Crook lost eighty-four men and used up twenty-five thousand rounds of ammunition. He did not ask and didn't bother to count how many had been injured.

With the little ammunition he had left, the General decided against chasing the warriors. He wouldn't be meeting with Custer or the rest of them. He and his men had been whipped and defeated mentally and physically. Crook's decision to take the remainder of his men and head south was an easy one.

The warriors came in from the battle late into the night. It was an unfinished battle and they did not know if they had won or lost. They had lost twenty-five warriors and many more were wounded. Many of the People came and greeted them. Some of the villagers and warriors stayed awake the rest of the night in celebration. Others tended to the wounded, and yet others mourned for those that had died in battle.

Standing Deer sat next to a small fire in his lodge, eyes staring at the opening in the roof of the lodge. The adrenaline and excess energy of the battle still raged inside of him.

He had to shake the hatred he felt burning inside his soul. It was eating away at him. He cannot hate all whites. He can't! Standing Deer concentrated on focusing his anger toward those who deserved it. He had to focus the anger and hatred toward the government officials who were trying to take his lands away, not the people themselves. They only knew what the newspapers wished them to know. He must concentrate on the soldiers who were following these orders from higher authorities and fight them.

Standing Deer needed his wife. He craved her gentle ways and her blessed eternal love. He ached for Spirit of the Mountain to be in his arms. His wife needed to be here to help the warriors who had been injured. Where was she? Why hadn't she returned to him?

He looked at the shield his wife had created with love. It had protected him well. Standing Deer turned the shield over and touched the backside. The bones had been crushed and severed by the impact of the two bullets that had slammed into it. He could be dead now, or seriously injured, if it hadn't been for this powerful shield she had made. He was a lucky man and he thanked the Creator.

When the celebration of the battle was over, the Chiefs waited and wondered why the One with the Red Beard had not followed the warriors to continue the battle the next day. A group of scouts had been sent out. When the scouts returned, they spread the word that they had found tracks that showed Crook had left and headed south, away from the village.

The warriors celebrated the victory of the soldiers from the One with the Red Beard. Mistakenly many believed this was the great victory of Sitting Bull's vision. Sitting Bull warned them that this was not his vision. His vision took place on the Greasy Grass. His vision told them the white soldiers would attack their village. The soldiers would fall dead into their camp.

Almost a week later, after they mourned for the braves and warriors that were now in the life beyond, Sitting Bull along with the other Chiefs decided it was best to move the camps. They headed to the Pazee Lawakpa; the Little Big Horn to the whites, the Greasy Grass to the Sioux.

It was one day's travel to the new camp when Spirit of the Mountain had arrived back at the village with her children. Standing Deer whooped with joy. He lifted her in his arms and swung her in the air. As he released her to the ground, Standing Deer bent his head and gave her a heady kiss on the lips. He quickly reached for Matthew and Jennifer and gave them each a bear hug.

"Where have you been?"

Spirit of the Mountain frowned and looked down to the bare ground of the lodge. Shuffling her feet, she felt like a reprimanded child.

"I'm sorry. At first, I needed to stay away and then I decided to just wait a few more days for the children to get out of school so they could stay here with the village. Please forgive me," she pleaded.

"I was sick with worry. You know all too well that there isn't a way for me to reach you. You cannot imagine all of the horrible things I thought had happened. Don't do that to me again. Please."

"Oh my love, I am so sorry. I had so much to think about. Before I could return I had to relinquish my anger that I felt toward Sings to the Wind. I understand why she warned them. I truly do."

"There are many of your friends here that are worried about you," Standing Deer admonished.

"Yes, I believe there are many that are worried. We will visit them after we eat."

"No, let us ride together first and then you can visit our friends."

Standing Deer and Spirit of the Mountain were silent as they ate their morning meal. The children kept the lodge filled with animated conversation about what their father had missed while they had been separated. Excitedly the children left after they ate to see their friends from the village.

Spirit of the Mountain felt the peace deep inside her that she longed for. It was a peace she used to feel when she was with the People. She was grateful that it was back. As the two rode through the woods, the dry leaves crunched under the horses' feet. She could smell the strong familiar aroma of the evergreens in the air. A slight breeze carried the late spring smell of the earth filling her with wonder and sweet peace.

She looked up into the large arms of the trees, stretching their branches out as if they were opening themselves to the world. They were opening themselves to anyone or anything that wanted to accept their embrace. So majestic they stood as they waited for the Creators creatures to come and eat under their leaves or shield themselves in the crooks of their arms.

She smiled and felt the wonders of the Creator. They stared at the suns rays as it sprinkled its way down to the earth. Birds of red and blue twittered and danced among the open arms of the trees and sang as the two moved on horseback through the dark woods.

As they exited the woods, Spirit of the Mountain looked up into the great azure sky. Closing her eyes, she took a deep breath and looked into her precious love's dark sultry eyes.

"I have done a lot of thinking in the past two weeks. There is still much unresolved between us. I believe so strongly that the children cannot continue living in two separate worlds. They can live by the way of the People without needing to see the tragedy that is coming," Spirit of the Mountain said quietly.

"I could have sworn, my love, that I did indeed agree with you. I had told you before that we could live in your world. I love you with all of my heart and soul. If this will help your mind be at peace then that is what we will do."

"Are you sure? They already know what is going to happen to the People. They don't need to live the tragedy, too."

"It is too late my love. Tragedy has ... ."

A sickly piercing animal-like scream filled their ears. Standing Deer took off at a quick gallop yelling at Spirit of the Mountain to stay behind. Ignoring his warnings, she raced quickly behind him.

Standing Deer slowly and cautiously approached a rickety old wagon with a broken wheel, laying on its side. He watched a washitu beating his wife with his handgun. The woman was fighting him with all her strength, trying to run away from him.

"No!" the woman yelled.

"Stop fighting me. I must kill you and then myself. We will never get out of here alive anyway!"

"No! Stop it! Let me go!" she yelled as she pummeled his face with her fists.

"You must die. I will never allow you to become a whore to any of those beasts, those savages."

The dark-haired woman fought viciously, repeatedly striking her fists against the man's chest and face. When the man dropped the handgun, she turned to run away and saw Standing Deer and Spirit of the Mountain.

"Aiyeeeee!"

Stunned, the man scrambled for the handgun. Pulling out her revolver, Spirit of the Mountain kicked her horse into a sprint and placed herself in front of Standing Deer. She watched the washitu fall to the ground, blood appearing slowly on his chest. Her shot had been quite accurate, in the heart where she had aimed.

So, what was that tug she felt on her shoulder? Why was she falling off her horse? Was she fainting? How odd ... why did the woman's scream sound so muffled?

The dark-haired woman screamed hysterically. Standing Deer carefully laid Spirit of the Mountain on her horse. Quickly he grabbed the hysterical woman and tied her to his horse. Then he stuffed her mouth to stop her screaming before they left for the village.

Why did she keep calling Spirit of the Mountain a witch? It was the second time he had heard someone call her a witch. The first time was John Colby. What in the Creator's name were these two washitu doing out here? Did they have a death wish?

When Standing Deer approached the camp, the villagers scattered to find Sitting Bull or Crazy Horse. The woman followed Standing Deer into his lodge and sat against the wall while he pulled his wife's deerskin dress down.

Hearing the news, Sings to the Wind raced across the village and entered the lodge. Soon Sitting Bull arrived, quickly followed by Crazy Horse. The village was in turmoil. Spirit of the Mountain had never been injured before. It was a bad omen.

Chapter TWENTY-FOUR

Lieutenant Colonel George Custer continued to push his men at a grueling pace of thirty miles a day. Daily, scouts rode out ahead of the regiments, pushing themselves twice as hard and twice as far. He watched a group of Reno's scouts approaching the marching regiments. Major Marcus Reno raised his arm, calling for a halt. He then dismounted and waited for Custer.

"What have you?" Custer inquired.

"Seems my scouts have found an abandoned camp of about four hundred lodges. They've also found signs of a fight."

"Well then, there's no need to stop now, lets go," Custer shook his head.

Tom Custer rode silently beside his big brother who seemed pleased. Tom believed without a doubt that this breakthrough was needed.

Pleased with the scouts and the discovery of the camp, Custer congratulated himself on the felicitous discovery. This good news would keep his men encouraged and ready to fight the redskins. Soon enough General Terry and General Gibbons would meet him at the Big Horn.

He was fortunate to have the Crow scouts join the group and improve his progress. Along with the Ree scouts and the Arikara, he would excel and success would be his. The best move he could make would be to follow the new trails that they were bound to find. It would lead him to the elusive

Sioux and Cheyenne. He and his men would continue to proceed up the Rosebud in search of the Sioux and follow the trail toward the Little Big Horn.

Custer had heard the rumors of the warriors leaving the reservation to meet with Sitting Bull. He also knew the reservations were denying it.

"You know Tom, I was thinking about the rumors of the reservation Indians leaving to meet with Sitting Bull. There couldn't possibly be as many as they say." Custer laughed and shook his head.

"We all know how rumors get blown out of proportion. One warrior may leave the reservation and rumors say it is ten. Even if it is half of what they say could possibly be there at Sitting Bull's camp ... that would mean we would only be fighting one thousand men."

"We could do it alone," Tom piped. "Without any problems. Your decision to leave the Gatling guns behind was a good one. They would have only slowed us down, causing more problems than necessary. Don't want anything slowing us down."

Custer nodded his head in agreement and grinned. He was going to beat the enemy. It was going to be one good fight. He scanned the vast abandoned campsite absorbing everything with the keenness of a panther. The scouts were scattered, making their particular observations. As he approached the abandoned site the scouts gathered to inform him of their findings.

John Colby and Isaiah left the group and approached Custer and his brother Tom as they dismounted.

"There were many Sioux here ... but nothing that the General cannot handle," John Colby informed him.

Looking at Colby with distaste, Isaiah interrupted. "There are many Sioux. Too many Sioux! Many soldiers will die in this battle. What you can see and beyond is all one camp, stretching across the miles."

"You must be mistaken. What you say is impossible," Custer frowned.

Custer knew better. He knew Indians and he knew them well. It was many different camps and they all didn't belong to Sitting Bull. When he heard Isaiah words, he knew they had to have made a mistake reading the signs. He also believed that the other camps did not follow Sitting Bull.

"We have enough soldiers to fight this camp," Colby chided Isaiah.

"No, we don't," Isaiah flushed red in anger. He had a deep feeling Custer wasn't going to stick with the original plan. "Custer, you must see there are too many Sioux and not enough soldiers to fight them."

"I don't need the scouts to fight with the cavalry. We can and will defeat the Sioux. You just get me to the Sitting Bull's camp and have the scouts take the Sioux horses so they cannot flee. The Seventh will do the rest."

Custer turned and walked away from the two scouts. He trusted Colby a lot more than Isaiah. Isaiah had helped him, too. But he had Indian blood in him, just like the other scouts, and trust was an issue.

Isaiah might turn on him, whereas Colby ... now Colby had fought with him in the war. He was a spy for the Union army. He had crossed lines of enemy territory posing as a Rebel soldier. Colby proved his worth to Custer many times over. He was a lucky man to have people like Colby fighting with him.

Custer knew whom to trust. He would not forget Colby or his Indian friends when he became President. This battle against Sitting Bull, with his brave Seventh Cavalry supporting him, would send him to the White House.

The Crow and Arikara scouts stood in the center of the largest campsite they had ever seen in their lives. There was no need to continue to walk around checking old fires or bones. They stood in the center of the abandoned site conversing quietly with each other.

The warrior scouts had already observed the many trails leading to the large encampment and were discussing the meaning of it. They were not pleased with what they saw and read.

Custer approached them with curiosity, Isaiah and Colby following behind him. Tom walked toward another group of Ree scouts near some wickiups. He stood with thumbs in his pockets and studied the shelter before him.

"Never," said Isaiah opening his arms out wide, "have I ever seen a Sun Dance shelter this big."

Isaiah's wizened eyes surveyed the sight. Flapping in the breeze were hundreds of rawhide straps hanging from the rafters. What he saw before his eyes proved to him that the Sioux had held one of the largest gatherings in history. He believed the Sioux would have the strongest medicine for this coming battle.

Custer stayed silent while Isaiah led him to an area that had drawings. Isaiah explained the drawings were meant for those Sioux searching for Sitting Bull's camp. It was a warning that there were soldiers coming up behind them.

Custer's eyes pierced through the scout in anger.

"They know?" his voice rumbled like the virulent growl of a dog.

Isaiah shook his head. "No, not us; someone coming from the south."

"By golly, that must be Crook's men," Custer exclaimed. A smile crossed his face and just as quickly Custer scowled and walked away. It was an expeditious change in moods and the men wondered how he could be pleased one moment and angry the next. Hadn't he just received excellent information?

Custer's mind was in frenzy. He must get to the Sioux before Crook or Crook would steal his victory. That can not happen. If Crook beat him to the Sioux, all his plans for Washington would go awry. He would not be able to go to Washington as planned.

"Mount!" Custer yelled.

"General! Wait!" Custer's brother Tom called. "You need to see this."

Tom brought Custer over to a wickiup where the Ree scouts had been lingering.

Custer observed the sweat lodge with irritation and shrugged.

"What do those drawings mean Isaiah?" he asked.

"This here circle of people depicts all the Sioux warriors. Over here you have more warriors and these, General ... are cavalry soldiers."

"And? Why are they drawn like that? What does it mean? Don't waste my time on stupid pictures."

Isaiah sighed. The scouts stood with eyes wide in astonishment. "Falling head first as these are drawn means death," Isaiah explained.

"I understand that, I'm not blind. The Sioux show my cavalry attacking their camp."

Isaiah pulled his fingers through his hair in frustration. With Custer's attitude spoiling for a fight, he would take great pleasure in shaking Custer into oblivion.

"No, it means your soldiers are dead," Isaiah said mordantly.

Custer rolled his eyes and laughed.

Walking away, he shouted, "Not me. Not my men. We're wasting precious time. Let's march!"

It was late when the warrior scouts rode into camp. They understood what the widened and scarred trail meant. Why wouldn't Custer understand that it was all one big camp instead of many small ones?

Now they have found more scalps from the recent battle along with the remnants of the celebration of their win. Maybe now Yellow Hair will comprehend the enormity of the camp they were following.

Custer held his lantern up to observe the scalps. Nodding his head, jaw clenched, he asked, "Where are they heading?"

"They are heading to the Greasy Grass, the Little Big Horn. There were many trails. The scouts say the trails are coming together and joining Sitting Bull's already large camp," Colby informed him.

"Good, now we know where they are hiding."

Isaiah cleared his throat. "They are not hiding, General. These Sioux just celebrated a victory over some soldiers. A group of soldiers that are bigger than this group. All these trails are coming together! Their emotions are ... ."

"They didn't fight my Seventh, Isaiah. They didn't fight the best regiment in the whole country. I have been given my orders. I have a job to do."

"I take it then that you are going to follow them."

Custer laughed and enthusiastically patted him on the back. "You bet I am. I'm going to follow that trail if it's the last thing I do on this earth as a soldier. We have to make sure those trails are not going away from the camp. I don't want them separating. It'll be a lot easier for us if they are all in one place."

Custer mounted his horse. Isaiah and Tom quickly followed. "General, can't you see that this is one of the largest gatherings the Sioux have ever experienced?"

"Yes, and well and good," Custer said cheerily, "then I won't have to chase them all over the place like a bunch of scared rabbits. I just hope they don't know we are coming. We're going to ride into that camp and do what our regiment does best."

"General, the Sioux are the best in battle of any tribe I know. You must understand what you are up against."

"Isaiah, don't tell me how to do my job. I know what I am to do. If we can't capture them, we will kill them. They are just Indians!" Custer spat in anger.

Watching Custer dismount, Isaiah shook his head in disgust and rode away with the other scouts following. Custer refused to see the truth.

"Tom, I want a meeting of the officers."

Custer stomped and paced in his tent. He was enraged and indignant that Isaiah actually had the gall to question his leadership abilities. He knew exactly what he was doing and he knew how to do it. This would be his last battle and then ... Washington. Custer smiled; President George Armstrong Custer did indeed have a nice ring to it.

John Colby stood in the shadows. When Isaiah was finished and Tom left to call a meeting, he entered Custer's tent.

Custer was surprised to see Colby awaiting him in his tent. Hanging his hat on a hook and showing off his shaved head, Custer haggardly faced Colby.

"What do you have to say, Colby?"

Colby pulled out his knife and started cleaning his nails. He nodded his head toward Custer's cook who was working discreetly in the background.

"Pour us some tea and then you may leave us alone, Maggie."

Maggie nodded her head and mumbled quietly, "Yes sir." Quickly she poured tea for the two men and left the tent.

"Spit it out, Colby. What say you?"

"Well sir, I think Isaiah and the other scouts are turning a bit yellow. There ain't nothing in those signs that tell me it's the largest camp ever. Nope, I think they are making it out to be worse than it is."

"Really? Why? I've known Isaiah a long, long time. It's a rare occasion indeed when that man is wrong. Never has he turned yellow before."

"You're orders come from the very top. Can't get no higher than the President of the United States. Those there orders are to take them Black Hills and get that gold for this good country of ours. Them Black Hills are sacred country to them Sioux. They don't care none about the gold. Isaiah now, he's getting a bit nervous about taking that sacred land from those Indians."

"You telling me he's lying to me?" Custer whispered with an uncharacteristic calm.

"No, not Isaiah. Isaiah and I don't quite see eye to eye but I'd never accuse him of lying. I think his eyes don't want to see the truth. He ain't lying to you on purpose. Only an idiot would accuse Isaiah of being a liar," Colby laughed.

Custer rubbed his jaw. "Hmmm, so you think Isaiah is worried about taking all those Sioux away from their land."

"Possibly. His superstitions are getting in the way of his better judgment and he just don't see it. That camp where the Indians held the Sun Dance was a big camp. I'll grant him that. But those trails ... they're leading away from the camp. That means some of them are heading out. There are just a few families here and there. They're going back to the reservations now that the Sun Dance ceremony is over."

"I don't want them splitting up on me!"

"No, General. Don't you worry about that. Most of them are still together. Like I said, just a few are heading back to the reservations."

"What about the rest of the scouts? I saw their faces when they looked at those drawings."

"I would say they pretty well agree with me. Isaiah is scaring them."

Custer squinted his eyes and Colby realized his mistake.

"Now why would Isaiah want to scare them? All of them would know how to interpret that story. None of them are stupid. That's why they were picked to be our scouts."

Colby cleared his throat. "I don't mean he intentionally is trying to scare them. He's just making it out to be bigger than it really is."

Custer nodded his head. He was tired and it had been a long day. "Enough for now. You're dismissed."

Colby left Custer's tent with a broad smile. Custer was so easy to convince and manipulate. With Custer focusing on the Sioux, he had him right where he wanted him. He'd be able to use Custer to fight the Sioux and do what Colby himself had failed to do: defeat and destroy the Sioux and that witch.

If the Sioux hadn't been so enamored by that witch, he'd be a rich man right now. He'd have all the gold he could possess and he'd have that pretty Indian piece every night, Sunshine in the Morning. Boy, he sure missed losing himself between her thighs.

Now the only way he'd get that gold was to destroy the Sioux and that witch along with them.

Oh, and he had tried. He tried burning them out by setting the prairie near their camp on fire when the warriors were on a hunt. That witch had organized a group of women and as he watched through his looking glasses, she had them burn the prairie in a wide berth to stop the fire from reaching the camp.

Then, he had sent that man with the small pox into the camp. They would all surely die from the pox. He had left knowing the camp was doomed, but they survived. He wishes he knew what kind of spell she used to save them from the deadly disease.

Maybe that couple he sent through the Black Hills will find the Sioux. He made a point to let the husband know about all that gold and the witch. Kill her, he told the husband, and you'll be the richest people in the world. The witch was a smart one, too.

He would have to keep Custer under his wing or this would backfire, as well. Colby laughed. It wouldn't be too hard to fool Custer. He'd done it during the war.

Colby lay down in his tent and laughed again. That witch was the only one who knew he'd fought for the South. Custer never even figured it out. He was a spy in Custer's regiment from the beginning. He rode back and forth to different camps throughout the entire North getting information and bringing it right back to the South.

Didn't do him any good. He still lost all of his slaves and his estate. As Colby dozed off into an un-restful slumber, his last thoughts were of finding gold and being a prominent citizen again.

The lodge was filled with tension. The dark-haired woman stared at the warriors and the woman as they bustled about in the bright lodge. She couldn't understand what they were saying, but could tell that all in the lodge were quite concerned about the witch lying on the buffalo mat.

"We will have to take the bullet out," Sitting Bull told Standing Deer.

"Can you see it?" Crazy Horse asked.

"Yes. Just barely! I'll cut around the wound and hold it open while you dig it out."

"Sings to the Wind, heat some water and get us strips of cloth to bind the wound," Crazy Horse ordered.

Sings to the Wind scurried about quickly preparing for the expulsion of the bullet. Standing Deer knelt at his wife's feet while he watched Crazy Horse and Sitting Bull.

Sitting Bull moved above Spirit of the Mountain's head while he cut incisions around the wound. Crazy Horse, sitting on her right side, soaked up the blood so he could see the bullet. The heated water was placed strategically next to him.

Slowly and carefully, with steady hands, Crazy Horse dug the bullet out of Spirit of the Mountain's right shoulder. Standing Deer grabbed her feet while Sitting Bull held her shoulders. Screaming, she balked like a raving buffalo bull.

Sitting Bull stuffed her mouth with cloth to muffle the screams as Standing Deer and Sitting Bull continued to hold Spirit of the Mountain down. Crazy Horse meticulously dug pieces of her deerskin dress out of the wound.

Sings to the Wind brought more heated water to the two medicine men. Together the men cleansed the wound. Silently, Sitting Bull leaned over and reached for his medicine bag.

Standing Deer had been holding his breath and was trying to keep himself calm. If anyone could save his wife, it was Sitting Bull and Crazy Horse. He prayed and watched in silence.

"The bleeding has slowed down. Should we cauterize it?" Sitting Bull asked Crazy Horse.

Crazy Horse shook his head no. Sitting Bull reached for his needle and thread, gifts from Spirit of the Mountain. He never believed he would be using them on her. Crazy Horse prepared a poultice while Sitting Bull closed the wound and left a small hole for drainage.

Sings to the Wind handed them the scraps of fabric after Crazy Horse applied the poultice. Hands shaking, she assisted them while they wrapped the wound in strips of cloths.

"We'll be back to check on her. Give her this to drink when she awakens. It will ease her pain," Crazy Horse instructed.

Chapter TWENTY-FIVE

Shaken by the tragedy before her, Sings to the Wind looked at Standing Deer with tears streaming out of her eyes. Feelings of anger, guilt, fear and pain overwhelmed her as she blamed herself for Spirit of the Mountain's misfortune.

"I've always thought of her as being invincible. Why in the world didn't she stay behind like you told her?" Sings to the Wind asked as she sobbed uncontrollably between gasps of breath.

"I don't know ... it all happened so fast. The woman" (pointing to the silent white captive sitting quietly against the wall of the lodge) "was fighting with her husband. It appears he was trying to kill her. When she saw us she started screaming. Before any of us realized bullets flew, Spirit of the Mountain took the bullet that was meant for me."

Sings to the Wind reached over to cool Spirit of the Mountain's forehead with a wet cloth. She felt helpless. Was there something else she could do to help her friend?

"We've been through too much together. I can't lose her now. I didn't tell her I was sorry."

"She's strong. We won't lose her," Standing Deer reassured her.

"Too much is happening in the village right now. I ask that you stay with the captive for me. Find out what you can from her. There'll be a meeting tonight. I'm not sure what should be done so I will ask the elders and we will decide then what to do with her," Standing Deer said as he kissed his wife on the cheek. Then he left.

Sings to the Wind looked at her dearest friend. I need you … don't die on me. She cried deep inside. How could you have been so stupid! What in the world made you take a bullet?

It was all her fault. She's the one who convinced Karen to come back all those years ago. If she hadn't been so nosy, her closest friend wouldn't be dying from a bullet wound. We've been through too much. It's been over eleven years since this life we have led with the Sioux began.

Eleven beautiful wonderful years since you were given the name Spirit of the Mountain. How could I chide myself for encouraging you to follow your heart? These have been the best years of our lives. They had grown and learned so much over the years.

Her friend had teased her for years calling her a Bible thumper. She could quote the Bible with the best of them. It wasn't until she lived with the Hunkpapa that she understood the meaning and teachings of the Bible. They had taught her more in their simple ways by living their day-to-day lives. The Earth and land were a gift from the Creator as well as all of its creatures. Everything has a life and a spirit. They were all placed on this Earth by a higher power to be treated with reverence. Things she had taken for granted, they taught her to appreciate it all.

Sings to the Wind continued to administer to Spirit of the Mountain with the cool cloth. She looked at her dear friend with love and concern. Even etched with signs of pain on her face she was a beautiful woman.

Spirit of the Mountain was a few years short of forty and didn't look a day over thirty. She wondered if their adventure through time had anything to do with it. She was three years younger, yet looked five years older than her friend did. She smiled. Some people had the luck.

Sings to the Wind had chosen not to travel back and forth. Two Feathers had become her husband, filling her life with precious memories. It had just been a few years ago when she had made the decision to stay in this world.

"Excuse me, I need to relieve myself," the captive said, interrupting Sings to the Wind's deep thoughts.

Sings to the Wind noted the cultured and well-spoken southern accent. Slowly, she looked over to the woman who was now standing near the entrance of the lodge with her hands and feet still tied together. Her dress was a pale yellow silk with an abundance of petticoats underneath; a gown that a very well-bred southern belle would wear to a debutante ball.

It was quite inappropriate attire to be traveling across the country. She looked more like she belonged on a huge southern estate. Sings to the Wind laughed to herself. She was the epitome of one of those women who work at Cypress Gardens in Florida.

Sings to the Wind untied her feet and showed the woman the appropriate place to relieve herself. She used hand motions and explained in Lakota that there were certain areas to relieve oneself and how to take care of it.

When they arrived back to the lodge, Sings to the Wind had the woman sit by the fire so she could tend to the wounds on her face.

Her hair was black as a crow, tied back in a twisted matronly bun. It was fastened so tight it looked as if it hurt. The woman couldn't have been older than twenty. Her husband had done a good job on her face. Both eyes were marked and swollen with a long purple bruise extending along the side of her jaw. Sings to the Wind shook her head in disgust.

"Disgusting," she said in Lakota.

The woman flinched as she dabbed at a cut near her eye.

"Sorry," Sings to the Wind said in English, then cursed herself for the slip.

"You speak English. Thank God, someone who can understand me."

"Surprised? You shouldn't be."

"You're an Indian," the woman said with an air of arrogance.

"No, actually I'm not ... not by blood anyway. I'm an American. I was born and raised in Massachusetts. Boston to be exact. Do I look Indian?" Sings to the Wind asked with a smile.

"Well," she tilted her head, "you're dressed like one. And your coloring looks Indian but your hair is a light brown. Not dark like an Indian's. You speak their language quite well from the way it sounded to me ... how long have you been a slave?"

Sings to the Wind laughed. "If you promise not to do anything rash or suicidal, I'll untie your hands. Do not leave the lodge without Standing Deer's knowledge nor mine. Understand?"

The woman nodded her head in agreement while Sings to the Wind unbound her hands.

"My husband is Hunkpapa, Sioux. The Sioux don't keep slaves. Never have, but they do take captives. Other tribes that are here in this village take slaves though."

"What will they do to me?"

"Anything they want. You are their captive, we're in the middle of the Indian Wars. What were you and your husband thinking when you came into Sioux Territory unprotected? That's practically asking for the death sentence."

Sings to the Wind rolled her eyes when the woman clucked her tongue and sniffed.

"Well, I am an American citizen and they must let me go unharmed. Besides, if that witch hadn't killed my husband ... I ... ."

"Would be dead," said Sings to the Wind. "Listen, lady ... ."

"Christine."

"Christine, this is war, not a game of croquette. You don't have a choice in what the council decides. You would be dead because your loving husband was going to kill you. The two of you were stupid enough to ride into Sioux Territory when there is bloodshed and fighting from both sides. You can't tell me that you had no idea of the risk you were taking."

Sings to the Wind moved over to Spirit of the Mountain and put a thermometer in her mouth.

"They do not have to set you free. They can trade you to another tribe member or sell you. They can keep you here to marry one of the Sioux ... if someone is interested. Or possibly someone might offer to take you in to help care for one of their elderly. They may even use you to trade with the American soldiers at the fort to get back one of their warriors."

"Once I've been touched and smirched by one of those Indians, no good decent man would want me. I'd be better off dead!" Christine yelled.

"Well, Christine, they're probably just as nauseated and repulsed by the thought of touching you as you are of them. It is extremely fortunate that your hair is so dark and your coloring is dark. That is an advantage for you at this point."

Sings to the Wind looked at the thermometer and grumbled to herself. Spirit of the Mountain's temperature was going up instead of down.

"You are Standing Deer's captive, he will have a strong vote on what to do with you. Chances are, he will vote to have you stay in the village. It would be safer, considering what is coming. If not, then you will probably be sold, traded or brought back to the fort. Then you can start worrying about being used and abused as a whore, depending on who gets you … or which fort." Sings to the Wind's voice was dripping with sarcasm as she spoke those last words.

Christine looked at Sings to the Wind with hatred and anger dashing through her dark eyes.

"I will have to stay with a filthy savage as his woman?" Then, pointing to Spirit of the Mountain, "That witch is a murderer. She killed my husband."

Sitting Bull walked into the lodge to check on Spirit of the Mountain and was greeted by a high-pitched, curdling scream. Sitting Bull jumped in alarm. With a perfect stone face, he told Sings to the Wind that he usually didn't have that effect on women, maybe he was starting to look like a bull.

Sings to the Wind started laughing.

"What's so funny?" Christine pouted, and then frowned when Sings to the Wind explained what Sitting Bull had said.

"He scared me. He just walked right in unannounced!"

Sings to the Wind laughed again, "That's because the outer flap is open. It's a sign to those in the village that the lodge is open to anyone to enter. If the flap was closed he would have called out to us and waited until we responded to enter."

"Oh, how civilized," Christine replied with sarcasm.

"Why do you keep calling Spirit of the Mountain a witch? And, by the way, believe me when I tell you that Standing Deer does not want you as his woman."

Christine looked at Sings to the Wind cautiously and then watched Sitting Bull tend to the injured woman lying on the buffalo mat.

"My husband and I met this man in Yankton while we were traveling with the wagon train. He had told us the best place to go was north of the Black Hills. He convinced my husband that there was an abundance of gold to be found. The man showed my husband the best route to take and we separated from the wagon train and came this way."

Christine breathed in a sigh of resignation. "My husband was warned numerous times about a witch who lived among the Sioux and that if we saw her to kill her instantly or death would come to us."

Pointing to Spirit of the Mountain Christine continued, "The man described her."

Christine stared at Sitting Bull in horror when he growled.

Sings to the Wind held Spirit of the Mountain up while Sitting Bull undid her wrappings. He arched his eyebrows and wished the woman would continue to speak.

"Please continue with your story. Do you know this man's name?" Sings to the Wind encouraged.

"Yes, I think it was Colby. He said she had magical powers, like a witch. She had the Sioux under her spell and they would do anything she wanted because her witchery was strong."

Sitting Bull started laughing and covered it by clearing his throat and coughing. He did not want the woman, Christine, to know who he was or that he understood her language. If the white woman had only seen or heard some of the heated discussions Spirit of the Mountain was capable of stirring, she would know that Spirit of the Mountain did not always get her way.

"My husband was offered a reward if we killed her and brought proof of her death. We were told she was wicked and played with the devil himself."

Sings to the Wind's mouth dropped open in astonishment.

"Wakansica? Witkotkoka." The devil? The fool! Sitting Bull whispered shaking his head back and forth.

"Why would you trust your lives to a complete stranger? He sent you on the worst path to travel through the west. I can't comprehend why you would leave the safety of the wagon train."

"The man was kind and helped us. My husband wasn't happy with the leader of the wagon train since someone robbed us. They stole all my supply of laudanum, our money and killed my father. He helped my husband find a new supply of laudanum for me."

Tears filled Christine's eyes as she recalled seeing the body of her father lying under the wagon. When they rolled the body over a large gaping hole showed where the shotgun fatally wounded him in the chest. Whoever had done it had shoved her father under the wagon.

"He helped us. I was so grateful. You must understand that I need my laudanum. What were we to do without money or gold? How were we to survive? He was honest, told us the safest way to travel, and warned us that the Indians used human sacrifices. He said that woman was the worst one of all of them."

Sings to the Wind's mind whirled. Christine needed laudanum. There's no way she would survive in the wilderness if she were addicted to the drug. Already horrified and appalled by Christine's story, Sings to the Wind gasped in shock from the last statement.

"They don't use human sacrifices! That's disgusting!"

Sitting Bull quickly stood and explained to Sings to the Wind that the wound had stopped bleeding and he'd decided to leave it unwrapped.

Hearing the acerbic words of the white captive put him in a furious temper. Why was this white man, Colby, telling such lies about the great and honorable Lakota? They had never used human sacrifices. Such human defilement was an ignominy to the People and the Great Spirit. How does this man claim to know so much about Spirit of the Mountain? And why does he keep referring to her as a witch?

His questions increased as he continued to his lodge. He will speak in her favor to keep her here, temporarily. He wanted to find out more information. Sitting Bull wanted answers to the strange accusations of the Lakota. He had reluctantly taken the position of War Chief, now he not only had to defend his land and family, but he must defend the honor of his Nation from more lies told by white men.

Sings to the Wind knew there was an unbelievable amount of prejudice against the Indians during this time period, but to make up lies to instill ultimate fear was ridiculous. No wonder the American people were afraid of the Indian Nations. People were escalating fears of the unknown and expounding on them.

Christine continued to babble on about the disgusting, savage Indians. Her attitude didn't stop with just the Indians, it included all men as well. Tired of her vitriolic attitude, Sings to the Wind was using all of her inner restraint not to slap the woman in the mouth with the back of her hand.

If Christine were going to be staying with the Lakota, or any of the other bands, she would be humbled soon enough. There was no need for her to make things worse by exploding in anger.

"Oh, please stop. They are good, honest and loving people," Sings to the Wind said quietly.

"What?" Christine yelled exasperated. "They scalp people and rape women, steal horses … . They allow that woman to stay in their village. How can you say they are good and honest people? They're heathens. That savage left my husband to rot in the sun. He didn't even get a decent burial."

"Just stop right there. One, the Dutch taught the American Indians all about scalping hundreds of years ago. Two, all sick men rape women. It doesn't have anything to do with color or nationality. Three, the soldiers also steal horses and scalp warriors. They have raped women, as well. This is war. A

Sioux will not steal from a Sioux, it is against their laws. And last but definitely not least, Spirit of the Mountain is a doctor, with a college degree. Not a witch."

"They kill our people," Christine exclaimed, ignoring the statement that Spirit of the Mountain was a doctor. "Doesn't that upset you?"

"The white man steals their land! There's a treaty that states this land is theirs and will be theirs until the rivers run dry. Yet, they come to take it anyway. Of course, it upsets me. Sometimes I feel as if I'm being pulled in two directions. But a treaty is a treaty and should be kept as promised. I can't stop the war."

Sings to the Wind continued, "If the Americans would stay out of Sioux Territory and stop digging in the Sacred Hills, then there wouldn't be a war. The Indians would not fight with America but would live in peace among themselves on their land. This is all that they wish."

"A treaty? There was a treaty granting this land to the Indians?"

"Yes, and now the government wants to break the treaty and take the land away from the Sioux because of the gold found in the Black Hills."

"Oh," Christine exclaimed. "I didn't know."

Sings to the Wind bathed Spirit of the Mountain with a cool cloth being careful not to get any water near the wound. "I can probably arrange to have your husband buried properly, would that make you happy?"

"Yes," Christine sighed, "even the worst of husbands deserve a decent burial."

Sings to the Wind chose not to pursue Christine's comment about her husband. She got up and called out to one of the children to find Two Feathers for her. When her husband arrived, she'd pass on Christine's request for her husband.

Moments later Two Feathers arrived. Christine exited the lodge with Sings to the Wind. Seeing only one extra horse for herself, she panicked.

Scared, she quickly turned to Sings to the Wind. "You are not going? I'm not going anywhere alone with these heathens."

"Quit being so ungrateful. This is my husband, Two Feathers. This is Spirit of the Mountain's son, Big Eyes, and you have met Standing Deer."

"I'm not going without you."

Exasperated, Sings to the Wind sighed. This woman was going to drive her mad. If this war wasn't so important to Two Feathers, she wouldn't have to be dealing with this woman. They would be living in her world where it was safe.

"I am heavy with child. I am not going. This is my first baby and I'm not going to take the chance of losing it because of your fears. You are either going to go with them or your husband will not be buried. They will not harm you."

Not waiting for a reply, Sings to the Wind turned and walked back into the lodge to continue her vigil with Spirit of the Mountain. When she heard the horses gallop away she relaxed. That woman had a lot to learn. She could definitely understand her fears, especially with all the propaganda in the newspapers.

Sings to the Wind lay down next to Spirit of the Mountain and caressed her swollen belly. She dozed with a gentle smile on her lips. If Christine had only known what they all had been through. So much ... so many memories ... .

Chapter TWENTY-SIX

"Bonnie," Spirit of the Mountain called out hoarsely. "Bonnie?"

Sings to the Wind, in the depths of a light slumber, wasn't sure if she had heard her friend's voice. Her half-closed eyes looked warily over to the injured woman.

"How do you feel?"

"I'm thirsty. Water, please."

Sings to the Wind nodded her head. Slowly she balanced herself holding her swollen belly as she curled into a stretch before getting unsteadily to her feet. Moving over to Spirit of the Mountain's left shoulder, she placed her arm behind her neck and helped her friend sit up.

Spirit of the Mountain drank the water. Gasping from pain, the injured woman slurped the water as quickly as possible. Sings to the Wind gently laid her friend back down.

"I was hit, wasn't I?"

"Yes, you were. Why didn't you use your kinetic ability? Why didn't you stay back like Standing Deer told you?"

Spirit of the Mountain flinched when she shrugged her shoulders. "I don't know. I just reacted. Is the bullet still in?"

"No. Sitting Bull and Crazy Horse worked together and took it out immediately. Your fever is increasing."

"There's infection. I feel as if I'm floating in air and burning in the fires of hell."

"Save your strength. I'll be right back."

Spirit of the Mountain nodded her head and was back in a fitful sleep before Sings to the Wind made it to the flap of the lodge.

Looking about she spied a group of boys playing hoops.

"Is Sitting Bull or Crazy Horse in the village?" she called.

Young Black Elk answered, "Tatanka Iyotanka, sha. Wakpa ekta un." Sitting Bull, yes. He is at the river.

"Thank you. Can you get him for me? Also, if you see Prairie Flower, will you tell her that her mother is awake? She will want to know."

The young spry Black Elk nodded his head and ran to the river to alert Sitting Bull. Several women from the village saw Sings to the Wind and came over to inquire about Spirit of the Mountain, all offering to relieve Sings to the Wind and assist as much as they can. Thanking them and assuring them she would be needing assistance and would let them know, she entered the lodge again.

Sings to the Wind sat quietly next to Spirit of the Mountain as she stitched new moccasins for the baby.

"Where ... where is Standing Deer?" Spirit of the Mountain croaked.

Sings to the Wind grabbed a wet cloth and started cooling her friend's face. Spirit of the Mountain's eyes were bloodshot and full of tears.

"He will be back soon. He is helping to bury the white man."

Spirit of the Mountain smiled and closed her eyes for a few moments.

"That is kind of him. I wish I knew who it was that sent him to the village."

For a few minutes, Spirit of the Mountain laid so restfully that Sings to the Wind thought she had fallen back to sleep.

"Who would be crazy or foolish enough to send someone into an Indian village when they knew the person had small pox? They must have known what would happen." Spirit of the Mountain asked Sings to the Wind.

"What?" the confused Sings to the Wind asked. That happened over five years ago. Just a moment ago, her friend had been lucid.

"Did we make it back in time to inoculate everyone? I hope we made the right decision. Too many Sioux were dying."

Sitting Bull entered the lodge and Spirit of the Mountain smiled at her friend.

"Kola," friend. "Did you finish 'Taming of the Shrew,' are you ready for 'Hamlet' yet?" Spirit of the Mountain asked Sitting Bull as she fell back to sleep.

Sitting Bull smiled at Spirit of the Mountain with concern in his eyes as he inspected her wounds. Those were the first two Shakespearean books he had read ... so long ago when she had taught him to read.

"She's been talking about the past for just a few moments. She was coherent when she first woke up," Sings to the Wind informed Sitting Bull.

Sitting Bull cleaned out the used poultice and replaced it with a stronger poultice he had made earlier.

"What has she been talking about?"

"The time when that man with small pox came into the Sioux village looking for Spirit of the Mountain to heal him."

"Yes, I remember that time. We lost many lives to that disease. She saved many lives. I remember the guilt she felt because the man said he was looking for her. Spirit of the Mountain believed she was responsible for the deaths of the People because she had not been here when the man arrived at the camp."

"She asked me why someone would intentionally send a dying man into the village."

"I think it might have been another way for the white man to try and kill us all. It was around the same time we found signs that someone had intentionally started the fire in the prairie. The whole village could have gone up in flames if she hadn't reacted as she did. I also recall Spirit of the Mountain saying that she believed it was intentional."

"What you say is true. But I believe they are separate occurrences," Sings to the Wind said. Sitting Bull nodded in agreement and waited for Sings to the Wind to continue.

"For years the white man have been killing the buffalo for their tongues and hide, leaving them to rot. The buffalo are hard to find now. This is intentional. They know that we need the buffalo to survive. They are trying to starve us to death. Just another way to annihilate the People."

Sitting Bull nodded in agreement, "I agree. But also, a while back Spirit of the Mountain told me she believed someone was trying to get to her. She evinced that some of the tragedies that have happened to the Lakota should not have happened. Now that I have heard what this white woman has been saying, I think Spirit of the Mountain is right. They are not just trying to kill off the People, someone is out there who personally wants to kill her."

Sitting Bull was concerned. Sings to the Wind and Spirit of the Mountain should not feel guilt because of the white man's avaricious nature. The question is who is this Colby person and why has he a vendetta against Spirit of the Mountain? This man is a very sick and dangerous person indeed.

Prairie Flower entered the lodge and silently sat down next to Sings to the Wind.

"Go and take some rest for yourself," Sitting Bull gently ordered. "Prairie Flower is here to help. I'm going to give Spirit of the Mountain some tea that will fight the infection and help her sleep. I will stay with her for a while."

Eyes filled with tears, Sings to the Wind nodded her head. "Sitting Bull, all whites do not want the Indians dead. There are people who are trying to help, fighting for the rights of the Indian."

"I know. Do not fill your heart with guilt for something you cannot control. Go. Get some rest."

"Tahinca Nazinpi?" Standing Deer? Spirit of the Mountain looked around, eyes blazing with fever.

"He will be back soon, my friend. Let me give you some tea, you need to rest."

"I must find him. I must tell him I was wrong!" With tears forming in her eyes, she took Sitting Bull's hand, "James Black Elk ... he told me I was fighting the will of the Great Spirit. I must tell Standing Deer about our son."

"He will be back soon. You can tell him then. Drink some tea and rest."

She was reliving her return to the village after the baby was born, ten years ago. Sitting Bull recalled the conversation as if it was only yesterday.

Spirit of the Mountain had taken what she called a "job" as a reservation doctor in South Dakota and had met a very wise man by the name of James Black Elk, who had taken her under his wing. Although James did not understand everything at the time, with his guidance and "Sings to the Wind's nagging," Spirit of the Mountain had finally realized she could not run away from her life the Great Spirit had so carefully chosen for her.

She came back to the village in search of Standing Deer, willing to try to make their relationship work. It had pleased the People of the Lakota to see her return. Sitting Bull smiled to himself as he recalled the times when he had counseled them. It had felt as if he was in the middle of a battle with two mountain lions.

Prairie Flower started crying. Her mother was dying, she was talking gibberish. Prairie Flower felt helpless.

Sitting Bull held the crying child in his arms murmuring words of comfort. Spirit of the Mountain looked at the child without recognition. Obviously the child belonged to one of Sitting Bull's friends, someone she hadn't met yet. She wondered idly why the child was so bereaved.

"How would you like to help me?" Sitting Bull asked the distraught child. When Prairie Flower nodded her head in agreement, Sitting Bull reached over to his pouch.

"I need some more of these herbs. There are some plants to the northwest of the river. They will help heal your mother. Bring a warrior with you when you leave camp."

Sitting Bull put a cold compress on Spirit of the Mountain's forehead as Prairie Flower was leaving the lodge.

"Drink some more tea, my friend."

Laying her back down on the buffalo mat, Sitting Bull held her hand while she fell into a light sleep. He closed his eyes and silently prayed. He was tired and as he leaned forward, he could feel himself falling into a light sleep.

Sitting Bull felt as if he was floating. It was a languorous feeling as if he was being carried by the wind under the wings of an eagle. It was an unusual sensation. He felt disoriented as he opened his eyes. The sight stunned Sitting Bull. The walls of the lodge were strange. They were blue and not like that of Standing Deer's lodge. They were different and had pictures of eagles on them. Looking down he saw that he was on a white man's bed. Against the strange walls of this chimerical lodge were tables, a bureau with a chair next to it and many books. There were so many books! As he surveyed his surroundings, he saw there was an opening but he could not see where it led.

Next to him on a table was an odd piece with a strange-looking coiled rope-like cord that was attached to it. He looked closer and saw numbers written on it and a blinking red light.

Sitting Bull closed his eyes, trying to understand this heretical vision. When he opened them again, he looked around and found he was back in Standing Deer's lodge. The chimerical vision was gone as quickly as it had come.

Sitting Bull concentrated on the meaning of the strange vision and what it could possibly mean. Why were there white man's furnishings in an Indian lodge? Could it be a vision from the Great Spirit warning him that the white man is going to take over their world? Regardless of what the Lakota try to do?

Standing Deer walked into the lodge with the white woman and pointed to a corner to instruct her to sit there. Christine's arms were full, as she had carried as much as she possibly could.

Quietly she dropped the contents in her arms onto the floor of the lodge, sat herself down and stared at the two men as they spoke with each other in their native tongue. She was at the mercy of these two heathens. Hopefully, if she stayed very quiet they would ignore and not touch her. She did not believe that these men did not have ulterior motives. Didn't all men want just one thing?

She looked at the woman asleep on the buffalo mat and out of the corner of her eye noticed Standing Deer's moccasins. The woman gasped in shock. The two men quickly turned and looked at her to see why she was so dismayed.

Christine quickly looked down to avoid their eyes. The moccasins were sewn by a machine! There had to be a reasonable explanation. Where would he have access to a sewing machine in this savage land? Maybe that woman Sings to the Wind had them made for him. Or possibly had them sent from her family in Boston. That was probably it. She had said she was a guest in the village and she had family in Boston.

"She has been asking for you," Sitting Bull told Standing Deer. "Her fever seems to be breaking but she is speaking of the past, my friend. She speaks of the time when the white man's disease came into the village."

Standing Deer could see there was something else on Sitting Bull's mind. He waited patiently for a few minutes until Sitting Bull finally spoke again.

"When I was sitting here with Spirit of the Mountain, I saw a strange vision. I was in a white man's bed with white man's furnishing around me. On these walls of blue there were many eagles, pictures of eagles. And books, I have never seen so many books. There was an opening but I could not see beyond to what was there. The walls were like that of a lodge, but different. There were many pictures of eagles on these walls." Sitting Bull shook his head in confusion and frowned.

"I have thought hard and looked deep in my heart but cannot fully understand what it means. Or maybe I don't want to accept what it means."

Standing Deer put his hand up in the air to stop Sitting Bull from talking. It was an unusual movement, normally taken as bad manners.

"When did you have this vision?"

Puzzled by the interruption and the question, Sitting Bull answered promptly, "Just about two hours ago, I was holding

Spirit of the Mountain's hand and felt myself floating as if I was soaring under the wings of an eagle."

Smiling, Standing Deer nodded his head in understanding. "You have gone and had a swift visit into Spirit of the Mountain's world."

"I would like to see more of her world but I believe Crazy Horse was right. I would not want to know what she knows. We must thank the Great Spirit for bringing her to us. She has done well and has protected us and cared for us through many tragedies over the years. I am proud to call her sister."

"She is proud to call you brother," Standing Deer replied.

"Standing Deer?" Spirit of the Mountain called out in English. "Where are you?"

"I am here my love, beside you."

"What? I don't understand your language. Speak English until I can learn more."

Christine's head bolted up in surprise and fear as she stared at the three in front of her. They knew English?

Sitting Bull looked over to Christine to see her reaction and then at Standing Deer. The woman's eyes were wide with fear.

Spirit of the Mountain had been fluent in their language for many years and with the help of the Hunkpapa had taught her children, Big Eyes and Prairie Flower, how to speak it.

"You must speak our tongue, my love."

"No, no. I don't understand what you are saying. I just know the few words that Laughing Flower and Sunshine in the Morning taught me. Where's the baby? How long have I been sick?"

"You need to rest, my love. Go back to sleep," Standing Deer continued to speak in Lakota.

Sitting Bull shook his head. She was getting worse. He leaned over and touched Standing Deer's arm. "You can stay here an extra day instead of leaving with the camp tomorrow. It may not be wise to move her."

"No," Standing Deer shook his head. "We will travel with the camp tomorrow. It is only a half days journey to our final resting camp on the Little Big Horn."

Standing Deer looked down at his beloved wife and remembered how hard she had tried to save Laughing Flower's life. She had cried unfettered tears when Laughing Flower went into the arms of the Great Spirit. She had begged for Two Feather's forgiveness.

It was Laughing Flower who had originally found the man with the small pox. She was filling the buffalo bladders with water when he had gone to the river. According to Laughing Flower, he was going to bathe in the river. She had seen the sores on his body and grabbed his arm to stop him from entering and polluting the water with his apparently diseased skin. She could see the man was seriously ill and did not want him to contaminate their water supply.

She grabbed his arm and pulled him away from the river. The man tried to resist her. Laughing Flower fell on top of him in the excursion. As they scrambled to get up, he had asked her if she knew where he could find Spirit of the Mountain. He had informed her that he was told to seek her and he would be healed.

That dreadful moment started a tragic legacy of death throughout the village. The warriors had been away battling the buffalo hunters and their camps. When the warriors had come home, they had arrived to death in their village. Soon after, Red Cloud had put his war ropes away and split the Sioux in two. It seemed at the time that everywhere one walked there was tragedy.

As time continued and the battles increased, Sitting Bull and the Sioux Nation became increasingly outraged by the presence of the whites in the Black Hills. Everyone knew they would eventually be forced onto reservations. If only in their minds they would continue tradition. From the time of the small pox epidemic to the present, the Lakota fought the inevitable. Unfortunately, most knew this time was marked and it was an end of their old ways of life.

Now as Sitting Bull stood outside of Standing Deer's lodge and scanned the multiple camps sites surrounding him, he saw that they were strong and his spirit felt strong. There were almost eight thousand people in his camp. All were going to the Little Big Horn.

Chapter TWENTY-SEVEN

Sings to the Wind watched as Christine finished unpacking and organizing her possessions in the lodge. Christine had been surprisingly helpful and pleasant throughout the last leg of the journey. It seemed that just in the few days they had been together a different, almost chimerical person was budding. Christine had laughed at herself and her own clumsiness as she had assisted Sunshine in the Morning while they put Standing Deer's lodge together.

While she changed Spirit of the Mountain's bandages, Sings to the Wind wondered what caused the transformation in Christine's attitude. Christine's temperament was as astonishing as Spirit of the Mountain's miraculous recovery. Already she was sitting up and patiently waiting for Sings to the Wind to finish wrapping her shoulder and chest.

"Okay, Doc, all set," Sings to the Wind said in English.

"Why, thank you, my good nurse."

Christine smiled at the two women. She had silently observed as practically the whole tribe had come to the lodge and asked about the injured woman. It was obvious that the woman was well-respected and loved by the People. How could that man have been so wrong? Could he have lied? Why would he have lied?

"Would you like some tea?" Christine asked Spirit of the Mountain as she started to put away some papers.

"Yes, thank you. What is that? Is it a newspaper?"

"Oh, no. They're Scientific American ... ."

"Scientific American? Can we read them?" Spirit of the Mountain was filled with effervescence. Someone had something to read in the village.

"Sure, here. They're about a year old. Anything worth reading is hard to come by, so I've saved them."

While the two women hungrily consumed the contents of the "magazines" Christine heated some water. She completely understood the need to read even though they were from March and May of 1875.

"Spirit of the Mountain, do you want some laudanum in your tea to help with the pain?" Christine offered.

Wide-eyed, Spirit of the Mountain stared at the woman and quickly recovered from the shock of the question. "No, thank you. Why in the world do you have laudanum?"

"It numbs the pain and helps me sleep." Christine replied.

"It's addictive. You do know that, right?"

"I only use it when I have to. Besides, I must make it last a long time if I am to stay here." Christine handed the tea to both women. Startled by a noise, Christine moved away from the women and stood transfixed with her head bowed.

A dark shadow fell across the entrance of the lodge as Standing Deer stood smiling in the doorway. Kneeling next to his wife, Standing Deer kissed her gently on the cheek. After speaking their customary endearing words to one another, he inquired in Lakota about Christine's comment about staying in the village.

"Standing Deer wants to know if you wish to stay."

Blushing, Christine continued looking down, acting submissive and emasculated. The change in personality was stunning to the women. One moment she was happy and animated, yet now she stood like a trained slave.

Christine nodded her head as if she was afraid to speak.

"We can arrange it if you would like," Spirit of the Mountain encouraged, eyeing her warily.

"It doesn't have to be here in this lodge. Perhaps I could stay with an old woman and help her with whatever she may need," was her quiet, subdued response.

"Little Red Hawk has expressed a strong desire for her. He wants her as a wife," Standing Deer whispered to Spirit of the Mountain.

"There is a young man who is interested in taking you as his wife."

Tears stung Christine's eyes. Her lips and hands trembled in fear as she backed away and stood with her head downward, leaning as close to the wall of the lodge as she possibly could.

"It will be fine for you. He is a good warrior. You won't have a problem fitting in, Christine. You have an exotic beauty and grace. Your hair is straight and black, your skin tone dark. You look Indian."

The woman looked as if she was going to faint. Spirit of the Mountain whispered to Standing Deer, asking if he minded letting them speak with Christine alone. She explained how her behavior had been happy and serene until he had arrived. It was then that her behavior had become quite obsequious and servile. Spirit of the Mountain was going to get to the bottom of this sudden change in personality. Standing Deer agreed as he acknowledged the woman cowering against the wall.

The moment Standing Deer left the lodge, Christine sat down and cried unfettered tears. It took Sings to the Wind a half-hour to coax Christine away from the wall of the lodge.

"Talk to us, Christine. What is it? What has you so upset and worried?" Sings to the Wind spoke quietly, as if to a small child.

"I can't. I can't do it all again." Christine looked at the two of them pleading for them to understand. Then it all came rushing out as if a bottle had burst before their very eyes.

"I was married for four years. It was awful. It wasn't like my parent's marriage at all. I was young when my mother died. I don't ever recall my father being cruel to my mother at all. I'm eighteen now and I know I should be married but it's awful. I'd rather be an old maid. Marriage is the worst kind of torture. I don't know how the two of you can do it."

She shook her head in dismay. "You look at your husbands with love. The marital bed is the worst part of it all. It is so painful and disgusting. It hurts so bad that I scream. That is why my husband gave me the laudanum. That's why I need the laudanum and I still bled every time we had relations. You can't even tell me you enjoy it!"

Spirit of the Mountain raised her right eyebrow but didn't interrupt. She was afraid it would stop the torrent of anguish coming out of Christine.

"Besides, I can't have children. Who in their right mind would want to marry someone who can't give them babies? My husband used to curse at me all the time and tell me how useless I was because I could not give him any children."

Silence sliced through the air like a machete. No one spoke for a long, attenuated time. Neither one of the women quite knew what to say.

"Please understand. I like being my own person. These last few days have been accelerating. I feel as if I can be myself and not worry about it. Except of course, when the Indian men come in the lodge. I don't have to worry about my husband approving or disapproving of anything I do or say," Christine sobbed uncontrollably.

"Every month I will have to hide myself again from everyone because of the punishment I will receive for having my monthly and not giving my husband a child. I do not want another husband who will beat me and accuse me of being worthless. I do not want to be punished for something I have no control over. If I'm to be a slave to someone, can't it be an old woman that would need me more? Please?"

Christine sobbed unsuppressed tears as Sings to the Wind cradled her in her arms as she would a small child.

"Poor child," Sings to the Wind comforted, "you will not be a slave. Little Red Hawk wants you as his wife, not his slave. He will treat you with love and kindness. He would never hit you. It would bring him shame and dishonor to do so."

Christine looked into Sings to the Wind's eyes with disbelief.

"You do not know that he would not beat me. I would shame him for not bearing him children."

"But we do know that he would not beat you. It is one of the worst ignominies that exist," Sings to the Wind repeated passionately.

"How do you know you are barren? Could it possibly have been your husband who could not give you children?" Spirit of the Mountain asked quietly.

Christine looked at Spirit of the Mountain in wide-eyed disbelief. "I never considered that it might be him. He was always so sure that it was me. He was intensely supercilious about the fact that I could not produce children."

"I suppose he wasn't very gentle in marital relations with you either." Sings to the Wind commented acerbically.

Looking down and wiping her eyes on the cloth Sings to the Wind had given her, Christine took a deep breath.

"Well, the first part of it wasn't that bad, except when I had to wait on my knees while he finished his drink in the parlor. But it was always what he called the grand finale that hurt so much."

Anger pounded in Spirit of the Mountain's head. "On your knees?" she growled.

"Of course, don't you do that?"

"No!" both women replied acerbically.

"He said it was all part of my wifely duties. At the end of the night he would send me to my room. I knelt next to the bed and waited for him to come up. If I wasn't kneeling when he entered my room ... I would have to face the repercussions."

In shame, Christine covered her tear-streaked face. "I remember the first time he did it. I regurgitated on the new carpet in my room. Then came the 'grand finale.' I screamed so loud he started beating me on the head with his fist while he held my stomach with his other hand."

Christine closed her eyes wincing from the painful memory. Her voice was variegated and hoarse. "I bled profusely. The next day I had a hard time relieving myself. Please, please you must understand. I would rather die."

"I believe, Christine that your husband was a very sick man. That is not what marriage is all about." Spirit of the Mountain's mind was in a tumultuous whirl. If the man wasn't dead already she might just go out and shoot him down herself ... again!

"Spirit of the Mountain, you could do a pelvic exam. Yes, and see if possibly there is a physical problem. Then you need to rest. You are still recuperating from a bad wound," Sings to the Wind suggested.

"A what?"

The two women explained to Christine what would be done, as well as the limitations of what they might find. Surprising both women, Christine consented.

Chapter TWENTY-EIGHT

Spirit of the Mountain could not imagine someone being so cruel to another human being as the lascivious behaviors of that man who called himself Christine's husband. She wondered what else he had possibly done to this woman. She was fourteen when they had married. Obviously, no one had prepared her for her marital duties or what was considered normal behavior. The woman's naiveté was astounding. How could her parent's have been so neglectful?

"Christine, you are still a virgin. There is a severe hemorrhoid problem probably caused by unnecessary stress on the anal area. Your husband was not engaging in normal sexual relations. This is why it was so agonizing for you to have marital relations with him. It is also why you could not bear any children. My guess is that he knew exactly what he was doing which makes him ... made him a very sick man."

Christine stared open mouthed at both women, "No, that can't be true."

"Oh, yes it is. Your hymen is intact. You have never been penetrated in the proper manner. You can marry Little Red Hawk and you will see what a real marriage is supposed to be."

Turning to Sings with the Wind, Spirit of the Mountain asked if she would find Standing Deer. She would speak with him about the rough and perfidious behavior of Christine's prior husband. When Sings to the Wind left, she then explained to Christine the appropriate and proper methods of sexual behavior between a man and a woman. Christine was prolific with her questions. They poured out of the woman-child with alacrity.

Standing Deer knelt next to his sleeping wife. Gently he caressed her cheek. To his eyes, she was the most beautiful woman in the universe. He was such a lucky man and never failed to thank the Great Spirit for bringing her to him.

Spirit of the Mountain languorously opened her eyes and smiled at her brave warrior.

"Bright Eyes, how are you feeling?"

"Firelike and lustful. Can you fit the bill, my stoic and proud warrior?"

"Wastelaka." I love you.

He laughed a deep lustful laugh. Gently he caressed the soft skin of her thighs, as he was leaning over her, careful not to hurt her wound. It was a quick and igneous bonding of the two lovers. Their souls were assured of their dance together. Afterwards they lay in each other's arms relishing the peace they invariably felt with each other.

"Where are the children?" Spirit of the Mountain laughed with guilt. She hadn't thought of them since her talk with Christine.

"With Two Feathers and Sings to the Wind."

"I need to speak with you about Christine. There's a slight problem ... ."

Spirit of the Mountain explained the beastly behavior of Christine's husband to Standing Deer. She asked if he would speak with Little Red Hawk before the marriage tomorrow night and explain the "infirmity" of her dead husband.

Standing Deer now understood Christine's fear and submissive behavior. He knew there were people like that in the world. He just couldn't believe he knew someone who had to live that way. It was indeed a very convoluted situation but he believed Little Red Hawk would understand. Standing Deer waited until his wife fell asleep and left to search for Little Red Hawk.

It was not too difficult to find him. He was in the story circle with a group of Sioux and Cheyenne. Little Big Man held the talking feather as he weaved and portrayed an adventurous tale. It would be a good story coming from him. The two men took a walk away from the crowds.

"Are you dissatisfied with the horse, Standing Deer?" Little Hawk inquired.

"No, and thank you for the horse. Although I told you that you did not have to give me anything, I appreciate the gift. It is a good horse. There is a problem though and you may change your mind about marrying the captive if you choose. I will not be offended."

Little Red Hawk waited in silence. There could be nothing he could think of that would change his mind about marrying the ravenous beauty. From the first moment he saw her, it was as if he had been struck by lightning.

Standing Deer hesitated, unsure of how to proceed. "Her first husband was wacinhnuni." Crazy. "He was a very sick man … in the head."

Standing Deer explained Christine's story to Little Red Hawk as delicately as he could without being too specific and without giving all the lascivious details of her husband's actions.

"She is still a virgin," Standing Deer finally concluded.

Gaping open-mouthed, Little Red Hawk looked at Standing Deer as if he had lost his mind. He shook his head in confusion. What could a man do that would still keep his wife a virgin? There is nothing that … suddenly his eyes opened in astonishment. His face flushed red with anger. The virulent anger streamed from the young man's eyes. The visions he had of the unscrupulous acts that played in his head made him nauseous. A lump stuck in his throat. Little Red Hawk wanted to cry for her pain.

Standing Deer watched the young warrior fighting the emotions. He stopped and looked him directly in the eyes, "There is nothing wrong with showing emotions, especially after what you have just heard. What she has been through deserves tears and animosity. I will leave you alone to decide if you still want her as wife."

Little Red Hawk's eyes watered with unshed tears, "I have not changed my mind. I don't care how long it takes for her to love me as a wife should, but I will be patient with her."

"You are a good warrior, Little Red Hawk. You make me proud to call you friend." Standing Deer left Little Red Hawk alone with his thoughts. Quietly he joined the story circle.

It was another blistering day. Custer and his men were drenched in sweat and covered with dirt from the dry prairie. Sitting atop his majestic stallion he removed his hat and wiped his shaved head with a bandanna. He felt the blond stubs against the palm of his hand and wished he hadn't been so impulsive with his decision to shave all his hair off.

"These tracks will lead us right to the camp," Custer unnecessarily explained to his brother. "I spoke with Colby. We're on our way, boy. We're going to make history. We'll be down in the books as the bravest and best cavalry unit in the history of the United States of America."

"Good morning. Have the children left already?" Christine awoke with cheer, surprised to see the lodge empty except for herself and Spirit of the Mountain.

"Good morning. Oh my, it's late," Spirit of the Mountain replied sleepily. "The children will be back in a few days. They've gone to ... visit some friends."

As Christine and Spirit of the Mountain fulfilled their morning chores, they chatted amiably. Christine was curious and asked many questions about the Lakota and their lifestyles that she had been observing.

"How did Sings to the Wind get her name? Do you think I will get an Indian name?" she bubbled in effervescence.

"Yes, sooner or later they will find a name that is appropriate for you, something that stands out about you that is special, I would imagine."

"Oh, I hope it is something beautiful like Bursting Flower or ... oh, I don't know," she laughed as they drank their hickory coffee.

"I'm sure it will be a beautiful name. By your cheeriness this morning, can I safely guess that you have accepted your pending marriage to Little Red Hawk?"

Christine scowled and then smiled, "So how did Sings to the Wind get her name?"

Spirit of the Mountain noticed the intentional change of subject. She would let it go for now. But the subject was not forgotten and the facade not ignored. She told Christine just that.

"After you tell me how Sings to the Wind got her name. She told me it was embarrassing but funny. She never got around to telling me how, though."

Spirit of the Mountain laughed, "Okay, I'll tell you. Several years ago we were in Paha Sapa, the Black Hills. Sings to the Wind had gone for a walk to be by herself. She was still unfamiliar with the area and it was getting dark. We were worried so a group of us started searching the Hills for her."

Spirit of the Mountain smiled with the memory from so many years ago. "Crazy Horse had found her. Actually he had heard her singing and followed her voice. As he explained it, she had been up on one of the flat peaks singing her heart out. Later she had told us that she sang because she was afraid and it made her feel safe."

"Oh, how sweet!"

"She was singing 'America the Beautiful' at the top of her lungs. Crazy Horse said she was so involved with the song that she jumped five feet in the air, started jumping up and down in one spot and screamed bloody murder when she first saw him. Then she hugged him and started bouncing up and down in excitement."

Spirit of the Mountain started laughing, "It must have been a sight. Sings to the Wind bouncing in excitement and Crazy Horse thinking she had lost her mind."

Christine started laughing, "Yes, it must have been quite a sight. Especially with Crazy Horse as serious and austere as he is. Now those two seem to be on the opposite ends of the personality chain."

"Yes, I guess it appears to be that way now. Crazy Horse has a lot to be worried about. There's a lot of responsibility on his shoulders. But let me warn you. Don't underestimate his sense of humor once you get to know him. He loves practical jokes. You will get to know him, too. Little Red Hawk is with Crazy Horse's band."

"I won't be with you?" Christine asked with panic in her voice.

"You will for a while, but the villages will go their separate ways in the future."

"But I want to stay with your village."

"Now that is up to Little Red Hawk. I'm afraid that decision may be solely up to him. It couldn't hurt for you to express your opinion though. But don't expect him to change his mind."

"I will do what I am commanded," Christine replied solemnly.

Spirit of the Mountain growled. It really irked her when women were so servile. Christine needed to straighten up and have some inner strength. She'll never make it with this lifestyle if she doesn't.

"You do not always have to agree with Little Red Hawk. He does not want a submissive slave. He wants a wife who will stand on her own two feet, work hard, and express her own opinions. But ... whatever you do, don't disagree with him outside of your lodge."

Christine nodded her head in understanding, "You must teach me the right way. I want to please him. I don't want to be punished."

General Alfred Terry had waited impatiently for news from Custer, Benteen or Reno. Too many days had gone by. With a mordant fear stinging his gut, Terry ordered his men camped on the Yellowstone River to move out.

Sitting Bull called out to Spirit of the Mountain and entered the lodge. Christine excused herself and promptly left to clean her laundry.

Spirit of the Mountain showed Sitting Bull the Scientific American papers while he took her bandages off. They decided to leave her wound uncovered for the time being.

He spoke with her about an article in one of the papers discussing the massive destruction of woodlands and how man needed to stop destroying the forests. Sitting Bull rolled his eyes. Spirit of the Mountain could see he understood that nothing would change. People would still chop down trees needlessly.

It was a sad thought. Even in her world they still crashed and burned. Wood, paper, etc., was still a necessity for the world and would continue to be for a long time. Assuredly, there were many groups fighting the destruction of the forests. The fight continued.

The night had been filled with celebration and cheer. As it grew later into the night, Christine's fear increased. She stood uncertain at the entrance of Little Red Hawk's lodge and watched as Spirit of the Mountain joined the story circle and wished that she could join them. Her heart pounded in her chest as fear rumbled through her head.

Little Red Hawk spoke with a few warriors as she entered his lodge. Slowly and methodically, she took off her dress and undergarments. Tears stung her eyes as she recalled Sings to the Wind taking her laudanum and refusing to give it back to her. Christine sat on the buffalo mat and brushed her long, straight, raven-colored hair.

As if in a trance, Christine took her small jar of petroleum jelly and dipped her finger in it. Her eyes stared at the entrance of the lodge as she absentmindedly rubbed the jelly along her teeth and inner jaws, preparing herself for her wifely duties.

Christine wanted to believe her new friends with all her heart, believe that it would be different. But, she had to be prepared, it was her duty. She knelt on the buffalo mat with arms by her sides and waited for her new husband.

The warriors joked with Little Red Hawk about how quickly he had taken Christine as his wife. They teased the young buck about not giving anyone else a chance to get to her before he had convinced Standing Deer to give her to him. They all agreed, she was a beauty. Even a washitu would not believe she was washitu. Maybe she had Indian blood in her. Little Red Hawk should ask his beautiful wife where her heritage lies.

Little Red Hawk opened the flap to his lodge. It had been a long wait and she had sat down wondering if he would ever arrive. Stunned and unprepared, Christine jumped to her feet and then dropped complacently to her knees. She looked down to the floor of the lodge in shame and fear because she had not been prepared for her husband.

With fear and tears shining in her eyes, she deliberately raised her head and opened her mouth. Little Red Hawk was confused for a moment and then appalled at the realization of what she was waiting for him to do. He cautiously approached her and took both of her hands into his. Turning them over, he knelt down and kissed each one on the palm.

He watched as unfettered tears fell down her high cheekbones and slowly made their way toward the crease of her mouth. Gently he pushed on her chin to close her mouth. Little Red Hawk reached around and encircled his new wife with his arms. Softly he spoke to her knowing she did not understand him. He laid her back onto the buffalo mat and held her closely to his rapidly beating heart.

Christine was very confused. Tenderly, he kissed her lips, eyes and neck. Little Red Hawk would go no farther tonight. Obviously, the nightmare of the life she had before him was worse than he could possibly have ever imagined. He would hold her like this every night for a year if that was what it would take for her to trust and love him with no fear.

Chapter TWENTY-NINE

The village was alerted. White soldiers had been spotted. The counsel meeting took place near the Cheyenne side of the village. All present were silent as Sitting Bull said a prayer and began the meeting.

"When I was a young warrior, the Sioux walked free on our Mother Earth. The sun would rise and set in our beautiful land and we would thank the Great Spirit for everything He has given us. We would cherish all that had been given us.

"We were powerful warriors and sent our enemies riding away in fear. We had ten thousand horsemen we could send into battle. Where are these praiseworthy warriors today? What has happened to all of the land that the Great Spirit has given us?"

Sitting Bull scanned the large group of warriors and elders surrounding the fire as he walked around the inner circle.

"Who here can say that I have ever stolen his lands or taken the white man's money? Yet, I am called thief! Find me a woman captive and ask her if she was ever treated badly by me. Yet, the white man says I am a bad Indian."

Sitting Bull pointed to a group of elders, "Who here could ever say that he has seen me drunk from the white man's fire water?"

Shaking their heads, the circle waited with the reticence of respect.

"Who has ever come to my village or my home and left with an empty stomach? Who can say they have ever seen me beat or abuse my wives or my children?

"The white man says I have broken laws. What law have I broken? Why is it in their eyes it is wrong for me to love my People and my country? This land is where my fathers have always lived. Why do they find it so hard to understand that I would die for my People and my country?"

A loud cheer fulminated through the air as Sitting Bull proudly walked over to Crazy Horse and handed him the talking feather. Crazy Horse stood silent and stoic as he waited for the cheering to die down.

"The treaty states that the land shall belong to the Sioux for as long as the grass should grow and the water should flow upon the lands. Eight years has passed since our elders signed this treaty. The whites want us to sell our land to them. We do not wish to sell our land on which we walk and live free."

Crazy Horse's face was staid. His voice was betraying the acrimonious anger inside him.

"The white man is like a nest of parasites destroying everything in their path to get what they want. They don't care who or what they destroy on the way. No matter where we go, they come to our land, kill our People, and destroy our country. No more! It is time to squash them like the parasites that they are!"

A Cheyenne stood and spoke, "We must remember Black Kettle and how he went to what the whites call Denver. He asked for peace. The Cheyenne were at peace with the whites. The whites wanted their hunting ground so they annihilated them without honor and mercy. Men, women and children at Sand Creek were slaughtered. The whites refused Black Kettle's request for peace.

"When the white soldiers came to his small village, he told the People not to be afraid. He had spoken to the white soldiers but they had not listened. The American flag flew high in his village for all to see.

"I heard that the white soldier, Chivington, said he had come to kill Indians and believed it was right and honorable to kill all Indians under their god's heavens. What kind of god do they have that would tell them to kill innocent men, women and children under a flag of peace?"

The talking feather was passed to another warrior.

"My grandfather was there. He spoke to me of the white soldiers who had argued with their white chief soldier. They did not want to fight the Cheyenne because they were at peace. Black Kettle was holding a white flag while he stood under the American flag. The white soldiers who refused to fight did nothing as they watched the women and children being beaten and mutilated.

"The brave warriors at Black Kettle's camp surrounded the women and children to protect them, but could not. There were too many soldiers. These white soldiers cut out the private parts of the females and carried them around like prizes in a kill."

Another warrior stood and yelled in unfettered anger to the crowd, "They want to exterminate us all. They cut down the living trees. They don't care about the land. They don't care that this land is our life. They have killed almost all of the buffalo knowing we cannot survive without them. Our families go hungry. We cannot shelter ourselves properly in the winter because we have fewer hides. No matter where we go, there are whites trying to kill us.

"They want us to go to reservations. They are prisons. They want to control us and make us live like them. There is no freedom there. I have lived on a reservation. If it weren't for Spirit of the Mountain, my family and I would probably still be there.

"The people on the reservations are dying from starvation and disease. They are supposed to bring food and clothing, but they do not. The food they do give us is rancid and full of bugs. We want to hunt for our own food. We want to take care of ourselves, but they will not allow it.

"They take our children when they are three and four years old and teach them the Indian way is wrong. They make them wear white man's clothes. No one is allowed to possess anything that is Indian. They cut their hair and take anything away that reminds our People of the old way of life. The parents never see their children again. They take them and the children never return.

"They have beaten us if we speak of the ways of the Indian, or speak our native tongue.

"If the whites do not kill them because of starvation and disease, they give them the white man's whiskey to destroy their minds. Brave warriors whom I have seen fight with the greatest strength fall down in oblivion not caring about anything around them. Their eyes are bleary and uncomprehending."

Crow Man gripped the talking feather with fervor and looked around to see the reaction on the faces of the distinguished warriors before him. "I have lived on a reservation. I want to be free. I want the freedom to live and choose for myself. I want to pray to my own God and practice my own religion. I want to come and go as I please, speak as I choose. Sitting Bull, didn't you tell me once that these soldiers fought for freedom and the right to choose for themselves? That freedom is why they came to this country?"

Sitting Bull acknowledged the question with a silent nod.

"We must do the same! We must fight to protect ourselves and have the freedom to live on our land in peace."

Two Feathers took the talking feather.

"They want our sacred Paha Sapa. They dig up the land looking for rocks they call gold. Those rocks make them crazy. They destroy everything around them and leave garbage behind when they are finished. They take more than they need and do not give back to the land.

"They make us sign a treaty and then they do not live by their own words. They are the liars and the thieves. They have no honor. I will fight to defend and protect our land, our ways and our families. I will fight to my death and I will die with honor in my heart."

Gall walked around the circle clutching the talking feather, "We are united! If the white man will stay out of our lands, we will have peace forever. If he does not, then we have war!"

"Men, we're on the right course. We've been traveling over thirty miles a day into enemy territory. Indian signs are every-where to be seen."

Custer scanned the group of soldiers in front of him. They looked ragged and exhausted. A rest will be needed, but not too long of a reprieve. The Sioux couldn't escape him now. He couldn't let that happen, not when he was so close to victory.

"We'll march tonight. We're going to find those Sioux and we're going to extirpate them. Their behavior will no longer be a worry to the American people once we have finished with them. Once this battle is over, we will no longer have to deal with those belligerent, pugnacious heathens.

"The scouts have apprised me the Sioux are gathering in a valley on the Little Big Horn. We're going to march this expedi-tion until we find that Sioux camp. Then, I'll make a decision on our attack. We'll rest one night and attack on the twenty-sixth." Hands clasped behind his back as he eyed a few of the scouts, Custer paced.

"We'll have the Sioux cornered between Terry, Gibbons and the Seventh. If the Sioux try and flee then, we'll have a problem if Gibbons isn't in position yet." Custer offered his men a sardonic smile and laughed, "We'll just have to stop them from running."

The men joined in with his laughter.

"The scouts tell me they have found evidence of four hundred lodges and wickiups. That'll be about fifteen hundred Sioux warriors."

Spreading his arms out in a theatrical and dramatic display of confidence, Custer continued, "Yes sir. The world will know that we, the Seventh Cavalry, with the help of Gibbons and Terry, beat and annihilated the fearless and invincible Sioux."

Custer looked around solemnly at his officers. He paused a few moments as he looked at them all, sustaining direct eye contact.

"Andrews," Custer pointed at the young man in front of him, "the scouts say there is a high spot up on the mountain where you can view the whole valley. I want you to go with them."

"Yes, sir. I understand you need eyes you can trust," Andrews replied with a salute.

"Darn right. I want to know what you see without me needing an interpreter. The rest of you, we leave tonight. No fires, no bugles. Everything will be ordered by word of mouth. Until then, gentlemen, dismissed."

Dusk painted the air. The deep azure sky was brushed with an intricate touch of reds and oranges. Lieutenant Andrews stood solemnly on the peak of the mountain beside the scouts. A cold vitriolic fear encircled and wrapped around his body, crushing him with a mordant unheard scream. There, before his very eyes, was one of the most capacious villages he had ever seen in his life.

The querulousness of the scouts sounded muffled and far away. The scouts kept saying many Sioux. "Many Sioux" was an understatement.

Dazed from the convoluted missive before him, he turned and watched as one at a time the scouts chanted their death songs. Silently he prayed to God for deliverance. Andrews reassured himself, glad he'd sent a note to Custer earlier when the Arikara first spotted the village. At least Custer would know the vastness of the village and would wait for backup before he attacked.

Andrews blinked. Out of the corner of his eyes he saw movement. Following his gaze, the scouts pointed out the dust that had suddenly risen. A few Sioux warriors who were now in a rush to alert the camp had spotted them. Andrews swayed, his entire body felt as if an unseen force was crushing him.

Custer, agitated and angry, stood next to Bloody Knife and Isaiah. The scouts stood back from the crowd of officers. A few of Custer's men stood on the peak of the mountain overlooking the valley.

"I don't see a darn thing," he growled at the scouts and Andrews. "There's nothing down there that tells me there is sign of one Sioux."

Isaiah pointed in frustration, "Over there. Can't you see the dust in the air and the herd of horses?"

"No. I can't see anything. There's nothing there!" Custer bellowed.

"General Custer, right in front of your very own eyes is the biggest herd of horses I have ever seen."

Bloody Knife shook his head in disbelief at the man standing before him, "What about the smoke from the fires? Can't you see them?"

Custer shook his head in anger, wondering what type of ruse these men were trying to accomplish. Were they turning yellow on him now? Now, at the greatest moment of his life?

"I see nothing. I told you, there is nothing there. We've been sent up here to look at nothing. Can't you get that through that thick head of yours?"

Isaiah's mouth dropped open and his eyes squinted in anger. Bloody Knife stood transfixed, fire blazing from his eyes.

"You, arrogant son of ... ."

"General," Andrews jumped in quickly before Bloody Knife could finish his sentence, "what about the Sioux warriors we saw earlier heading toward the village? They had to have seen our tracks. They crossed them on the way to the village."

Custer's jaw was clenched in anger. One of his best men was seeing ghosts. These scouts must have really spooked him. Shrugging, he walked away.

Stunned, the men on the peak watched as Custer stomped away from the group muttering to himself.

"I don't believe you saw anything, Lieutenant," Custer called back to Andrews.

"General, those Sioux scouts have already alerted the village. I know what I saw. Our scouts know what they are talking about. That is one of the strongest and largest Sioux gatherings that has ever happened."

Custer slowly turned to face Andrews. "I know you aren't arguing with me. Are you, Andrews? This is balderdash! Your insolent behavior is unacceptable, Lieutenant. My reports say that the reservations have an accurate count of the Sioux and none have left the reservations. There is no way there could ever be such a large camp."

"General," Isaiah said quietly as he cautiously approached Custer. "It is not just Sitting Bull's camp. It is many camps that have joined with him together for the Sun Dance ceremony we saw earlier. There is proof that Sioux have left the reservations."

Custer pointed his finger at Isaiah, "You are here to help me find the Sioux. I will take care of the rest."

He looked around at the scouts and officers standing before him. "We'll go back and have an officer's meeting. Then we'll attack."

On the way down the mountain to join the rest of the regiment, Custer's brother Tom was solemn and silent. It was an unusual sign coming from his normally happy demeanor.

"Speak up, Tom. What is it?" Custer sighed.

"Don't get me wrong. I want to whip some Sioux as much as you do. But shouldn't we wait until the men and horses are rested? We've been pushing pretty hard the last few days."

"Though I don't believe him, if what Andrews claims is true, he wasn't seeing ghosts. The element of surprise is gone. I can't have those Sioux running away like scared little kittens and hiding in those mountains. We can't allow them the time to leave the camp. It needs to be done now."

"The Sioux warriors and their horses will all be fresh and ready for a strong fight. Our men should have the same advantage," Tom said quietly.

Custer sighed. "Yes, that would help. I have never led you in the wrong direction before Tom. I won't start now. We have the best regiment there is in all of these United States. If we wait, they'll be gone. I didn't see a darned thing up there on that peak. Those scouts insist there's Sioux in that valley. If there is, then we're going to get them."

Tom nodded his head in understanding.

"I'll send Matthews to Gibbons with information to let him know what we are planning," Tom told his brother.

"Too late," Custer snapped.

"Too late? Why?" Tom snapped back.

"No time for us to wait for their arrival. Besides, we don't need Gibbons' or Terry's support. We'll attack as soon as we can."

The officers watched Custer walk down from the peak. All were stunned. Custer was doing exactly what General Terry did not want him to do. He was going against orders to achieve his own fame. They were numb with the realization that Custer was ignoring the scout's warnings that this was one of the largest gatherings of the Sioux Nation.

Watching Custer walk away from him, Tom looked at his brother incredulously, wondering if he had ever intended to obey General Terry's orders.

Chapter THIRTY

The scouts prepared themselves for battle, painting each other and chanting war songs. Some sang their death songs. Their instructions were to steal the horses. Bloody Knife walked up to Custer, Reno and Benteen as they were finishing their coffee.

Grabbing a cup for himself, he turned to Custer, "You are my friend. I warn you to move carefully and cautiously. There's a very good reason why those Sioux left those scalps and beards behind after their battle with Crook and his soldiers."

Hearing the conversation, Isaiah approached the group, "I have known the Sioux for a long time. They have always treated me fairly. They will not willingly go to the reservation. You will have the biggest fight on your hands."

Bloody Knife nodded in agreement, "Your army does not have enough ammunition to kill all the Indians in this camp."

Custer shrugged. "You two ladies," he emphasized, "and the rest of the scouts keep telling me that ahead of us is the largest Indian camp on the North American Continent. I'm not backing down now. We are going to attack it. If you want to stay behind like two sniveling women ... ."

Before he could finish his statement, Isaiah bounded forward and grabbed his shirt, shoving Custer onto the ground. Bloody Knife and Curley quickly grabbed Isaiah and pulled him off Custer.

Spreading the word among the scouts, each one watched as their comrades started singing their death songs. Isaiah quietly said to Bloody Knife that they would never come out of this battle alive. The two men walked away shaking their heads in disgust.

Custer brushed off his shirt and buckskins. In a deceptively calm voice, he spoke to Captain Frederick Benteen, "Sound the command for battle."

After silence for so long on the trail, the sound of the cry for battle pierced the air. The day had arrived. There was no need for silence any longer.

The march was on. The soldiers were tired, worn and sunburned from five weeks on the trail heading west. They had traveled through the cold of May. Now they continued in the sweltering heat of the sun on this hot June day. The clouds were starting to dissipate from the intense heat.

Standing in front of Standing Deer's lodge, Sunshine in the Morning called out to Spirit of the Mountain.

"Sings to the Wind's child comes early. It is ready to be born."

"I'll be right there!"

Spirit of the Mountain grabbed the special herbs needed to help with labor and pain. As she exited the lodge and walked with Sunshine in the Morning, she noticed Thunder standing next to their lodge. Why is Thunder here? Spirit of the Mountain looked around and saw that many of the warriors also had their war-horses near their lodges.

"What's going on, Sunshine? Why are the war horses in the village?"

"A small group of white soldiers was spotted about twenty miles from the camp. Some of the families are taking down their lodges and will be heading north. Gall said not to worry.

If the soldiers attack, they will not attack until morning. Besides, it would be suicide for such a small group of soldiers to attack such a large camp. We are safe."

Spirit of the Mountain looked around warily. Something wasn't right and she couldn't put her finger on it. The battle at Rosebud had to happen first. According to history, there hadn't been any skirmishes in the month of June. It is possible that this sighting of the white soldiers will cause them to return to the Rosebud. She nodded to herself. Then the battle will occur the first week of July, just as history has it.

No one had bothered to tell her about the Rosebud battle. They had concentrated on her wounds and her health.

Spirit of the Mountain and Sunshine in the Morning entered Two Feathers' lodge. As they guided Sings to the Wind to the birthing area, their minds were only on the thought of the coming child.

The sounds of eagles flying overhead were heard as they approached the vast green valley. They rode their weary horses down the slopes of pine and cedar trees. Custer called a halt and a meeting of the officers just as they reached the valley.

"Captain Benteen, you have the advance. D and K Companies will go with you. You will proceed southwest."

"Begging to differ, sir. Wouldn't it be best to keep the regiment together?"

"Captain, your job is to obey orders. Mine is to give them," Custer replied rigidly.

He cleared his throat. "Yes sir," Benteen replied.

"Watch for the Indian village. Your job is to stop any hostile Indians from fleeing up river. Get the companies together and ride out."

"Yes sir." Benteen saluted and walked away.

"Major Reno, you will take Companies A, G and M."

"Yes sir, and my orders?"

"Your orders? You wait, Major. Proceed down the left bank and wait."

"Yes, sir."

John Colby stood in front of Custer, "I request to ride with Reno, Sir."

Custer nodded his head in agreement as he watched Colby leave the group to prepare for the battle. He studied those men who remained waiting for the rest of the orders. They now understood that he was planning a three-sided attack.

"The pack train will be left behind. The rest of you ride with me. We will be prepared for rear guard. We don't want those Sioux coming up behind us. I have a nagging feeling that the Sioux are going to flee. We'll know what we have to do when we approach the village. Let's move."

It was high noon and Two Moons was bathing in the river while he watched his wife and a group of women digging for turnips. As he turned to stretch his neck and arms, he saw a great cloud of dust bursting in the air. Quickly he called to his wife as he rushed toward the camp to warn the People.

The sound of a freshly newborn baby's cry was music to everyone's ears. The ebullient cheering and chatting were cut short by the fulminating sound of the racing horses and warriors that had been sent to investigate the dust cloud seen by Two Moons and his wife. The warriors were shouting warnings of white soldiers approaching the camp.

Custer met up with Reno and his men. The scouts had informed them that there were too many Sioux. More than this regiment could handle. A small group of warriors was spotted just out of rifle range. To Custer, they had not appeared worried in the least.

The group of warriors raced into the village to alert their friends and families. Many of the People were not fearful for they felt the white soldiers would attack at dawn, not in the middle of the day. Many more had not received the warnings for they had stayed up late celebrating the night before.

Most of the warriors found it hard to believe that such a small group of white soldiers would attack a camp that was so large. They believed the white soldiers were blood thirsty but not stupid. It would indeed be suicide if the white soldiers attacked the village. As it was now, there were more than eight thousand men, women and children in the vast village.

"Major Reno, take your men across the river and charge the village. We'll be your rear guard. Isaiah, I want you to ride with Reno."

Reno cautiously made his way down the slopes of the winding path and readied his regimen to cross the river. From the hills, he and his men saw many Indians bathing in the river, walking around the river and trees. They did not appear as if they had been warned of soldiers.

As they approached the river, Reno caught sight of the tops of lodges. He had never seen so many in his life. He promptly sent a messenger to alert Custer of the sighting and to verify Custer's support.

As Custer was receiving the message from Reno, Bloody Knife returned from the hilltop. Bloody Knife informed Custer that there were more lodges to the north than could be counted. The village appeared to go for miles.

Custer frowned. The element of surprise may already be gone. The camp must surely know the soldiers were coming to attack. The Sioux would be preparing for battle as he sat here on his horse. He had a job to do for his country. By separating the twelve companies into three groups, success would still be his. They had to surround the village.

As Major Reno was attacking the front of the village, Custer's five companies would ride up a mile or so and attack the top of the village, surrounding the camp. With Benteen riding the river, they would be able to attack from three sides.

"Attack!" Reno shouted.

In a rush, the hooves of the horses pummeled the ground, kicking up the dry dust into the air causing the shapes of his men to appear ghostly as they moved forward in the attack. Reno's men entered the mouth of the village, attacking the Hunkpapa camp.

Surprised and unprepared warriors raced out of their lodges. Some ran out unclothed, awakened by the explosions of the rifle shots. Women and children dodged bullets, racing to the rear of the camp as quickly as they could run.

Gall and a group of warriors created a wall to protect the women and children as they escaped from the Hunkpapa camp.

Sitting Bull raced through the village shouting, "Brave up boys, brave up! It will be a hard fight!" He watched as Crazy Horse grabbed Standing Deer's horse, Thunder, and raced up and down the village calling out to the People and the warriors.

"Poca he! Poca he! It is a good day to fight! It is a good day to die! Strong hearts to the front! Weak hearts to the rear!" Crazy Horse then dismounted and left Thunder behind Standing Deer's lodge. Kneeling down in a rifleman's position, he started shooting.

Spirit of the Mountain raced out of Two Feathers' lodge. No! This shouldn't be happening. What is going on? This is not supposed to be happening yet! Oh, my God!

Massive chaos encircled her. She looked around, stunned and terrified. Everything seemed to be happening in slow motion. Yellow Bird, just two years old, lay five feet to her left. An open wound in her chest was pouring blood onto the dusty ground.

She ran across the village as a warrior was downed by another bullet. Spirit of the Mountain looked to the front of the village and watched as Isaiah, the black washitu, fell off his horse and onto the ground. She ran over to the fallen warrior. Cradling him in her arms, she cried tears of anguish to the dying man as she apologized for not knowing this was going to happen this way.

John Colby stood sheltered behind a lodge and spotted Spirit of the Mountain. He would enjoy killing her. She had destroyed his chances of digging for gold and becoming the rich and powerful man he should have been before the Civil War.

If it hadn't been for her, he would not have had to leave the Sioux village over ten years ago. He would have been able to dig for this gold. He would not have had to worry because the Sioux would never have expected him to do such a thing.

Crazy Horse saw Spirit of the Mountain holding the dying man. Out of the corner of his eye, he saw a white soldier hidden behind a lodge. The man rode toward Spirit of the Mountain. The man's rifle was pointed at Spirit of the Mountain's back. Crazy Horse heard a loud whooshing sound as if a thousand eagles' wings were flapping in rhythm.

The white soldier was pushed back as invisible hands shoved him away from Spirit of the Mountain. The white soldier attempted to move forward again and was knocked down from his horse.

The sound of the eagles' wings continued to resound in Crazy Horse's ears. As the white soldier raced his way on foot toward Spirit of the Mountain, Crazy Horse steadily moved his rifle into position. With a slight squeeze of the trigger, the white soldier lay dead.

Spirit of the Mountain was oblivious to what was happening behind her. She would never know that Crazy Horse had saved her life from the crazed man. The shot coming from Crazy Horse's rifle was just another deafening repercussion of the many bullets fulminating in her ears.

Crazy Horse watched the front of the village as Reno started to retreat. He grabbed his bow and raced toward the Cheyenne section of the village to organize his men.

On top of the bluff Custer watched Reno's vitriolic attack. He was able to witness the men, women and children as they were killed on the east side of the river. Curiously, he watched a rider approach on a lathered horse.

"Private McCarthy, sir. Major Reno said to report that he is under attack and requests your backup. There are too many warriors, sir."

"Yes! Great!" Custer clapped his hands together and gave the man a big grin. "We'll head north and attack the village."

"Sir? Did you hear what I said?" The young soldier blinked in amazement, "General Custer, Major Reno has asked for your support!"

Private McCarthy still heard the haunted screams of his regiment echoing inside his mind. At this point, he didn't care who he was speaking with. They needed backup, now.

"He's getting my support, Private," Custer snapped. "We're going to do it from the top and work our way down."

"Aren't you coming to back him up, sir?"

"No. He's started the battle and I'm going to finish it. Since your horse won't make it back to Reno, go join F Company."

Desperately, Reno gradually retreated across the river assuming defensive positions. As he retreated, hundreds of warriors continued to come forward and attack.

Captain Benteen sensed the asperity of Reno's battle with the Sioux. Calling to his battalion, Benteen issued orders for his men to back up Reno. Benteen's felicitous arrival prevented Reno's annihilation.

Leaving McCarthy in the dust, Custer rode up and down his column shouting orders. They would head north and cross the river to attack the top of the village.

Custer led his men up the river riding behind bluffs to mask them from the village. He and his men could hear the shots ringing in the distance. They could see Reno's men at the southern part of the village. Dust randomly covered their sight of the battle. He rode on and continued to study the village through his binoculars. Puzzled, he couldn't see many warriors. There didn't appear to be much activity in the village at all. Possibly, they were all fighting Reno. Or they could be out hunting buffalo. Custer started laughing. This was too good to be true.

Elated, he yelled to his men, "They're all ours now boys!"

A cheer rose among the eager soldiers. All were itching for a good Indian fight. Some had felt left out of Major Reno's fight at the mouth of the village and were more than ready to go.

"Lieutenant Andrews, I want you to ride back to Benteen and then the pack train. I want both here now. Tell them it's a big village and we need back-up." Custer stopped as he strained his eyes to look through the binoculars. The village was much bigger than he had expected. As they were riding steadily north, they could see more lodges.

"Tom, look at this. This village is huge!" Custer's eyes were glazed and wide with anticipation. Custer licked his lips.

"What are we going to do?"

"Attack, of course. We're going to squash some Sioux. We need to attack so we can relieve Reno. We'll get them Sioux going in so many directions they won't know which way is up. Lets go!"

Custer kept his eyes peeled for an opening. The soldiers were on edge, impatiently waiting for the command to attack. Custer spied the opening he had been searching. Pointing in the direction he wanted his men to go, he dramatically lifted his arm up into the air.

"Attack!"

Chapter THIRTY-ONE

Custer sat atop his horse and watched as simultaneously the regiment raced their horses forward. The dry, acrid dust was so thick it blinded the cavalry as they thundered forward. The shapes of the men were ghostly as they plunged toward the bend.

The clash with the enemy was shocking. As the first regiment of the cavalry rounded the bend, arrows and bullets struck them with deadly accuracy. The men reigned their horses to a complete stop as more dry dust filled the air. Custer's men could not see where the bullets were coming from and did not know how many enemy warriors were before them.

No one knew where to direct their firepower. They were being picked off one at a time as if it was a deer hunt.

The four warriors hiding behind the trees were among the best riflemen the village had. The dust from the cavalry's horses was an advantage to them. They could see the enemy but the enemy could not see them. There wasn't a single bullet that flew into the dust cloud that did not hit a soldier with deadly accuracy.

Now that the Reno attack had been held back, Gall and his men started to race toward the battle to assist Crazy Horse. Iron Hawk quickly grabbed his attention. Another group of soldiers had been spotted just outside of the San Arc of the camp.

"Take no prisoners!" Gall screamed.

The taste of revenge was choking him, enflaming his anger to a blindness that only those who have experienced this type of warfare could understand. In his eyes, Gall saw his wife and children, dead, blown away by the white man's bullets. This was their land … their home! They were supposed to be at peace here. What kind of man attacked another man's home and killed his wife and children? In his eyes and those of his brothers … a man like that deserves to live no longer!

Up the slopes he led his warriors to battle. They would fight for their freedom, their land. They would destroy these white soldiers who were trying to take it away from them, Gall vowed to himself, one by one until the last soldier breathed his last breath.

Crazy Horse, Gall and Standing Deer were riding toward Custer's Seventh Cavalry. They were ahead of a group of one thousand Sioux warriors. Crazy Horse's plan was to attack the white soldiers from behind and surround them. The warriors spurred their horses forward at the sound of the rifle shots.

Spirit of the Mountain dragged a dying warrior to the side of a lodge. Turning, she watched the chaos of the village. Horses were stampeding toward the rear of the village with Hunkpapa and Oglala warriors chasing them down and bringing them back. Many warriors were running toward the brush and trees where they could fight the soldiers that had stopped and dismounted from their horses.

She crawled on her belly toward their lodge. The bottom of the lodge was fastened securely to the ground and she had to cut an opening to crawl through. Taking her bow and arrows, she quickly rummaged through Standing Deer's bags and grabbed ammunition for his gun. Grabbing her rifle and as much ammunition as she could carry, she exited the lodge the same way she came in.

She was filled with igneous and feral anger. These men were killing everyone in the village. It wasn't a battle of men.

It was an annihilation of a village. Women and children lay on the village grounds dead. She was not going to sit and watch without fighting back.

Spirit of the Mountain crawled to a bush where she spotted the Cheyenne, Dull Knife. Dull Knife's empty rifle lie beside him. He was shooting off arrows as fast and meticulously as she could bullets. Realizing that his rifle was the same as Standing Deer's, Spirit of the Mountain gave Dull Knife Standing Deer's ammunition. She had a modern-day rifle and her bullets would not fit his gun.

Methodically, as if in a horrific dream, Spirit of the Mountain raised her rifle. The shot was accurate. This was war .... .

At the top of the hill, Custer watched wide-eyed as the group of warriors raced toward his men. The recovery of the instantaneous clash was quick. His shock and panic of knowing their attack was no longer a surprise was quickly squashed.

The cavalry's thirsty horses started whimpering as they tried to get closer to the water. Looking through the cottonwoods, Custer viewed the village that appeared to him to be abandoned.

Rifle shots continued to ring out. Human and inhuman screams pierced the air. The pummeling tumult of the battle and the clouds of dry dust were enough to disconcert even the most experienced of soldiers. Custer watched in disgust at the chaos of armed soldiers running around in confusion. Injured men ran to the back of the formation while the dead were mercilessly pushed away from the battlefield. The horses' deadly hooves were pummeling those that had not been moved.

Standing Deer and Two Feathers used their pistols. Those who were without firepower shot arrows. Anything possible was used to attack. Neither Crazy Horse nor Custer had expected the enemy to be so close. Crazy Horse's men recovered quickly and battened down for the fight.

Custer yelled over and through the confusion. He had to calm down his men now! Most of all, he had to stay composed.

"Fall behind! Dismount!" The veteran soldiers shouted orders to calm the inexperienced, forming them in a half circle. They were being lambasted by arrows and bullets. The wounded were being placed behind them.

Custer could see that they had to get out of the coulee. More and more warriors were coming into position to fight. He watched the large group of warriors crossing the shallow waters of the river. Many more were hidden in the ravines and gullies. He had to get his soldiers away from level ground. They were going to be cornered and surrounded if they didn't move now. They had to get to higher ground.

"Tom! I want Companies C, E and F to hold their positions and press the warriors. Watch my back until Benteen arrives and then follow me in. We're going to attack the village."

"What?" Tom stood and looked at his brother open-mouthed and stunned. He rubbed his face to control the panic that was trying to seize him. Was his brother not seeing the same thing he was?

"Don't question me now, Tom! Just do it."

"Seventh Cavalry! Mount!"

He had to move fast and pray that Benteen would as well. Tactical warfare was where Custer was trained best. Reno would push the warriors back to his Seventh and they would take care of them at the top.

A lump stuck in his throat as he looked over the crest and watched Crazy Horse. The warriors swept down the ridge attacking and crushing everything that lay before them.

Private Wilson approached Reno on his lathered horse and dismounted. The horse walked a few feet away from the soldiers and collapsed. The Private managed to pass on his message: "Sir, General Custer requests a back-up."

Reno looked at the young boy and saw the fear emanating from his eyes. Arching an eyebrow, he spread his hands toward the group of Sioux in front of him.

"We're not going anywhere. We can't. You, Private, cannot go back up there, either. I want you to get another horse and go on to the pack train. Get them up here now."

"Thank you, sir. I mean ... yes, sir." Relief spread in his face as he mounted another horse and raced away from the battles.

Reno turned and looked at Benteen. Neither man said a word. They didn't have to. Their jaw muscles twitched as they tightened their mouths together. They knew what they were doing when they chose not to send relief to Custer.

Crazy Horse split the almost one thousand Lakotas and Cheyenne warriors into three groups. The warriors screamed blood curdling war cries as they flew through the valley of soldiers like ghostly shadows. The clash of the battle was so thunderous it seemed almost deafening.

The cavalry soldiers broke formation and ran. Some of the braver men fought to the end. The warriors would not mutilate those soldiers. They fought bravely like true men and deserved to die an honorable death. But die they would.

Standing Deer watched as un-mounted horses ran out of the dry, acrid dust whirling through the valley. He and the warriors attacked the cavalry like waves pounding against the rocks.

There was a fierce determination to prove themselves better than the white soldiers before them. The feral and angry warriors crushed the soldiers, releasing a virulent grudge against the white man. Each warrior took their anger out on every one of Custer's men.

The regimen again lost their organization right before Custer's eyes. Some tried to retreat seeking higher ground as they fought the savage and feral attack. Many of the men shot their horses for protection. Racing down the hill as he fired off shots, Custer yelled out orders to his men. He needed to reorganize the massive chaos in front of him.

"Retreat! Up to the hill!" Custer shouted quickly as one of his Seventh fell beside him, shot in the face.

Confusion filled the Seventh as they tried to rush up the hill. Soldiers were being pierced side to side by arrows. Those that had fallen were beaten to death and scalped. Custer watched as shameful soldiers killed themselves and each other to avoid torture. He watched in dismay as the warriors were cutting those men to pieces.

A few uninjured soldiers were returning random shots as the ever-increasing warriors hiding behind the cottonwoods beat and pummeled them. As they retreated up the hill, Custer watched as Sioux and Cheyenne warriors surrounded them.

The sounds around them were deafening. Rifle shots filled the air. Ear-piercing, frightening war cries carried themselves among the torturous sounds of the battle. Horses screamed in fear, combining with the yells of the men that were being tortured and killed.

"Dismount! Form lines!" Custer yelled as he dismounted from his horse.

Custer's head snapped up in astonishment. All of a sudden there was deathly silence. The warriors had stopped shooting. The war cries had stopped.

Fear gripped and choked the throats of Custer and his mighty Seventh.

Chapter THIRTY-TWO

Custer and his officers ordered the remaining soldiers into formation. They were ready for another wave of warriors to attack. Movement had stopped on both sides. A silence lay heavy in the air.

As the dust began to settle, the sky became filled with a massive outpouring of arrows. The warriors were randomly shooting into the air and letting the arrows fall where they chose. Then the bullets flew from all corners.

Custer and his men were surrounded and pinned into place from every angle. The lull was over. Each direction he looked there were feral warriors attacking in waves. There wasn't anywhere for them to retreat. His men couldn't avoid the onset of the attack. Helplessly, he watched as arrows randomly killed his men.

His stomach churned as his heart was being choked by an invisible hand. A thick blanket of acrimonious fate settled above him. He couldn't see the clear azure sky any longer. All he could see was the dry dust of the battle and feel the taste of defeat in his throat. He needed Reno now!

The dull thud of a lone bullet tugged on his chest. Blankly, Custer looked down and felt the pain as the impact pounded through his chest. The battle became distant as he looked around at his men. Stunned and dazed, he looked toward the waves of warriors and lost his grip on the reins. Lieutenant

Colonel George Armstrong Custer was hit, knocked from his horse. A bullet had slammed into his heart.

Quickly, his officers brought him to the rear of the battle.

Many of the soldiers were shaken that their invincible leader had been shot for the first time ever in battle. They spread themselves in front of their beloved general as a protective barrier while the officers moved him to a better place.

Time slowed to a crawl for the Seventh Cavalry. The battle was at an all time climax. It was as if they all had been joined in the same nightmare. Only this was real, a real hell worse than any battle the experienced soldiers had ever been in.

And Custer was down.

The warriors circled the soldiers on their horses. Some laughed in euphoria as they watched the soldiers group themselves into a cluster. Amazed at the cowardice they saw among the soldiers, they watched some soldiers kill each other and then themselves.

It was like a buffalo hunt. But instead of buffalo, it was a large regiment of soldiers grouped for the kill. As they continuously rode around the frantic soldiers, one by one the warriors shot them with arrows and bullets.

Gall and his men watched in amazement as some shot each other or themselves. The cowards made it easy for the warriors. Their shameful behavior angered Gall and the warriors. What were these soldiers doing? He wanted the satisfaction of watching them die by his hand, not by their own. He wanted to hear the dull thud of a bullet or see arrows pummel into the white men's bodies.

From atop the hill the two officers who had assisted Tom with Custer watched stunned as the soldiers had been corralled by the warriors as if they were cattle.

Dazed, he sat up with assistance from his brother and groaned out an order for the left flank. He fought to stay conscious. His mind was focused on his men and the tactics of battle and survival.

"Hold that left flank!" Tom yelled.

"Hold the hill ... ," Custer croaked.

The orders were passed on. The officers continued to attempt regaining control and order of their men.

The anxiety of seeing their strong General hit and down was numbing. He had never been injured in battle before. The men weren't sure how to deal with it. The officers knew that as long as the men from the Seventh could see Custer sitting up, their hope would be strong. With Custer being able to lead them, they would not lose.

The officers reasoned among themselves. Reno and Benteen would be here any moment and they would have a reprieve. The soldiers knew they would make it.

"Get them back into ranks," Custer spoke in a raspy, death-caressing voice.

The regiment's doctor had been killed. Tom bound the wound and gave his brother a drink of whiskey. Custer gagged on the hot spirits sliding down his dry throat. He never imbibed in spirits and was unaccustomed to the taste. His eyes watered.

Tom gently laid his brother on the ground.

"Tom ... Tom ... ."

"I'm here. Try not to talk. You need to rest."

Custer shook his head, "I'm sorry. Tom, I'm sorry."

Time seemed to have stopped. Custer could only see his brother. His eyes tried to focus as he struggled to speak. In the distance, he could hear the cry of an eagle.

"Tell ... tell Libby ... I ... love ... her."

Custer saw no more. The battle was done for him. His battles in life were over. His legacy will become one of controversy for all time. Holding his brother in death severed Tom from the real world. He never heard the warriors approach until it was too late.

Tom focused his eyes on the moccasins standing next to his brother's body. The sight brought him back to reality. He screamed in terrifying fear as he slowly reached for his pistol … knowing that his death would be immediate.

The last handful of soldiers threw their guns onto the ground as they were surrounded by a group of warriors.

"We surrender! Take us as prisoners!"

"We take no prisoners!" the warriors shouted as they shot them down. The Sioux would not take prisoners. No one would stay alive this day.

Sitting Bull kept the village organized and calm. Once the initial impact of the attack was over the People joined the fight. After the soldiers retreated and the battle was away from the village, the bodies of the dead soldiers were gradually moved. Anyone who was strong enough dragged the bodies of the soldiers to the front of the village so the regiment could come and retrieve them when the battle was over.

Isaiah lay fatally wounded, face down in the village, knowing this was the final setting of the sun for him. Sitting Bull approached the black washitu and turned him over to see if he still lived. He was surprised to see his old friend.

"Isaiah, what are you doing here? Why did you bring our enemy to our camp?"

Isaiah opened his death filled eyes and saw his good friend.

"The orders … were to take … you to … reservation. Custer was … to wait … for the rest … of the army. He … didn't …

listen. We told ... him ... there were too ... many. Too many ... Sioux. We ... warned him ... not to ... attack ... ."

Sitting Bull gave his old friend some water and held him as he died in his arms.

Spirit of the Mountain and the other medicine men were kept busy tending the warriors and their wounded families. Her children, Big Eyes and Prairie Flower, were among the group of children running for water from the river. As she was placing a poultice upon an elderly woman's leg her heart was with both the soldiers and the warriors fighting their deadly battle a short distance away. Star Dancer watched her with concern.

Spirit of the Mountain could not understand why the battle was happening now. The Rosebud battle wasn't supposed to happen until the second of July. Little Big Horn Battle should not happen until the end of July. Why is it happening now? Could Sings to the Wind's interference change history that much? What would it do to the future?

When she was done, Star Dancer patted her on the shoulder. "Don't worry, Little One. Our warriors will be fine."

Guilt lay heavy upon Sings to the Winds chest. What could she have possibly done to have changed history so dramatically? If she hadn't warned them about the Rosebud Battle and the Little Big Horn Battle, this wouldn't be happening.

She looked at her newborn's sleeping face while unfettered tears slid down her cheeks. If it hadn't been for her opinions and actions many warriors would still be alive. No one was supposed to die at the Rosebud Battle but many warriors did.

Only sixty-six were supposed to die at this battle. What damage had she done here? How many more would be mourning because of her ignorance? Sings to the Wind could hear the mourning cries of those who had lost loved ones. She could hear the random spattering of bullets as the warriors volleyed with Reno and Benteen.

She had to get up and leave the lodge. Her People needed her help. In her heart she knew that no one would blame her. Except ... except Spirit of the Mountain. She prayed that her closest friend would forgive her. She prayed that Two Feathers and Standing Deer would survive. Hugging her baby tightly, she held on to her soul, praying she could forgive herself.

Spirit of the Mountain had just finished tending another wounded warrior when a band of warriors from the battle on the hill came riding into camp. With hope in her eyes, she looked for her beloved Standing Deer. The warriors brought in more wounded and dead. The cries of mourning filled the village.

Gradually bands came riding in and each time she would look with hope in her eyes. She looked for the one and only man who owned her soul. The only man who had ever possessed her.

Two Feathers called out her name. Slowly Spirit of the Mountain turned to look at the warrior approach her on his horse. A wounded warrior lay across his lap. Tears filled her eyes. It felt as if a knife cut through her heart. It wasn't just any warrior. It was her warrior. Two Feathers carried Standing Deer into his lodge with Spirit of the Mountain flying behind his heels.

She cut his bloodied doeskin shirt and looked at her love's stomach wound. Her whole body started to shake in spasms. His eyes were closed, his body still warm. Two Feathers had informed her that he had been shot at the beginning of the battle.

"Oh, my love," she choked on her tears.

Standing Deer turned toward the sound of his wife's voice. With his eyes closed, he spoke his words of love, "Do not mourn for me my love. We will be together again."

She kissed his face and grabbed both his hands as she laid her head on his shoulder.

"Love. Hear me, please. The past ... begins the circle of life connecting us ... to the present and then to the future. Leave your mind open ... . You must believe ... our souls will be together again. Look to the past ... and see the future with your heart ... see what is true in your soul and believe I will never leave you."

"No. You cannot die. NO!"

"Do not cry, my love. We ... will be reunited again ... as one being ... one soul."

Standing Deer's body shook as he took one last deep breath, to never breathe in this lifetime again.

Chapter THIRTY-THREE

The call of eagles sang in her ear. They were telling her to be strong, letting her know that their guidance was with her. She did not want to be strong. Spirit of the Mountain's body trembled in shock. Her soul, her life's spirit, had been cruelly taken away from her. Their life had been mystically joined across time, becoming one. Now her soul was separated from that blessed union. She felt as if she was torn apart.

How would she survive without her one and only true love? What was she supposed to do? She would be a lost soul living through the motions of life without him.

"You can't leave me," she sobbed. "I don't want to live without you ... ."

Her eyes were wide with anger and sorrow. An animal-like scream of agony pierced the air and joined the other terrifying screams of sorrow that filled the village. She lay against Standing Deer, holding her husband as tears flowed freely. Spirit of the Mountain was oblivious to the blood staining her skin and clothing. She absently slung her leg over his thigh. Gripping his shoulders tightly she kissed his lips and laid her head on his shoulders. Endless, racking sobs filled the lonely lodge.

The more she cried, the more her anger festered. It grew like a greedy cancerous lump. The bitterness overwhelmed her, becoming as bitter as a termagant. It boiled inside her being drowning reason from her blood as it pounded through her. Anger and hatred poisoned her as they slowly consumed her. It was controlling her very being.

The front flap of the lodge snapped against the exterior wall as Spirit of the Mountain ran through the doorway toward Sings to the Wind. The bright sun blinded her temporarily as she raced toward Two Feathers' lodge. She would start with Sings to the Wind and then work her way to the White House. She would destroy anyone who was brave enough, or ignorant enough, to get in her way.

Stunned, Sitting Bull and Little Red Hawk saw the murderous glaze in her eyes. Little Red Hawk reacted quicker on his feet than Sitting Bull and grabbed Spirit of the Mountain as she raced across the village. Blinded by anger, she fought like a mother grizzly defending her babies.

Crazy Horse was riding into the Hunkpapa section of the village and saw the struggle between the three. He watched as Little Red Hawk was trying to drag Spirit of the Mountain to her lodge. Sitting Bull was trying to hold down her flailing arms.

Spirit of the Mountain knocked Sitting Bull off balance and onto the ground. Reaching over, she flipped Little Red Hawk onto his back. She growled as she patted herself on the back for taking self-defense courses. She just never thought she would be using them on her friends. Her goal was Sings to the Wind and no one was going to stop her!

Quickly Crazy Horse rushed over and interceded. Without giving her a chance to react, he leaned down and threw her over his shoulder. Spirit of the Mountain pummeled his back in anger as he carried her to the lodge.

"I'm going to kill her! Let me go!"

"Hiya," Crazy Horse spoke calmly.

"Let me go!"

"Hiya."

Crazy Horse plopped her down onto the buffalo mat next to her husband. If Spirit of the Mountain hadn't been so angry, she would have been humiliated by the chimerical fashion in which she had been returned to her lodge.

"Don't move," Crazy Horse demanded.

Spirit of the Mountain crossed her arms and glared at Crazy Horse.

"It is not her fault. It was to be. You know in your heart I speak the truth. You cannot blame her for the greed of the white man."

Spirit of the Mountain covered her face and burst into tears just as Prairie Flower and Big Eyes entered the lodge.

"Ate!" Big Eyes yelled.

"Daddy! No!"

The children bent over their father's lifeless body. Spirit of the Mountain held Prairie Flower as she wept with unabashed tears. Putting her other arm around Big Eyes waist, she rocked her children to ease their grief. Big Eyes clenching his jaw, lips trembling as he held back the flow of tears.

Crazy Horse silently backed out of the lodge to leave the family alone with their grief. Big Eyes pulled himself out of his mother's arms and raced by him blindly running toward the river.

After a few moments, Crazy Horse joined Big Eyes at the river. A soft breeze cooled the tormenting heat of the sun. The clear river flowed freely before them. He watched the young boy break a twig in multiple pieces. Sadness reflected in Crazy Horse's eyes. War was never easy but it was hardest on the young. Triumph only lasted until the mourning began.

"Eya niyan, cantesica." Cry, Mourn.

Big Eyes shook his head no.

"I can't. I must be brave."

Without realizing it, Big Eyes replied in English. If he hadn't been so filled with grief, he would have remembered that Crazy Horse refused to learn the white man's language.

"I do not understand the white man's words."

"I can't cry. I must be a man now. I must be brave and strong for my mother and sister." Big Eyes whispered in Lakota.

Crazy Horse looked silently across the curling water of the river, rudely reminding him that nothing stays the same. With brotherly compassion, he laid his hand on the grieving boy's shoulder. "To mourn and cry does not make you less of a man. A man must be true to his heart, true to himself. If his heart wants to cry, then he should cry."

"Do you cry, Crazy Horse?"

"Yes, I have cried many tears. I am not ashamed to admit this to you."

"You joke with me. I find it hard to believe that a great warrior and brave like you would cry."

"I am a simple man, Big Eyes. I have had many different kinds of sorrow in my life. Sometimes, crying can make you feel better. There is nothing wrong with crying if that is how you feel." Big Eyes put his arms around Crazy Horse and cried unfettered tears. Crazy Horse tenderly hugged the child until all his tears were shed.

Later that evening as the sun was setting upon the village, groups of warriors gathered around the fires. They spoke of the regiment's attack and the victory of the battle. Sitting Bull joined a group of warriors near his lodge as they sat and smoked.

The warriors knew the battle was the fulfillment of Sitting Bull's vision. Many wondered how the white soldiers would react to this defeat. How far would they have to go now to live in peace? Where could they live so that the soldiers would not hunt them? Surely, revenge would be in the hearts of all white soldiers after they hear of this battle. They looked to Sitting Bull for guidance.

Sitting Bull spoke to the group of warriors before him.

"We did not kill Custer. He did this to himself. Custer was a vain fool and rode to his own death."

Sitting Bull looked around at the faces before him as they all agreed with his words. The warriors sitting before him had fought bravely to secure their village and protect the women and children.

"My heart bleeds in sorrow. Many great warriors and braves were killed defending our village, protecting our families. Many brave white soldiers were killed, dying for what they believed in as well."

He smoked from the pipe and passed it on to the warrior beside him.

"We just ask for peace and want to live our lives as we choose. These white soldiers attacked our village. They attacked our families, killing our wives and children. They forced us to fight. What did they expect us to do? Lay down our weapons and let them kill us like animals? When they force us to fight then we must fight to defend ourselves and our loved ones."

A few bullets interrupted the words of Sitting Bull. There were still warriors south of the village holding Reno and Benteen on the hillside. Again, he solemnly looked around at the men and bowed his head in sadness.

"Tonight we shall mourn. Tonight, we shall pray for the souls of our dead warriors. We will mourn and pray for those brave white soldiers who also fought in this battle and shall never see the sun rise again."

Sitting Bull danced and chanted prayers to the Great Spirit. He prayed and sang for the souls of the one hundred and fifty warriors and the twenty-three women and children who now travel in the afterlife. He prayed for the souls of over five hundred men killed in battle that were under the leadership of Custer, Benteen and Reno.

The sun rose in the azure sky to another cloudless day. The heat was already stifling and suffocating those who had risen in the early morning hours. The village was filled with the bustle and urgency of pending disaster. Tension filled the air. The largest village ever known to the Sioux was packing up and going their separate ways. Within a few hours, all the lodges would be taken down and packed on travois.

Villagers who were already finished helped those around them. Conversations were filled with a forced calmness. The People were saying their goodbyes, wondering if they would ever see their friends again.

Many would go to Spirit of the Mountain's hidden camp in the hills. Some would return to the reservations and some would go with their respective bands under the leadership of their chiefs. The rest would travel in whatever direction the wind chose for them.

Spirit of the Mountain watched as Young Buck placed Standing Deer's lodge on his travois. She had given it to the young warrior and his pregnant wife. They had been living in a wickiup during their stay on the river. In the future, she would stay with Two Feathers and Sings to the Wind. The young couple would have more need for her lodge.

Dressed in deerskin, Christine approached her warily. She had heard of Spirit of the Mountain's anger the day before. Many of the women had spoken about it at the river while they took their morning baths.

Spirit of the Mountain gave her a strained smile.

"Do you need some help? I have finished helping Little Red Hawk with the packing."

"No, thank you. I'm done."

An awkward silence fell between the two women until finally Christine could not hold her tongue any longer. Although she had changed greatly living among the Sioux, patience was not one of Christine's virtues.

"Why are you giving away your lodge? Aren't you staying with Sitting Bull's people?"

"I won't be needing it any longer. I'll be staying with Two Feathers and Sings to the Wind when I am in camp."

"You are no longer angry with her?"

Spirit of the Mountain shook her head no, flinching at the reminder of her uncharacteristic behavior of the day before.

"I can't stay mad at her. She didn't deserve my anger anyway. It is not her fault. Just like Crazy Horse said, she cannot be blamed for the white man's greed."

Christine nodded her head as she nervously smoothed imagined wrinkles in her dress. Looking around at the small groups working together to prepare for their travels, she felt uncomfortable and unsure of herself.

"Do you need help with Standing Deer's burial?"

Gritting her teeth and jaw, Spirit of the Mountain took a slow deep breath. Standing Deer had been baptized a Christian in her world. He would be buried, as a Sioux brave deserves. Carefully, she explained the Sioux beliefs and that Standing Deer would receive those proper burial rites.

Again, awkwardness draped the two women. Quickly, Christine changed the subject.

"Little Red Hawk said he spoke with you and we would be going to your ranch. He said we would be safe there."

Spirit of the Mountain nodded her head. She could not say anything. She knew they would only be safe for a few years.

"I want to thank you for giving me to Little Red Hawk. We can't understand each other's language yet, but we do have an agreeable relationship. He is so good and kind."

Christine giggled, "It took me three days to understand that he didn't want me waiting on my knees for him anymore. He kept saying 'stop' in Sioux and pointing to the buffalo mat. He kept using hand signals I couldn't understand. I thought he wanted me in a different position. It was quite comical at first."

Christine watched as Spirit of the Mountain's eyes filled with tears as she recalled the precious memories when she first came to the Sioux so many years ago. She kicked herself for not knowing when to keep her mouth shut.

"Oh! I'm sorry! Here I am babbling about how happy I am and your heart is broken."

"Don't apologize. I am happy for you." Spirit of the Mountain wiped away a stray tear, "Excuse me, I must go and speak with Sitting Bull."

"Did you really flip Little Red Hawk onto his back?"

Spirit of the Mountain was agape at the question and then giggled. "Yes and when I apologized he laughed at me. Thank the Creator he has a sense of humor. I really must go. I have not told Sitting Bull my plans yet."

Christine watched as Spirit of the Mountain walked away. Her heart went out to her new friend and the many others that had lost their loved ones.

The day after the battle, in the middle of the afternoon, Sitting Bull and the rest of the village left the desolate camp. The warriors burned the prairie behind them to cover their tracks as they headed toward Big Horn Mountains.

When they arrive at the new campsite, they would first mourn and then celebrate the victory of the battle. The People did not consider it a massacre. To them it was the greatest battle of all. It was a battle their warriors could be proud of and speak about for generations.

It was another blistering day when Terry arrived at Benteen and Reno's camp. The day after the Sioux abandoned the campsite, General Alfred H. Terry approached the battlefield with his entourage. One lone horse stood silently before his eyes. Comanche, Captain Miles Keough's cavalry horse, stood faithfully next to his dead un-mutilated master. He had trusted Custer with six hundred fifty-five of his men. Red-faced with anger, he stared at the sight as Reno and Benteen told him that less than two hundred had survived the battles.

"And Custer's men?" Terry roared.

Benteen looked down at the General's feet,. "None sir. None survived that battle."

The soldiers under Reno and Benteen's command had escaped mutilation. Those that had been killed in the village had been scalped but otherwise had died as brave soldiers should, with honor.

The regiment approached the field where Custer's battle had taken place. At the sound of the pounding hooves, vultures took to the air. Terry scanned the sickening battlefield where Custer and his men had fought. As he stood in the coulee, he could see almost all of the soldiers were scalped. Many had been trampled by horses. A handful lay un-mutilated. The unspoken question of why was answered by a scout.

"Sir, those that have not been mutilated fought bravely and honorably in the eyes of the Sioux."

The general nodded his head in acknowledgment as he prayed he would not lose his breakfast. He observed some of the men racing into the trees to regurgitate the contents of their morning meal. Two soldiers called him up to the hillside. As he walked up the hill, he could see six bodies lying on the dusty ground.

Two were scalped, but not mutilated. Custer lay before his eyes, shot twice in the left temple and heart. One of Custer's fingers was cut off and one of his ears had been severed. Terry looked closer and realized his ear had been stabbed with a sewing awe. Later he was told it was done so Custer could hear better in the after world.

About a dozen feet from where Custer lay, a grotesque disfigured body was found. It had been so badly mutilated that they couldn't tell who he was. A young officer identified the body as Custer's brother, Tom. The officer was able to identify him only by of the tattoo on his arm.

Chapter Thirty-Four

Spirit of the Mountain sat on the edge of the campsite staring at the moon and stars as the breeze blew her knee-length hair. She was going to cut it all and give it to Standing Deer as his gift from her for his travels to the afterworld. Sings to the Wind had convinced her against it, explaining how much he had truly loved her hair and would want her to keep it.

At the burial, Spirit of the Mountain had ceremoniously cut a chunk and braided the piece with his hair. It was a startling contrast to his raven-colored hair.

Closing her eyes, she felt the tears run down her cheeks as a painful lump caught in her throat. The battle wasn't supposed to happen this way! She was afraid to leave and go home to the modern world. The fear of what this disaster did to change the future was overwhelming.

Squeezing her eyes tighter, she tried to erase the memory of the dead soldiers from her mind. Before they left the campsite on the Little Big Horn, she and Sings to the Wind went up to the hillside with some of the other women to see where the battle with Custer had taken place.

It had reeked of death. Bodies lay on top of bodies. So many had been mutilated and trampled by horses. When Sings to the Wind had found Custer's body, Spirit of the Mountain had to hold back the bile as she watched her friend remove a sewing awe from his ear. Quickly she looked around to see if anyone had seen her do this. She closed her eyes as Sings to the Wind hid the awe.

"I don't know who to hate," Sings to the Wind croaked.

Pulling out her hunting knife, she grabbed Custer's hand. "I love my country. I love being a Lakota, but this, this is not what America stands for ... ."

Tears rolled down her cheek while Spirit of the Mountain watched wide-eyed as Sings to the Wind cut Custer's finger off.

Sings to the Wind stood up with tears in her eyes.

"This ... this is America. We the people declared our independence for freedom. Freedom to live the way we choose. This is the land of the free. Why can't they understand that the Indian want to be free and live their lives as they choose. This is Sioux land. It is the land of the free as well ... the home of the braves."

Sings to the Wind covered her face and cried.

"I'm so sorry I did this. Please forgive me, Spirit of the Mountain."

Without a word Spirit of the Mountain put her arm around her friend and walked back to camp, away from the feral battle site.

Opening her eyes, she winced while she chided herself for reliving the gruesome memory. Guilt was not an easy thing to live with. She felt overwhelmed with guilt. She would not want to be Sings to the Wind. Her guilt must be three-fold.

Feeling a presence, Spirit of the Mountain quickly turned toward the camp. Crazy Horse came out of the trees where he had been standing, while he waited to speak with her. Opening her arms to him he stepped forward and held her tightly as she cried in his arms.

"You are a good friend. I am surprised that you don't hate me."

"I could never hate you. You cannot control what the white soldiers do."

"I am white. You do not like whites, more now than ever before."

"Your heart and soul is with the Lakota. Besides … ," Crazy Horse chuckled, "your white skin is darker than mine, especially in the summer when the sun tans you."

Crazy Horse playfully tugged on her hair, "Except, this gives you away. I remember when you wanted to make it black. I recall a certain brave was so mad he could spit out a horse."

Spirit of the Mountain laughed as she stepped out of his arms, "If I remember properly, you also tried talking me out of doing it. You told me I was trying to hide from the real me. I couldn't change the color of my hair anymore than you could get rid of your waves and curls."

Crazy Horse smiled at the memory, "Let us walk for a while."

Spirit of the Mountain nodded. As the two lifetime friends walked, she waited patiently, knowing that he would speak his mind soon enough. Crazy Horse was an abstemious and humble brave. In her eyes, he was a hero. In his own, he believed what he did was common. He believed he was like any other warrior.

Spirit of the Mountain believed differently, just as many of the Sioux did. He was one of the bravest and most honorable warriors she had ever met. His legend belonged where it was because he earned it. His fealty to the People was everlasting.

"My friend, you are among the very few who know my heart. You understand and accept what has happened to me and the mistakes I have made in my life. You know why I will never take a wife. You know that my commitment is to all the People.

"Guilt is a hard emotion to live with. I do not want to see that bitterness destroy your heart. The best part of your heart is that you see something good and positive about everything.

"I was surprised to see your anger. I have never seen that strong of anger come from your heart. You were so filled with a desire to kill that someone told me Two Feathers' lodge had been shaking."

Pausing, he touched her cheek and put his arm around her, "Do not blame the battles on yourself. Do not feel guilt over the Battle of Rosebud or the attack on the village at the Little Big Horn ... ."

"Battles?" Spirit of the Mountain uncharacteristically interrupted. "What do you mean by the Battle of Rosebud?"

Crazy Horse tilted his head and looked quizzically at Spirit of the Mountain, "You were not told of Rosebud?"

Spirit of the Mountain shook her head and listened as he told the tale from his eyes.

"I could have warned the People about the attack on the Little Big Horn if I had known about the Battle of Rosebud. Don't you see history was already changed? It wouldn't have mattered if I had forewarned you of the attack!"

"No, my friend. The Creator did not wish you to interfere and you did not. We had scouts out every day. The soldiers had been spotted. We knew they were there. We did not believe they would attack when they did. White soldiers always attack in the morning. We were expecting a battle the next morning. Not in the afternoon like it happened."

One week later ... in the modern world.

The morning star twinkled above Spirit of the Mountain as she unlocked the office of the clinic. Numbness enveloped her being. Here in the modern world she was Karen.

Why couldn't she go back and right the wrongs? The Creator had given her so many powers to use in the past. Why hadn't any of them helped the People? The motions of life continued around her and she was at a standstill. She had kept herself locked up at home and finally decided to show her face again in the modern world.

She had distributed all of Standing Deer's possessions that he kept in the Lakota village except for his medicine bag and wedding band. The medicine bag now hung on the wall above the bed with the wedding band tied to it. She had given his bow, arrows and lance to their daughter, his pipe and knives to their son. The rest of his belongings were given to those in need, and to his closest friends.

With Charlene's help, all of Standing Deer's modern possessions were placed in the living room of their home. She had already spoken to Jim Black Elk and he had spread the word of Standing Deer's death. Tonight she would open her doors to greet her friends as they came to give their condolences. Again, she would part with his possessions and give them to friends and those in need, following the traditional ways of the People.

Before she realized it, the morning had flown by. Karen had a few moments to spare before Jim would arrive for their luncheon. She read her e-mail and some Native American newsletters she had received.

With a deep sigh, Karen deleted the spam mail and opened a newsletter. Saving the information she received about the Adopt a Child and Elder program, she waited patiently for the next letter to open.

Her mouth dropped open in despair as she read about the numerous teen suicides happening at the Standing Rock reservation. Tears filled her eyes as she cried out, "Why ... why ... why ... ?"

Jim Black Elk stood at the doorway. "Are you okay?"

"I just read about the suicides. I've been so caught up in the past that I've lost the present. What is going on?"

Jim shook his head, "We're doing all we can. We're not sure if it's some kind of suicide pact or not. The children deny there is a pact. A pen pal program has been started and we now have notices sent out on the Internet looking for counselors."

"I can't believe so much has happened just in one week."

Puzzled by her statement Jim again shook his head, "This has been happening for months."

Karen sighed, "I'll probably have to cut lunch short. I need to go over to the hospital and check on some of my patients. Let them know I'm still around."

Again, Jim looked at her in puzzlement, "Why would you need to go to the hospital? Don't you assign them to a different doctor when you send them there?"

"Why would I do that?"

"Wouldn't it be just a bit time-consuming for you to be constantly driving to Standing Rock?"

Karen was stunned by the question. "Standing Rock? Why would I go there? What's wrong with the hospital here?"

"Karen, we don't have a hospital here ... well, it's not finished yet anyway. They had it completed and realized they didn't put in the telephone lines. Are you feeling okay?"

Karen put her head on the desk and groaned. She couldn't believe there wasn't a hospital. What happened to it? Did it just disappear and erase itself because of ... oh, no. What else has changed?

"How's your brother? I take it he's still at Rosebud."

"Karen, he's never been at Rosebud. He's at Standing Rock. You called the doctor to get him transferred here when the hospital is finished. Don't you remember?"

"Yes, and no. I thought I called the doctor at Rosebud Rez."

Jim shook his head again growing more puzzled as the conversation continued. "There isn't a hospital at Rosebud. It's just a clinic like this one. What is going on with you?"

"I ... I just need time to adjust to all the changes."

He nodded his head. "Well, there is good news."

"Good. I could use some." Karen said dryly.

Jim laughed. "My brother is out of his coma. About a week ago the doctor called me. He said he'd never seen anything like it. My brother took a deep breath and then sat up. Wide-awake as if he had been jolted. It happened on the anniversary of the Little Big Horn Battle. What's strange is that he keeps complaining that his stomach hurts. They've done all sorts of tests and can't find anything. They're releasing him tomorrow."

"Oh, that is wonderful. I can't wait to meet him."

"You will. Now, let's go eat. I'm starving."

Matthew held his breath as his mother looked in his room to check on him before she left for work. Like a predator, he kept his ears open, waiting for the sounds of the engine to reach the end of the road before it turned to head toward the clinic where she worked.

When the silence returned, he crept to her room and lay down upon her bed. He was going to time-travel and see what kind of adventures awaited him. Matthew stared at the ceiling as he waiting for sleep to come and spiral him away to another world ... .

Matthew awoke to the sounds of pans clattering and soft voices. Slowly, he opened his eyes in anticipation. Disappointment flooded through him as he realized he was still in his mother and father's bed.

What was he doing back here? He was supposed to be off in some exciting adventure, like his sister did. Walking over to the door, he peeked out to make sure he could leave the room without being caught. As Matthew tiptoed to his bedroom door, his heart sank when he realized his bedroom door was open.

Charlene Laughing Bird silently walked up behind the unsuspecting boy.

"Well, young man, what do you have to say for yourself?"

Jennifer stood beside the woman with her eyebrows raised in curiosity. Matthew fumbled for excuses. He could not lie, regardless of the consequences.

"Jennifer did it!" he yelled in his own defense.

Charlene shook her head, "I'm not talking about Jennifer. But since you brought it up, she and I will discuss that later. I want to know why you went into you mother's room when you know the rules."

"Matthew! You little ... !"

"Enough, Jennifer. I want to know, Matthew."

Matthew looked at Charlene. He had never seen her so angry. For an older woman, she was very intimidating as she stood in front of him with both hands on her hips.

"I just wanted to see where I would go."

"And?" Charlene and Jennifer replied simultaneously.

Matthew frowned. "I woke up in Sitting Bull's tent and fell back to sleep and ended up here."

"Did he see you?"

Matthew nodded his head. "Yes, he asked what I was doing there and if Mom knew I was coming to him. I told him I wasn't supposed to be there. I needed to go somewhere else," Matthew frowned and shrugged his shoulders. "Then I woke up back here."

Charlene shook her head and sighed. This family has never had normal discipline problems. How was she supposed to handle this one?

"Go and do your chores. Your plans are canceled for the day. I will discuss this with your mother when she gets home tonight."

"And you, young lady. Come in the kitchen. You are in hot water as well."

Jennifer gave Matthew a shameful look and stomped into the kitchen to finish her chores. Charlene was two steps behind her.

"Well, young lady?"

"I had a bad dream and I wanted to be with Mom."

"I'm listening ... ."

Jennifer took a deep breath. "It started out awful. Then it ended really nice. There was a bunch of people dressed like pilgrims ... like in the movies. And they spoke like that, too. Funny ... 'thy, thee, thou.' It was weird. They pricked this lady with something and accused her of being a witch. They ... I watched as they burned her."

Tears filled Jennifer's eyes as she recalled the screams and the chanting.

"I ran so fast and far. I finally stopped running when my lungs felt like they were going to explode. Then I heard men's voices behind me and I started to run again. That's when an Indian boy grabbed me and helped me hide. He took me to his father and brother."

Charlene sighed.

"They were Narragansett Indians. It was the only word I recognized. We spoke with sign language. It was a little different than the sign I have learned but we were able to talk. Then I woke up and was back here."

An uncomfortable silence filled the air.

"Are you going to tell Mom?"

"I have to, dear. You know the rules. Jennifer, you are not old enough to deal with time-travel. You could have been hurt or killed. Both of your parents have warned you. You know what your mother went through, wondering whether she was losing her mind ... afraid she would be institutionalized. Don't you understand that no one would believe you? Think about how long it took me to understand. I still find it hard to believe."

"I want to go back."

"No. You must promise me you will not do it again without your mother's permission. That bed has powers. Powers that only the Creator understands. You are not prepared to accept the gifts the Creator has given your mother. These gifts were meant for your mother. Promise me that you won't do it again."

Jennifer looked down at the dishes she was washing and frowned.

"I promise," she mumbled.

Chapter THIRTY-FIVE

Six weeks after the Battle of Little Big Horn, Sherman placed the Plains Territory under military control. In August, Congress insisted the Sioux turn over the Powder River Country and the Black Hills.

"Sign or we will cut off all rations ... ."

Spirit of the Mountain sat in the circle listening to the arguments of the warriors before her. The meeting had become heated with frustration. The government had threatened the Indians again.

The group at the ranch had dwindled down to about fifty. In the last few months, many of the People had gone back to the reservation. Red Cloud had cunningly informed the officials at the reservation that the warriors had voluntarily left the ranch and decided to come back to the reservation. It was the safest way to protect those that were still living on the ranch.

Now the group was in an uproar, furious at the continuous lack of compassion the government had for the Indian lands.

Yellow Moon of the Hunkpapa tribe stood and spoke, "I do not believe we should give up so easily. Spirit of the Mountain started this ranch to help the People and protect the buffalo. To burn and destroy the ranch would be a great tragedy."

"I believe we should burn it to the ground and hide in the mountains where they will never find us. The mountains are big. They will not follow us," Wild Raven shouted.

Two Horns stood with arms raised, "Listen to me. They will find us. They will hunt us down like animals. I suggest that we stay here on the ranch as long as we can. When there is a threat, we will burn the ranch and hide in the hills until we are safe."

"Will we ever be safe?" Christine asked.

Silenced voices sliced the air. The crackle of the firewood danced in all of their ears. A lone hawk screeched above them. The screech of the hawk was an omen, a bad omen. Chills ran down their spines.

No one seemed to have a response to the accurate yet innocently-asked question. Would they ever really be safe again? Would they be able to adapt to the lifestyles that the road was taking them to?

They were given the freedom to live as they chose on the ranch. All who sat around the crackling fire knew it wasn't that way on the reservation. Here they could practice their religion. They could pray to the Great Spirit without being punished. They could hunt as warriors do.

Little Eagle broke the silence. "Many of the warriors have accused us of living like the washitu. I have been told that I was becoming washitu. I am San Arc. I am not on a reservation where they give me rancid meat and tell me I cannot speak my native tongue.

"If I have to adjust my lifestyle and live on this ranch like a washitu, then that is what I will do. Here I am a free man, a warrior. At the reservation, I would be a prisoner and must do what the white man tells me to do. I chose freedom. To destroy this ranch would take away our last hope of freedom."

"I agree with Two Horns," Spirit of the Mountain spoke quietly. "He has made a good point. Nothing should be destroyed until there is no other option left to us. Shall we take a vote?"

She looked around the campfire as each member nodded their heads in agreement, "It must be unanimous. All who agree we should wait?"

"Keya!" Agreed, the group shouted.

"All who oppose?"

"Hiya!" two voices shouted.

One of the opposing warriors stood before the group, "We should forget this ranch and go live in the mountains. We can't continue to keep buffalo like the white man keeps cattle."

"Why can't Christine keep the ranch when Spirit of the Mountain is not with us. She is washitu."

"Look at me," Christine replied in a fluster. "My skin is as dark as yours. I am half-Filipino and half-Spanish. My hair is as black as the night. One look at me and they would see an Indian woman. I don't look washitu. It would never work."

With frustration written on his face, the warrior sat down.

"Do we agree to continue on the ranch until we no longer have a choice?"

All agreed, there wasn't opposition this time.

EPILOGUE

1877: Chief Crazy Horse surrendered with eight hundred Oglala warriors and families at Fort Robinson. Fear was rampant that he would go on the warpath and his arrest was ordered. As he was entering a guardhouse, he was alerted to the manipulation. Resisting arrest, Crazy Horse was stabbed by a soldier. He died later that night.

President Hayes invited Chief Red Cloud and Chief Spotted Tail to Washington, DC, to discuss a possible settlement between the Sioux Nation and the American Nation. Red Cloud and Spotted Tail failed to retain the Black Hills. The Fort Laramie Treaty was broken and the Black Hills were taken. The gold rush to the Black Hills was on.

Jim sat across from Karen rubbing his temple with his left hand. The diner was quiet and they were waiting for their food to arrive. Karen had just informed him of the vote to have the ranch burned if they were found.

"It's been a rough couple of months hasn't it?"

Karen sighed.

"Are you sure you want the ranch burned?"

"It may be necessary. They will wait until there is a threat of being found. They might have another year before they are forced onto a reservation. The buffalo will be safe ... regardless of what happens. I'm hoping that Christine and Little Red Hawk can pose as ranchers and prevent it. The meeting lasted all night. It's what the people living on the ranch agreed on. Christine and Little Red Hawk will dress in white man's clothing to try and fool anyone who sees them from a distance."

Jim nodded his head and frowned, "Not an easy decision. Sometimes I wonder how you cope."

The waitress came over to bring their food. After a few moments, Karen inquired about Jim's brother.

"He's still acting strange, not the John I knew. He seems to be searching for something. The other day he sat on his horse staring at the sunset. That's something I would do, not him."

"Is he still interested in helping at the reservation?"

"Yes. That is why he originally came back. But he seems discontented as if he is missing something or lost something and doesn't know where to look."

Jim was silent for a few moments as they continued with their meal.

"He is still complaining about stomach problems."

"You haven't convinced him to come see me yet. Why is he so adamant against seeing a doctor?"

"I don't know," Jim shook his head. "He was never like that before. He has returned to the reservation with many issues."

"Tell him issues belong in the ... ," Karen's beeper went off. She excused herself to use the diner's telephone.

Rushing to the table, she threw money down for the waitress, "It's your brother. He's at the clinic having severe stomach pains again."

Karen and Jim came in through the back door of the clinic.

"Sorry, but he seems to be in some serious pain. Here, I did some x-rays while you were on the way. I don't see a thing."

Denny explained as Karen waved her hand and mumbled that it was okay.

Karen studied the x-rays and shook her head. She saw nothing unusual either, "Where is he?"

"Room three."

As the three rushed down the hall the lights blinked on and off.

Karen looked up surprised. It had been cloudy outside but it hadn't looked as if it was going to storm.

"Whew, hear that wind?" Jim asked. "Where did that come from so suddenly?"

Karen opened the door to room three as she frowned at the howling of the wind outside. Denny and Jim followed behind her.

"Temperature is normal, BP is normal, dilation of the eyes … normal."

Karen nodded her head. Paul lay on the bed with his eyes on her and Jim as he winced in pain.

"Hello, I'm Dr. Anderson. Glad you finally listened to your big brother, John."

"Didn't have a choice this time."

John was a very tall man. His feet hung over the edge of the bed. He must be at least six foot five or six. His long dark hair was pulled back in a tail. Karen looked at his flushed face. His skin was clammy and cold.

"Do his BP and heart rate again."

As Denny scurried to obey orders, Jim stood back and watched Karen. The winds outside were howling, shaking the windows with their force.

"BPs up. Heart rate is at seventy-two."

Karen felt his lower and upper abdomen for swelling and pressure. Nothing … there was nothing.

The howling winds pounded against the clinic windows. Jim looked out the windows expecting to see a tornado at any moment. He saw only a cloudy sky.

"What did you eat last?"

"Eat?"

Karen nodded her head. The wind was so loud it seemed muffling. The pounding on the windows sounded like distant rifle shots as the clouds burst with the force of cannons.

"I had chili tacos with extra hot sauce. But I've never had a problem with eating it before. That can't be it."

Karen smiled. Standing Deer used to react the same way to hot foods.

"Never?"

"Well, not before my accident. My stomach could take anything. Now I seem to constantly have stomach problems. I've reached the point where I don't drink beer anymore because I get stomach pains. I stopped drinking soda, too. That helped. But this is the first time I had stomach pains from eating tacos."

The wind and rain bursting against the windows as if a war of the winds was going on outside. Thunder roared in their ears. The lights blinked on and off casting an eerie glow in the room.

Standing Deer couldn't eat tacos with hot sauce or drink alcohol either.

"Maybe it was the hot sauce," Karen suggested.

Turning to Denny, Karen spoke over the howling of the wind, "Make up some mint tea with honey."

"Mint tea?" John asked, puzzled. A washitu doctor who prescribed tea?

"Yes. It will help relieve the stomach pains. I believe you have developed a diversion to foods you were once normally used to eating."

John thought about it a few moments.

"Well, I feel really foolish."

"You shouldn't. It is unusual for the body to have such a reaction like that. If it does happen, it's usually a gradual thing and it may be just one or two items of food."

"Thank you. Maybe in some past life I had problems like this and the accident brought it back. It was really strange the way I came back from the coma," John laughed.

"Well, that is true. Jim told me about it. It was the same day my husband passed away," Karen frowned. Her whole body shivered with goose bumps. She rubbed her arms and looked at the man sitting in front of her.

Slowly she turned to look at Jim and then out the window. The howling wind stopped. A peaceful rain pattered on the windows. The thunder slowed as it crossed the distant prairie.

John laughed and raised his hands outward, "You never know. Since my accident I have learned and grown. I never quite accepted some of the beliefs of my People. But now ... now, I believe the past begins the circle of life. It connects us to the present and then to the future. If we leave our minds open then we can believe. Our souls will be together again in the circle of life. If we look to the past, we can see the future with our hearts. We can see what is true in our souls ... ."

Stunned at hearing Standing Deer's words come out of John's mouth, Karen dropped the clipboard. Her heart clenched into a tight ball. She looked at Jim with tears in her eyes and then she looked at John Black Elk and said ...

"And believe I will never leave you," Karen bent over and stared into John's eyes.

"What did you say?" he whispered.

"The words you just spoke are what my husband said to me just before he died. His last words were … 'and believe I will never leave you.'"

"You … it is you that I have been searching for all these months."

Thunder echoed in the distance.

John reached up and unbound Karen's hair. It fell into a cascade of autumn colors as if a waterfall had been held back and suddenly released. Slowly their lips met. The electric surge pounded through their bodies. It again connected their souls, joyously releasing their eternal dance of love.

www.ingramcontent.com/pod-product-compliance
Lightning Source LLC
Chambersburg PA
CBHW032139010726
47494CB00002B/280